Praise for
A BLADE SO BLACK

"With memorable characters and page-turning thrills,
A Blade So Black is the fantasy book I've been waiting for
my whole life. Alice is Black Girl Magic personified."
—ANGIE THOMAS,
#1 *NEW YORK TIMES*–bestselling author of *THE HATE U GIVE*

"I loved the 'our world' framing and the 'other world'
adventure so deeply. They were at such odds,
but the overall effect was just chefkiss.gif perfect."
—E.K. JOHNSTON,
#1 *NEW YORK TIMES*-bestselling author of *STAR WARS:
AHSOKA* and *A THOUSAND NIGHTS*

"Wholly original and absolutely thrilling—*A Blade So Black*
kicks so much (looking gl)ass."
—HEIDI HEILIG, author of *THE GIRL FROM EVERYWHERE*

"Mixing elements of *Alice in Wonderland* and *Buffy the Vampire
Slayer* . . . a delectable urban twist on beloved fairy tales."
—*ENTERTAINMENT WEEKLY*

"This really is Lewis Carroll by way of *Buffy*, and it makes for a fun, gritty
urban fantasy . . . will set the new standard for teen readers."
—*NPR*

"A dark, thrilling fantasy-meets-contemporary story
with a kickass heroine."
—*BUSTLE*

"Retold fairy tales have been a popular trend . . . but you've never read
one quite like *A Blade So Black*."
—*NERDIST*

"An action-packed twist on an old classic,
full of romance and otherworldly intrigue."
—*THE MARY SUE*

A DREAM SO DARK

A DREAM SO DARK

L. L. McKINNEY

NEW YORK

[Imprint]
MAKE YOUR MARK

A part of Macmillan Publishing Group, LLC
120 Broadway, New York, NY 10271

A DREAM SO DARK. Copyright © 2019 by Leatrice McKinney. All rights reserved.
Printed in the United States of America.

Library of Congress Control Number: 2019932727

ISBN 978-1-250-15392-0 (hardcover) / ISBN 978-1-250-15391-3 (ebook)

Our books may be purchased in bulk for promotional, educational, or business use.
Please contact your local bookseller or the Macmillan Corporate and Premium Sales Department at
(800) 221-7945 ext. 5442 or by email at MacmillanSpecialMarkets@macmillan.com.

Book design by Heather Palisi

Imprint logo designed by Amanda Spielman

First edition, 2019

1   3   5   7   9   10   8   6   4   2

fiercereads.com

Writing books takes a whole lot of work,
Lots of love and a few minor quirks.
So let's all do our part
To not steal people's art,
Because that's just the move of a jerk.

This book's special, so treat it with care.
Please don't steal it, or hurt it, that's fair.
Magic rests in these pages
To curse you for ages,
So all pirates had better beware.

For my little brother, Carl III aka Noogie.
You were and are so loved,
and I'll see you again, someday.

It's no use going back to yesterday,
because I was a different person then.

—LEWIS CARROLL

A DREAM SO DARK

Prologue
'TWAS BRILLIG

'Twas brillig, and a mortal's tones
Did stretch a day beyond the braced;
A princess slain, dead to her bones,
A world distraught, a knight disgraced.

Portentia, Queen of Wonderland,
A crown of grief upon her soul,
Vowed to repay the world of man,
With mother's tears and pain untold.

Addison, keeper of the realm,
Now plagued with guilt from duties failed,
Swears to uphold his Lady's whelms,
Unyielding faith, but conscience veiled.

And so, they two a war will wage,
The Black Queen and her trusted Knight,
For all to know a mother's rage
And all to feel her daughter's plight,

While sibling girls of white and red
align against their mother's will.
They share her pain, their sister dead,
But they would not innocents kill.

The Queen's defeat is at their hands.
They strip her of her powers black,
then bind her to the Nightmares' lands
and split her crown and all it lacks.

Behold the Heart! Behold the Eye!
For here the Black Queen's power sleeps.
Leave them to rest, and by and by
The world will mend the broken deep.

For if these artifacts awake,
Surely then, too, the Queen shall rise.
And all will suffer in her wake
Beneath the blood-soaked, screaming skies.

Beware the Heart! Beware the Eye!
Beware the Blade so Black!
He left it dead, and with its head
He went galumphing back.

One
GONE

Alice couldn't run. She couldn't hide. All she could do was sit there as her mother *went. In.*

"Must be out your got. Dayum. Mind. Just doing whatever you please." Mom paced in front of the coffee table, her steps barely muted by the carpet. She'd kicked off her heels and abandoned one near the door while the other lay over by the fireplace. This alone was a sign Alice was well and truly screwed. "Like you run things 'round here. Like you pay bills, do you pay bills?" Mom whirled on Alice, who had pressed so far back against the couch she felt she might slip between the cushions and be lost.

"No, ma'am." Alice's voice sounded as small as she felt in the face of her mom's fury.

A little muscle in Mom's jaw jumped as she ground her teeth together. "I can't hear you."

"No, ma'am," Alice managed, louder this time, the words thick with the emotions coursing through her. Fire licked at the center of her face, and a feeling like fingers around her neck closed off her throat. She just wanted to go to bed. Couldn't she go to bed?

"Got the school calling me 'cause you decided you just wasn't gone show up, I guess. Now I'm missing work, and for what? For *what*, Alison? Knowing I didn't raise you like this, *knowing* this wasn't gone fly. Then walk in here covered in lord knows—what is that mess?" Mom flapped a hand at Alice, indicating the black splattered against her clothes and skin. "And *what* is that smell?"

Alice stared at the stains. Yeah, that inky shit stank to high heaven, but that wasn't why her eyes started to water. It wasn't why her chest went all tight, like the space was suddenly too small for her lungs. She smoothed her fingers over the rusty red splotch on her shirt. A handprint hidden under all the other yuck. *His* handprint.

The heat behind Alice's eyes filled the rest of her face.

"I know you not ignoring me." Mom's tone went razor sharp.

Alice wanted to answer, but the words tripped over her tongue and hit the back of her teeth. What escaped instead was some sort of whine.

Mom's eyes widened slightly. Her arms unfolded from where she'd crossed them under her chest, and she shifted as if to reach out to Alice, but lifted a finger in warning instead. "No, ain't no crocodile tears gonna fix this."

The tears came anyway. They welled up and spilled over

Alice's cheeks as she stared at the floor while fighting to keep from all-out sobbing. The carpet's shaggy white tufts went brown and green, the memory of the shredded football field dancing in and out of her vision. The rumbling snarl of Fiends and the shriek of clashing weapons filled her ears. Her heart knocked against the inside of her chest, its *thump-thump* rising to join the crash.

Voices surfed the waves of chaos.

"Side, on fire!"

"I-it'll be okay . . . you'll be okay."

Lies.

You lied to him.

She flinched. She hadn't meant to lie. She gave everything she had to try and save him! The Black Knight, he was the one that didn't keep his end of the bargain. He was the one that let those monsters tear her friend apart! Chess was gone because of *him*.

Maybe, but Chess would be at home right now if you hadn't pulled him into this.

"Alice," Mom barked.

If it wasn't for you, he'd still be alive.

A buzzing prickled beneath Alice's skin, spreading over every inch of her. It pressed at her temples and filled the space behind her eyes.

You did this. You killed him.

Her vision darkened at the edges. Her jaw throbbed, the muscles so tight her teeth ached. She couldn't cry. She couldn't—if she did, she wouldn't stop.

Just like Dad.

The sobs tore free. Hard, unforgiving things that clawed their way from the depths of her. They stole her breath, shook her frame, and bent her in half until something deep inside cracked open and bled familiar shades of shame, anger, and regret.

Fingers played against Alice's shoulders before the cushion beside her dipped with sudden weight. The smell of floral perfume reached her before Mom's arms tucked around her.

Let me go! Alice wanted to scream, but she could only cry and gasp and cough and cry some more.

"Come 'ere." Mom drew Alice up, then guided her deeper into her embrace. "I don't know what's going on. You don't tell me nothing, you just out running these streets. Is something happening at school?" She rubbed at Alice's back, her fingers pressing steady circles between her shoulders. "Talk to me, baby."

Talking. That wasn't possible. The very idea of words shriveled in Alice's mind. Whatever managed to make it to her tongue just dissolved entirely. A groan slipped free, muffled against Mom's shoulder, but that was it.

"Okay, baby, okay." Soft shushes and faint humming filled the silence between hiccupped sobs. Every now and then a whispered *Jesus* accompanied them.

Jesus had nothing to do with it, Alice wanted to say.

Eventually, the sobs died away enough for Alice to cobble together a couple words. "H-he's gone." She coughed like she was six years old again. Snot slipped over her lips, between them. She rubbed at her mouth. Her throat burned.

"Who's gone?" Mom smoothed hands over Alice's braids, then wiped at her cheeks. "Is this about your daddy?"

Alice shook her head. The action made her dizzy and left wet, slick patches on what felt like one of Mom's really nice shirts.

"Look, whatever's going on, you don't have to deal with it by yourself." The arms around Alice tightened in a squeeze. "We'll get through it. Together, okay?"

A sudden edge of anger scissored through her thoughts. *Together. What, like with Dad?* There wasn't much "together-ness" in dealing with her father's death.

"But you gotta tell me, baby. I can't help you if you don't talk to me."

That anger sharpened. Alice had tried to approach her mom after Dad died, but the woman either retreated so far into herself it was like she was looking for Narnia, or she threw herself in the opposite direction and got lost in her work. Meanwhile, Alice ended up crossing into another world and killing shit as a hobby.

And say Alice *did* have a sit-down with her mom or whatever, how in the hell was she supposed to explain any of this? Hatta, the pub, Wonderland? Chess . . .

Would Mom even believe her? And if she did, what then? She'd probably forbid Alice from going to Wonderland or seeing her friends. She might go off on some mess about how she believed Alice believed what she was saying, then make her "talk to someone" about it. Maybe she'd yell at her for making shit up and never trust her again.

Or maybe, just maybe, Mom would understand for once, or at least try to. A small, hopeful part of Alice latched onto that barest sliver of a silver lining. Maybe all this could be one less thing she had to carry, to hide. Maybe it *would* be okay. Mom wasn't a liar, like her.

But Alice had no idea where to start.

Begin at the beginning, something whispered against her mind. A gentle touch. A calming press.

The night Dad died. The night she met Hatta. The night everything changed.

Her racing thoughts settled on the memory. It was so crisp and clear in her mind she shivered at recalling the cold press of stone against her back. The stink of the fetid puddles and heat-soaked dumpsters nearby stung her nose. She could practically taste the salt of her tears. Then a beast slithered out of the throbbing dark, followed by a monster slayer, an invisible boy bright and shining.

Begin at the beginning.

Alice took a slow, deep breath. She sniffed and swallowed and swiped at her nose "I—I . . ."

"Yeah, baby?" Mom encouraged.

Alice licked her lips. "It . . . a-after Daddy . . ."

"Take your time."

Her throat closed up, *again*.

The rest of the words refused to come. They gathered at the back of her tongue, piling on top of each other like rocks after a landslide, heavy and broken. It was as if part of her still wanted, needed to keep the secret.

Something shifted in Mom's expression. The corners of her mouth turned downward, and Alice felt the tightness in the arms still wrapped around her.

Get it together, Kingston. She had to say something.

Janet Jackson and company belted *We are a part of the Rhythm Nation* from Mom's pocket. She huffed in annoyance before pulling her phone free. "It's Courtney."

Alice blinked, surprised. Court just left not twenty minutes ago, after getting her own cussing-out. The flutter between Alice's lungs agreed. Something was wrong.

Mom slid her thumb across the screen. "I can tell her to call back, so we can finish talking."

"She probably left something." Alice hoped she didn't sound too eager as she wiped at her still-aching face. "Or I left something in her car."

Mom squeezed Alice, rubbing at her arm, and lifted the phone. "Yeah, honey?"

Court started screaming.

Mom jerked the phone away from her ear, her expression twisting, before telling Court to calm down and try again. Alice couldn't make out what she was saying, but whatever it was, it didn't sound good. The fluttering in Alice's chest turned to full-on flailing.

A frown wrinkled Mom's forehead. "Chester is where?"

Alice's insides went cold.

"A what? Oh lord, hang on, baby. Here." Mom held out the phone. "I can't understand her."

Alice reached for it, her fingers shaking. She didn't want

to take it. Whatever was going on had to be bad, and she was so done with bad, but Mom was already pressing it into her hand. Chewing at her lower lip, she lifted it to her ear. "Yeah, Court?"

"Alice! Ohmigod, I'm coming to get you."

"Wait, what? Why?"

"Something happened with Chess, we need to go to the pub."

"Som—" Alice blinked rapidly, her brain misfiring for a second. Did she hear that right? "With *who*?"

"Chess! Hatta called and said we had to come back, right now." The rising panic in Courtney's voice mirrored Alice's. "Then someone started hollering and he hung up."

Alice shook her head. "No . . . he's not . . ." Her chest tightened all over again. She couldn't catch her breath, and it left her with a feeling like water sloshing around her thoughts.

Mom leaned forward to catch Alice's attention. "What's going on?"

"I tried calling back," Courtney said. "But no one's picking up!"

For a few seconds, Alice couldn't remember how to speak. Her mind was working so fast trying to keep up with what Courtney was saying, what Mom was saying, with her own thoughts, and it kept misfiring.

Something happened with Chess.

Hatta said to come back.

But Chess was dead.

They had to hurry.

Chess . . .

"O-okay." Alice finally managed, one hand pressed to her mouth. She shut her eyes and tried to focus on breathing as the burn of tears made a comeback.

"I told your mom Chess was in an accident and we're going to see him. I—I didn't know what else to say!"

"Okay," Alice repeated, her voice thin.

"Shit, this is so fucked up." The sound of sniffles and whimpers carried over the phone.

"C-Court?" Alice croaked. She swallowed to ease the ache in her throat.

"I'm okay! I'm okay." Court sniffed again and whispered something Alice couldn't make out. "I'm okay. ETA two minutes."

"O—" Court cut the call. "Kay." Alice lowered the phone. Her heart buzzed in her ears as her mind continued to tumble over everything. Something was wrong with Chess. But Chess was dead. Hatta said to come. Something was wrong. Hatta said . . .

Bad. All bad.

"Alison!" Mom snapped her fingers in Alice's face. The sound sent shards of pain dancing behind her eyes. "What's happening?"

"U-um, Chess." The words got stuck again. She pressed her hands over her face and groaned. Her fingers came away wet with fresh tears. "S-something—oh my god. He was in an accident? Court's coming. We're gonna go see him. Please, Mommy." Her voice cracked on the plea. "Please. I—I—I know, I'm grounded, but I have to see him. It's bad. It's real bad, *please*. Please."

Mom pinched her lips together and held Alice's gaze, her brown eyes questioning. For a perilous stretch of seconds, the only sound was Alice's harsh sniffles and choked breaths. Mom licked her lips and glanced to the side before sighing through her nose.

She's gonna say no. Raw, unrelenting panic jolted through Alice and knocked an equally unforgivable idea loose. "O-or! You can take me. He's at Grady."

The small sound Mom made at the mention of the hospital sent Alice's stomach plummeting. It was a low blow, and god, she felt a whole ass for doing it, but she *had* to get out of here.

Swallowing the sour taste at the back of her throat, she pressed on. "You can drop me off on your way back to work, and I'll call when I'm ready."

Another handful of seconds passed.

Mom pursed her lips and leveled a look at Alice. She opened her mouth, and the blast of Courtney's horn made them both jump. Mom shut her eyes, pushed to her feet, and started pacing in front of the coffee table again.

Alice glanced at the clock. Both hands stood nearly straight up, putting the time at just noon. "Or you can, um . . . pick me up when you get off. Please," she pressed. She had to sell this. Sniffing, she wiped at her nose. "Court can bring me home, whatever works, I just need to—"

Mom lifted a hand, gesturing for quiet. She paced a bit more. Her shoulders hitched when Court blew again, but Mom remained focused on Alice. "I don't know what's going on with you. And I hate thinking I can't trust you."

Alice couldn't deny she had that coming, but it still hurt to hear it. She fought to hold her mother's gaze.

"But you're not leaving me much of a choice here, Baby Moon," Mom continued.

"I know." The words leaped free before Alice even realized they'd hit her lips, her mouth suddenly dry. "I know. I—I'm sorry. I just . . . there's a lot—"

Another blast from Court's horn. Mom grunted before stalking over to the door, yanking it open, and stepping partway onto the porch. "I will rip that horn out and choke you with it, lil girl!" Then she turned back to Alice, letting the screen bang closed behind her. She eyed her a bit longer before jerking her head toward the door. "Come on."

With her heart in her throat, Alice hopped up, grabbed her bag, and hurried after her mother, who padded down the front steps. Her feet had to be freezing—pantyhose didn't do much protecting from the cold. Alice followed close behind as they headed down the driveway, toward Court's Camaro.

Court's wide green eyes, red and puffy from crying, watched them approach through the passenger side window, which she rolled down after Mom twirled her finger.

"Here's the deal." Mom bent forward so she could meet Court's gaze, then glanced back and forth between both girls as she spoke. "The *instant* you get to that hospital and find out how Chester is doing, call and let me know, and not from Courtney's phone. Use the phone in his room, or the nurse station, or information booth, or security, or something, I don't care. Then you can sit and visit for a little while. Just a little while." Mom looked to Alice. "Your ass is in this house by three o'clock. Not three-oh-one."

"Yes ma—" Alice started, but fell silent when Mom lifted her hand again.

"I'm not playing with either of you. This is it. Last damn chance. If you mess this up, you two won't see each other outside of school until college." She swung a manicured finger back and forth between the girls like the sword of Damocles. "I mean it. I love you, Courtney baby, but you will *not* be allowed in this house for the rest of the damn year." The finger stopped at Alice. "And I'm putting bars on your window. Don't. Test. Me."

"Yes, ma'am," both girls chimed together. Alice's voice shook almost as much as she did.

Mom tucked her hand into the crook of her elbow, arms folded again. "What time I say?"

"Three o'clock," Alice answered.

Mom peered into the car. "What time I say?"

"Three o'clock," Court answered as she swiped at her flushed cheeks. Her whole face was bright red.

Mom stepped back and gestured for Alice to get in the car, which she scurried to do. She was fastening her seat belt as Mom practically leaned in through the window to stick them both with a healthy dose of side-eye. "*What* time did I say?"

"Three o'clock," the girls said together.

With a nod, Mom threw an arm over Alice to give her one of those awkward half hugs that she did her best to return. "Drive safe."

Court waited until Alice's mother had backed up a few feet before pulling off. Neither girl seemed to breathe until they turned the corner, but Alice could feel her mother's glare following them, like heat from Nana Kingston's comb on the back of her neck. Court kept her eyes on the road, her grip on the wheel so tight the color had drained from her knuckles.

"What all did Hatta say?" Alice asked, anxiety crawling through her. She fought to keep her breathing even, but it felt like her whole body had turned against her, still trembling as she sunk farther into the seat.

"S-something happened with Chess a-and, um . . ." Court took quick, deep breaths and blinked rapidly. "And we needed to get back there right now."

"What kind of something happens with a . . . a—a dead . . . He's dead . . ."

"I know!" Court slammed her fist on the wheel. "That Duchess woman started screaming in Russian and Hatta hung up! I don't—" She pursed her lips and stared ahead.

Shit. Alice glanced around. "Where's your phone?"

Court pointed to the cubby under the center dash. Alice snatched the phone up, punched in the lock code, and hit the pub's number.

It went straight to voice mail and Alice's body went tight. A wave of . . . of rage washed over her. How the hell you say some shit about someone's dead friend, hang up, then don't answer when they call back? Alice had to force herself to relax or she might crush Court's phone like she did hers. She waited a bit, then hit redial. It rang this time. And kept ringing.

Voice mail.

She tried again, her knee bouncing.

Voice mail.

"Damn it!"

On the fourth try, someone finally picked up.

"Looking Glass."

Alice's heart jumped at the sound of Hatta's voice. There was an edge to it, an unease that plucked at the already frayed whispers of remaining strength barely holding her up. "Hey, it's me. What's going on?"

For a moment the line went so quiet she thought the call had dropped. She even pulled the phone away to double-check. Then Hatta said the absolute last thing she could've expected.

"Chess is gone. And he took Maddi with him."

Two
HELLA

"**What do you mean *gone*?**" Court jerked the car to the side, dodging around a slower truck as she shouted the same question Alice had asked Hatta a few minutes ago.

"That's what Addison said," Alice murmured, her mind buzzing as it worked to fit information together. "That Chess got up and walked out into the middle of the pub." She'd understood his words, but they didn't make any sense.

Court glanced back and forth between Alice and the road repeatedly. Each time she snapped her head around, the crease between her brows smoothed, until it vanished and her eyes went wide. "Wait . . . he's *alive*?"

The girls stared at each other, as much as Courtney could while trying to drive. Neither of them said a word. A swell of joy surfaced in the sea of Alice's confusion. Her heart fluttered, filling her chest with this dizzying, fizzy sensation.

"He's alive," Alice eventually repeated, for Court as much as for herself. "He's alive!" A smile broke over her face, and a laugh followed. "He's alive!"

"Yes!" Court slapped the wheel. "Yeeeeeeeeeeesssss!"

Alice screamed, which melted into sobs, and those bubbled over into laughter. She doubled over and shouted into her knees, her eyes stinging, her fingers pulling at her hair. Chess was alive.

Court rubbed at her back, babbling something, Alice couldn't hear her. Alice sat up, wiping at her face, then leaned over to wrap her arms around her best friend. Oh god. Chess was alive.

Thank you! Thank you . . .

Alice pulled back into her seat. She shook out her hands as pins and needles danced through her limbs. It felt like she'd been dunked in ice water then hung out to dry.

"H-how?" Court squeaked.

"I—I don't know." Alice closed her eyes and tilted her head back against the rest. "I don't know." It wasn't possible. She'd watched him die. She'd felt him . . . felt when the last of him faded, and all that was left was his torn body still bleeding in her arms.

"Maybe it's some weird Wonderland shit," Court offered.

"Lot of that going around." Magic *was* the first thing that came to Alice's mind. Maybe he was under a spell, or possessed? That . . . massive Nightmare she fought last night had formed right on top of his body, swallowing it. Then, for a moment, the monster had had Chess's eyes. Alice thought she might've imagined that part, but now? Now she wondered if maybe any of that had something to do with whatever was going on. And if that was the case, this might not be the blessing she thought it was.

"But he's gone," Alice said. "And he took Maddi."

The smile melted from Courtney's face. "Took her? Like kidnapped?"

"According to Addison. He said he'd explain in person. Easier that way or something. But they're both gone."

Silence descended. Uneasiness rose between them, devouring the joy they'd shared seconds ago. A headache wormed its way behind Alice's eyes, and an ugly, black feeling filled her middle. The number of times Nightmares messed her up, Maddi had been there to make it better. Maddi was the one who got her back on her feet with her potions and salves. Maddi watched over her when she was lying in bed, beat all to shit. Alice didn't understand what the Poet was saying half the time, but that didn't matter. Maddi was her friend.

This couldn't be happening.

◊ ◊ ◊

The pub door banged shut, and Alice froze at the top of the steps that led down into the bar.

"Whoa," Court murmured, voicing Alice's own shock.

Glass littered the floor in massive shards and glittering flecks. The splintered remains of a barstool and a couple chairs were strewn about. A table had been halved, one part tossed to the side, the other nowhere to be seen. Behind the bar, some of the shelves were cracked in half. Broken bottles and shattered sections of the mirror spilled onto the counter below. Pools of amber and clear liquid peppered the floor. Some of the paraphernalia had been ripped from the walls, leaving holes in the plaster in a few places. One of the TVs lay cracked and dark against the floor. The tangy smell of booze clung to everything.

Two pairs of blue eyes looked up from where the Tweedles sat on the small step up into the area with the pool table. Blood smeared Dem's left cheek, and he cradled that same arm, while Dee sported a freshly blacked eye, still mostly swollen shut. A matching set of bruises was already starting to purple against their pale skin.

On any given day, Dimitri and Demarcus Tweedlanov were not to be fucked with. They were a well-oiled team of monster-killing murder machines, and they'd been Dreamwalkers *years* longer than Alice. Seeing them like this? Clearly on the receiving end of a beatdown? It shook something inside her. They were the strong ones. They were the steady ones. And right now? They looked less like defenders of the realm and more like two boys who'd gotten their asses handed to them on a playground.

"Must've been a helluva fight," Court murmured.

"Who you telling?" Alice said.

The Duchess knelt in front of them, a first aid kit opened near her feet. Her rope of red hair swept across her back as she leaned in to inspect Dee's eye, murmuring something in Russian. Anastasia Petrova was also not to be fucked with. She trained the twins after all, same as Hatta trained Alice, and was usually a bit of a hard ass. But she spoke gently as she looked to their wounds. It was . . . interesting seeing her like this.

Alice moved down the steps, picking her way through the mess and toward the three of them. "You guys all right?"

"I've had worse." Dem winced. His puffy jaw meant talking probably hurt.

"Shhh," the Duchess hissed before applying a salve to a cut Alice noticed as she got closer. He grunted in return but remained otherwise silent.

"Your friend is good fighter, for a dead guy." Dee looked less happy than his brother about the new scars they would no doubt be sporting, his brow furrowed despite it scrunching up his shiner.

"About that," Alice started.

"Addison wanted to know when you arrived." The Duchess didn't glance away from her work on the twins. "He's in his office."

Alice nodded, even though the woman wasn't looking at her, and glanced at Court. "I'll be back, with answers hopefully. Help where you can, yeah?"

"I'll be here." Court moved toward the bar, setting her purple Brahmin on the counter. She still hadn't put on any makeup today, and her face was bright red from the cold and the fight against tears.

Alice headed for the hallway, glass crunching beneath her shoes. It was impossible to avoid all of it.

Behind her the Duchess spat something in Russian followed by a low "Stop fidgeting."

"What can I do?" Court asked.

Alice, already partway down the hall, couldn't hear if any of them answered. As she walked, she wondered where

Odabeth and Xelon were. She didn't figure there was much the daughter of the White Queen, heir apparent to one of the dual thrones of Wonderland, and her Lady Knight could get into in midtown Atlanta. Then again, maybe royal beings from another realm liked to sightsee? She didn't have much time to dwell on it, stopping outside the open door to Hatta's office. She lifted a hand to knock against the frame, though paused as she took in the sight of him.

Sitting behind his desk, Hatta bent forward so his elbows rested against his knees. His head bowed, he held his face in his hands, dark green strands of hair falling between his fingers. He looked so . . . broken? So not like his usual, sarcastic, charming, brighter self.

In all this time Alice had known him, from meeting him the night her dad died, through his training her to fight Nightmares, then the two of them working together to protect the Western Gateway, she'd never seen him looking so defeated. Well, that wasn't 100-percent true. She'd catch glimpses of him here and there, when he'd be in his office or behind the bar, and he'd get this far-away look on his face. Like he was someplace else. He used to stare in that fancy mirror of his with that expression. Before said mirror was discovered to be part of a shattered artifact of dark power and used to reforge that artifact, thanks to deception, a tiny bit of betrayal, and . . . yeah. Man, this past week had been a lot.

Across from him, the locker in the far corner hung open, and inside it, suspended in the air, was the Vorpal Blade. Sheathed, the blade so black didn't drink up the pale office light, but darkness thrummed along the length of it, waxing and waning just so, painting the air around it with a shiver of shadow. The weapon was supposed to be one of a kind, from Hatta's days as the original Black Knight. The new Black Knight had one, too. Hatta's was bigger. A bit scarier, too. There was a joke in there, somewhere.

"Did it used to do that?" Alice asked.

Hatta's head snapped up and he spun toward her, banging his knees against the desk in the process. "Shhhhhhh . . . mmph."

She winced in sympathy. "Sorry."

"No worries." Standing, Hatta closed and locked the cabinet doors. The key vanished into his pocket as he did a little sidestep Alice was sure was supposed to mask a wince—he was still wrapped in bandages and pretty banged up after the fight this morning—but it didn't work. Coming around the desk, he tilted against the front of it and released a slow breath that was damn near a groan. "What were you saying, luv?"

"The Vorpal Blade." Alice pointed at the now closed locker. "Did it used to do that?"

"Do what?"

"That *whonm-whonm* thing with the light." She flexed her fingers in the air to emphasize her attempt at describing what she'd seen. "I mean, I know it sucks up light, but this was different. Like the dark part of it was having trouble staying on? I don't know."

Hatta arched an eyebrow slightly, glanced at the locker, then back to her. "It's not doing anything special."

Alice had only ever seen the Vorpal Blade, *Hatta's* Vorpal Blade, a few times, but she'd definitely have remembered if it did whatever that was. She pulled her mouth to the side. "We still keeping secrets, then?"

"About what?"

She thrust her hand toward the closed locker. "Don't tell me it wasn't doing something funny, Addison. I know funny acting when I see it, and that sword was acting funny."

A shade of his usual smile pulled at his lips. "Do you, now? In any case, the Vorpal Blade isn't behaving oddly at all. At least, not for how it should be behaving."

That's how it is, then? Okay. Grunting, she wrapped her arms around herself. "If you say so."

"I do." Hatta looked her up and down with those multi-colored eyes of his. It sent warm fuzzies through her. "But that doesn't mean you don't."

"I don't what?"

"You don't say."

"*What?* No, never mind. What happened to Chess?" The fuzzies fizzled out, replaced by an ugly twisting somewhere near her center that warred with the excitement from before. Her friend was alive, even if he was . . . she wasn't sure. "What you said on the phone didn't make no kinda sense."

"I'm afraid I don't know the answer to that, milady." Hatta's tone was polite enough, but the way his eyes darkened, how the color fled to their very edges and the faintest spark of fire flickered to life at their center, told a completely different story. "Or why he took Madeline captive."

Alice's throat worked at a lump forming at the back of it. "This has to be the Black Knight, right? I mean he stabbed Chess with that sword and it did something to him. Plus, he was d-d . . . in no condition to do nothing like this. Not on his own."

Hatta's shoulders sagged, and a touch of the visible fury faded from his gaze. "Perhaps. Perhaps not. Come. It's better you hear the recounting firsthand." He moved to step past her.

Out in the bar, everyone was doing what they could to try and straighten things up. Dem held a trash can while Dee tossed in broken and empty bottles from the back of the bar. The Duchess righted tables and chairs that hadn't been smashed, and Court swept twinkling shards into small piles along the floor. The four of them looked up and paused in their respective tasks.

"Gentlemen." Hatta moved to take the trash can from Dem. "Glad to see you're back on your feet."

Dem snorted. "I keep telling you we've had worse." He started to fold his arms over his chest but looked to think better of it when something popped, making him flinch. Instead, he pressed one hand to his side. "And we weren't trying to hurt him."

"Uspokoysya." Dee looked from his twin to Hatta. "We're fine."

"Mmm. In that case, please bring Alice up to speed on what happened this morning." Taking the trash can with him, Hatta moved behind the bar. He set it aside and started, of all things, to gather up glasses and bottles to mix drinks.

The twins shared one of their creepy glances, then turned to her.

The Duchess kept cleaning. Court had paused, eyes on the boys as well.

"We had just gotten back from taking care of things at the field," Dee started. "The place was a mess, but we did what we could."

New guilt wormed its way through her. Here they were cleaning up after her. Again. Today was definitely a Category Five on the You Done Messed Up chart. "I'll go back and purge everything soon as I can."

"It should be fine for at least a few days," Dem said.

"We hope. There is no telling with Nightmares on this side of the Veil." Dee looked to the Duchess, as did his brother.

As if sensing their stares, she glanced up, but only briefly before returning to her task. "I would suggest within the next twenty-four hours. Let us not take any chances."

Alice nodded. It might take a bit of finagling with her mom to get it done, but she'd manage. She had to. "You were saying?"

"We heard a shout." Dee frowned, or tried to. It was more a grimace, thanks to the black eye. "Then footsteps. It's your friend."

"Your dead friend," Dem muttered. "Only not so dead anymore."

"He has Maddi," Dee continued. "We're surprised, but ask if she's okay because she does not look okay. So I grab his shoulder. He did this." He touched fingers lightly beneath the shiner. "I didn't even see it coming."

"I make a move on the asshole." Dem picked up the story.

"That asshole is my friend," Alice said.

"That asshole punched my brother."

"Point," Alice conceded, not in the mood for a fight. She gestured for Dem to continue.

"He drops Maddi and turns on me. Guy is fast. Really fast. And strong. I almost cannot keep up, because I don't want to hurt him, since he's your friend."

"We try to pin him down. He just—" Dee waved with his good arm, the other in a makeshift sling. "Throws us off. I hit the wall." He pointed at the broken shelves and cracked mirror behind the bar.

"I hit the table." Dem pointed to a pile of wood pieces.

Alice was having a really hard time trying to imagine Chess—who'd never so much as raised his voice for as long as she'd known him—fighting not one, but both Tweedles. And winning.

"We don't need details, mal'chiki." The Duchess tied off her now full trash bag and set it aside. "Skip to the important part."

"Right," both respond, chagrined.

"There was something wrong with his eyes," Dem said. "They were black, with circles around them."

"And he wouldn't answer us when we tried to talk to him. Just kicked our asses—"

"Not mine."

Dee shot a glare at his brother. "Kicked our asses, picked up Maddi, and went out the door. Then disappeared."

"Poof." Dem wiggled his fingers in the air. "Left black goop all over the sidewalk."

"Like from Ahoon," Dee offered. "Remember what we found in that house?"

"I remember." She wouldn't be forgetting that trip anytime soon, especially since it was when the Black Knight jumped her and started all this mess. He'd been waiting for her, had probably planted that goop to draw her out. If she had quit beforehand like she planned, would things have gotten this far? Maybe if she'd walked away without taking one last mission, he'd still be waiting, and Chess and Maddi would be here and fine. The dark, twisty feeling from before flared with a vengeance.

"That stuff was also all over the battlefield." Dem polished off his drink in one go.

Dee took his much slower. "Purged with little problem, though."

"We found the twins afterward." Hatta moved to offer a couple more drinks to the boys, who reached for them with eager thanks. "I tried to pick up any possible trails, but it was too late."

Dem tapped the bar for yet another refill, earning a few words from his twin, likely something about slowing down. The two started bickering in Russian.

Hatta poured another round, his expression pinched in concern.

"What *is* that goopy junk?" Alice asked. The twins had taken a sample in Ahoon, and she'd all but forgotten about it after everything went sideways. "Is it doing . . . whatever is happening to Chess?"

"It's called Slithe, and perhaps." Hatta took a deep swig of his own drink. "Think of it as Nightmare blood. If blood was also flesh, skin, bones, organs, all of . . . that."

"So, Nightmare juice?" Alice scrunched her nose as an uneasy feeling filtered through her.

Hatta rolled his shoulders. "Yes. And no. On its own, Slithe is simply Slithe. It's relatively harmless and flows through

Wonderland like water. It's only in the Nox, where there's a high concentration of fear, anger, pain, all of the negative yuck of the human psyche, that Slithe becomes toxic enough to form Nightmares."

Alice frowned, memories of this morning flooding her thoughts. She tried to recall if there was something, anything, that might help them figure out what was going on with Chess. "The Black Knight summoned a bunch of that stuff on the field. It swallowed Chess and became whatever the hell that creature was. If Slithe is natural to Wonderland, what's it doing here? In our world? What's it doing to Chess?" She managed to keep the edge of fear from her voice, but just barely.

"Everything natural to Wonderland comes from this world," Hatta said, like it was supposed to be common sense and *not* them talkin' 'bout the goings-on of a secret realm hardly no one knew existed. "As far as what it's doing to your friend, I'm not sure."

The Duchess said something in quiet . . . was that French?

Hatta's brows lifted. "Whitechapel?"

The Duchess nodded, her expression drawn.

Hatta stroked at his chin before shaking his head and responding. In French.

What the hell?

The two of them went back and forth a little before he finally said something that seemed to placate her. Then he poured himself a second drink, which she swiped for her own, ignoring his annoyed look.

"Um . . . what was that?" Alice asked.

"What was what?" Still glowering at the Duchess, Hatta

didn't bother getting another glass and instead capped the bottle.

"Whatever y'all said just now. About Whitechapel?"

"Old business." Hatta set the bottle to the side. "Let's focus on the matter concerning your friend."

Alice got the distinct feeling she was being brushed off, but as much as that irritated her, she agreed they needed to concentrate on whatever was going on with Chess.

Court slid onto a stool beside Alice. "Y'all told us he was dead." There was an accusatory bite in her tone.

"There was no pulse. Maddi and I both checked." Hatta licked at his lips then pressed them together. "We truly believed he was gone, otherwise we would've treated his injuries. However, given present circumstances, it's possible we made a mistake, and he was merely comatose."

"That's one helluva nap," Court murmured.

He felt dead, though. And the way his eyes had gone dull? Staring at nothing? A chill slid down her back at the memory. That wasn't a coma. She rubbed at the goosebumps rising on her arm. "Can . . . can Slithe bring back the dead?"

"No," Hatta answered, a little too quickly. "If it were possible, there never would've been a Black Queen, or a war."

He's right, Alice realized. If there had been a way for Portentia to resurrect her daughter, she never would've given herself over to the darkness of the Nox.

"A what now?" Court asked.

"Okay, so, you know how Odabeth is a princess?" Alice asked. "And there was a war in Wonderland a long time ago?"

Court nodded.

"Her grandma was Portentia of Harts, High Queen of All Wonderland, and everything popped off when one of her daughters . . ." Alice glanced at Hatta. He met her gaze, his expression calm but his jaw tight. *Sorry*, she wanted to say, but she looked back to Courtney and continued. "Died suddenly. No one knows what happened except she'd been playing with a human girl right before they found her."

"Wow . . ." Court murmured.

"Yeah. The Queen was devastated." The image of Portentia weeping over the tiny crystal casket would be stuck in Alice's mind forever. "So much so, she went to the Nox, the part of Wonderland where Nightmares are born, and tried to use that power to resurrect her little girl. But she failed, and the darkness consumed her. She became the Black Queen, and she blamed humanity for her loss. So she set out to destroy the human world, which would've destroyed Wonderland. Her own daughters—including Odabeth's mom—had to fight her to save everyone."

Courtney lowered her hand from where she'd pressed it over her mouth. "That's some heavy shit."

"Tell me about it." Alice couldn't imagine the pain of losing a child. Losing her father was bad enough; she saw what happened when her mom just thought about it. Mom would definitely go off the deep end if anything happened to her. "So, if the Slithe didn't do this to Chess, what did?" Alice asked, pushing away the sickening mental image of her mother crying over her casket.

Bzzzzt. Bzzzzt. Court's phone rattled against the bar top. She snatched it up and glanced at the screen. All color drained from her face. She lifted wide eyes to Alice. "It's your mom."

Instant panic wrapped Alice's mind, tight and suffocating. *Shit!* She'd forgotten they were supposed to call!

"Should I answer?" Court asked.

"Yes!"

"But we don't—"

"If it goes to voice mail, that's both our asses."

"What is going on?" Hatta asked.

"I was supposed to—hold on . . ." Alice trailed off as Court tapped her screen.

"Hi, Mrs. K. Yeah, we're here. No, we haven't seen him yet. Yeah, she's right here." Court held the phone out and mouthed, "Sorry."

Alice took a steadying breath. Just the potential fate of the world hanging on this, no big deal. She pressed the phone to her ear. "Hey, Mom."

"*What* did I tell y'all?"

"I'm working on it. I'm at the information desk right now staring the receptionist lady in the face."

"Put the woman on the phone."

"On . . . on Courtney's phone?"

"*Now,* Alison."

"Okay, one second." Alice hit mute and screamed into her arm. This was not happening. This. Was. Not. Happening.

Court winced in sympathy. "That bad?"

"She wants to talk to the receptionist."

"But there's no receptionist."

"There's no receptionist!" Alice didn't mean to scream in

her friend's face; it was just—volume control was a thing of the past, like her life was about to be. She spun in another circle and screamed again. Everyone stared at her, their eyes wide. Hatta, the twins, the Duche—the Duchess!

And like that, an idea was born. A bad idea. A horrible idea. Terrible, really, but it was the only one Alice had.

Clutching the phone in both hands like a set of prayer beads, she half slid, half fell off her stool and hurried over to the Duchess, who actually recoiled a bit. "My mom thinks we went to the hospital to see Chess after he was in a car accident. It was the only way she'd let me leave the house. I need you to pretend you're the receptionist and tell her we're at Grady."

The Duchess's gaze fell to the phone, and her nose wrinkled. "You want me to lie to your mother?"

"Yes! If you don't, I'm on lockdown until I go to college, and probably even then, meaning I won't be able to help figure out what happened to Chess or Maddi."

"Alice?" Mom's muffled voice called. "Alice, pick up this damn phone."

Instead, she pressed it closer to the Duchess. "Help me, please."

At first the Duchess stared at Alice like she was a stain on a nice blouse. She eyed the phone, then held out her hand expectantly. "What is your friend's full name?"

"Chester Dumpsky." Relief poured through Alice. "The hospital is called Grady Memorial." She unmuted the phone, then offered it over.

"Mmm." The Duchess cleared her throat and held it up to her ear. "Hi, this is Anne Smith with the Grady Memorial information center. Why, yes, she sure is, standing right here in front of me."

The Southern accent that came outta that woman was so stereotypically thick and syrupy she sounded like a KFC commercial. Alice did not expect that, and neither did anyone else, given the looks on their faces.

The Duchess kept it up, unbothered by the room's collective what-the-fuckery. "She asked to visit a Chester Dumpsky. Yes. Yes, he came in earlier this morning after a collision. I'll have a room number for her here shortly. Why, yes, ma'am. Of course. Here she is." The fake-ass smile on the Duchess's face vanished as she held the phone out.

Shook, Alice picked her jaw up and took the phone back. "Hello?"

"Three o'clock. Tell Courtney to text me when you hear how he's doing."

"Yes, ma'am."

"Bye, baby."

"Bye." Once the call ended, Alice's legs gave out, and she dropped into a crouch, her arms folded up over her knees. "Ohmigaaaaaaawd." That was uncomfortably close. Like, when someone looked at you through the crack between the stalls in the bathroom levels of uncomfortable.

"She bought it, huh?" Court asked from somewhere above her.

"For now." But she wouldn't be able to keep this up. Not with things escalating like this. And man did she want this to be the last time she'd lie to her mom like that, but who the hell was she kidding. Lifting her head, she breathed a "th-thank you" to the Duchess, who simply shrugged.

"Now that that particular crisis has been averted." Hatta came around the bar to offer Alice a hand up. His smirk sent another flutter through her. "We need to make some adjustments to our plan, which is why I asked you and Courtney to return. And to give you these." He squeezed Alice's fingers before pressing the leather strap of her dagger belt to her palm. "Can't have you out there unarmed. Keep these on you as often as you can."

"New?" Alice asked, a little surprised as she pulled one of the weapons from its sheath. The light caught in the silvered glass blade, highlighting the faintest whisper of webwork cracks.

"Afraid not," Hatta said, confirming her suspicion. "Just a patch job, but they should hold. You're much Muchier than you were before. Plus, I don't think a sword would fit in your backpack."

"True. Thanks." These were small enough to fit in the bottom of her pack if she wrapped them in the pair of emergency sweatpants she kept in case of surprise!periods and monster-gut stains. "So, what're these adjustments that need to be made?"

"I have decided to return to Saint Petersburg," the Duchess said before Hatta could answer. "I fear I have left my Gateway unprotected for too long, a worry compounded by the presence of so many Nightmares on this side of the Veil. However, the boys will remain, as our focus will now be divided."

"Divided?" Alice arched an eyebrow.

Hatta nodded. "You, Xelon, and the princess will return to Wonderland to begin looking for the Heart."

Alice's own heart kicked against the inside of her chest. Christ, she'd forgotten all about the Eye and the Heart for a second! The Black Queen's powerful artifacts that she used to build an army of Nightmares to try and wipe out the human world. Those same artifacts were used by her daughters to seal her away after the war.

The Black Knight was after them—it's why he started all this, no doubt intending to bring his Queen back. They couldn't let that happen. That and they needed the Heart in order to cure Odabeth's mother and Addison of the Black Knight's poison. The only way to find the Heart was with the Eye, and worry for Chess and Maddi had tossed the plan right outta Alice's head. "So the Eye is okay?"

"It and the princess are fine." Hatta jerked a thumb over his shoulder, toward the hall leading to the back. "She and Xelon were resting when your friend made his escape."

"He had to be under the Black Knight's control."

"Maybe." The Duchess stroked at her chin like she was in some sort of TV show. "If he was, it makes little sense that he would focus on capturing Madeline instead of attempting to retrieve the Eye, as it was his primary objective. It seems even in defeat the Imposter remains one step ahead of us."

"Which is why both you and Xelon need to accompany Her Majesty to Findest as soon as possible." Hatta's expression darkened. "Madeline knows our intentions, and she's a strong one but . . . it's smart to make moves just in case."

In case he pulls the info out of her. Poor Maddi . . . "How long does it take to get to Findest?"

"Longer than it took to reach Legracia," both Dee and Dem said together.

That journey was nearly a week in Wonderland, and a couple of days out here. Being gone for that long was *not* gonna fly, especially not after the way Mom chewed her out this morning.

"Meanwhile, the Tweedles will take up search efforts for Madeline and your friend," Hatta continued. "I'll aid them on that front."

Alice nodded, her mind still working over just how she was going to work all of this out with her mom. "I need a day to get ready. To get my mom ready."

"We can come up with some excuse to buy you some time." Court set a hand on Alice's back as she came around her other side. "If anything, I'll kidnap you or something. Go on a road trip without letting you out of my car."

"She'll definitely send the cops after you."

"I'll just cry some white tears, and they'll let me go. Easy peasy Becky cheesy."

Alice blinked before busting out laughing. She had no idea why, but that was the funniest thing she'd ever heard. And just when she felt it dying down, the vaguely confused look on Hatta's face only made her laugh harder. She was practically doubled over and struggling to breathe by the time she regained control. "Lord, I love you."

Court squeezed her shoulders. "Love you, too."

"Okay." Hatta glanced back and forth between them.

"Tomorrow, then. I know it's soon, but we can't risk anyone getting to the Heart before us."

Alice threw a glance at the purple cat clock, which had managed to stay in place high on the wall behind the bar, but it still appeared to be broken, or out of batteries. "We probably need to get going. I'm supposed to be home by three."

"That reminds me." Court pulled out her phone. "Telling your mom Chess is stable but unconscious." The "keys" clicked under her thumbs.

"I'll walk you ladies out."

Alice said a quick good-bye to the twins and the Duchess, all three of them going back to cleaning up, before she hurried after Courtney and Hatta, who'd already stepped out onto the sidewalk. Even in the sun, his skin was still a sickly sort of pale. The green of his hair appeared dull, and the circles around his eyes had darkened. "Listen, I'd hoped we'd get at least a few days to try to recover, but we can't afford the time now. I'm sorry." He shoved his hands into his pockets.

"It's not your fault." Somehow, she felt it was all hers. Still hers. Always hers. She let her friends get involved in this, and now? Now one of them was under some sort of zombie spell. And to think she'd been about to tell her mom about all this. Like hell that was happening now.

"No one's fault, but I'm still sorry. These can both be a thing, you know." His smile widened as he reached to set a hand on the side of her face.

Court made a soft sound and spun on her heel. "I'll bring the car around," she called as she hurried toward the parking lot.

Alice shook her head, gazing after her friend before

turning back to Hatta. Eyes flickering over his face, she pushed onto her toes as he bent forward. Their lips met, and a wave of warmth moved through her. The funny flutterings from before returned, dancing up and down her spine, along her arms and legs. His arms slipped around her waist, and hers wrapped around his neck, their bodies meeting in the middle. Her fingers slid into his hair, and his danced up her back, earning the faintest shiver. The kiss was slow, careful; he was still healing.

When he pulled away, Alice could barely hear anything over the beating of her heart. She pressed another quick kiss home for good measure. This was really happening. One good thing to come out of all this mess.

The sound of the Camaro rumbling toward them made Alice draw back, but not too far. Her hands slid along his arms, minding the bandages. "Now I have to figure out how I'm going to get away from my house long enough to go on another mission so soon."

"Still in trouble?"

"All the trouble." She withdrew from him reluctantly as the Camaro pulled up.

Hatta held the door open as she climbed in, then closed it behind her. "Be safe, ladies." He waved as Court drove off.

Once they were on the road Alice shoved her fingers into her hair and tugged. Tomorrow. How the hell was she going to manage any of this by tomorrow?

They reached a red light, and Court tapped her fingers against the wheel. "So, it really might come down to me fake abducting you to get this done, huh."

"Maybe. I got no other ideas right now."

"What if we kept driving? You hang out at my place, and I don't even take you home until after you get back."

"I can't do that to her. And I can't be responsible for what she'll do to *you*."

The corners of Court's lips pulled back in a grimace. "That bad, huh?"

"Courtney, you know my mom."

"Yup, yup. So, on a scale of one to ten, just how screwed are we gonna be at the end of all of this?" Court asked as she guided them through traffic.

"Hella."

Three

LOST

Alice made it home a whole twenty-five minutes ahead of schedule, waving to Court as she headed for the front door. She didn't get halfway up the stairs before Mom came out, purse on her shoulder, keys in hand.

"Good timing." Mom twisted the deadbolt and checked the handle.

"What for?" Alice stepped to the side as her mother moved past her and down the stairs.

"I got a call from Valencia Hills. Gotta go see what your grandma's up to, come on."

"You want me to come?" Normally Alice loved visiting her Nana K—who was a riot, and could throw shade with pinpoint accuracy, to hilarious results—but she only had so much time to prepare and come up with an excuse for pulling another disappearing act tomorrow. "What for?"

"You ain't got nothing better to do than sit up in that room, and I can't trust you to do that, now can I?"

Alice winced. *Still fair, but ow.*

"Besides, it'll give us a chance to continue our talk, so hurry it up," Mom called before ducking into the car without waiting for a reply.

Heaving a sigh, Alice clomped down the stairs after her. The absolute last place she wanted to be was stuck in close confines with her mother for half an hour, likely answering more questions about Chess, which would just lead to more lies, or trying to pick up where they left off before Courtney's call.

Alice couldn't believe she'd almost said something about Wonderland and all that went with it. Now she'd have to come up with a believable reason for her breakdown earlier.

"How's Chester?" Mom adjusted her mirrors, which was her shifting them, then shifting them back, since those things were always perfect.

"He's stable." Alice glanced out her window, not really looking at anything. The lies used to come so much easier. "Didn't wake up while we were there. Think it was the pain meds."

"Poor thing. Think I'll make some cobbler tonight so we can take it to him tomorrow." Mom backed them into the street.

A jolt of panic straightened Alice's spine. "We?"

"Oh, yes. You're still grounded, so next time you go, it'll be with me. This thing with Courtney was the last time. I wasn't playing."

ShitshitshitSHIT. Her mind sputtered over any intelligible responses that didn't involve words that would end with her momma knocking the taste out her mouth. She stammerred out an "o-okay," but it wasn't okay. Now, on top of coming up with a plan to get away tomorrow, she had to figure out how to keep her mom from popping up at Grady asking for a missing boy who was injured in an accident that didn't happen.

Groaning, Alice slid down in her seat slightly.

"S'wrong now?" Mom asked, eyes on the road.

"Just tired."

"Ahh. Staying up late to sneak outta the house will do that." There was an edge to Mom's words that laced the side-eye she shot at Alice. Luckily the look was brief. "So, you gonna tell me what all that was about, this morning?"

"All what?" Alice fidgeted with the end of one of the straps on her pack and did her best to ignore the *Really?* look her mom aimed at her.

"All that blubbering. You said 'he's gone,' and when I asked if you were talking about your daddy—" Her voice caught the slightest bit, but Alice still noticed. "You said no. So what's going on?"

Mayday, mayday. Her thoughts went about three different directions at once, but ended up going nowhere. "I . . . That was . . ."

Janet Jackson started singing again, her voice echoing through the car. Alice's gaze pinned to the screen on the center dash where the words *The Office* hovered over the Answer and Decline options.

Mom grunted. "I gotta take this." She tapped her steering wheel. "Hello?"

Alice nodded, trying not to look as relieved as she felt. Rescued by the Queen once again. She was gonna have to write Janet a letter or something after this second save, out here doing the lord's work.

That call kept Mom occupied for most of the ride. Apparently, she'd worked from home the rest of the afternoon, which explained why she was there soon as Alice got home. Mom and a few coworkers had a trip coming up this weekend, and today was supposed to be one of their prep days. Hard to prep when you're not there to . . . to prep.

Every time Mom apologized for the inconvenience of it all, she shot a this-right-here?-is-your-fault look across the car. Even though Mom still had the rest of the week to get things taken care of—at least that's what she kept telling Carlos, who sounded like a worrier—Alice was sure she'd hear about it sooner rather than later, since she was the reason Mom had to leave work in the first place. And *especially* since those looks had progressed to I'mma-kick-your-ass and this-ain't-over, respectively.

They stopped long enough for Alice to run in and get Nana Kingston some fried chicken and okra from her favorite place before pulling up to the large senior residence where Nana lived now. She moved in maybe six months ago, after it was determined she couldn't be by herself. Her episodes happened more frequently; she'd forget who she was, where she was, or she'd think she was in some other time completely. It was like her mind had been rewound some years and started playing again right at that point in the past. Those were the hard ones because sometimes her mind would wind back to a year before Alice was born. Talking to your grandma while she had no idea who you were was heartbreaking.

Even with all that, Nana K was still able to function, but the minimal staff here made sure she always had someone around to help ground her, and made sure she took her meds.

Two glass doors leading into the building parted, and Alice braced herself for a frankly disrespectful blast of heat to the face. The whir of the industrial fan clashed with the otherwise peaceful decor. It was like a *Better Homes and Gardens* magazine had a baby with HGTV, and that baby threw up everywhere. Not that Alice had ever seen more than a cover for *BH&G*, but she felt it fit. She wrinkled her nose, the smell of plastic plants, a hint of dust, and spices from the food she carried mingling together. All of that was suddenly and completely overpowered by a wave of extremely floral perfume, which meant Ms. Clara was manning the sign-in desk today.

"Hey, Clara," Mom called to the receptionist, a woman around her age or a little younger. Alice figured forty-ish.

"Hey, girl!" Ms. Clara beamed at Mom. The two of them had only known each other a few months but greeted each other like old friends with loud laughter and smiles. It made Alice grin. She liked Ms. Clara.

"How're the kids?" Mom went on.

"Somewhere bothering they daddy and not me." Ms. Clara had two small children that Alice had met a couple times. Both boys. Nice, polite young men, according to Nana K. "What you bring me?" Ms. Clara made a show of sniffing dramatically, her round, light-brown face all rainbows and joy. She was the only person who probably wore more makeup than

Courtney and looked twice as fly. Nothing against Court, but there was no besting Black women when it came to a beat face.

"This for Momma." Mom gestured to the plastic-bag-wrapped Styrofoam in Alice's hand and moved to sign the two of them in.

"She been wild today, y'all, watch out. Hey, Alice." Ms. Clara waved, flashing purple nails long as Alice's fingers.

"Hey, Ms. Clara. What my nana up to?"

"Chile, you know how she be." Ms. Clara flicked the end of some luscious lashes with one of her nails. "'Bout to run these nurses right. Allegedly, she shook up a whole case of Coke that was headed to this private party for one of her neighbors, old white woman who can't mind her business." Ms. Clara sniffed a laugh. "We try and tell folk not to be bothering Mrs. Kingston, she not here for no foolishness, but what do we know, we just young and ignant."

Alice couldn't help laughing, shooting a glance at Mom, who looked equally amused. "She really did that?"

"I said allegedly. Her neighbor certainly thinks so, but there's no way to prove it. No one saw your grandma till after the party, and she goes, 'Looks like you shook things up, Susan.'"

Mom's eyes went wide. "She did *not*."

Ms. Clara grinned and shrugged, sitting back in her chair. "You didn't hear it from me, though." The spray-painted *Fat & Fabulous* that curved across her chest in colorful cursive matched her bright eyeshadow, and her fire truck red curls matched her lipstick.

"Other than alleged soda vandalism, how's she doing?" Mom asked.

Some of the joy left Ms. Clara's face. "Yesterday was bad after you left. She kept asking for Sydney. Took her a while to get to bed."

At the mention of her father, Alice felt a twist in her chest that sent a sharp sting to the back of her throat and eyes. Mom nodded and released a somewhat shuddering breath. "Thank you, Clara."

"Anytime, girl. Y'all tell her I said hey, and she need to come down here and visit me soon!"

Mom led the way into the main atrium, through the sea of couches and chairs strewn about, past the little café that hardly ever had more than a couple sandwiches and some huge slices of vanilla cake in the display, and toward the elevator. The facility was nice enough, the little apartments pretty fancy.

On the way up, Mom muttered to herself. "She was fine when I left, she was *fine*."

Alice reached to take her hand. "Sounds like she's doing better today. And I know she'll be good when she gets some of this chicken."

Mom released a slow breath and nodded, smiling. "Nothing like Max's to make you feel right."

On the third floor, Alice led the way down the hall toward Nana Kingston's little apartment. She had a corner, so her place was a bit bigger than the others, which was a good thing because this woman was a pack rat and a bookworm all rolled into one.

Alice knocked loudly. At first there was no answer, and right when she started to try again, she heard a voice holler from inside.

"That better be Midge with an apology for talkin' shit like she won't get hers, or I'll—" The door yanked open, and a plump, dark-skinned woman that stood eye-to-eye with Alice, unless the silver Afro atop her head counted, stopped mid-rant. She blinked brown eyes so rich the color seemed to swirl behind her gold glasses and smiled wide enough it made your face hurt. "My baby!"

Alice returned the smile and pressed forward into the tight hug. "Hey, Nana K."

Nana K pressed loud kisses all over Alice's face, then swiped at the burgundy lipstick she no doubt left under one eye. "My girl. Hey, Missy," Nana K called to Alice's mother.

"Hey, Mom. We brought you Max's," Mom sang and gestured to the bag.

"Oh, my girls and my favorite chicken, thank you, Jesus." Nana K clapped her hands together then led the way into the apartment, though she paused and threw a suspicious look over her shoulder, eyes peering over the rim of her glasses. "You get the okra?"

"Two larges." Alice patted the bag.

"*My* girls. Come on, come on!" Nana K shuffled into the small kitchen, gesturing for the two of them to sit in the den/dining room.

She busted out some plates, forks, and Pepsi cans, and it didn't take long before the three of them were cackling and talking around and between mouthfuls of food. It felt nice to laugh, even if it was about a lot of nothing. Mom caught Nana K up on some gossip at church, Nana K pleaded the Fifth about the soda incident, it was all good.

Then Mom took a long drink from her can. "Mom. Clara said you were having some trouble last night?"

"Alice, baby, you full?" Nana Kingston asked.

"I'm okay, thank you, though," Alice said, glancing back and forth between her mom and grandma.

"Mom," Alice's mom pressed, though gently. "You lost track of things last night? How you feeling today?"

Nana K lifted her chin slightly. "So I got a lil turned around, ain't nothing to worry yourself about, nothing for Clara to be worried about, neither. That why you're here? She call you?"

"She's just concerned." Mom arched an eyebrow. "She said you ain't been down to visit her for a while."

"Well, I was down there just last . . . last . . ." Nana K trailed off. She looked around the room, her eyes going glassy and far off, like she wasn't really noticing Mom or Alice or anything. Then her hands started shaking, and she reached for the sweater on the arm of the couch, pulling it in and pressing it to the lower half of her face.

Alice exchanged a look with her mom as something in her stomach wound tight. "Nana K?"

Nana Kingston whispered under her breath, the words lost as she glanced around, with her face scrunched up in fear. Then she shut her eyes as tears rolled down her cheeks. "Not here. I lost him. W-where did he go . . ."

The burn behind Alice's eyes slid to her throat, and suddenly it was hard to breathe. "N-Nana K?"

"Mom." Mom tried as well.

"He's late . . . so late . . . important." Nana K kept bunching the material of the sweater in her fingers.

"Mom. Hey." Mom slid out of her seat and onto her knees in front of Nana K. "It's okay. We're here. We're right here. See?" She took hold of her elbows gently and leaned in to catch Nana K's wandering gaze.

Nana K blinked through tears, her eyes finally focusing on Mom. She sniffed once, then twice. "I'm late."

"It's okay, Mom. Where're you supposed to be going?"

For a few moments, Nana K didn't say anything, just sniffled and fidgeted with her sweater. Then she gradually lowered it to her lap, wiping at her face.

"Do you need to run some errands?" Mom asked.

Nana K shook her head so hard her jaws trembled a little.

"To the store?" Mom tried next, careful to keep her tone soft. "Do you need to go to the store?"

Another few moments of silence before Nana K started nodding slowly, lifting the sweater again.

Mom nodded in turn. "Okay, we'll go shopping." She started cleaning up the plates and leftovers.

Face hot and achy from the effort it took not to burst into tears, Alice moved to help when a gentle touch at her shoulder made her look up.

Mom smiled at her, brown eyes glistening with her own unshed tears. "I'll take care of this and get your nana ready. You go and grab us some iced coffee for the road. You remember how she like it?"

Nodding, and shaking a little, Alice got to her feet. "H-half-and-half, no sugar."

"That's my baby." Mom kissed her cheek and took the plate in her hands.

Alice fidgeted briefly before stepping past her grandma but pausing long enough to kiss the side of her head. She didn't get so much as a sidelong glance.

Swallowing thickly, her crumbling heart in her throat, Alice hurried from the apartment, shutting the door behind herself. That's when the dam broke, for the second time that day. The helplessness and frustration from before rushed back in, for a whole new slew of reasons. God she hated seeing her grandma like that. Hated that she didn't know how to help, that she locked up. Then there was this . . . sour feeling that always crept in, telling her she was failing her grandma. She was being a bad granddaughter, a bad person. Most days she could fight that feeling back, but today? The lingering sting of her recent failures only made it worse, and she fought to breathe around sobs as she hurried for the stairs.

By the time she reached the café, she'd managed to rein her wild emotions back under control. Slow, careful breaths helped keep it that way. The little lobby café was never really busy, but it was almost closing time, so a few folks were down here for last call. Two white women stood at the counter, perusing the menu like there was more than five options. It wasn't a damn Starbucks.

When they asked the bored-looking Indian girl behind the counter what kind of beans went into the vanilla bean latte,

Alice rolled her eyes so hard she swore she saw the inside of her scalp. Man, she wished she had her phone, if just to pass the time.

"Good night," Ms. Clara called to whoever was on their way out.

"Night."

Alice's whole body went rigid at the sound of that voice, and she spun toward the exit. A white boy paused just inside the automatic doors as they parted. His brown hair jumped slightly as heat blasted him in the face.

It can't be . . .

The boy turned. Violet eyes found and held Alice's for a heartbeat. Then he spun and stepped out the door.

Four

BOO-THANG

"Hey, baby, where's the fire?" Ms. Clara called, but Alice didn't stop or even glance back as she bolted past the reception desk and for the exit. The doors didn't open fast enough, and she nearly crashed into them, rattling them as she twisted to push through sideways.

Slamming to a halt outside, she drank in gulps of cold air, her head whipping around in search of Chess. That was him, she was sure of it.

A sharp whistle split the air. Alice whirled to spot him standing along the sidewalk that circled the building. His hands shoved into his pockets, he watched her with his face completely blank. He wore the Paramore T-shirt she'd gotten him for Christmas last year. The two of them and Courtney had gone to a concert that summer. He'd said it was the best night of his life.

Alice hesitated, her heart pounding in her ears. She took a step toward him. He didn't move. She took a few more, slowly closing the distance between them. He watched her, violet eyes tracking her.

As she approached, she looked him over. Cuts and bruises stuck out here and there along his arms, but most of them were faded, nearly gone. She lifted a shaking hand. He still didn't move as she pressed it to his chest. A breath escaped her when her fingers made contact. The softness of his shirt. The firm muscle beneath. He was real, solid and warm against her fingers.

"H-how . . ." she croaked, her throat closing off.

Without a word, he lifted his shirt.

Alice's stomach roiled at the sight of pale skin split open, the edges ragged, ripped. Where there should've been blood, something more like oil festered, slick and glistening. Slithe. She slapped a hand to her mouth as she recoiled, unable to help it. "Oh my god . . ."

Chess touched the edge of the wound that had surely killed him, the same wound Alice remembered pressing her hands to, trying to stop the bleeding. But his life had poured out of him anyway. He traced the darkened flesh gently, his fingers coming away stained black.

"She told me you did this." There was something off about his voice, something deep, something sad, and so not like him. "You left me to die in the dark."

"I—I . . ." Every inch of her went cold, and her insides melted away. How . . . *how* could he think . . . Alice wanted to say it wasn't true, but the denial dried up on her tongue. Chess had gotten hurt *after* the Black Knight took him, but that only happened because she let it. She put her friends at risk. Her vision blurred. She bit hard into her lower lip, hoping this pain would distract her from the ache threatening to crack her open.

There was no denying her part in it all, but one thing was true.

"I didn't leave you." The trembling started there, in her words, and spread until her whole body was taken by it. "Even though I th-thought you were gone. E-even though I saw you fade." Tears streaked hot along her cheeks. "I'd *never* leave you." She held his gaze, needing, begging him to believe her.

That's when she noticed the violet in his eyes had dulled, and the warmth had gone clean out of them.

Something's wrong. Wait, the fuck did he say? ". . . She?"

His expression remained blank, though a single brow had arched slightly. "Mmm?"

"You said *she* told you. Who's she?"

Chess frowned as if he wasn't sure he understood the question, then his expression smoothed out like someone had hit a reset button for his face. "My lady."

"Your who?"

"My lady," he repeated. "My . . . queen. She says you have to come with me."

Alice's stomach dropped at those words. She was suddenly very aware that she was out here by herself with him, and that sent a tremor of fear through her. Before today, before this very moment, Alice would've never thought Chester was capable of hurting her, or anyone, but he *did* attack the twins. And he took Maddi.

"How about you come with me, instead," she said. "You're

not well, and I know people who can help you." She offered him her hand. "*I* can help you."

"Help me."

"That's right. I can help you." Despite something inside her screaming at how wrong this was, she inched nearer to him. "Let me help you. Then we can help my other friend, Maddi. Do you remember Maddi? From the pub?"

His frown returned. His entire face twisted with it. "Maddi."

"Mmhm." Another step brought her within arm's length. Tensing, and anchoring her weight just in case, she reached for him. When he didn't so much as blink, she closed her fingers around his. They were icy cold. "What's happening to you?"

"I'm not . . . I'm supposed to take you . . ."

She pressed her free hand to his chest again. Warmth washed over her palm.

He jerked away from her, his hands going to his head. "Take her. Take . . ." He made a noise that was something between a whimper and a groan, clearly in pain.

She started to steady him, but before she could, he jerked his head up, eyes wide and bright. They danced around for a second, frantic, before settling on her.

He blinked. "Alice?"

Frozen, her hands still in the air, she nodded slowly. The way he said her name, like he wasn't certain it was her but desperately wanted to believe it was, sent a not-unfamiliar thrill through her. "It's me." She gripped his shoulders, her fingers digging in. "I'm here. Are you—"

He closed the distance between them. Something in her shouted to pull back, but she was rooted to the spot. His lips were warm as they pressed to hers. Soft at first, then firmer. The kiss was clumsy, hungry. He tasted like honey, rich and slightly sweet, and she chased that flavor, surprised at how much she wanted more. Her heart hammered against her ribs. Her breath escaped where it could. When he finally broke away, she let him.

Her senses buzzing, her lips tingling, Alice held to Chess where her arms had gone around his shoulders. His fit around her waist. Panting, he swallowed thickly and shifted out of her hold. "You need to stay away from me."

A different kind of buzzing moved through her now. "What?"

"I don't want to hurt you, but she'll make me." He gritted his teeth and shut his eyes. "Damn it, I almost—I can't fight her, not now. Please, Alice, promise me you'll . . ." He trailed off, his gaze drifting past her. His eyes widened.

Confused, Alice whirled to spot Nana Kingston stepping out of the building, Mom behind her. *Dammit*. She turned to Chess again, another question on her lips, but it dried right up.

He was gone.

Her chest tightened, and she spun in a circle, scanning the parking lot for any sign of him.

"Alice," Mom called, a hint of annoyance in her voice. "What happened to getting the coffee?"

Reeling as her mind raced, Alice backed toward her mother and grandmother, her eyes still playing over the handful of cars, searching. "I . . . I ran into a friend from school."

Mom and Nana K eyed her with disbelieving and amused looks, respectively.

"Uh-huh," Mom said.

"Plus, there were these two white ladies taking forever to do nothing."

"So we found out." Nana K sipped at her freshly poured drink, offering up a similar cup to Alice, her wide smile taking a decidedly sly turn.

Alice blinked and took the drink with murmured thanks, which she repeated when Mom handed over her bag. She hadn't realized she'd left it, and her daggers, in Nana K's apartment.

"The hell you got in there, girl?" Mom led the way to her car. It *beep-beep*ed as they approached.

Weapons forged in another world meant to kill interdimensional monsters. "Books. Got a test next week." Alice glanced over her shoulder one last time. Still no sign of Chess.

The three of them climbed into the car, Alice sliding into the back seat. Thankfully, Mom and Nana K—who seemed to be herself, for now—chatted up about the alleged soda incident, leaving Alice alone with her very flurried thoughts.

My lady, Chess had said.

Three guesses who . . . But did that mean she was awakened? No, they still had the Eye. Maybe it was someone else. Someone able to do what the Black Queen couldn't.

◊ ◊ ◊

Two department stores down, and halfway through Cumberland, Alice was exhausted, partly from being on high alert in case Chess or his mystery lady popped up, but mostly from carrying *all* the bags.

"You young!" Nana K had explained.

Yeah, she was young, but after nearly three hours of shoe shopping, purse shopping, eyelash shopping, pretty much all the shopping, not even youth was enough to ward off fatigue. At least she was getting a new pair of Chucks out of it. Nana K had insisted, though Mom said she couldn't wear them until she was off punishment. Fair.

Alice munched on a pretzel where she sat hunched on one of those couches wrapped around a support beam. Nearby, Mom was trying to talk Nana K out of a pair of sunglasses from a random kiosk. Nana K was a staunch believer in retail therapy, so long as it was done right, which meant getting what you wanted and telling buyer's remorse you weren't taking calls until next week.

"I look fly, though." Nana K patted at her Afro as she eyed her reflection in a little mirror then spun around, arms out. "Ain't that what the kids say? They fly?"

Alice grinned and licked salt from her fingers. "You supa fly, Nana."

"Haaaaaay." Nana K snapped her fingers and turned back to the mirror.

Mom shot a look at Alice, who glanced away innocently. Eventually the two joined her and their bags.

"Whew. I'm pooped." Nana K flopped down and tapped at the arm of her new Ray-Bans to make them wiggle.

"Can you even see in those?" Mom asked. "They're not prescription."

"I can see fine." Nana K stared pointedly at a couple of guys coming out of the Nike store, Black dude and a white guy.

They looked to be around Mom's age. "Juuuuuust fine." Nana K lifted her eyebrows, then set her glasses back into place.

Mom sighed and shook her head. "Okay, but you surely can't see right wearing them *inside*."

Nana K pushed the glasses up so they rested atop her head, sunk into her Afro. "You happy now?"

Mom chuckled and sighed. "I'mma go get the car." She started for the door at the end of a nearby corridor. "Finally." They'd been on their way out when Nana K stopped at the sunglass kiosk. Twenty minutes ago.

Nana K watched until Mom stepped around an Asian family and out the door before pulling something from her purse and shoving it into Alice's hands. "Here, baby."

Alice nearly dropped her pretzel, setting it aside and turning what looked like a random drawstring baggie over in her hands. "Thanks?" She pulled it open and gasped faintly when a glasses case fell into her hands, the shiny black Spade on the side glinting in the light.

"I know Missy got your shoes on lockdown, so keep those hidden or say you got them a while back." Nana K nudged Alice with her shoulder, smiling.

"Wow." Alice popped open the case. Big, round aviators gazed up at her with reflective lenses that shifted along a spectrum of blue to purple to pink. A diamond checkerboard pattern covered the arms, the borders glinting as she plucked them free. "These are gorgeous, thanks!"

"You're welcome, baby." Nana K returned her hug, kissing her all on the side of her face again. "Now, then."

Ah, damn. Alice put her sunglasses away and braced for

the talking-to those two words meant in *that* tone. Mom probably told her about her sneaking out.

"What's this I hear tell you missing curfew and sneaking out and such?"

Called it. Talking to Nana K wasn't a bad thing, even when Alice was being scolded or whatever. But this wasn't something she felt up to discussing. She rolled her shoulders and went back to her pretzel. "Nothing."

"Enough nothing to get you grounded."

"It . . . There was some stuff with Courtney and her birthday, and we just stayed out later than we intended a couple nights."

"And the sneaking out?"

"Just hanging out with some friends, that's all." Alice flicked a bit of salt to the side. *And saving the world.*

"Mmm. This have anything to do with the cutie you were talking to at my place?"

Alice jerked around in surprise. If it wasn't for her Dreamwalker reflexes, she would've dropped her glasses and her pretzel. Instead, she only lost a nearly empty cup of cheese. "W-what?"

"Oh, I'm old, but I know mack'n when I see it." Nana K plucked her sunglasses from her 'fro and, with a dramatic flair, placed them over her eyes. "That the boyfriend?"

Suddenly very aware of the rising temperature in her face, Alice glanced around, almost afraid Court or someone else she knew would materialize within earshot, then back to her grandma.

"I don't have a boyfriend," she said a little too quickly.

"Uh-huh. Bae, boo-thang, whatever y'all call it now. He's cute. What I saw of him."

"That wasn't—"

"Got you a white boy. My baby like the swirl?" Nana wiggled her shoulders as she smiled.

"Nana!"

"What? Ain't nothing wrong with it!"

"There's no boyfriend," Alice insisted. Yeah, there was Hatta, but she wasn't sure what she and Hatta were, and *boyfriend* didn't feel right. Maybe there wasn't a label for them. What do you call the guy from another dimension you're kinda talking to but not really but you kissed a couple times and you definitely have feelings but it's too early to tell? Also, that boy has been around since the Middle Ages but technically isn't even twenty yet because of the whole *from another dimension* thing.

"So you kissin' not-boyfriends like that?"

Alice's eyes slowly went wide, and a feeling like cold fingers slipped down her spine. "You saw that?" she whispered.

"Mmmmmmmmmmmmmhmmm," Nana said, drawing it out. "While ya momma was getting our coffee. Don't worry, I didn't get more than a glimpse. I don't be in other people's business like that."

Alice whimpered faintly. That shouldn't have happened. She should've . . . She didn't know what she should've done, just not that. She rubbed at her face and shook her head.

"Calm down, baby, I won't say nothing."

"Thank you." That was a relief and a half.

"He got nice lips?"

"That's not—"

"They seemed nice, the way you was hangin' on 'em like that."

Alice set her stuff down and hid her face in her hands. "Ooooh my goooood."

"Just tell me you using protection."

She bolted upright at that. "*Nana!*"

Nana K leveled a look at her that said she wasn't joking about this bit.

Alice sighed, but it was more like a groan. "It's not even like that. There's nothing to protect." She crossed herself and held up her pinkie. "Promise."

Her grandma eyed her before copying the action and hooking her pinkie around Alice's. "Okay. Gotta look out for my baby. I'm great, but I'm not ready to be a great-grandma just yet."

"And I'm not ready to make you one. It wasn't anything. He's not even the one, so."

"So we've moved on from total denial to 'the one' at least." Nana K smirked. "Good."

Alice was two seconds from sinking right through the less-than-comfortable, cheap leather cushion, when Mom came strolling up unwittingly to the rescue. "You two just not paying attention. I've been sitting out there for a couple minutes, you weren't watching?"

"Sorry." Alice tucked her glasses into her bag, then grabbed it and the shopping bags, taking large bites of her pretzel to wolf it down.

"I had her distracted, talkin' 'bout her boo-thang." Nana K sang the last word, shimmying her shoulders again.

Alice choked on her last bite of pretzel. *Kill me now.*

"Boo-thang?" Mom asked, her tone incredulous.

"No boo-thang." Alice scurried to throw away her trash and started for the exit at a near run. "Doors locked?"

"Alice, what boo-thang?"

Five

FREE

Mom grilled Alice about potential boo-thangs all the way back to Nana K's place, and it wasn't until Nana K—looking far more entertained than she ought to—told Mom she was just teasing that Mom let it go.

"And so what if she had one? So long as she's smart about it, shouldn't be a problem," Nana K said as they pulled into the lot in front of her building.

There were fewer cars, as now the residents and overnight staff were the only ones here.

"There shouldn't be nothing to be smart about." Mom slammed the car into park like it'd insulted her honor or something.

"Can we not talk about my nonexistent sex life? Thanks," Alice called from the back seat.

Mom twisted around to glower at her. "You shouldn't be able to spell *sex life*."

"Oh, come on, Missy, she's not a baby. Next year she'll be old enough to vote and go off to war. Those aren't half as fun."

"Mom!"

Alice tried not to snicker, but failed spectacularly.

"Tell me I'm lying," Nana continued. "Besides, I said I was playin', so leave the girl alone, yeah? Alice, baby, help me take my bags up?"

"Sure thing." Alice moved to climb out of the car as Nana K kissed Mom's cheek. "Thanks for taking me out. Gotta escape now and then."

"Just keeping you outta trouble." Mom gave her a side hug. "See you, Mom."

Nana K blew Mom a couple kisses as she shut the door then led the way inside. Ms. Clara wasn't at the desk, replaced by whoever was on watch tonight, an old white man Nana K greeted with a passing "Hey, Doug."

He saluted them with a pair of chopsticks he'd just used to shove half an egg roll into his mouth.

Once they were upstairs, Alice set the bags down by the front closet and Nana K wrapped her up in a hug. "Thanks, baby, I had fun today."

"Me too." Alice returned the squeeze, smiling. "And thanks for not telling Mom about the kiss."

"My secret. At least until the next time I see her, so y'all better talk before then, okay?"

Alice winced but nodded.

"Good girl. Oh, lemme grab something I meant to give

your momma. Be right back." Nana K ducked down the short hall that led to her bedroom.

Alice shuffled back and forth while she waited, soaking in the lingering scent of chicken from earlier. On top of that, Nana K's place always managed to smell just slightly like sugar cookies.

"Alice."

"Yeah?"

"What's that, baby?" Nana K shouted from the back.

Alice blinked, glancing down the hall. "Did . . . did you call me?"

"Uh-uh. Be out there in a second. Where did I put that—"

"Alice."

She went still. That definitely wasn't her grandma's voice. It was softer, pitched slightly higher, and did *not* come from the back room. Her hands went to her hips, but they were bare, the daggers in her bag in the car. Feeling a sudden rush of vulnerability, she spun in a slow circle. Her head whipped around, her nerves buzzing.

"Alice." More insistent this time, and from her left.

She turned and nearly fell over backward when she spotted her reflection in the large oval mirror on the wall by the door. Her reflection gazed back at her, but not like how you look at yourself in the mirror. There was an awareness behind her eyes, and her clothes were different. A dress sewn from light fell over her form, the skirts glowing bright white. It was the same dress she'd seen in her dreams, and then at the pub when she'd pulled the Eye from the mirror after Odabeth used a Verse to reform it from the shattered pieces.

"Alice," Reflection-Alice said. Her voice held the faintest bit of an echo. "You have to free it."

"F-free . . ." Alice chanced a glance at the hallway and her grandma's half-closed door. The last thing she needed was her Nana coming out here and finding her talking to herself. Or worse, talking to . . . herself. She looked back to the mirror, her breath catching as it started to come quicker. "Free what?"

Reflection-Alice placed her hand against her chest. A spark of red flickered to life beneath her hand. Once, twice more, it spilled out from between her fingers and illuminated her dark face in soft red.

"I—I don't understand," Alice whispered.

"It's trapped. In darkness. In fear." Reflection-Alice grimaced, her other hand joining the first, both clutching at her glowing chest. "It can't survive like this. It will give in."

"Okay, baby," Nana K called.

Alice glanced in the direction of the bedroom again, then back. Reflection-Alice reached *through* the mirror, her arm translucent where it hung in the open air. Alice wanted to pull back, but she stood, frozen, as Reflection-Alice's see-through fingertips touched the center of her chest. The same red light that poured from Reflection-Alice now poured from her.

"W-what!?"

"Free it," Reflection-Alice whispered before vanishing. So did the light, leaving Alice holding just her chest as Nana Kingston came around the corner.

"Sorry that took so—baby?"

Panting and clutching at her shirt, Alice stared at her

grandmother, not sure what to say, or if she could form words at all.

Nana K frowned and moved forward, her hand falling over Alice's. "You okay? What's wrong?"

Alice shook her head, swallowing thickly as she glanced to the mirror, then back again. "N-nothing. I saw myself in the—" She gestured at the mirror. "My reflection scared me." It was true.

Nana K looked to the mirror as well, then to Alice, and arched an eyebrow. "Your reflection."

Nodding, Alice hoped her grandma couldn't hear or feel how fast her heart was beating. "You know how you forget a mirror is there, then see yourself and think it's a whole other person?"

Nana K looked to the mirror one more time. "That happens to me sometimes. C'mere a second." She set a Target bag by the door. "That's for your momma, but I got something for you, too." She took Alice's hand and led the way toward her bedroom.

Alice stole another glance at the now-regular-looking mirror before following obediently. Nana K's room looked like something out of a fairy tale. Hunks of stained and painted glass stuck to the walls, forming this sort of Technicolor path that flowed across all four walls. Strings of small, soft lights hung from the ceiling in a web work of illumination. Their glow caught in the reflective surfaces and bounced around, dancing like it was alive. No matter what direction you looked, your face was cast back at you in fractured starlight.

An old, plush burgundy chair sat in the corner, with a

fancy footrest in front of it. Two equally old dressers lined the walls, the wood scuffed in a few places and shining with fresh polish in others. One was covered in random pieces of jewelry, the other in palettes of makeup, bottles of perfume, scarves, stuff like that.

Nana K gestured for Alice to take a seat on the high queen bed that sat against the wall, in front of the only window, the flowy curtains drawn closed. The white pipe frame creaked a little when she settled against the mattress. The velvet of the deep purple comforter tickled Alice's palms. Nana K had always had this bed, and it was forever covered in at least a dozen pillows of varying size and fluffiness and shades of red. Alice used to dive into these pillows when she was little.

"Where did I put that thing?" Nana K started opening and shutting drawers, banging around between them, going back and forth between dressers and sometimes drawers she'd already searched.

"Um." Alice eyed the large mirror at the back of one of the dressers, half-afraid Reflection-Alice would turn up again. "What're you looking for? Maybe I can help."

"No, no, I know I put—aha!" Nana K plucked something free.

Joining Alice on the bed, she held out a small jewelry box. At least, Alice thought it was a jewelry box. It was shaped like a jewelry box, a little purple treasure chest with a ruby on the front, though there was no latch.

"Thanks?" Alice reached for it.

Nana K shook her head. "Open it."

Alice hesitated, unsure, then gripped the thing and tried to pry it open.

"Push the gem, honey," Nana K said, peering over the top of her glasses.

"O-oh." Embarrassed, Alice pressed her fingers to the ruby. It caught the light with a faint twinkle, and the lid popped open.

Inside, nestled against a bed of blue satin, was a black chain. The links glistened in the light, shining like they were coated in oil and sprinkled with diamonds, the night sky poured out and forged into a necklace.

"Wow."

Nana K nodded and Alice plucked it gently from its resting place. The chain was long but light, the surface warm to the touch. A charm dangled from the end, a single crystal rose. Alice let the necklace pool in her palm, then ran her thumb over the glittering petals.

"I got that from your great-grandmother." Nana K closed the box and set it aside. "She got it from her mother, and her mother, and so forth. I didn't have any daughters." Her voice thickened with emotion, breaking on the last word. She cleared her throat and huffed faintly. "But I was waiting to be able to pass it to you." She plucked the chain free and gestured for Alice to turn around.

When the barely-there weight of the chain settled against her chest, right near the center, she laid her hand over it.

"There." Nana K took Alice's shoulders and turned her to face her. "Beautiful. The both of you. I would've given it to you sooner, but you know how forgetful I can be."

"I love it." Alice smiled and leaned in to hug her grand-mother, earning a squeeze in return. "Thank you."

"You're welcome, baby. Here, take this with you." Nana K offered the little jewelry box. "And put the necklace inside whenever you're not wearing it, okay?" She stressed that last word. "Don't want it getting scratched or lost. Every time, I say."

Alice took the box. "Yes, ma'am."

"Good girl. Now, you better get, before Missy come call-ing or come up here." Nana K walked Alice to the door, where she grabbed the Target bag, stole a final side-glance at the mir-ror, and slipped out.

She couldn't help looking around for any sign of Chess on her way to the car. He'd turned up out of nowhere before, and part of her hoped he would again. The other part of her balked at the memory of that sludge oozing from his side. What the hell was going on with that? With him? She needed to talk to Hatta, to explain what she'd seen. The Slithe was definitely keeping him alive, or part of what kept him alive, even though that was supposed to be impossible. Then there's what Chess had said about this . . . lady. But Alice still didn't have her phone! She'd have to wait until tomorrow when she could use Courtney's.

"About time," Mom complained as Alice slid into the pas-senger seat. "What took so long?"

"She wanted me to bring you something." Alice held up the bag, which looked like it held some random article of clothing. Nana K was always giving mom clothes—old clothes, new clothes she bought but never wore, all the clothes. "Then she had to look for something she wanted to give me." She touched the chain, which shimmered faintly in the dark.

"Mm, pretty." Mom backed out of the spot and started for the street. "You still took forever and a day."

"Well, I ain't got my phone, else I woulda called and told you what was up, but alas." Alice smirked and glanced sidelong at her mom, who scowled and twisted her lips to the side.

"Uh-huh, don't get cute, or you'll never get that thing back." She guided them out into traffic, which should have been light, considering it was close to nine. "Okay, but seriously, though, what's this about a boo-thang?"

Six

ENOUGH

After straightening the living room, doing the dishes, cleaning the bathroom, and doing her homework, Alice finally flopped across her bed, even more exhausted and now a little sore. Mom wasn't kidding about this grounded mess, which meant Alice was going to be doing every chore in the house, when she wasn't doing homework.

The housework was a nice distraction, for the most part. But now that her hands weren't busy, her mind was. She couldn't stop thinking about this lady Chess mentioned. Did she tell him to kidnap Maddi? Why? Was that the only reason she brought him back?

So many questions. Alice sighed and rubbed at her face. Her hands smelled like Lemon Pledge. Hatta and the others needed to know what was going on. And maybe they'd have an answer or two with this new information. But all of that would have to wait until school in the morning.

Groaning, she rolled onto her stomach and pressed her face into the pillow tucked in her arms. This was gonna be a long ass night.

"You never seem to be having an easy time at things, princess."

Fear jolted down Alice's spine, and her head jerked up and around. Like before, the Black Knight sat just inside her closed window. His legs folded lotus style beneath him, he rested his elbows on his knees and his chin in his hands.

Alice was on her feet in an instant, snatching up her bag and yanking the daggers free in the same movement. She slid into a ready stance, muscles tight, weapons lifted.

The Black Knight watched in silence before heaving a sigh. "It really didn't have to be like this. All you had to do was hand over the Eye. Instead, you tried to pull a fast one."

Anger poured through Alice, fresh and hot. It roared in her mind, filled her mouth, then poured free. "You. Killed. My. Friend."

The Black Knight rolled his shoulders. "He didn't look dead to me."

"You killed him." Alice's hands and voice shook. "And then used that shit to bring him back."

"*I* didn't do anything, kitt—"

"Then some lady or whoever the hell!"

He sucked in a breath, the air hissing through his teeth. "He told you about her, didn't he. He wasn't supposed to. She won't like that."

"*You* weren't supposed to hurt him! You lying asshole."

The Black Knight lifted a finger. "Which, if we're being totally honest, makes two of us. You didn't bring the Eye." He waved his hands as he lowered his legs to stand, still midair.

"Save your bullshit. I'm not here for it." Alice flexed her fingers around the hilts of her daggers. "Where's Maddi?"

"She's safe. And thus far, unharmed. I can take you to her, if you like."

"I'm not going anywhere with you, you backstabbing sonuvabitch."

He lifted his hands. "Hurtful. But fair. Very well, just give me the Eye and I'll be on my way."

"You have five seconds to get the hell out of my house before I put your ass through that wall." A white-hot fury crawled through Alice. She wanted him to stay, to test her, but that's just because the only thing she wanted more was to cause him pain. To hurt him the way he hurt Chess. She wanted to make him bleed. That desire poured through her, settling in her limbs. Her head buzzed with it.

The Black Knight sighed. "Look, this . . . this isn't what I wanted." The tone in his voice shifted, dipping lower, heavier. If Alice didn't know better, he almost sounded sorry. "Not what happened with your friend, not what's happening now."

"If you didn't want this, why the fuck are you doing it?"

"It's the only way to . . . to protect you."

Alice barked a laugh. "Protect me?"

"*Exactly.*" Gravity took hold of him, and he stepped through the air as if descending stairs until he stood on the ground. "My lady doesn't care whether you live or die, so long as her plans proceed, but I do. And, despite appearances to the contrary, I don't want to hurt you, Alice. I *never* wanted to hurt you. But I had to." There was an odd catch in his words, and he paused, as if gathering his bearings. "I *had* to, so she wouldn't send someone else, or come herself, and do worse. You'd likely be dead, and I—" He bit off the rest of the words, fingers curling into shaking fists in the air. "I couldn't let that happen. I still can't let that happen. Please just . . . give me the Eye, so I can go, and this can be the end of it."

For a moment, neither of them said anything. Alice stared at him as the urge to punch and kick until she felt flesh give and bone break roiled inside her. It was a foreign feeling, but she gave herself wholly to it.

He pressed his hands together as if in prayer. "I am *begging* you not to make me do this."

She shifted her weight in her stance just a tad, and narrowed her eyes. "Fuck you."

It was like someone cut the strings holding him up. Every part of the Black Knight slumped, his hands and shoulders dropped. His head tipped forward. His very presence seemed to deflate. He reached back to grip the hilt of his sword, drawing it free slowly.

The inky blade came into view. Light seemed to bend around it, folding away, then back again as it moved, like someone had cut away the air and left it open, full of nothingness. "As you wish, princess."

That was all the warning Alice had before he came at her. She twisted to bring up her daggers, meeting his drive with her own. The sound was like a sonic boom, leaving her ears ringing. Alice shifted with the momentum of his attack, guiding him past her and into the door with a bang. She nearly tripped over her feet as she danced around in the small space between her bed and her dresser.

This wasn't going to work; she needed to get him out in the open. Darting forward, she lashed out with a kick. The Black Knight lifted his arm to block, but her foot connected and drove him backward and through her bedroom door with the thunder of splintering wood.

"What the hell!?" Mom screamed, somewhere to the left.

Shit!

Panic bolted through Alice. This was happening, right here, right now, in her house. Her mother was going to see. But there was no time to worry about that. Alice dove forward, through the remains of the door still clinging to the hinges, striking at the knight in a flurry of blows. She pushed him toward the stairs, or at least tried to.

Mom shouted Alice's name and something else, but she couldn't make it out over the sound of weapons clashing and her heart thrashing in her ears.

The Black Knight parried her attack and brought his sword around in a swing Alice barely managed to duck. She kicked out again, sweeping at his legs with her feet. He tried to dodge but caught himself against the railing overlooking the living room. Another kick sent him stumbling down the stairs with a shout. Alice bolted to her feet, backing toward her screaming mother.

"Get in the room!" Alice shouted.

"What is thi— What are you doing!? Alice! ALICE!" Mom

snatched at her, trying to pull her back, but Alice shook off her grasping fingers.

She threw out one arm in front of her frantic mother as the Black Knight regained his feet. "Mom! Just go!"

"You shouldn't use that tone with your elders, princess." He stalked toward them, dragging the tip of his sword along the pegs of the railing. It bounced against the wood with a heavy *thunk-thunk-thunk-thunk*.

Mom grabbed Alice again, throwing her off balance just as he darted forward. Alice flung herself to the side, colliding with her mother, and the two of them tumbled into the wall as the knight's blade cut the air.

Alice scrambled to her feet, hauling her mother up and shoving her toward the stairs. "Go!" She slid between her and the Black Knight as he turned, sword lifting.

"You can still turn this around, kitten. Give me the Eye. She's just going to keep coming for you and the people you care about if you don't." He extended his arm, pointing the sword at Alice's chest, then angled it away just so, at her mother.

"I'm not giving you a damn thing." Alice darted forward, ignoring her mother's scream. She thrust one dagger toward his chest, twisting around to drive the other at his side when he blocked. The blades collided in flashes of white, shrieks of metal against glass rising into the air.

Anger blazed through Alice. It filled her body, pushing her to move faster, strike harder. She twirled in and out of his faltering stance, pushing forward into thrusts and parries, pouring every bit of strength into her blows. This asshole poisoned

Hatta. Killed Chess. Took Maddi. Now he was in her house again, and threatening her mom?

Enough. "You wanna play with me?"

Alice dodged outside of a swipe, then brought her knee up, slamming it into his stomach. He *whuuf*ed and stumbled back, but not before she spun around and hammered the heel of her shoe into his helmet. He staggered with a cry.

Enough. "These little games of yours?"

A feeling like lighting burned along her arms, cold and powerful, but also painful. She tightened her hold around the hilts of her daggers. If past instances were anything to go by, she wouldn't be able to hold this for long.

Enough! "I'm done." Heat exploded from her palms and engulfed her fingers. Light flared along her daggers, bright and blinding. The Black Knight threw up a hand to shield his eyes, despite his helmet.

"And so are you." With a roar, she was on him. He brought his sword up to defend himself. He even managed to block her attacks, but in exchange he gave up ground as he backed away from her wild and furious onslaught. She drove her weapons home, pouring her rage, her fear, into every strike. Each blow reverberated through the blades. Their light pulsed up her arms and down her legs. It filled her, fueling her.

The Black Knight buckled under her barrage. His back hit the door frame leading into Mom's room. He was boxed in.

"Kitten—"

"You don't talk to me!" Alice whirled into a spin and pushed every ounce of fury and energy flowing through her into the blades. With a *boom*, two white arcs exploded forward.

The Black Knight managed to dodge one, but the second caught him full on, and he went flying, tumbling into Mom's dark room.

Body thrumming, shaking, Alice hurried forward. She slapped on the light. Her mom's blue comforter and sheets were thrown aside from where she'd probably raced from bed at the sound of the fight. Two grooves sliced deep into the floor, singeing the carpet and wood beneath. The dresser across the way was mangled, split in half, its smoldering contents spilling out like guts, the dark wood finish peeling back under the faint glow of dying embers.

The Black Knight was gone. He was *gone*!

"Ahhh!" Alice drove the pommel of one dagger into the wall. The plaster caved, and a thick crack zigzagged a few feet across the wall like lightning.

"A-Alice?" Mom's small voice called from behind her.

She turned to see Mom running shaking fingers over the groove the arc had left in the doorjamb. Brown eyes found hers, wide and confused and fearful. The anger pouring through Alice started to fade. She realized it had been the only thing holding her up when the trembling in her limbs intensified. Groaning faintly, she leaned back against the wall and slid to the floor.

Mom made a small, frightened sound and hurried over to her.

She lifted a hand. "I'm okay. Just tired. Fight took a lot out of me."

Mom stopped in the doorway, looking between the charred grooves in the floor, the mess that was once her dresser, down the hallway, then at Alice.

"Wha-what the hell just happened?" Mom flung her arms into the air. Her bonnet had slid partway off and dangled from the curlers wrapped in her hair. A few had come loose, leaving black curls sticking up here and there. "Who the hell was that? What the hell is going on!"

Shutting her eyes, Alice couldn't help the bitter laughter that bubbled up. Of course this was how it would go. Why not? The last thing she needed right now was her mother finding out her little secret, and what happened? Said secret shows up outta nowhere and rips holes in her house.

"*Alice!*"

"You might wanna sit down, Mom."

Seven

WHAT HAD HAPPENED WAS . . .

Alice managed to calm her mother down enough to convince her to have a seat on the bed. It took several reassurances that she herself was all right and twice as many insistences that they didn't need to call the cops before she was able to plunge into her story.

She started at the beginning, the night Dad died. She explained the Nightmares, Hatta—though she left out a few details concerning recent kissy developments—her training, Wonderland, then everything that had happened the past week with the Black Knight.

At first, Mom kept interrupting with questions, but as Alice dove further and further into explaining, Mom fell quiet. Her face went ashen. Her eyes widened. She'd pressed her hand to her chest about fifteen minutes ago and now had the collar of her nightshirt in a stranglehold.

"So that . . ." Mom cleared her throat as if the words refused to come. "That's why you been sneaking out and not coming home? You out there fighting those things?" Her gaze trailed toward the grooves in the carpet again. "Out there fighting him?" Her voice dried up toward the end of her sentence.

"Yeah." Alice tilted her head back against the wall. She hadn't moved from the spot she'd sunk to after the fight. She tapped one Figment Blade idly against her thigh. The other rested on the bed. Mom had asked to see it. Alice had handed it over, and it only took a few seconds before it was tossed to the sheets.

"That thing on the news, 'bout the field being torn up by vandals." Mom smoothed her collar out only to twist it up again. "That was you?"

"Yeah," Alice repeated. "Only it wasn't someone doing donuts or whatever they think happened. We fought a Nightmare." She'd skipped the part about this being the biggest damn thing she'd ever faced. She also skipped over how it nearly killed her. And all the other times something almost took her out. "I had help, though. I've had help this entire time."

"And that's how Chess got hurt. *Not* a car accident." There was an accusatory lilt to Mom's words.

"Y-yeah." Alice also left off the part about him dying, especially since that was still up in the air. "He was trying to—he got caught up. And that ass—that jerk I was fighting is the one that hurt him. I have to stop him before he hurts anyone else."

Mom pursed her lips and nodded as Alice spoke, though she shook her head a few times as well. The fingers of her free hand went back and forth between tapping the blanket and twisting in it. They brushed the dagger, and she jerked her hand back as if burned, staring at it.

Several seconds passed. Then several more. Mom just eyed the weapon.

Alice shifted where she sat as her mother's chest started to rise and fall faster and faster. "Mom?"

"Oh my lord," Mom wheezed. "Oh my lord, what—what in the world are you thinking? You can't be doing this shit!"

Alice surrendered a sigh. *Here we go.* "I'm one of the few people in the world who can."

Mom shook her head, her curlers bouncing. "Mm-mm. Mmmmm-mmmm, nope. Nuh-uh. Not my child."

"Mom—"

"This is chaos." Mom lifted her hands. "This is madness, and you'll have no part in it."

"I'm already part of it." *And you don't wanna know about the* actual *Madness . . .*

"Then stop!"

Alice blinked. "Stop . . . what?"

"This!" Mom flung her hands up. "You stop. You just stop. You're done."

Alice snorted so hard her throat burned. "I was gonna! I was gonna quit, tell Hatta to find someone else. Then all this popped off, and . . . and now I gotta fix it."

"No." Mom jumped to her feet and started pacing. "No you don't. You don't gotta fix nothing, you're just a baby. *My* baby. And I'm not having it."

"I have to do this, Mom."

"No, you don't. And you not."

"If I don't, people could die."

"*You* could die. Let them other folk handle it." She waved a hand, continuing to pace.

"They need my help."

"What did I say?" Mom shouted, her voice cracking, as she whirled to face Alice. "It stops today, right now, all of it. The lying, the sneaking out, the . . ." Her eyes trailed to the grooves yet again, and the pacing resumed. "You're finished. You're gonna tell those people you're not doing this anymore, you hear me?"

Alice watched her mother while drawing patterns in the carpet with the tip of her dagger. Funny, she expected to be freaking out about having to go over all of this, about having her mom finally learn her secret, but for real? She was relieved. No more hiding, no more lies. And even though Mom was having a damn cow, screaming and carrying on, just like she'd expected, Alice was actually kinda chill. It was weird as hell.

"I can't stop now," Alice said quietly. "That guy, he's trying to resurrect his queen. It's a long story, but the point is she tried to literally destroy the world once. If we don't stop him, she'll try again. Then I'll die anyway. And so will you. And Nana K. And everyone else."

Mom made a sort of wounded sound as she waved her hands again.

"Didn't you see me kick his a—butt?" Alice pushed to her feet, holding the dagger out between them. "I was trained to do this, Mom. I got powers and—you saw that fight. I'm fast. I'm strong. I'm a legit superhero."

Mom shook her head again. Her shoulders hunched, her fingers working at each other. "No. I said no, didn't you hear what I said?"

"And you hear me, right?" Alice sighed and moved to catch her mom's shoulders, forcing her to stop. "I've been doing this for over a year. And I'm good at it."

Mom met Alice's gaze, hers bright with fear and something fiery, all mixed beneath a furrowed brow. "So, so what? What, I'm just s'posed to let you run off to fight some damn demons just cuz you beat up on some lil boogeyman?"

"Nightmares. They're called Nightmares. And he's not the boogeyman. Not really." The boogeyman probably wasn't as dangerous. "And yes, I have to fight him. And beat him. Then I'm done." Technically, she would have to find this lady and deal with her, *then* she'd be done. But there was no reason to get into that right now.

Mom stared at Alice, frown still staunchly in place. "This is some mess." She pulled away and stepped over to her ruined dresser. "Lord help me, this is too much." Her bare toes trailed the edge of the carpet where it was scorched, like testing the water in a pool or something. "My house. Oh my god. A-are we safe here?"

Alice rolled her shoulders, unsure. "We should be. I mean, I chased him off. But he could come back. Has before." At that, she moved to grab the other dagger from the bed. Inspecting the blades, she noticed the cracks had deepened, and a few more had formed. They probably wouldn't last another fight.

"You want something to eat?"

Alice blinked, not sure she heard right. "What?"

"I need to eat." Mom stepped around the bits of door still dangling from the doorjamb. "Gonna make breakfast."

Alice stole a glance at the clock on the nightstand: 1:13 a.m. "U-um." She wasn't really sure how to respond to that. "Yeah, I can eat, I guess."

"Mmhm." Mom's half-rollered head disappeared down the steps.

Left standing alone in her mother's partially trashed room, Alice pushed out a hard breath as her whole body sagged slightly. "That could've gone better." It also could've gone much, much worse. Running a hand over her face, she glanced around at the damage again. This was getting outta hand. She needed to let Hatta and the others know what was going on. If only she had her phone.

Wait . . . She hurried over to the nightstand where Mom's phone lay facedown. Her phone was somewhere in here, but it also probably wasn't a good idea to go looking for it while Mom was processing, or whatever she was doing down there. Instead, Alice grabbed Mom's and pulled up Courtney's number.

> It's Alice. Saw Chess.
> He's full of that Slithe stuff.
> Black Knight came to my house again.
> Fought him. He ran. Tell Hatta.
> I'll try and get there tomorrow.
> Mom knows.

The response was almost instantaneous, despite the late hour.

Oh shit . . .

Alice glanced at the door, then back to the phone.

Yup. Don't text back. See you tomorrow.

She waited a second to make sure nothing came through—Court was the type to say okay or something to a request to shut up—then deleted the messages. More lies. More secrets. She didn't wanna keep that going, but Mom was in a delicate place right now, and random texts about all of this might not be the way to go. She set the phone back on the nightstand. That was when she smelled it, the acrid, tangy scent of smoke.

Something was burning.

Fear flickering fresh in her chest, Alice hurried from the room. "Mom?" she called over the railing as she moved down the hall. No answer, even though light poured in from the kitchen. "Mom?" Fear turned to panic as she raced down the stairs and bolted into the kitchen. "Mom!"

Smoke hung thick in the air, enough so Alice's eyes stung. The tightness in her chest eased when she spotted her mom at the sink, running water into a skillet. Something thick, black, and grimy flopped out of the pan into the drain. Relieved, Alice waved a hand in front of her face as she approached her mother. Any second now, the detector was gonna start chirping.

"What happened?"

"Burned the eggs." Mom sniffed and wiped at her nose with the back of her hand.

Alice froze. *Oh no.* "Mom?"

Mom sighed and let the pan slip free with a clang. She turned on the garbage disposal, and the gurgling whir filled the air for a few seconds. After turning it and the faucet off, she faced Alice. Red tinted her eyes and tinged her cheeks just a tad if you knew where and what to look for.

"I was just thinking, how I'm s'posed to protect you. How I'm s'posed to take care of you, raise you right, make sure you're safe. Here you are running around behind my back fighting people and killing *monsters*. Monsters . . ." She shook her head. "I knew something was up, that you were hiding shit from me. I was scared it was some lil boy and you were pregnant or something. Especially after w-what your nana said. Never did I imagine . . . *this*."

"No, I'm not pregnant. And there's no boy." At least, not a human one, but they'd talk about that later. "This is better, right? Than me being pregnant?" She smiled, hoping to ease some of the tension coiling through the air.

Mom scoffed. "If you risking your life for months without me realizing counts, I guess. You really could've ended up dead, and I would never—I'd never know it." Her voice broke again, and she pressed a hand over her mouth.

"No, no, that wouldn't happen." Alice moved forward then, wrapping her arms around her. "First of all, I'm good at what I do, Mommy. I mean really good, you seen me. And if anything ever did happen—it won't—Hatta would make it right. You'd know."

"And that's supposed to make me feel better? God, I'm in here wondering what I did or what I did wrong, that made you do this—lie to me all this time or make all this up." A shuddering breath shook its way out of Mom. "But it's not made up. Much as I want it to be. There really was some . . . dark knight here. He tore up my house."

"I may have helped with that," Alice offered, still trying to inject a bit of humor into the situation. She hated seeing her mother cry. It pulled at parts of her she'd locked away after her dad died, parts she didn't want making a comeback. Not right now.

Mom cut her a look, but it was brief. She sniffed. "You really out here being some hero, huh? Like one of those silly shows you be watching, Player Moon or whatever."

"*Sailor Moon*." Alice smiled.

"You know what I meant." Mom sighed, shaking her head. "This is a lot." She reached to finger one of Alice's sheathed daggers. "I'm not okay with it. At all. I don't know what I am, but I am *not* okay. I'mma need time. Wrap my head around this."

Alice stayed quiet. The one thing they didn't have was time, but she didn't wanna push. Mom was right, this was a lot, even for Alice, and she'd been at this for a while.

Mom wiped at her face then spun on her heel and made a beeline for the fridge. "I'm glad you kicked his ass. Messing up my furniture." She pulled out a tub of butter pecan ice cream and grabbed a spoon from the nearby drawer. "How am

I supposed to explain this to the insurance people? It looks like a big ole bear or something been running around up there." Mom shoveled a spoonful of ice cream into her mouth and grunted before proceeding to talk as she chewed. "I can't tell 'em what actually happened, they'd lock both of us away."

"We'll come up with something." Alice reached for the spoon.

"Uhp." Mom pulled the tub and thus the spoon out of reach. "Get your own. I ain't sharing with you, I'm still mad." She took another bite to emphasize her point.

Alice couldn't help laughing. "Fair." She wasn't really hungry, anyway. The faint twisting in her stomach was something else, something that had more to do with the unease moving through her.

Her mom was here, okay, and somewhat accepting of what had been going on all this time. But the Black Knight had still been in her house, had attacked her outright. Why? She didn't have the Eye here, and he didn't even look for it. He just showed up and started poppin' off. It didn't make sense, and usually that meant something more was going on.

Crap. He was up to something. And Alice had a feeling that, by the time she figured out what, it would be too late.

◊ ◊ ◊

Out in the den, Alice finished stretching a sheet over the air mattress that now occupied the middle of the space, the tables pushed to the side. She threw a couple blankets in place and was tossing in some pillows when Mom emerged from the kitchen, a plate in hand.

"Do superheroes eat brownies?" Mom set the plate on a nearby table.

A chocolaty, buttery scent filled the air, and Alice groaned as she reached to take one.

"This one does." She bit into the warm gooeyness, and her eyes crossed. "So good."

"Figured this slumber party needed proper snacks."

After Mom balked at the idea of staying upstairs tonight, Alice suggested they both sleep together in the living room. That way Mom could keep an eye on her while she kept an eye out for the Black Knight. Once it was decided, Alice pulled out the air mattress and Mom whipped up a batch of her should-be-world-famous butternut fudge brownies.

"And now that things have calmed down, we need to have a *proper* conversation." Mom settled onto the couch and kicked her feet up on the mattress. "About this whole situation."

Alice figured this was coming. Their earlier talk was just to get everything out in the open, but now that Mom had a chance to process while baking, it was no doubt time to get into the nitty-gritty, as Nana K said. Alice took another brownie and waited.

"I said I am not okay with this, Alison, and I meant it. I'm not sure in what world you ever thought I might be, but this surely ain't it." Mom drew a slow breath as she picked at a brownie herself.

"I know." Alice came around to sit beside her and was

instantly wrapped in soft arms and the smell of vanilla jasmine something or other. It was Mom's favorite.

"I'm *not*." Mom's voice cracked before she sniffed a little.

Silence stretched between them, and Mom's hold seemed to tighten with each passing second.

Finally, Alice shifted to draw back but not completely free. "I wasn't either. Not at first, but . . . I don't know. I was so . . . *angry* after Dad died. And you . . ." The familiar irritation started bubbling up.

Mom, her trembling lips pursed, gazed steadily at Alice, her eyes glassy with tears.

The anger fizzled.

"You were dealing with it, your way. This turned into my way. I don't know what I was doing, just I *could* do it. And, like I said, you seen how good. And it's more than that, I'm doing something important." Alice let a little bit of space open up between them. "I . . . I couldn't stop what happened to Daddy."

"Oh, baby, that wasn't your fault."

"I—I know. I still couldn't stop it. But I'm stopping a lot of other bad stuff from happening. At least, for a little while." She smiled faintly. "I told you I was actually planning on quitting last week. But this mess hit the fan, and . . . I gotta finish this, now. I can't just let it go, or people could get hurt real bad."

"What about you?" Mom stressed. "What about you getting hurt?"

"That . . . happens. But! But I came back from all that, and I'll come back from this."

Mom puffed her cheeks and blew out a slow breath. "Can't nobody else do this?"

"It would take months for Hatta to find someone else and train them. Besides, it's not just me in this. I have a lot of friends who're just as good as me, better even, and they got my back." Alice reached to take her mother's hands, squeezing them. "I gotta see this through with them. I can't make them handle it all alone. Afterward, I'll be done."

Mom shifted in her corner of the couch. "Completely finished? No more sneaking out to kill monsters?" She blinked. "Lord, I sound like one of you and your daddy's wild Japanese cartoons."

Alice laughed and nodded. "Anime, Mom, and no more of any of it. The fighting, that is—there'll still be lots of anime."

Mom shut her eyes, resigned. "It's just that, I'm your mother, and it's a mother's job to protect her baby." She set trembling fingers against her lips. "I can't do that if you're out there without me."

"Nooooo, Moooom. Don't cry." Alice scooted toward her mother, feeling the burn of her own tears. Damn, she was crying a lot lately. She tucked herself against her mom's side, head on her shoulder. "You have protected me. You showed me what it means to look out for someone you love, no matter what. It's because of you I'm able to do this, even though I lied to you about it."

"I'm not okay with *that*, either." Mom sniffed and wiped at her face before curling her arms around Alice again.

The two of them sat there wrapped in each other and the

quiet of the house for a bit. Alice closed her eyes while her mother stroked her fingers along her baby hairs. It felt . . . good to have everything out in the open. Amazing, really. Funny, if it wasn't for the Black Knight showing up like that, she'd still be trying to figure out how to sneak out tomorrow. The next time she saw him, she'd thank him, right after kicking his nuts up into his chest cavity.

"You know," Mom started. "I'm pissed, but I'm also proud."

Alice blinked up at her. "You are?"

"Oh yeah. I may not be happy about how it's happening, but my baby out here saving the world, apparently. And tearing up my house in the process." Mom's tone shifted to mock irritation.

Alice grinned wide. "Speaking of, we still have to figure out what you're gonna say to the insurance company."

"I'll say we came home to find it like this." Mom grunted. "Now you got me lying."

"Sorry."

"No, you ain't." Chuckling, Mom pressed a kiss to her forehead. "Your daddy would be proud, too."

The burn from before returned, and Alice's throat tightened. "Y-yeah?"

"Oh yeah. And also angry 'bout the lyin' and sneakin'. But oh so proud."

Pillowed in her mother's arms, Alice's thoughts strayed over all the things she'd ever imagined her daddy would say if he knew about everything. She'd hoped he'd be proud of her, and hearing her mom say it was the next best thing to hearing him.

You doing good, Baby Moon, but more importantly, you doing right, like I always knew you would.

With exhaustion pulling at her—she hadn't slept in nearly two days now—and nestled between sweet memories of her father and the loving embrace of her mother, Alice eventually drifted off to sleep.

Eight

TEST

Alice weaved through the throngs of students and made a beeline straight for Courtney's locker. Court waved when they caught sight of each other—which was easy thanks to how tall she was in her usual: a pair of pumps—then hurried to meet her.

"Oh my god." Court threw her arms around Alice and squeezed. "You're okay!"

"Until you choke me out," Alice grunted, wriggling slightly.

"Sorry!" Court eased up, but didn't let go. "Sorry. I'm just . . . I don't think I could lose two best friends in the same week."

"I know what you mean." Alice glanced up and down the hall. No one seemed to be paying them any attention particularly. "Were you able to give Hatta my message?"

"Mmhm. He said to call him as soon as you get the

chance." Courtney held out her phone, which was wrapped in a pink-camo case with an angry cartoon bunny face on the back. That was new.

Alice didn't say anything, merely arched her eyebrow before hitting the pub's number. She had about eight minutes before they had to get to class.

"Looking Glass," Hatta droned.

"Hey, it's me."

"Are you all right?" His tone sharpened. "Courtney told me about the Imposter showing up at your place again."

"I'm fine, just tired, really. He got the worst of it." Alice chanced another glance down the hall. Courtney shifted to hide her somewhat from the crowd.

"And your mother?"

"She's fine. Pissed, but fine. Lissen, I don't have alotta time, but I saw Chess. I don't think he recognized me at first, but then he seemed to come out of a trance of some kind? He said some lady—literally called her 'my lady'—had rescued him from the dark. Then he showed me h-his wound, the one he definitely should've died from. It was filled with that Slithe stuff."

The line went silent for a few seconds, and then, "When you say filled . . ."

"I mean like someone had packed it in there like . . . I don't know, where there should've been muscle and blood, there was that shit."

"Curiouser . . ."

Irritation spiked at the base of her skull. "This isn't a curiosity, Addison, this is my friend."

". . . Sorry, milady, I wasn't trying to make light of the situation."

Alice sighed and pinched the bridge of her nose. "I know. I'm sorry, just . . . do you know what's happening to him?"

"It sounds like a morfasil. Remember when Madeline tended your wounds and covered the one on your side with a thick substance that then shifted to match your skin tone?"

"Yeah?" Alice pressed a hand over that injury, or what was left of it. Dreamwalkers healed quickly, especially when Maddi looked after them. The "bandage" had shrunk as the wound did, and was nearly gone.

"That's a morfasil. Or a type of one—they have many uses."

"So the Slithe is a bandage for the wound?"

"That's what it sounds like. I'd have to see it to be certain, but that's unlikely to happen anytime soon."

"So . . . so he's really not dead, then?" She lowered her voice.

Courtney cleared her throat, loudly, and waved at a couple white girls who glanced their way.

"Alice, I assure you, Slithe cannot bring people back from the dead. When an attempt is made, the results are . . . grotesque."

Alice nodded, relief pouring through it. It wasn't that she didn't believe Hatta the first time, just . . . she'd *seen* the light go off in Chess's eyes. He looked, he *felt* dead. "O-okay."

"But this revelation of the Slithe-based morfasil concerns me. And you said it was inside the wound?"

"Mmhm."

"Mmm." Another pause before Alice heard someone

speaking to Hatta on the other end. His voice was muffled, and she couldn't make out what either of them was saying.

Brrrrrrrriiiiiiiiiiiinnnnnnnng!!!

Alice jumped as the shriek of the three-minute-warning bell filled the hall, and kids started to move with purpose toward their homerooms. Locker doors banged shut in a percussive sound-off.

"Hatta," Alice called into the phone. "Hatta, I have to get ready to go."

"Sorry," he said more clearly now. "I was talking to Anastasia. She suggested that this might be the result of him being stabbed by the Imposter's sword."

Alice winced at the memory of Chess's body jerking as the blade plunged into it. The Black Knight had said there wouldn't be any problems so long as they brought him the Eye. Another lie. She bit down the sudden swell of anger.

"Or," Hatta continued. "Another likely source is a Poet, and a powerful one. Powerful enough to enchant the sword with a latent verse. That's what happened when the Imposter gave you that 'message' for me."

Alice remember that night clearly as well. The Black Knight had cut open her palm and filled it with some black sludge from her hand. Likely Slithe, but she hadn't known at the time, and she hadn't said anything until it was too late and the verse took hold, poisoning Hatta.

"Wait," Alice murmured, blinking out of her rising anger. "If it's the same thing as what happened to you then . . . can we use the Heart to help Chess?" Now hope sparked to life in her chest. They were already going after the Heart to help

Odabeth's mother—the White Queen—and Hatta. If this helped Chess as well . . .

"Maybe. It could be the same Verse, it could be a similar Verse with a different remedy. Either way we—"

"Alice." Court tugged at her shoulder. "We need to go, or we're gonna be late."

"O-okay." Alice fell into step behind Court as they hurried down the now mostly empty hall. She didn't want to cut the conversation short, but detention would throw a massive monkey wrench in getting to the pub on time. "Hatta? I have to go. I'll be there later today."

"All right, luv. See you, soon."

Warmth slid through her at that. "Bye." She hung up just as she and Courtney all but stampeded through the door to their homeroom, right as the final bell sounded.

◊ ◊ ◊

"Waitwaitwait. Back up." Court glanced around the lunchroom, then scooted her chair closer to Alice's. "So he just kisses you and vanishes?"

"Mmhm. Now I know what the twins meant when they said poof." Not that there were a ton of ways to disappear, but she hadn't imagined they meant literally.

The sound Courtney made reminded Alice of a wounded animal. Her face had gone bright red, and she blinked rapidly, no doubt fighting back tears. With a sniff she refocused on her meal. "I'm really glad he's okay."

Alice reached across the table to squeeze her friend's hand. "Me too. Even if he is acting shifty as hell."

"And that your mom didn't end your short but beautiful life."

Alice snorted. "Yeah. She even said she was proud. Hella pissed, but proud."

"That still could've gone *way* worse."

"You ain't lying." Alice covered a yawn and rubbed at her face. The pain setting in behind her eyes said this was gonna be a long day, especially after the most sound but brief sleep she'd had in a week. Passing out after nearly being killed before Courtney's party didn't count.

"So does that mean you're in the clear to get things handled?" Court stole another glance at Chess's empty chair. They'd both been doing it since they sat down.

"Sort of. She wants to talk more after school, about just what I'll be doing, how long I'll be gone, how safe it'll be." Alice pilfered a sprout of Courtney's untouched broccoli.

"Man. I did not think I'd see the day when your mom would find out you were secretly an ass-kicking monster killer and be okay with it."

"For the record, she's not okay with it, but she understands what's happening is important. That I don't want the world, her, my grandma, or my friends to end up caught in the middle of an interdimensional war."

"Legit." Courtney took a moment to reapply sky blue lipstick. It was the only makeup she had on today, which was still something to get used to. Their homeroom teacher had even asked if Court was all right after she came in with a naked face. "What time did you want to go to the pub?"

Alice was all packed up and ready to go. She just had to stop by home long enough to grab her stuff and reassure her mom everything would be all right. Hopefully. "ASAP. Though I need a favor after you drop me off."

"What's that?" Court clicked her compact closed.

"Check on my mom while I'm gone. I don't want her to be by herself." Normally Alice wouldn't be too concerned about that, especially since she was never gone for more than a handful of hours in the past. But this time she could be gone for days. Even if Mom knew what was up, she was likely to worry herself into a catatonic state. It would help to have Courtney around to engage.

"Of course. I mean, long as she doesn't murder me. I lied to her for a whole year, too."

◊ ◊ ◊

The rest of the day dragged by, as it tended to whenever Alice had something she wanted to do after school. She told Court she would meet her in the parking lot after a run to the bathroom. It took longer than she would've liked—why was there always a line?—and she eventually pressed her way toward her locker.

She nearly stumbled over her own feet when she caught that violet gaze staring from the end of the hall. She hadn't expected to see him so soon, if ever again, to be honest, but there he was, and there he went.

He turned and moved on, heading for the back of the school. And, like before, Alice hurried after him. She pushed through the waning throng of kids, tossing *sorrys* and *excuse mes* over her shoulder as she went. Pushing through the door, she surveyed the back lot from the top of the stairs. Students filed past and swept between the remaining rows of cars. Her eyes ping-ponged over each head of brown hair.

There. He was already at the end of the lot, and still going.

"Chess!" Alice shouted. A few kids glanced at her, then across the lot at him.

He didn't look back.

"Dammit." Leaping down the stairs, she took off at a run, dodging around a pickup truck and nearly getting hit by a little Toyota, the tires squealing as she danced out of the way.

The girl driving shouted something, but Alice wasn't paying attention.

"Chess, wait!" She hit the edge of the parking lot where she had to duck around a line of trees.

Chess had somehow already made it halfway down the block. He'd stopped, though, and turned to face her. Waiting.

She slowed, panting, her head buzzing from the lack of oxygen and the rush of blood. As she approached him, something was . . . off. She couldn't put her finger on it, though.

She stopped several feet away, chest heaving, tongue thick in her mouth. "Chess, please. I don't know what's happening, but I can help you. Let me help you."

"You think I need your help?"

"Yes! This, whatever's happening to you, it isn't right. I don't know what this lady is doing to you, but I know it's not good."

"You don't know the half of it." He tilted his head back, the sunlight flickering in his eyes. That's when Alice noticed the color. They were black, not violet.

She drew back a step, fingers twitched toward her bag, her daggers hidden inside.

Chess extended his hand, the tips of his fingers blackened.

Alice's eyes widened as inky gunk shot from his hand. She threw herself back with a shout, twisting as he turned to follow. Dodging around another deluge, she turned to run for the school, only to nearly tumble forward when her foot snagged against—she didn't know. And when she turned to see, she found that sludge covering her shoe and wrapped around her ankle.

Chess chuckled, his hand re-forming, though there was something off about the laughter. It lightened, pitching higher, shriller. The smile that stretched his face nearly reached his ears. His teeth sharpened, the whites of his eyes fading to black.

Fear slithered through Alice as she struggled to get free from the goop ensnaring her.

"What's wrong, princess, don't like my new look?" Chess's lips moved, but a woman's voice passed through them. "That's what he calls you, isn't it? No." He tapped a long, sharp, black finger against his lower lip. "No, that's not it. Milady? Milady, that's right. Now then, milady, let's have a chat, mm?"

"Who are you?" Alice asked, her voice much steadier than she felt. This wasn't Chess, and the voice? The voice was familiar, tapping at some small part of Alice's brain that knew it, but couldn't place where from. "What have you done to my friend?"

"Don't worry, he's fine. I simply borrowed his likeness to test out my newest creation. And because I knew you'd follow him, just as you did last time." Fake-Chess lifted his hand, his pale fingers darkening, the skin loosening before dripping like melted wax.

The roiling in Alice's stomach intensified. She withdrew as much as her trapped foot would allow.

"Marvelous, isn't it? Fear, refined to its purest, most potent form, easily manipulated if you know what you're doing, and so many uses. Like reviving and controlling your little friend." Fake-Chess turned those dark eyes on her. "I'm curious to see if I can control one such as you."

Alice struck before she could even think about it, fear launching her fist forward. It connected with Fake-Chess's cheek, but instead of striking flesh, tissues, and bone beneath, his face gave, folding around her fist, cold and wet. Her breath caught as a chill raced up her arm.

"I see you need to be taught some manners," Fake-Chess said, the words muffled by his lips being squished together.

Alice tried to pull away, but her hand was stuck. The fluid flesh of Fake-Chess's cheek began to climb up her wrist and slurp down her arm. With a shout, she twisted to get at her backpack and the Figment Blades tucked inside. The strap slid down her arm, and she swung it around, only for fingers to curl around her wrist and yank the bag from her grip.

"Uh-uh-uh." Fake-Chess grinned and tossed the bag aside. "Can't have that."

The goop continued to swallow more of Alice's arm, and now the fingers around her wrist blackened and spread.

"No," she gasped. "No! Get away from me!" She pushed and pulled, but her arms were trapped. The gunk on her foot spread up her leg. It covered her body, pouring over her clothes, against her skin, cold and wet. "No!"

It reached her face, and she screamed, the sound soon muffled as it closed over her mouth. She pressed her lips together against the slithering sensation, twisting and pulling, but it was no use. It crawled over her face.

She shut her eyes.

Nine

MISSING

Addison pressed his fingers to his temples hard enough to feel his pulse behind his eyes. It did nothing to ease the ache building at the center of his skull, sweeping outward, slowly but surely eating away at his thoughts.

It won't hurt anymore if you just give in.

"No."

Fighting it will only make things worse for you. You know this.

"Fighting is all I can do."

It will be unbearable.

"I am accustomed to pain."

A knock at the door banished the hissing between his ears as his head snapped up. The pounding intensified with the jerky movement, and he groaned faintly. "Yes?"

The door opened, and Anastasia filled the entryway. Her

expression pinched, she looked less than pleased about something. Then again, she often was.

"Alice's little friend is in the bar. She says something is wrong and wants to talk to you about it."

Addison felt the frown pull at his brow. "Courtney?" He pushed to stand, coming around his desk. "She's alone?"

"As far as I can tell." Anastasia led the way down the hall and into the bar, the rope of her red hair swinging past her hips.

As promised, Courtney paced near the entrance, clutching something to her chest as she stomped back and forth, those ridiculous shoes of hers clicking against the floor.

"Courtney," Addison called as he approached.

She glanced up, her eyes wide and rimmed. Her pale face still lacked the sweeps of color and glitter she usually wore.

"What's the matt—"

"Is Alice here?" She stumbled over the words, speaking them almost too quickly to be understood.

"No, she's—" He glanced to the Tweedlanovs, who both sat at the bar, for confirmation. The two of them shrugged simultaneously, then turned twin looks of concern to Courtney. He faced her as well. "Should she be?"

"Oh my god, I knew it, I *knew* it!" Courtney pressed a hand over her mouth with a hiccup as more tears followed the faintly slick trails along her flushed cheeks. She then shook that same hand as she drew a shaky breath. "There was something wrong, I don't—I was waiting for her in my car, and she went off to the other side of the lot, and I should've followed her, but I thought she was talking to someone, I don't know. And she took forever, so I started to drive around, and she screamed, and I tried to hurry, but I was too late!"

Those words shot through Addison with the pinpoint accuracy of an arrow through the heart. They stole his breath just as easily. "Wait, slow down, what happened?"

Courtney wiped her nose and sniffled as she shook her head. "I—I—I don't know," she squeaked. "I don't know! This *thing!* There was this—this black thing with her, then everything just went white, it exploded with this light, and when it went away, she was gone!"

Twin shouts of disbelieving shock rose from the Tweedles as they practically leaped from their seats, approaching Courtney. She hugged whatever was in her arms tighter against her chest.

That's when Addison noticed it was Alice's pack. He reached for it despite himself.

The twins quieted.

Courtney tightened her hold for the briefest moment, then relinquished the bag. "This was left on the ground."

Addison held the bag carefully, like it might crumble in his grasp. Little figurines dangled on keychains hung from the zippers, tiny dolls with huge eyes, ridiculous hair, and little skirts. He'd teased Alice about them once, asking if she was too old for toys.

"Addison." Anastasia's voice cut through the memory.

He looked up to her, then to the sobbing Courtney, who still stood in front of him, her face buried in her hands. Alice was missing.

"Ah." With a thick swallow, he set a hand to Courtney's shoulder and guided her toward the bar. "Did anyone else see what happened?"

She shook her head.

"Was the black thing a Nightmare? Like what chased you the other night?"

"N-no. This was like . . . I can't really describe it. Just black stuff!"

Anastasia turned to the back of the bar area, glasses tinkling faintly before she faced forward again and set a large jar against the counter with a clack. "Did it look like this?"

Inside the glass, what could only be described as some sort of living mud rolled about along the bottom of the jar. It flowed in over itself, unending, even as it flopped about and glopped up along the side.

"Yes!" Courtney aimed a finger tipped with a pink nail at the jar. "That's that Slithe stuff, right?"

"Da. This was covering the room where your friend was this morning, likely left over from the same method he used to abduct Madeline." Anastasia's voice dropped just so, and her gaze wandered around the room before finding his again. She was putting on airs, but she was worried. They all were. About Maddi, and now Alice.

You knew this could happen. You would have been strong enough to prevent it if you'd given in.

"Silence!" Addison shut his eyes tight, pinching at the bridge of his nose. "Just . . . leave me alone."

Fingers squeezed his shoulder.

"Addison?" Anastasia's voice pressed gently.

He shook his head, drawing a slow breath. "I'm fine. Leave it be."

"Ahem."

Addison blinked open his eyes and turned, same as everyone else, to find Xelon standing just outside the hallway to the back. She looked so strange in human clothes, a pair of jeans that were just the right side of ill-fitting and a brown Thanksgiving sweater with a cartoon turkey stitched into the front. Her white hair fell across and around her shoulders.

"Once my armor is repaired, the princess and I will be ready to depart for . . ." Xelon's pale eyes flickered between them, lingering over Addison's left shoulder—doubtlessly on a crying Courtney. "What's wrong?"

Addison started to answer, but the words stuck in his throat. A sudden tautness between his lungs stole his breath and the ability to speak. *Alice is missing,* he was going to say, the weight of those words heavy enough to pull at him from the inside. His hold on her bag tightened, same as Courtney's had. Clearing his throat, he tried again. "Alice is missing."

◊ ◊ ◊

After two more explanations of what Courtney had witnessed, once for Xelon, then again for the princess, a plan had been devised, and now the princess stood in the center of the bar, the Eye in hand. Dressed once more in flowing silks and glistening cloth, she looked every bit like her mother. Addison hadn't seen the White Queen in decades, but the memory tugged at his heart, all the same.

"Open my eyes." The princess finished the Verse, and the Eye burst to life with light. She tilted her head back, and the jewel rose from where it rested against her palms before fixing itself at the center of her forehead.

As before, light tumbled down her body. It coated her limbs and filled them from the inside out, casting her in radiance. And, also as before, she approached the mirror set behind the bar and pressed her hand to it. The surface rippled as if it were water pricked by stone, the image wavering, the few remaining unbroken bottles and shelves fading.

Addison waited for the image to solidify into a location, but it continued to swell, the waves cresting and falling. And then they stilled. Silence filled the room. Heads swiveled as people glanced around and at each other.

"I don't understand." The princess's voice with its dual-toned echo breached the quiet.

"What is it, Your Highness?" Xelon lifted a hand as if to touch the princess but refrained.

"I can't see her." Odabeth tilted her head this way, then that, angled it back and forth like she was trying to peer around or through some unseen obstruction. Her hair swam about her head as if caught underwater. "I can't see anything."

"Concentrate, Your Majesty," Anastasia encouraged. Her eyes moved between the empty mirror and the glowing Odabeth.

"I'm trying." Her words were strained. Her bright fingers flexed against the glass.

The image bubbled. Something flickered briefly into existence. Odabeth bowed her head, her shoulders hunching. The image returned, more defined this time. Black erupted from the center, shards of darkness, jagged and sharp. The ground was ash and wasteland, cracked and broken. Thunderous clouds stained the sky, their mass cut by flashes of red lightning.

Ice rolled through Addison, familiarity chilling him through to the bone. Fear followed, just as cold and twice as sharp.

"Bozhe moi," Anastasia whispered.

"What?" Courtney asked. "What is it?"

Home . . .

"The Nox." Addison tore his gaze away as the pounding in his head intensified. "But that's impossible, she can't be there."

"That is what I see," the princess gasped, her voice tense.

"Princess." Xelon did take hold of her shoulders this time. "You need to release the vision."

"Wait," Anastasia called. "It's changing."

Addison lifted his eyes to the mirror. As Anastasia said, the view of the Nox was shifting, swirling into a whirlpool of black and silver.

Odabeth whimpered.

"This is too much," Xelon cautioned.

"Just a moment longer," Addison said.

"Strewth, it's hurting her!"

Odabeth lifted a glowing hand for silence just as everything settled. A cliff rose against the pink sky above, tinged with blue and red as the day ended. The edge curved outward, then dropped into a wide chasm, and in the distance the same roiling, thunderous skies of the Nox winked crimson. Across it all, a sort of gray haze settled in the air, like peering through smoke. But even with such a landmark, Addison could not place this location.

"Does anyone know where this is?" he asked.

"It is unfamiliar to me," the Duchess murmured.

The twins shook their heads, as did Xelon.

"N-not there," Odabeth panted. "Not here. No . . . nowhere . . ." The mirror shifted again, darkening. Then a face flashed against the glass, razor sharp, framed in jagged lines, red flickering in its eyes. "Auhn!" With the princess's cry, the image shattered. So did the mirror, with a sound like thunder. Shards showered the bar as everyone took cover, Xelon throwing herself over Odabeth.

As the roar faded, an echo of laughter chased after it. His ears ringing, the throbbing behind his eyes worsened, Hatta struggled to his feet. "I-is everyone all right?"

"The hell was that?" Courtney complained as Dee helped her to stand.

Dem picked himself up.

So did Anastasia, muttering in Russian the entire time. "That was impossible. *Impossible.*"

But it wasn't, was it?

Addison pressed a hand over his eyes. "Mmph."

It was her . . .

"No . . ."

"Princess?" Xelon croaked. "O-Odabeth?" Panic danced at the edge of her voice.

Addison made his way over to the knight and her lady, Anastasia close behind. Lying in Xelon's arms, the princess had reverted to her natural form, the light of the Eye no longer filling her. The eye itself lay on the ground, a short distance away. Anastasia went to fetch it while Addison pressed fingers to Odabeth's pulse. It leaped beneath his touch, weak but steady.

"I think it just took a lot out of her, is all," he murmured.

"She will need to rest." Anastasia took up the chain attached to the Eye and draped it around Odabeth's neck. "I will prepare a rejuvenation potion to help combat her fatigue."

With thanks, and help from Anastasia, Xelon managed to regain her feet, Odabeth cradled in her arms. The two then headed for the back.

Addison slid onto the nearest barstool, nearly slumping against the counter, eyes on the splintered remains of the mirror. That voice. It couldn't have been her.

But what if it is?

She was still dormant. She had to be; the Eye was here.

You know that voice. It calls to us. We should answer.

Digging his fingers into his temples, Addison pushed to his feet and went around to the other side of the bar, crunching over glass along the way. He grabbed the nearest bottle of amber liquid, not sure what it was and not really caring, so long as it was hard, unscrewed the top, and tipped the neck to his lips. One, two, three, four strong pulls later, the burn in the back of his throat and the thick buzzing behind his eyes were signs that he might regret this decision later, but for now at least he'd have his head back, for a time.

He hadn't expected the old urges to rise so quickly or so sharply, not after burying that part of himself so deep for so long. And without Madeline, they would continue to grow, until he couldn't distinguish the part of his mind that was lying from the rest of him. He took another couple of pulls, then set the bottle on the counter, taking deep breaths. Lifting his gaze, he found the twins and Courtney all staring at him, their expressions equal parts concerned and impressed.

"What now?" Courtney asked quietly.

"Now." Addison retrieved three glasses, poured a finger of what he now realized was whiskey into each, then shoved them toward the other three. They each took a glass and knocked it back, wincing. "Now we find her."

"No one knows where that was." Dee gestured at the remains of the mirror.

"How do we find someone in a place no one has ever been?" Dem asked.

"Or find a way to find said place?" Dee asked.

True, no one here had recognized that location, but there was one individual who knew Wonderland better than most, and half as much as all. He'd be up to the task, if the old man was sober. If not, well, he'd better be up to it anyway. Addison pulled his phone from his back pocket. "I know a guy."

Ten

DOWN IS UP

Alice jolted, her eyes flying open. Her heart thundered in her ears. Her chest heaved, gasping for breath, she couldn't breathe, she couldn't . . . she . . .

Something was wrong. That inkling skittered along her nerves, and she wrapped her arms around herself even as the urgency of the feeling faded. Like trying to hold on to a dream just after waking, she couldn't remember *what* was wrong, exactly, only that it was. Whatever it was. And it was starting to make her head hurt.

"Ugh, where am I?" Blinking, she glanced around. She stood at the edge of a chasm with vast emptiness before her and the broken Wonderland sky above. At least, it looked like the Wonderland sky. Purple clouds bloated with blue moonlight coasted across the fissure as Dust fell like fine rain. In the distance, the darkness of the Nox waited.

"What am I doing here?"

Was she on a mission? Her hands fell to the pommels of the daggers at her hips, more for comfort than anything. No, she was searching for someone.

"You can't stay here," a familiar voice said from somewhere behind her.

She glanced over her shoulder, meeting a gaze identical to her own. Alice stared at herself, rather a reflection, a perfect copy, save for the massive, flowing white dress caught in the breeze. It was beautiful. She was beautiful.

"Why not?" Alice asked once she pulled her attention away from following the beading around the bodice. Something about the glint in the jewels tugged at her.

"You know why." Reflection-Alice looked out over the chasm. Down in the deep, something shifted in the shadows, bubbling. "We can feel it."

Alice followed her gaze. "The Darkness."

"It stirs. She stirs."

Alice looked back to her reflection. "Can we stop it?"

"Not without the Heart."

"Do you know where it is?"

Reflection-Alice set her hand over her chest. "Hidden."

"Hidden where?"

"In a place that cannot be seen, only felt."

"That helps." Alice faced the chasm again, peering into the depths. Then she raked her gaze over the horizon once more, pausing when she noticed a familiar rise of stone in the distance. The shape, the color, the splotch of brightness where it was carved out. She didn't believe it at first, but the longer she stared, the more certain she was. "Is . . . is that Stone Mountain?" she asked, incredulous, looking back at herself.

Reflection-Alice nodded.

"What in the world is Stone Mountain doing in Wonderland?"

"It's not."

"But." Alice looked to the monument again, and sure enough, there it was. But something caught her attention just past it, a flicker of light glinting off of something. Just beyond the mountain, the crystal-like spires of Legracia, the White Palace, reached for the sky. "That wasn't there a second ago. Where did it come from? What's it doing here?"

"It's where it belongs," Reflection-Alice said, gazing into the distance, her skirts flowing around her.

A throbbing picked up behind Alice's eyes, part confusion and part annoyance. "I don't—what the hell is going *on*!" Wonderland was weird AF, but this? This was *Inception* levels of ass-backward. Stone Mountain next door to Legracia, and was that Coke Museum? *Oh hell no.* "This . . . this isn't possible. It's finally happened, I'm losing my damn mind."

"Not entirely," a new voice called.

Alice turned, as did her reflection, to spy the last person she ever expected half strolling, half stumbling toward her. The smell of booze reached her before he did.

Hiccupping around burps, Sprigs shuffled over to stand just behind the two Alices. The old Black man scratched at his mostly bald head, the two tufts of white hair sticking up on either side of that dark brown dome. It was strange to see him outside of the pub—the guy practically lived on a barstool—and *here* of all places.

"Okay." Alice took a slow breath and nodded. "I'm dreaming. That's what this is."

"Mmm, you're half right. But mostly wrong." Sprigs's voice slid along his tongue and between his teeth like butter over hot metal. He had that old Black man voice Daddy used to call sanded; the roughness was smoothed by a life long lived, but the cracks were still there. *He's seen some thangs*, as Daddy would also say.

Daddy . . . Normally thoughts of her father would send Alice's emotions wild, but she kept her head, stayed steady. Weird.

"This is the In-Between." Sprigs scratched long, knobby fingers along the white scruff coating his chin. "The point where your world and my world meet."

"Your world?" Alice asked, only to be met with a look. "Right, Wonderland, duh." Of course the oldest, longest regular of the Looking Glass Pub would be Wonderlandian.

"This is the Veil." Sprigs gestured. "It's not here, nor there, nor anywhere. So it's pretty much everywhere."

Alice blinked and looked back over the horizon. A few more familiar locations had popped up, like her church and Ahoon. "I get it. I think. These are all places I know, from both worlds."

Sprigs nodded. "Normally you're passing through here too quick to linger, to see anything, but now that you are . . ." He shrugged, as if to say, *This is what you get.*

"Right. So how do I get out?" Alice asked.

"That's the tricky part," Sprigs muttered, glancing around. "Not sure."

Well, that's helpful. "How'd *you* get here?"

"I'm here because I can be here," Sprigs offered, as if that made all the sense in the world. He glanced around, looking more than a little nervous. "Though I'd like to be somewhere else. It's gettin' late."

"Okay, so show me the way out."

"Can't. You gotta—" He went quiet, eyes widening as he glanced around. The jerky motion made him waver on his feet, and Alice reached as if to steady him, though he spun full circle, throwing her off. "Too late. Go down. Down is up. Up is out."

Alice blinked, not sure she was hearing right. "Down is, wait, what?"

"Too late, can't stay. Go *down*," he stressed before backing away from her.

"Hey!" she called, reaching for him, though the dirt beneath him flashed white, a swirl of light as the ground opened up. He jumped in and was gone.

Alice stared for a few seconds, not entirely sure what she'd just seen, or what to make of it. "Down is up," she repeated quietly. "Up is out." She glanced to her reflection, who'd stood nearby without saying one word that entire time. "You have any idea what it means?"

"It means what it means," Reflection-Alice murmured.

"Ugh! Right. Of course." She spun, glancing around, her eyes falling to the chasm and the darkness below. "Well, that looks like the only way down." Did that mean she had to jump? Because that was not happening.

"Have courage, Alice." Reflection-Alice set her hand over her chest again. "Trust yourself. Trust your hear—ahh!" She screamed as a black blade burst between her fingers.

"No!" Alice shouted, eyes on the metal slick with blood. It ran down the weapon, soaked into the white fabric of the dress, washing the entire thing red. Reflection-Alice gagged in her struggle to breathe before going limp, an arm encircling her from behind, keeping her upright.

The Black Knight's head appeared at her shoulder, his mask trained on Alice.

Anger flared through her, drying up her shock. "You!"

"Run, kitten," he murmured, more pleaded.

Alice's hands went to her weapons, but before she could draw them, a sword erupted from her chest, same as her reflection. She cried out, panic blanking her mind. There was no pain, only the feeling of ice crawling through her, over her.

Fingers tangled in her hair, wrenching her head around. A woman with white skin and fiery hair pulled atop her head sneered, red lips split in a vicious smile. "Poor precious one. You've lost your heart. Here, let me help you." She twisted the sword and yanked it upward.

Alice heard her bones snap, her flesh tear. There was no pain, but she threw herself forward with all of her strength, her mind filled with nothing but the need to get away. The sudden jerk took her by surprise as she all but flew out of the woman's grasp.

"No!"

The scream followed Alice as she pitched forward and over the edge of the chasm. Then she dropped into the black, smacking into it with a feeling like hitting water. The cold filled her. The darkness consumed her, and she started falling, tumbling end over end, her arms and legs flailing, useless. She screamed.

Thud. Alice grunted as she hit something solid. Pain radiated through her body. Air exploded from her lungs, and they struggled to draw more in for a few seconds. Her eyes flew open, her heart racing. She gagged on the precious oxygen her body fought to take in, though eventually she coughed and choked her way to breathing.

Her arms felt like noodles as she pushed herself up, tingling fingers patting herself down. It took her panic-stricken mind a few seconds to realize she was alive, and mostly well. She glanced around.

The pink sky above, the beginnings of purple clouds drifting along in the light. Purple grass beneath her, the blades fizzling in and out of sight, giving it the image of wind cutting through them. There weren't any trees, really, just these scraggly-looking yellow things that were more like cacti with branches.

This definitely looked like Wonderland. She took a slow breath, and a faint scent of citrus and bubblegum filled her nose, mingling with dirt and the sharp smell of peppermint. And it smelled like Wonderland.

She sank back, shifting gingerly as her ribs ached faintly with the motion. Pain. Pain was good. It meant she wasn't dreaming, or stuck in the Veil, or whatever the hell had been going on.

Whatever that was before, with her Reflection, that had to be a dream. But Reflection-Alice had been showing up more and more in the real world, so maybe not.

Alice tugged at her collar with one hand and patted at her chest with the other. Her dark skin was slick with sweat but unmarred. She could practically see that blade sticking out of her chest, coated in her blood. She checked the rest of herself over as well.

Relief started to rise through her—until she realized her bag was gone, and with it, her weapons. Of course it was gone, that . . . mess that was pretending to be Chess had thrown it off somewhere. So not only was she in Wonderland, still unsure the hell how, but she was somewhere in Wonderland she didn't recognize/had never been, and she was unarmed.

Great. She huffed, wincing as she shifted to get her feet under her. She stood slowly, carefully, her knees knocking a little as her legs held her weight. *Okay. Okay, this is fine. I'm fine.*

Then something cold, hard, and sharp pressed to the side of her neck.

"Ugokuna."

Eleven

PETS

Shadows crept along the floor, carpeting it in darkness. In fact, everything was darkness and mist. It covered the walls, clear up to the high ceiling. It filled once-vibrant corridors, now decrepit and broken. It crawled over solid surfaces and coiled in the air, a living, breathing thing that had infected this place.

The Black Knight did not like the darkness, even though it did his bidding. Like now, when he paced the open area of what had once been a grand dining hall—the lengthy tables and chairs broken and crumbling, strewn across the floor. The darkness was quiet, contemplative. It allowed things that shouldn't be to take shape, to come to life, like his traitorous thoughts.

For as long as he remembered, he had been loyal to his lady. He did as she requested, performed every task she set before him, even so much as attacking an unarmed enemy and her daughter. He was unwavering. Until the night he met *her*.

He gestured, and the darkness gathered, swirling to coalesce into a more corporeal form, nearly identical to his, but at the last minute, he flicked his fingers and the puppet shifted. The body slimmed, the hard lines of the armor softened into clothes. Hair flowed from its head, twisting outward in coils and curls. Alice.

When he drew his sword, so did his shadow puppet. They faced each other, and for a time, neither moved. He stared at it. At her. There was something about Alice Kingston that . . . *affected* him, especially when it came to causing her harm. Yes, he did as ordered. He attacked her. He used her to poison the traitor. He went after her friends to force her hand. And every time he caused her pain, a part of him broke. Like bits of stone being chipped away, his resolve faltered. This weakness could not stand.

He struck. The shadow puppet countered. Where there should have been a clash of metal there was silence. The Vorpal Blade slammed into the shadow sword. The Black Knight felt the impact in his arms, but darkness was swift and silent. They danced around each other, the puppet pushing into and out of his guard, testing it.

When it left itself open, he moved to strike but froze when it looked up at him with that face. It wasn't hers, not really. There was no light in the eyes, no defiance, no warmth. There was only the cold black, but still he couldn't bring himself to cut her down.

The puppet didn't share his qualms and, with a quick twist, its shadowy blade drove up at his face. He threw himself back, barely avoiding being skewered.

Panting, eyes wide, his heartbeat quickened. He . . . hadn't seen that coming. The puppet held the lunge briefly before drawing back, almost dramatically, and taking another ready stance. He stood there reeling, until the damned thing lifted a hand and beckoned with a curl of fingers, taunting him. Impossible.

Irritation smoldered like coals within him. He tightened his grip on his sword to stop the trembling in his fingers. If he wasn't careful, that anger would rise to full flames. That was why he was training, hoping to burn some of it away.

"Knight," a raspy voice called from the shadows lining the hall. A Fiend padded forward, materializing from the black.

Ignoring it, the Black Knight pushed into another attack. The puppet lifted its blade to block, then twisted out of the pin and into a swipe, driving him back. It followed up with a flurry of jabs.

The Fiend watched with a single yellow eye at the center of its head. "Her Majesty summons you."

He didn't stop. Instead, he spun into another attack, which the puppet barely managed to counter. Pressing his advantage, he drove his opponent back.

"Knight!" the Fiend snarled, its needlelike teeth glinting.

He remained, focused on the puppet. The two exchanged blows and strikes, neither gaining the upper hand nor losing it.

Another Fiend formed beside the first. "Her Majesty

summons." Three glowing blue eyes fixed on him from various points of its head.

Deflecting a thrust, the Black Knight lifted a hand. The puppet halted. It held the sword above its head, motionless as it dissolved, leaving curls of shade floating in the air until they faded.

"Tell her I come," he muttered.

The Fiends turned and disappeared once more into the darkness, leaving him alone.

Whirling, the Black Knight exited the dining hall and moved through the blackened corridors, his stride swift. It carried him quickly enough toward the center of the palace, and the throne room. The grand doors swung wide when he shoved them aside, far enough to slam into the attached walls and rattle the hinges. The resounding clang echoed through the hall, clear up to the high ceilings that weren't visible due to the swell of shadow looming overhead. Flickering torches lit the space; chandeliers were suspended from chains that seemed to float in the air, attached to nothing above.

His steps thudded against the carpet trailing from the door to the throne, a massive seat of metal and glass that looked like it had been split from a mountain, the edges jagged and deadly despite the deceptive softness in their shine. He stopped at the bottom of the stairs and reached to press his fingers to the sides of his helmet. A seam materialized beneath his touch, and he parted it, drawing the helmet free and shoving a hand through his hair. Her Majesty always insisted he remove the helm in her presence. He did so, even though she was not here. Not yet. And while the throne was empty, the room was not.

Chained to a table, the links rattling and scraping against the stone floor as she moved, the Poet girl worked diligently. Her hands shook; this was visible in the slight sloshing of liquids in the jars and containers she used. She threw a glance toward him as he approached, her eyes wide and frightened.

"Crimson."

He looked away from her, pretending to survey the room. "I told you to stop calling me that."

"Red awash away." She turned from the table. The chains clinked and drew her up short. She couldn't go far. "Lost in a sea of say."

"Then we can agree that you don't know me, and you can be done," he snapped.

"Sparkle and shine a tale to tell!" The Poet, Maddi the others called her, shifted to face him as much as she could, her arms drawing back toward her work. "Not who, not how, not when." Her voice cracked the faintest bit, and she sniffed.

"You should get back to work." He tucked his helmet into the crook of one arm. Where was Her Majesty? If his summons was so urgent, surely she would be here.

"P . . . please." Maddi strained against her bonds. She swallowed thickly, her face screwed up in pain, as if speaking hurt. "T-talk . . . me. To. Addison's woe . . ."

Ire spiking to fury, he whirled on her, hand going to his sword. "Shut. Up," he warned darkly. The ferocity of his anger surprised him. Strewth, could he not control himself? His concern for Alice, his anger at Addison, both had been growing steadily since he initiated phase one of Her Majesty's plan.

Maddi had gone quiet, her lips pressed into a thin line.

She stared at him with such sadness. If he didn't know better, he'd believe she knew him. Well, she believed it, at least.

"T-truly lost to me?" she asked, her voice small.

"You should focus on your work," he repeated, relaxing, his hand dropping from his weapon. "Her Majesty does not like to be kept waiting."

"You know me so well," a voice called from somewhere behind the throne, the tones deceptively melodic, like crystal bells.

Maddi squeaked and turned back to the table as Her Majesty strode forward, the shadows at her feet constant companions, swirling beneath her. Pale and swathed in silk and satin the color of blood, she didn't look half as lethal as she had the potential to be. She watched him as she approached, her eyes fixated until she came to a stop in front of him where he stood before the throne. "And yet you kept me waiting."

He stood silent for a moment, his muscles aching with the tension of his earlier restraint. "Apologies, Your Majesty. I was training and did not immediately hear the summons."

When she lifted her chin, he dropped to one knee.

"Milady . . ." he murmured.

With a hum she turned and climbed the few stairs to the platform cradling the throne. The Black Knight remained as he was, his head bowed until she lowered herself into the curve of the seat and waved a hand. "Rise."

He straightened on command. That was when he saw the human standing to the right of the throne. He'd likely come in behind Her Majesty.

Beneath his armor, the Black Knight's skin crawled. Something about the human unnerved him.

"Oh, you don't like my new pet?" She reached to play her fingers against the human's arm. "Shhhhh, he didn't mean it." The boy remained unresponsive.

Crash. The Black Knight looked to the table where Maddi plucked the pieces of a shattered vial from the floor.

Her Majesty gave a sound of annoyance. "I really wish you wouldn't break the nice things I've given you to work with."

Maddi whimpered.

"Which reminds me, how close are you to finishing?"

Maddi turned, though she didn't look up. "T-trying—"

Her Majesty cleared her throat loudly.

Maddi dropped to her knees, her chains clanking.

"Better. Go on."

"F-flutter and fruit, not a tide but a stroke. Shade and smoke . . ."

The smile faded from Her Majesty's face. She held out a hand as if to rest it against the air. Darkness crawled forward from the walls, pooling beneath her palm and stretching outward. It solidified into muscle, inky fire, white fangs, and red eyes, glowing with menace as black lips curled.

"I invite you to my home, give you a place to sleep, materials to do potentially your best work, and you insult me like this. My babies are not pleased."

Maddi clapped her hands together, lifting them over her head. "Pass! Pass through the night, feathers and stardust."

Her Majesty sighed. "Very well. You shall have more time.

But remember, if you fail me, I'll add your friends to my growing menagerie." She ran her fingers over the Fiend's head.

The monster snarled, its form flickering as if struggling to hold together. Paws shifted to inky fingers, then back again. The maw flattened briefly to an unfamiliar face before reverting.

"I always have room for new pets."

Maddi drew back, bumping into the table. The jars and vials shivered against the wood. She hurried to her feet and went back to mixing her tinctures for . . . whatever Her Majesty desired. She hadn't shared the details around the Poet's capture with him, why she wanted her. He wasn't foolish enough to ask her to explain herself, but he had inquired as to why she hadn't just sent him to capture the Poet.

"Because you're making a bad habit of failing me" had been Her Majesty's answer. It had cut deeper than he anticipated. Then she poured salt on the wound by saying the human—Chess—would be running errands for her now. She needed someone she could trust with the important things.

"Now then," Her Majesty cooed, snapping him back to the present. "While Madeline is a dear and works on my contingency plan, I need you two to do something for me."

"As you wish," the Black Knight said, frowning when Chess said it as well. The sound of their voices overlapping sent another unpleasant shudder through him.

"Chester, dear, if you would fetch the Eye for me, I would appreciate it. Burn that place to the ground and search the ashes if you must."

Chess bowed.

She smiled and set a hand on his head. Then she turned her attention to the Black Knight. "There is something . . . about the girl that intrigues me. Her abilities suggest there is more to her than any of those fools may realize." She stretched out along the throne, her body shifting, skin moving in and out of view. "I'd expected trouble from Hatta—still do, truth be told—but the girl is proving . . . resourceful. I want you to find her and bait her into a fight." She played those red nails against her chin. "A fight where she has to protect someone. Test her. Push her. Then report back to me."

The Black Knight hesitated, not really wanting to know the answer to his next question. "Am I to leave her alive?"

Her Majesty eyed him, her gaze knowing. For a moment he feared she would order him to slay her, just to test his loyalty. After all, even when ordered to cause Alice harm—as much as it twisted something inside him to do so—he always made sure it wouldn't be enough to kill her. He'd almost failed on that front.

"If she falls, she falls. I am merely curious."

The Black Knight bowed. "Of course, my lady. Might I voice a concern?"

She arched a thin brow.

"Not for myself, for . . ." He trailed off as his eyes moved to Chess, still kneeling beside the throne. "Addison Hatta is still a formidable opponent, even with the Madness eating away at him. Then there are the Duchess and Xelon to deal with."

She chuckled. "Worried for my new pet?"

"Not in so many words. Worried he won't be able to complete the mission on his own. I wasn't, after all." He couldn't keep the bitterness from his tone. "And I like to think I'm a bit better at this than a corpse." He didn't like being replaced. It bothered him more than he was ready to admit, and she seemed to enjoy pressing him about it.

"So rude, my knight. Chester is not a corpse. Those are dead. They lack purpose. And I've given him one." She played her fingers through Chess's hair almost lovingly, were she capable of such a thing. The Black Knight doubted it. All she knew was devotion and rage, perhaps fondness one might keep for creatures, but not love. He'd known love well enough to recognize it, and it was not in her.

He blinked, brow furrowed. He wasn't . . . Now his very mind was getting ahead of him. Know love? The idea didn't bother him, but he didn't know where it came from. Still, he schooled his expression. She already did not trust him with finding the Eye; he couldn't give her reason to go beyond that.

"Perhaps you are correct. The traitors are formidable." Her Majesty sighed dramatically, then waved a hand. The shadows around her shifted, oozing toward the throne. Her expression twisted, as if the exertion brought her pain.

Several black globs broke away, solidifying into Fiends as they came to gather at the base of the staircase. They hissed and snarled, the sounds keening as their bodies continued to morph until what appeared to be humans stood before him.

"Take them." She gestured, sinking back against the throne. "Both of you. And do not fail me."

His skin crawling beneath his armor, he bowed then turned to depart. He could hear Chess fall into step behind him, until they exited the throne room and the Black Knight turned left, heading for the rip in the Veil Her Majesty had forced open in order for them to travel back and forth between here and the human world.

Some of the Fiends followed after Chess. The rest stayed with the Black Knight.

Find Alice, bait her into a fight. That would be easy enough.

"Famous last words," he muttered to himself before gesturing to the Fiends. "Sniff her out."

Twelve

THE EASTERN GATEWAY

Alice knew the feel of a blade against her skin well enough to tell when someone had a sword on her. Any other time, that would probably be funny. Right now, it sent a cold wash through her body, her muscles freezing, her breath catching as her eyes darted to the side, trying to catch a glimpse of whoever the hell this was.

The pressure from the blade eased slightly but did not draw away. Alice resisted the urge to swallow, fighting to keep her breathing even. Not only was she in some unknown place in Wonderland, unarmed, but now someone had a weapon on her.

"Nani shiteru no, koko de?" The words were fast, clipped, but Alice recognized the language, even if she didn't understand it.

"I'm sorry," she started, her voice slightly shaky. "I don't understand."

"What are you doing here?" A Japanese accent coated the words.

Alice's mind danced over possible answers. Hatta had told her once that many Wonderlandians weren't all that fond of humans, especially since one started the war. Most were fine or indifferent toward them, but was it worth the risk? "I don't know, really. I mean, I didn't mean to come. At least, not this time."

"This time? You've been here before?"

"Yes, I—"

"How?"

Alice hesitated, but only long enough for the pressure at her neck to increase slightly. "The Western Gateway."

"The *Western* Gateway?" The blade withdrew.

Alice released a heavy breath, her hand going to her neck, though she froze when something moved at her right and a Japanese girl stepped into view. She moved carefully, clearly a fighter, carrying her body just so, ready to strike or defend. She gripped the hilt of a long Figment Blade fashioned to resemble a katana. Daylight glinted along the length of it.

The girl stood a little shorter than Alice, her cropped black hair falling around her face, just reaching her chin. Wide, dark brown eyes flickered over Alice.

"You're really from the Western Gateway?" the girl asked.

"Uh, yeah." Alice glanced to the side, then back to the girl.

"Who guards it?"

"Addison Hatta?"

"All right. That would explain the accent." She twirled the sword up and then slipped it into the sheath just over her right shoulder. The black strap stuck out against her white blouse, which she wore over a pair of black leggings and matching boots. "But not how you survived that fall."

Alice shook her head as her brain tried to wrap around this bit of information. "Wait, what?"

The girl aimed a finger upward. "There was a *boom*, like thunder? Then you fell out of nowhere." She whistled as she swirled her finger toward the ground. "Flop! I thought you were dead. You should be."

"Hol' up." Alice glanced at the sky, shielding her eyes with one hand, then looked back to the girl. "You're telling me I just dropped out of the sky?"

"Like a sexy comet."

Wait, *what*? Alice blinked rapidly, caught off guard. Her mouth worked for a second while her brain didn't. "U-um, I—where am I?" There, that was a safe question, and one she actually needed to focus on, not the sudden uncomfortable heat in her face and flutter in her chest.

"Hikari no Aterie. Aah . . ." She bit at her index finger as she tapped the toe of one boot. "You can call it Fusasa Forest."

Alice nodded, glancing around at the funky yellow cac-trees. "And what do I call you?"

The girl extended her hand. "I'm Haruka."

Alice couldn't help the little squeak at the back of her throat but covered it up with a faint cough before shaking Haruka's hand. "I'm Alice. And I'm hella lost."

"I can tell. The Western Gateway is not close." Haruka shifted her weight, glancing around in a few directions as she chewed on her finger again. "Why are you here?"

At that, Alice flung her hands up. "I got no clue. I don't even know *how* I'm here. I was . . ." She trailed off, remembering the altercation in the parking lot with that thing wearing Chess's face. Groaning, she rubbed at her eyes. "It's a long story, but I need to get back."

"To the Western Gateway? That's weeks in that direction." Haruka pointed. "You don't look like you'd last more than a few days, though."

"Weeks?" The sinking in the pit of Alice's stomach worsened. "This ain't happening, man."

"Mmm." Haruka nodded. "It may be simpler, and faster, for you to go home the conventional way. Come with me." She started off, sure in her steps.

Alice hesitated a moment before moving to follow the other girl. Usually she wouldn't be so quick to trust some random person wandering through Wonderland, or anywhere else really, but Haruka had the chance to shish-kebab her and didn't. Plus she had a Figment Blade, and looked relatively normal. Human normal, that was.

"So, when you said I'd have to go home the conventional way?" Alice's eyes wandered over the other girl. "What did you mean?"

Haruka glanced over her shoulder. "A plane."

◊ ◊ ◊

The two of them walked for what felt like at least an hour, though the time was spent with Alice explaining what the hell happened right before she apparently dropped out of the sky.

Then she had to explain things with the Black Knight, which Haruka knew a bit about, as the other Gateway guardians had been informed of what was going on and were on alert, just in case. Turned out Haruka was on her way to the Red Palace to try searching for the Heart again, and Alice dropping in sort of derailed things.

Alice offered to go with her, but it was decided they should go back first for a few reasons: One, Alice could call and let everyone know what happened and that she was okay. Two, she needed weapons; this was still Wonderland, and it wasn't smart to go unarmed. Three, Haruka didn't have enough supplies for two people to make the trip. This point was driven home when Alice's stomach gave a gurgle. She had skipped breakfast and then didn't eat much of her lunch, so she was pretty much starving by this point.

Haruka paused long enough to pull an energy bar out of the satchel she was carrying. "Here. It doesn't taste great, but it'll calm the beast." She smiled in a way that sent a wash of heat through Alice, some of it settling in her cheeks.

"Thanks," she murmured, taking the bar and unwrapping it, though she didn't take a bite until Haruka turned back to lead the way. Alice devoured the bar in three rushed bites. She could practically hear her mother lecturing her to slow down, chew her damn food, or at least taste it, before swallowing.

Shoving the wrapper in her pocket, she froze as a low roar filled the air. Ice stampeded down her spine, and her hands went for her daggers, but they weren't there.

"Shit!"

Haruka glanced over her shoulder, blinking. "What is it?"

"You don't hear—" Another roar sounded. Alice hunched her shoulders, head whipping back and forth as she searched for the creature making that noise.

Haruka blinked, glancing around as well. "Oh, it's the Furies. You have no need to fear them." And like that, she faced forward and continued.

Alice hesitated, still in her ready stance, but as distance grew between them, she dropped it and hurried along. "Furies?"

"Mmhm." Haruka pointed off to their left. "They're dragon-like creatures. They live here and in the deserts to the north. A few in the seas to the south." She paused, a thoughtful look crossing her face. "That gives me an idea. Come on, we're almost there." She took off at a jog.

Alice hurried after her, pitching a couple of glances in the direction of the roars as they went.

Dragons . . . in Wonderland. It didn't really surprise her, but it still kinda did. In that moment, she realized just how little of Wonderland she'd explored, or seen. She wondered what else was out there.

The plains eventually bled into forests thick and lush, blue and yellow leaves of varying sizes springing from trees thick and thin. Pink vines curled through the overhang, blossoms of varying colors and textures sprouting along blue bark. The canopy stretched overhead, blotting out the still pink skies. Shadows crawled along the jungle floor, shifting as the girls picked their way through the underbrush.

Alice ducked under leaves as wide as her bed and climbed

over roots shooting along the ground like thick veins. It took a bit of doing, especially at this pace, and *especially* since she was unfamiliar with this area. Right when she was about to ask how much farther they had to go, the brush parted and they stepped into a small clearing.

There it was, the Eastern Gateway. It looked exactly like the Western one, only instead of alabaster marble making up the stairs, platform, and columns, they were a bluish green that shimmered in the daylight, the color shifting and never quite settling.

"Romi-san," Haruka called as she climbed the few stairs to the platform. Her steps echoed, the sound bouncing from the columns, the air humming faintly with it. "Romi? Doko ni iruno?"

Alice made her way up to the platform, turning to take in the area. Where the Glow was light and silver, this place was soft shadows and rich color.

With a whoosh of sound, the air at the center of the platform split in the same way Alice had seen many times before. The slices curled backward, folding open, and light spilled free. A figure wreathed in brightness stepped forward, boots sounding against what looked like jade as they emerged.

Alice blinked a few times, caught a little off guard by the sight that greeted her. A woman stood in the Gateway. She was already taller than Alice, but a pair of platform boots added several inches to that. The boots climbed her calves, and blue and purple striped tights went the rest of the way to a pair of high-waisted cigarette shorts. Over those was a bright orange sweatshirt cropped short, but just long enough to be modest.

Ish. The woman had the hood pulled up, and a pair of cat ears rested atop her head.

She took a slow drag on a vape pen, the whine from the mod just loud enough to hear, then blew a cloud of bright pink smoke into the air. Alice followed the sugary puff as it rose above their heads and vanished. She looked back to the woman, who watched her with hooded amber eyes so bright they seemed to glow.

The woman said something in quick Japanese, and Haruka answered in turn. Alice heard the words *Western Gateway* in there somewhere.

The woman looked back to Alice, took another drag, and blew smoke into the air. This time, it was green.

"So." The woman rolled the word along her tongue. "You're Hatta's girl." Her Japanese accent wasn't as pronounced as Haruka's.

Alice's face flamed, and she swallowed before clearing her throat. "I work with him, if that's what you mean, yeah."

"My condolences." The woman clicked her tongue. "You're a long way from home, Miss . . . Alison, right?"

"Alice."

"Alice." The woman nodded. "I'm Romi. Welcome to the Eastern Gateway."

Thirteen

WHO ARE YOU?

Romi turned and stepped back through the way she'd come. Haruka moved to follow and, after the briefest moment of hesitation, Alice hurried after them.

She stepped into the bright haze, blinking as her eyes stung slightly. The whirl of the Gateway closing behind her filled her ears. A wave of unease rolled through her.

"U-um, you should know that I get—" Before Alice could finish, gravity loosed them, flinging them into the unknown.

Alice's insides tumbled about as wind rushed in her ears and stung her cheeks. She squeezed her eyes shut tight, biting back a whimper that was lost to the roar of sound.

Open them, something whispered inside her.

She shook her head, resulting in a wave of vertigo.

Open your eyes.

Against her better judgment, she pried one lid up. The other quickly followed, and her eyes widened.

Wonderland spread out beneath her, growing smaller and smaller as they shot into the air. She swallowed thickly, her feet dangling, the wind tugging at her limbs, pressing them to her sides.

To Alice's left, Haruka was in a similar position, her eyes closed. To Alice's right, Romi had her arms folded, her eyes open, gazing at Alice with an expression she couldn't quite read, though it made her insides squirm a bit.

Tearing her gaze away from the Gatekeeper, Alice lifted her head and nearly screamed as the bright pink of the Wonderland sky came toward them at a rush. She threw her hands up in defense, as they blew right through it.

Nothing happened.

They just kept going, the wind screaming in Alice's ears, the roar rivaled only by the thunder of her heart. Wonderland had vanished beneath her feet, replaced by the cracked earth and unending abyss from before. She recognized the distant darkness of the Nox, the glittering towers of Legracia, the metallic glint of downtown Atlanta, all crowding the horizon. This was the In-Between.

They were quickly rising above it, shooting toward the lightning streaked clouds overhead. They barreled through them, light erupting as they reached the other side, blazing so bright Alice had to shut her eyes again.

Something solid pushed up beneath her feet. Her legs went watery, and she dropped to the floor with a pained grunt, flopping against the hard surface. Her left hip and side ached where she'd landed on them, the same leg tingling where it was pinned beneath her at a less than comfortable angle. She groaned as her stomach roiled and the energy bar Haruka gave her climbed toward her throat.

With the sour sting of copper just behind her tongue and a gurgling retch, she threw up. Pressing her fingers over her mouth did little more than make sure she ended up covered in it.

The lights clicked on. Alice blinked to clear her vision.

Either Haruka or Romi sniffed in disgust. Embarrassment rolled through Alice, turning her insides even more.

"Ugh, s-sorry . . ." she whimpered, her voice abandoning her. She wiped at her mouth.

Romi said something in Japanese, her already deep voice dropping slightly in pity. Haruka stepped away. A door creaked open behind Alice, and Haruka's quick steps rushed away, leaving the pungent smell of dust and pine behind her.

Alice kept her eyes down, looking herself and her mess over. Her embarrassment spiked, and she felt the sting of tears against the backs of her eyes.

No, no! She wasn't going to cry on top of all this.

A hand fell to her shoulder, and she jumped. Romi crouched beside her, leaning in to catch her eye. "The passing is rough on you." Her voice was quiet but matter-of-fact.

Alice nodded, swallowing, and instantly regretting it as the bitter taste of sick coated her tongue. It was almost enough to make her retch again.

Steps pounded toward them, and Haruka pushed into the

little space, calling out in Japanese again. Romi nodded at her, answered in turn, then rose and stepped aside. Haruka took her place, holding out a pink towel that smelled heavily of bubblegum.

"Here."

Alice took it with murmured thanks, wiping her mouth and hands as Haruka dumped a bottle of something over the mess. The scent of citrus filled the air as the substance bubbled up and over it all. Haruka then took a second towel and started mopping it up.

Now, on top of feeling embarrassed as hell, Alice felt guilty for Haruka cleaning up her mess. "Sorry," she said again.

"No real harm done," Romi said from somewhere over Alice's shoulder.

She turned to find the woman taking another drag from a different vape device, this one a bit bigger. The smoke she blew into the air swirled yellow, with faint sparkles dancing through the cloud.

"Haruka will show you where to get washed up. And we'll get you some clean clothes." Romi looked her up and down, her amber eyes bright with intelligence and something judgmental that made Alice shiver. "Then she'll bring you out front and we can chat."

Romi left the room, glittering smoke trailing behind her.

Haruka continued pouring that liquid and mopping it up. As she worked, Alice glanced around the room. It was bigger than the broom closet at the pub, but not big enough to be much use as anything else. Unlike the closet, it was completely empty, the dark walls bare, the wood floor equally so.

"Finished," Haruka said. It took two towels, which she dropped into a bucket Alice hadn't noticed her bring in. She grabbed the handle with one hand, and caught Alice's elbow with the other, lifting them both as she got to her feet.

Alice was grateful for the help; her legs were still wobbly, but they held. Haruka looked her over before letting go, though she hesitated as if waiting to see if she would stay standing.

"I'm okay," Alice said miserably, her stomach tumbling for a different reason as she avoided the other girl's brown gaze. "Thanks."

Haruka nodded, then led the way out of the room. Alice followed her into a narrow hallway that was decidedly brighter than the little room, not just because of the sunshine pouring in through the skylight overhead, but because the high walls were covered in white wallpaper peppered with sakura blossoms. The paper was worn, torn here and there, and the carpet under her feet was equally weathered. Undoubtedly old wood creaked beneath her feet. Haruka ducked through a doorway, pausing long enough to beckon Alice to follow.

Inside was a little nook where the floor dropped and then rose again to meet a door. Alice was confused for a second until Haruka started taking off her boots. Hurriedly copying the other girl, Alice set her shoes to the side, then followed Haruka into the adjacent room.

A wide bathroom opened in front of them, all sharp, modern edges and earthy browns, so different from the hall. The rush of running water drew Alice's attention to a tub set in the floor. The smell of roses wafted through the air.

"Um." Alice fidgeted, sticky fingers tugging at the hem of her shirt. "That's for me?"

"Yes." Haruka poured the bucket of towels into a funky-looking washing machine tucked in a nearby corner.

"I don't think I need a whole bath." Though she couldn't say she didn't want one. It was just weird to take one in some random stranger's house, fellow Dreamwalker or not. That's how people ended up missing, their pictures on the eleven-o'clock news.

Haruka stepped over to the tub and turned off the water. "The bath's not for washing. That is." She pointed at a small, tiled area set into the wall. A shower, Alice realized.

"The tub is for soaking afterward," Haruka continued. "Figured you might want to relax after earlier."

"Y-yeah. Thanks," Alice murmured, embarrassment rising up inside her all over again as she watched the other girl work.

After setting a small tub on a nearby shelf, Haruka faced Alice. "Put your clothes in"—she pointed at the washer—"and hit start. First button on the left. Towels are over there. I'll bring you something to wear until your things are clean." She slipped from the room and slid the door closed behind her.

Alice stood there for a second, just glancing around, not entirely sure what to do with herself. She was in a stranger's house halfway around the world, without her weapons, with so many questions and no idea what the hell was going on. Frustration welled inside her, but she swallowed it down and took slow breaths.

Breathe, Baby Moon.

Okay, first things first. She couldn't go wandering around looking and smelling like this. Checking the door for a lock and sliding it into place, she peeled out of her clothes, grimacing as the cloth slid, slick with sick, against her skin here and there. Careful not to let any bits fall off onto the floor, she threw her shirt and jeans into the washer and hit what she hoped was start. The machine started up, filling with water.

Glancing at the door and the lock, still firmly in place, she undid her bra—careful not to touch too much of it with her sticky fingers—then stripped the last bits of cloth off and hurried over to the shower. There was a rag and what smelled like vanilla soap waiting for her, that she used to scrub at her skin. Once she was certain she was good and clean, she rinsed off, then waddled over to climb into the tub. The water sloshed a little bit as she sank into it, the bath rising just above her chest. Its heat soaked into her as she eased her way down. Warmth spread over her, the smell of roses and something spicy growing heady. Her skin tingled faintly.

Much as she wanted to linger, and even with Haruka's invitation to relax a little, she figured it wasn't a good idea. Ten minutes. She'd give herself that long, then she needed to go figure out how she was going to get home. Ten minutes to rest her eyes.

Knuckles tapped against the bathroom door, and Alice jolted slightly. "Y-yes?"

"Are you all right?" Haruka's muffled voice called. "You've been in there for nearly an hour. I've got some clothes for you."

"What!?" Alice flailed, sloshing water a bit, as she clambered out of the tub. An *hour*? How did—damn it, she must've dozed off! "Sorry! Sorry, I'm coming."

"No rush. I just wanted to make sure you hadn't shriveled up. Or drowned." There was an amused lilt to Haruka's voice that made Alice's face warm. Again. It needed to stop doing that.

"Nope! I'm good. And . . . not drowned." Alice snatched up a towel and wrapped it around herself before hurrying over to the door. She fussed with the lock for a second, then slid it open. Haruka offered up folded swaths of cloth that Alice took with thanks.

"Um, I don't wanna be rude or anything, but I was wondering if you had some lotion?"

Haruka pointed to the mirror over the sink. "Do you need anything else?"

"No, thanks again."

"You're welcome." Haruka wandered off, and Alice closed the door.

Setting the clothes down, she went searching for lotion. The medicine cabinet was full to the brim, with plenty of labels that mixed both English and kanji. She wasn't sure why that surprised her, but it did. Throwing on some deodorant and what she'd assumed was lotion—but considering how watery it was, she was having second thoughts—she went for the clothes. Thankfully Haruka had included a single pack of new underwear with the plain white T-shirt and a pair of shorts that were almost too small. If her mom ever caught her in something like this, it would be her ass.

She stepped out into the little nook to pull on her shoes, then ventured further into the hallway. The right led back to the doorway where the gate was held, so she went left and around a bend. There were a couple closed doors along the way, but the hall eventually emptied into a somewhat large room with tall walls and a stained-glass dome overhead depicting a cluster of colorful mushrooms.

Books covered every surface where there wasn't an old painting or a funky lamp jutting out of the wall, casting a cone of light along one of the black metal walkways wrapped around the room. There were two, the first looking to be at least ten feet above the floor, and the second ten feet above that. A few spiral staircases here and there provided access to the additional levels, and set into those levels, Alice could see tracks for rolling ladders. The room itself was neither square nor round but more oblong, bowing in and out like Play-doh that had been stretched wide and snaked along. It curved the walls here and there, making it look as if books could just fall free in a couple places, or that the patrons perusing the shelves would lose their balance and topple down, but they didn't. A man moving along the first level shifted to where he was walking almost parallel to the floor for a second, before being righted as the wall straightened, not missing a step.

At the center of the warped space sat a circular desk with some old-timey lamps along the surface, like from old-day libraries. Settled inside was Romi, her orange hood dropped against her shoulders, revealing thick, steel gray waves of hair pouring down her back. She sat puffing away on a kiseru now as her eyes played over the pages of a huge leather-bound tome. Alice ducked around a couple of girls perusing a paperback with a parasol on it and headed that way.

Romi glanced up as she approached, looking her over again. "All cleaned up?"

Alice's face heated, and she fought to keep from fidgeting. "Yeah. Sorry about the mess . . . and thanks for the clothes."

Romi waved a hand. "It's just a loan. Your clothes should be ready soon enough. Thank Haruka, if you're going to thank anyone."

Nodding, Alice glanced around the oddly shaped room once again. It was actually pretty neat, like something out of another world. And the instant that thought entered Alice's head, she felt ridiculous. *Of course this place looks like—shut up, Kingston.* "Nice place."

"Thanks," Romi rasped before taking another drag and blowing out the closest thing to normal smoke Alice had seen this entire time, only the cloud took the shape of a rabbit and bounded off through the air, leaving tendrils of vapor trailing behind it. The air was suddenly thick with the smell of blue-berries. "Welcome to the Hon no Mushi, or the Bookworm."

Alice turned from where she had been staring after the bunny and blinked wide eyes. "Aptly named." So the Western Gateway was a bar, and the Eastern Gateway was a bookshop. She wondered what the North and South were.

"I let Addison know you were here, and in one piece." Romi puffed out a blue cloud. No animal emerged, to Alice's slight disappointment. "He was thrilled to hear it."

The way Romi's tongue rolled over *thrilled* made the heat in Alice's face intensify. "Good. I need to get back as soon as possible."

"That may prove difficult." Romi lifted one finger when Alice opened her mouth to protest.

The girls Alice had passed stepped up to the desk. Romi greeted them in cheerful Japanese with an equally cheerful smile. They conversed a bit as she rang them up on a register Alice hadn't noticed tucked onto a lower surface circling the inside of the desk. Placing their books in a cream paper bag that sported a little fat worm chewing on a book, Romi waved as the girls headed for the exit.

When she turned back to Alice, the smile fell away. "Fastest way to get you back to the States is by plane, but you have no passport."

She hadn't thought of that, and now a faint spark of panic lit inside her. "You mean I'm *stuck* here?"

"There's always the way you came." Romi clicked her teeth against the mouthpiece of the pipe, her fingers dancing along it like it was a flute.

"Haruka said that would take weeks," Alice complained.

"And it will." Haruka stepped up beside Alice and dropped an armful of books onto the upper surface of the desk. "Unless we take Chou."

Romi's eyes rounded slightly, their color sharpening.

"It's the fastest way, and the safest, for both of us." Haruka flipped open the cover of a book in her pile, placed a little sticker on the inside corner, then set it aside. She repeated the action with the others. "I'll take her to the Western Gateway, then come right back. Three days there, three days back. Simple enough."

Romi sat back, an irritated look on her face. She puffed on her pipe again, loosing a purple plume. This one swam away as a school of fish. She said something in clipped Japanese that Haruka returned without looking up from her task. They went back and forth a few times, Romi sounding a little more terse each time she opened her mouth. Haruka grew quieter in turn, until the last thing she said was barely above a murmur. Romi sucked her teeth, and a wide smile spread over Haruka's face. Apparently she won the argument.

"He does not like strangers," Romi murmured, still looking none too pleased.

"But he likes me." Haruka finished with the books and handed the pile down to Romi. "And so do you, so wipe that look off of your face."

Romi stuck her tongue out at Haruka's retreating back. "It seems we found you a way home, though it will take an hour or so to prepare. In the meantime, you can catch me up on all of this nonsense going on with a Black Knight and the Eye."

"I mean, I'll try, but it's a long st—"

"Question one." Romi lifted a finger, and Alice sputtered into silence. "Who are you?"

Alice blinked, glanced to the side real quick, then back to Romi. "I'm . . . Alice."

"Yes, yes, I know, but who *are* you?"

Confused, Alice shifted her weight where she stood, not entirely sure how to answer because she wasn't entirely sure what was being asked. "I . . . don't understand the question?"

"It's fairly simple." Romi tilted back in her chair and kicked her feet up. "Who are you? Who is Alice? You don't seem like much, but looks can be deceiving."

Alice felt a ping of irritation, and a bit of wounding to her pride. "I'm more than you could imagine," she said lowly.

"We'll see." Romi puffed out more colorful smoke. "You'll have to be, to ride my Chou."

"What's a Cho?" Alice had a feeling she might regret asking.

"A who." Romi turned to more customers as they stepped up to the desk. A line was starting to form as the sound of bells rolled through the bookshop, followed by a soft voice speaking in Japanese.

Alice didn't understand the language, but she knew a "we're closing soon" announcement when she heard one. She moved away from the desk to avoid standing there all creepy like and perused some of the titles on the nearby wall. She hadn't seen where Haruka had disappeared to, and until Romi was finished checking people out, there wasn't much more for her to do. She wanted to call Hatta, to call Courtney and her mom and let everyone know she was all right.

After the last customer was rung out, Romi rose from the desk and followed the man to the door, locking it behind him. She flipped the sign in the window and strolled toward the side hall, beckoning Alice to follow. Opening one of the doors Alice had passed earlier, Romi stepped into another hallway, this one wider. The smell hit Alice first, hot and spicy, thick and rich, the scent of frying meat and vegetables. Her stomach gave an eager churn.

A set of wood stairs led upward at least one story. Romi sat on a bench against the wall and went about the task of unlacing her boots. Alice followed suit, tugging her shoes from her feet and setting them aside. Romi's boots sagged slightly, bending over as if they were tired from a day of being worn.

Upstairs, they entered a somewhat large apartment, loft style, with a high ceiling and walls at least three times Alice's height. Some of the walls were lined with floating shelves stacked with books and small statues. Others were covered in various types of art, from fancy-looking paintings in thick old frames to wall scrolls and basic posters, all depicting traditional Japanese art or what Alice assumed was either anime, movie, or music posters.

Haruka moved around in the kitchen, the source of the heavenly smells simmering on the stove. Alice's mouth watered, but she had more pressing matters to deal with.

"Can I use your phone?" She trailed after Romi to where the woman flopped onto a couch.

Romi dug into a back pocket and produced a phone wearing a rubber R2-D2 case. "He's the most recent call."

Thanking her, Alice found and hit the number. It rang a couple of times before someone picked up.

"Yeah?" Hatta asked, sounding more than a little irritated.

Alice's heart jumped in her chest. It was so good to hear his voice, even though it hadn't been all that long. "Addison, it's me."

"Alice." Hatta's tone softened. "Are you all right? What happened? Courtney said something about a Nightmare swallowing you. Not a Nightmare exactly, but I'm sure you know what I mean."

"That's . . . pretty close. I don't really know, it looked like Chess but then it went all black blob on me, pulled me in. I wound up in some place called the In-Between."

"I know. Nathan said he was able to find you, but then started yammering about it being too late and went straight for the bourbon. Hasn't made any sense since."

"Nathan?" Alice asked.

"You all call him Sprigs."

"Oh. Right." That was a deceptively normal name for someone who, apparently, was also from Wonderland. She should probably just assume everyone connected to Hatta was. "He got all scary and peaced out, then . . ." The memory pushed against Alice's mind, insistent. "Then the Black Knight showed up. And there was a woman."

"Who?" Hatta pressed.

Alice shook her head, then realized he couldn't see her. "I don't know. She had red hair. Pale skin. I've never seen her before."

Hatta went silent, likely thinking. She could almost hear his frown.

"She stabbed me. It didn't hurt, it just . . . was cold. Then I fell, and woke up in Wonderland."

"Are you all right?" Concern coated every word.

"Yeah. A little sore and hungry, but I'm okay. Romi and Haruka are excellent hosts." Romi gave a thumbs-up from where she was puffing on yet another vape device. "We're trying to figure out a way to get me home that doesn't take three weeks to cross all of Wonderland. I can't fly, no passport, so I'm taking a . . . Cho."

Hatta made a faint choking sound. "*Chou?*"

"Yeah. Romi said it was a who." Alice thought she heard Romi snicker, but when she glanced up, the woman was sunk into the couch, her head laid back against the top of it, blowing various impossible shapes into the air: a sphere, a couple cubes, a star.

"Chou is Chou. Listen, Odabeth and Xelon are getting ready to head to Castle Findest. That's where the Heart was last, according to the Eye. Hopefully if Odabeth stands in the spot the Eye showed her, then tries the locator Verse, it will reveal more. Xelon is more than capable, but I'd feel better if they had some extra muscle along for the ride."

A smirk pulled at Alice's lips. She liked being thought of as the muscle. "What about the twins?"

"They're still going to focus on tracking your friend and Madeline. At the moment, I've sent them on a supply run."

"Supply run? For what?"

"Bandages, painkillers, that sort of thing. Without Maddi, we have to make adjustments in our preparations." There was no mistaking the somber twist in his words. "Speaking of preparing, think you can borrow a weapon from Romi and meet up with Her Highness and her knight? If Haruka is available, we could use her help as well."

Alice glanced at the Dreamwalker at the mention of her name. She was setting food out on the low table. "I'll ask. Where will we meet them?"

"Excellent. There's a village near Ab—"

A loud *boom* sounded on Hatta's end of the call, along with a crash of wood and glass. Someone screamed.

"Hatta?" Alice's grip on the phone tightened.

No response, just the muffled sounds of someone shouting.

A low growl picked up, a sound Alice would recognize anywhere. Nightmare. Hatta grunted, the sound ending in a choked cough.

"Addison!"

The line went dead.

Fourteen

WHICH WAY?

Addison didn't know anything but pain. It coursed through him, jarred his senses and rattled his bones. It throbbed along his limbs, pounding in time with the beat of his heart.

There was another noise under the thumping in his ears. He couldn't really make it out at first, but then it grew louder, more insistent.

"Addison!"

It was a voice, one he knew. Or one he thought he knew. He tried to answer, but only groaned as his body refused to listen to his orders to move. The pain remained persistent, rising and falling in a steady rhythm as well.

"Addison!" the voice called again. "Damn it, Hatta, if you die on me." Hands gripped his face, turning his head.

He forced his eyes open, his lids heavy and uncooperative. Light filled his vision, bright and blinding.

"Bozhe moi." The image of the Duchess faded into view as he blinked. She was upside down, her face twisted in concern and something else. She spat a curse and looked over her shoulder.

"A-Anastasia?" The word came out more of a rasp. His mouth was clumsy and felt like it was full of sand.

The Duchess whipped back around, her green eyes wide. Her hair was wild where strands had come loose from her braid, and a fresh slice beneath her left eye bled freely. "Addison, can you move? I need you to move."

"I can try." He shifted, flexing fingers and toes, then arms and legs as his muscles strained to pull him upward. Pain continued to ricochet through his body, radiating from his middle as the pounding picked back up again.

She moved in behind him, slipped her arms under his, and lifted.

"What happened?" he asked as the two of them got him on his feet. They stood in the mouth of the hallway leading to the back of the pub. The small space tilted slightly as his vision continued to swim.

A roar filled the air.

"Fiends. Tore the damn door down. Pulled you out of it, but we have to get back in there." Anastasia extended a sword to him. "Can you fight?"

It took a second for the question to register, then he braced one hand against the wall and took the sword with the other. "Do I have a choice?"

Smirking, she turned and darted toward the bar. The sounds of battle folded in around her and settled in over the ringing of his ears. More snarls and growls. Xelon shouted, and something shattered. Steeling himself, Addison pushed forward the last few steps and out into the bar.

Anastasia drove her blade into one of the beasts. It flailed and pitched over in its death throes, spewing black and yellow across the floor. Xelon drew out of a crouch over another corpse, her arm thrown out to shield the terrified Odabeth and Courtney, huddled together in a corner of the bar.

Another three Fiends stalked through the hole in the wall where the door used to be. A figure strolled in behind them. At first, Addison thought it was the Imposter. He wore similar armor, but no helmet.

"Chess!?" Courtney stared, her eyes wide, her mouth open.

Two more Fiends filled the doorway, flanking him.

Anastasia spat a curse.

Addison seconded the sentiment. With Xelon it was three against five, but two of them were still recovering from their battle with the Imposter. With Odabeth and Courtney to look after, things would likely go bad in a hurry.

"Chess, what're you doing?" Courtney shouted at him.

He didn't answer, instead unsheathing a sword at his back. The metal gleamed in the hazy light of the bar.

"I'm afraid Chess might not be in there," Addison murmured.

"Give me the Eye," Chess said. "And you can keep your lives. I won't ask again." He played his gaze over the lot of them. The Fiends snapped and snarled at his sides, hackles raised.

Addison tightened his hold on his weapon. Beside him Anastasia untucked the whip from her hip. It unfurled with a hiss.

That was when the Fiends pounced, or at least the first of them tried to. With a crack, Anastasia's whip tore a hole into its side. It tumbled into a heap, yowling in pain. Meanwhile Anastasia stepped forward, twirling her arm overhead. The whip obeyed and, like a thing alive, snaked through the air at breathtaking speed. It circled her and lashed out again and again, striking at the Fiends, keeping them at bay. It whirled around Addison as he drew near.

Just like old times. He smirked.

Chess drew back a step as his eyes flickered over the whip's movements, searching for an opening. Hatta's smirk widened. There would be no opening. So long as Anastasia had the strength to keep the whip in motion, there was no getting past her. But if you knew her well, like Addison did, there would be a break from the inside, allowing those who fought at her side to drive at the enemy. It'd been a while since they fought together, but he could still read her movements. There.

He darted forward, sword up.

Crash!

Metal slammed into metal as Chess ducked in to meet his charge.

Impossible. Shocked, Addison froze up just long enough for Chess to twist his weapon, pushing it down the outside of Addison's sword and penetrating his guard entirely.

He shouted as pain flared white hot across his side when steel bit into flesh.

"Addison!" the Duchess shouted. "Xelon, get the princess out of here!"

Addison flipped his blade to counter the swipe. At the same time, Anastasia twisted to fling her whip out. Chess had to withdraw to avoid having his skull punctured, but he'd already done his dirty work.

Blood poured wet and warm against Addison's side. He stumbled back and into Anastasia.

Impossible, his mind kept screaming. No one should have been able to read the whip defense like that, and certainly not this human.

Anastasia flipped her whip into a recoil and snatched a jewel from her ear in one fluid movement.

"Etigni'ta!" She held the jewel aloft.

Just as the Fiends pounced, light exploded from her hand. Addison shielded his eyes. Arms around his waist guided him toward the hall. Behind them the Fiends yowled in pain. The Verse would only last a few seconds.

"Run!" Anastasia screamed.

Ahead of them, Xelon and the girls bolted down the hall, toward the only way out: the Gateway.

Behind them, there was a sound like water going down a drain, only at light speed. The Fiends howled, their claws clacking as they recovered and gave chase.

"Get the door!" Xelon shouted.

Courtney reached it first. Wood slammed against wood as it was flung open and they raced into the dark. Someone slammed the door shut behind them. It rattled on its hinges when the Fiends hit the other side.

"Hold on!" Anastasia called.

Light exploded around them as she didn't open a path so much as rip into it, and they were plunged between worlds.

The sudden drop sent a wave of vertigo through him. His limbs flailed helplessly as he tried to regain his balance.

Alert, he could see Anastasia's bright red hair to his left. He tried to spot whoever else was falling with them, but everything went dark. Wind screamed in his ears and snatched at his clothes, slapping his face. He was still falling, but . . . something was wrong. Why couldn't he see?

He blinked his eyes rapidly, but that did nothing. He tried to call for Anastasia, but the wind snatched his words from his lips.

A sound like thunder shook through his entire body, and light exploded across his vision. He blinked to clear it, and a bright expanse of sparkling pink water unfolded beneath him just before he hit the surface. The water cradled him, but his side screamed in agony. It nearly robbed him of his ability to move, but he had to.

He forced his legs to kick, his arms to stroke. It was like swimming through pudding. Eventually he broke the surface and, with everything he had, pushed toward the nearby shore. He hauled himself along the sandy surface, his lungs and muscles screaming.

Panting, he flopped onto his back and stared up at the pink Wonderland sky, still fractured from the Breaking. Where was he? This wasn't the Gateway.

"Oh my gaaaawd," a familiar voice whined from nearby.

Addison turned his head to find Courtney pulling herself from the water the same way he had. She coughed and sputtered, flopping onto the yellow grass. Xelon was beside her on hands and knees, panting. Her white hair hung in around her face like a soggy cloud.

"P-princess," Xelon sputtered before glancing around. "Odabeth!" When there was no answer, Xelon staggered to her feet and started for the water.

"Wait," Courtney called. "Sh-she's not in there. I saw her and the Duchess go flying off into the distance." She coughed and pushed herself up on trembling arms, then froze as she caught sight of their surroundings.

Addison enjoyed watching humans during their first visit to Wonderland. The awe on their faces was amusing, among other things, but there was no time for that now.

"Which way?" he said as he shoved himself onto his side.

Both Courtney and Xelon turned to him.

"Hatta." Xelon came toward him, favoring her left leg in a slight limp. She reached to help ease him into a sitting position. Even with her careful touch, agony spread through him.

"Are you okay?" Courtney asked, her green eyes wide as she crawled over to them.

"Define okay," he huffed, an arm around his throbbing middle.

"Alive will do for now," Xelon murmured as she made her way to the edge of the water. She splashed some of it on her face, rubbing away the purple sand.

Addison would have nodded his agreement, but his head

was still pounding. He fixed his still slightly wavering gaze on Courtney. "Which way did you see them go?"

The girl looked confused for a moment before realization brightened her face. "Oh! Um, that way." She pointed, then lowered her arm. "Or maybe that way."

"Shit," Xelon hissed.

"Sorry." Courtney rubbed at her pale arms and sniffed. "I was falling a million miles a second, I only got a glance."

"It's not your fault," Xelon said, though she was still tense. "We need to find them."

"If she's with Anastasia, she is well protected." Hatta scanned their surroundings, trying to get a feel for exactly where they were. It wasn't the Western Gateway, but it couldn't be far from it, the ache in his chest from the Verse that exiled him was only mild beneath the burn of other injuries. He shifted to stand, only for his breath to escape him in a gasp as a feeling like glass peeling away skin tore along his side. He slumped into a half-seated sprawl against the grass.

"Move slowly." Xelon lifted his shirt, examining the wound. "He got you good."

"Yeah, he did." The slice was clean but deep and bleeding freely. Hopefully he hadn't nicked anything important. His skin was purple along his ribs, and when Xelon touched her fingers to them lightly, he jolted in pain. "Ah! Shite . . ."

"Looks like they're bruised. Maybe worse. Probably from the blast. Bastard blew in the front door."

"I'll send him a bill." Hatta winced as Xelon continued to examine him.

"Jesus." Courtney stared, her hands cupping the lower half of her face. "I—I . . . Chess, he . . ."

"He's still under the Imposter's control—ahh!"

"Sorry. If we don't do something, you're going to bleed out." Xelon straightened, glancing around. Wading out into the shallows of the river, she knelt and rooted around in the mud.

"Can we save him?" Courtney asked quietly.

"Maybe," he murmured. He felt for her, and Alice. It wasn't easy to see a friend like that. It wasn't easy being that, either. "If I can come back, there's hope for him." Though he wasn't fully himself, not as he was before. "Right now we need to regroup, figure out a plan."

"You need to hold still for a bit." Xelon returned with two pink, muddy handfuls. Moving to kneel beside him again, she held out one hand. "Brace yourself."

He did. It didn't help. The pain was excruciating, and the mud was icy as hell, but he gritted his teeth and endured.

Courtney watched from nearby, brow furrowed. "Aren't you supposed to clean a wound, not pack it with mud?"

"Yes, but this isn't any ordinary mud. The silt gathered here is partly composed of Dust. It's a magical substance that falls from the heavens when the sky cracks open around what humans call midnight."

"Huh." Courtney tilted her head to the side. "That sounds kinda neat."

"It's breathtaking." Xelon talked while she worked. "Dust is used for many things, like forging weapons for Dreamwalkers or in potions and salves for healing. In its raw form it's not as effective, but it's better than nothing and should stop the bleeding, buying enough time for us to get some help."

"Good." Courtney nodded. "H-help is good."

"Did Odabeth have the Eye on her?" Addison grunted when Xelon touched a particularly tender area.

"Sorry." Xelon nodded. "And yes."

By the time Xelon finished dressing the wound with the clay, he was a bit dizzy but otherwise fine. "That may buy us some time, if he searches the pub first."

"You have a plan?" Xelon straightened from where she'd finished tending to him.

"The beginnings of one. What's the damage?"

"Bruising, possible breaks among your right ribs. You've got a nice knot here," she pointed to somewhere behind his right ear. "Possible concussion—be careful while moving. I did what I can, but I'm no Made . . ." She trailed off.

Addison set a hand to her shoulder. "You got me on my feet."

"Almost." Xelon stood and offered her hand. Courtney hurried in to help. His side twinged when he moved, and it hurt to breathe, but he was in one piece and upright. "There. *Now* you're on your feet, and if you want to stay that way, you'll take it easy. So, this plan of yours?"

"You were supposed to go to Findest. We go to Findest."

Xelon scoffed. "We were supposed to go to Findest with supplies, my armor, my weapons." She ticked these things off on her fingers. "With none of the above, how long do you expect we'll last? Especially with this Chance—"

"Chess," Courtney corrected.

"Sorry. Especially with Chess and his Fiends hunting us?"

Addison didn't suspect Chess would be after them; he'd most likely go after Odabeth and the Eye, but that was if he knew she had it.

"Won't he go after the princess?" Courtney voiced his musings, hugging herself, a couple of bruises purpling along her arms and legs.

"Not necessarily. He doesn't know the princess has it, and he's suspected me of having it this entire time."

"You did," Courtney murmured.

"I had one sixth of it. Technically."

Xelon shook her head.

"My point being, if he thought I had it before, there's no reason he wouldn't think I have it now."

"Unless he learned otherwise from a reliable source," Xelon said, her voice lowering. She meant Madeline, of course. There was no way to know if she'd been compromised, so they would have to assume she had.

"Even if he did, it doesn't change anything. We need to get to Findest as soon as possible. Anastasia will feel the same and likely encourage the princess to do likewise."

"So we're going to hike through Wonderland like this?" Courtney asked, looking more than a little pale.

"We don't really have a choice."

Courtney glanced out over the river, as if she could somehow go back the way she came. That wasn't an option for any of them.

"Okay, so which way?" Courtney sniffed and wiped at her face.

Xelon stepped off a short ways, shielding her eyes from the daylight with one hand against her brow as she surveyed the area. This was the Rangwarid River, meaning they were somewhere far south of the Glow. That could be a good thing, considering they needed to head that direction, but whether they were farther east or west could prove problematic.

"Findest is at least two weeks that direction." Xelon pointed.

"We won't make it two weeks," Addison pointed out. Little food and water aside, *half* that long out here unarmed would not end well.

"I won't make it two days," Courtney said. "Just being honest," she added when Xelon glanced her direction.

"If you two will let me finish. Findest is at least two weeks that direction, *but* the nearest town, if I recall correctly, is about a day that way." She pointed southwest. "Maybe two, at a slower pace."

Courtney groaned softly. "She died as she lived: Young and Beautiful."

"What?" Xelon asked.

"That's what I want them to put on my gravestone." Courtney nodded. "My legacy."

Addison chuckled, then regretted it when his ribs throbbed. "We should get moving. Lead the way."

They started the direction Xelon had indicated, with her in the lead. She set a slow, testing pace, likely to see if he and Courtney could keep up.

Addison took stock of his condition. A dull ache had settled between his ears, but it was nothing compared to the hurt in his torso. He was light-headed, a little nauseous, but nothing severe. He could hold a steady pace, for now, but who knew how long it would keep up.

Courtney fell into step between them, glancing around once more, still taking it all in. Xelon looked around similarly, though her gaze was hard and direct, surveying the area for very different reasons.

And so they loped along, three sopping wet, hobbling humps roving the hills, a trio of perfect targets.

Fifteen

MESS

"**Addison!**" Alice shouted again, even though the phone had returned to Romi's home screen, which was a picture of cat holding an umbrella.

A cold feeling bubbled in her stomach, then spread down her arms and legs as she hit redial. Her body iced over completely when a woman's robotic voice told her the number had been disconnected. She tried again. And again. No change.

"What is it?" Romi asked, her pipe held as if she'd been about to take a puff. Instead she gazed at Alice, her eyes narrowed.

"I—I don't know." Her hands shook as she tapped in Court's number, screwing it up twice. "It sounded like an explosion or something! And . . ." The growl.

The phone rang. And rang. And rang. Court's voice mail picked up. "Hey! It's Alice. Something's wrong at the pub. I need you to check it out. *Don't* get out of your car, though, unless you know for sure it's safe. I think . . . I think a Nightmare might be there. Be careful. Call me back at this number."

She hung up and started to dial Chess, but her fingers froze. He wouldn't answer. His phone was still in his car, parked somewhere near the school, unmoved. This was day two or three of him missing? His family would probably call the police soon if they hadn't already . . .

Tears stung her eyes, and her throat closed up. No, she couldn't think about that right now. The twins were handling—

A pair of fingers thrust into her field of vision and snapped. Blinking rapidly, her heart jumping, Alice looked up to find an annoyed looking Romi glaring at her.

"There you are." Romi snatched her phone. "What is going on, *Alice*? What's this about a Nightmare at Addison's place?"

Alice swallowed thickly. "I . . . I definitely heard an explosion, but I think I heard a Nightmare, too. Something growling before the phone died. Now it's disconnected." Alice shook her head. "I have to get back there, now."

"To the possibly exploded place full of Nightmares." Romi took a draw and released red smoke.

"It was just the one. Maybe. At least, I only heard one."

"Believe me when I tell you that Addison Hatta is more than capable of dealing with a single Nightmare. The explosion thing might be cause for concern, though." Romi stuck the pipe into the corner of her mouth. "I heard him say something about you and Haruka meeting someone?"

Alice stared for a second before shaking her head. "That doesn't matter right now! I need to get back there and—"

"And what? Get caught up in whatever may be going on?" Romi narrowed her eyes. "Anastasia has kept the rest of us mostly informed on what's happening, and it sounds like the focus needs to be on finding the Heart."

"Yes, but—"

"Then that's what you do. When shit hits the fan, you follow through and do your job."

"They could be in trouble!"

"They'll be in worse trouble if that Black Knight bastard gets what he wants. What would running in half-cocked do but make it worse?"

Frustration bubbled up inside Alice, along with this helpless feeling in the face of the fact that Romi was probably right. She didn't know what the situation was at the pub, and even if it was . . . the worst . . . that meant the Black Knight had the Eye, and they couldn't let him have the Heart. Whether she liked it or not, she'd have to leave Hatta and the others to whatever fate befell them and finish her part of the mission.

Her throat tight, her eyes burning, Alice nodded.

A smile pulled at the corners of Romi's lips. It wasn't amused, more . . . impressed? "Good. So, what was Addison's grand scheme? He always had one of those."

After a couple of deep breaths to keep the trembling in her gut from shaking her voice, Alice laid out the plan, at least as well as she could with what Hatta had told her. They were supposed to meet up with Xelon and Odabeth. "In some village near . . . He was cut off. Sounded like it started with Ap or Ab."

"Ap, Ab, Ap, Ab." Romi went back and forth repeatedly as she stroked her chin with her free hand. "He could've meant Abdicur Pass. That's the only place between here and the Western Gateway with a village nearby."

"We have to go there," Alice insisted.

Romi shook her head slowly. "That's just a guess. He could've been about to say several things, there's no way to tell. Was there anything concrete?"

Frustration pounded at Alice's temples, but she took a slow breath and thought over their conversation. "Findest. They're going to Findest."

"Findest?" Romi took another puff, blowing the blue smoke to the side. "We searched that place from top to bottom." A smoky pink butterfly curled free from her lips.

"S'what he said. But when the princess used the Eye to look for the Heart, it showed her Findest. Everyone figured going there and having Odabeth try again might reveal something more. Maybe."

"This is a lot of movement and planning to hang on a maybe." Romi clacked her teeth together slightly. "It'll take nearly as long to reach Findest as it would the Western Gateway, maybe longer."

"Not with Chou." Haruka had set the table and was removing the apron tied around her waist. "Remember?"

Romi grunted, then said something in irritated Japanese. Haruka answered easily. The two of them went back and forth a handful of times, the conversation not necessarily heated but energetic. It ended with Romi heaving a sigh.

"Thrice damned Addison Hatta, pulling me back into the field." Romi shook her head and flicked a bit of ash from the smoking end of her pipe. The ash didn't fall so much as vanish from thin air.

"You . . . you two didn't get along?" Alice asked.

The look Romi gave her could've fried her edges. But then the woman's expression softened and she heaved a sigh. "No. We got along better than most, the four of us."

"Four?"

Romi nodded. "Addison, Anastasia, Humphrey, and myself. The Royal Guard."

"Humphrey?" That was a new name. "Not Theo?"

"Mmm? No. I didn't meet Theo until after the war started."

"And Xelon?"

"Never heard of her."

Alice blinked, taken aback. "She . . . she's the White Knight."

Romi snorted. "Oh, really? Well, guess they couldn't leave the position vacant after I left."

"Wayment." Alice shook her head and lifted her hands. "*You* used to be the White Knight?"

"Mmm. It didn't mean what it means now, it was just how people who didn't know my name referred to me, because of the armor and all. Mine was white, Humphrey's was red, Addison's was boring silver so people just called him the knight. And Anastasia didn't wear armor, unless flowing gowns, body drapes, and sometimes poofy dresses count as armor."

"I know a few cases where it might." Alice grinned.

Romi returned it. There was a genuineness to it that wasn't there the other times she smiled. But it was gone as quickly as it appeared. "So we called her the Duchess."

Alice laughed. "That sounds about right."

"That was us. And Addison was our leader." The whimsical look on Romi's face shifted, darkened. "Until he betrayed us. Sure, he got his head out of his ass just in time to defect to our ranks and help mount one last attack against the Black Queen, but he'd only spent years pounding our forces into dust at her behest beforehand, so, yeah. I'm a little bitter."

"Mmm." What do you say to that? Alice didn't think Addison should still be in exile, but that didn't mean the people he hurt had to forgive him. Paying his debt didn't come with full and complete absolution. "For whatever it's worth, I'm sorry. I . . . know what it's like to have someone you care for betray you." Chess's face flashed across her mind.

Romi puffed out a purple flower. "You didn't do anything. Except end up connected to someone I spend most of my time angry at, and that wasn't your fault." After another slow drag, she nodded. "Ahhhhh, fine. We'll leave for Findest first thing in the morning."

"Morning?" Panic shot through Alice. She'd almost forgotten what they were discussing at first! "We need to leave now!"

A hand fell to her shoulder. Haruka squeezed. "We have to prepare, food, water. And you will need proper clothes for traveling."

"And weapons." Romi got to her feet. "You two, eat. I need to get things ready for Chou." She lifted a hand when Alice started to protest. "We will leave sooner than the morning, but we can't rush this. We can't afford to be caught with our guard down because we are tired and ill-prepared."

Okay, so that made sense. Swallowing her retort, Alice followed Haruka to the table. Romi slipped out the door, saying she would be back shortly. The sound of her thumping down the stairs faded as Haruka placed a helping of something that smelled heavenly in front of Alice. She wasn't in the mood for food, but the eager twist in her stomach said it was.

Alice used the chopsticks offered to shove some into her mouth. Man, it was delicious.

"How did you meet Hatta?" Haruka asked between bites.

"You know him?"

Haruka shook her head. "I know of him. I know what Romi has told me—he is a Gatekeeper, he fought in the war."

"That they were friends?"

"Yes. They still talk, but not often. Usually about updates on Nightmare activity, and to ask for favors. She likes the smoke he makes."

Alice frowned. "Smoke?"

Haruka nodded and mimicked Romi's posture in holding her pipe.

"Oh! Oh." Hatta made tobacco? Or whatever the Wonderland equivalent was. Go figure. "He saved me," Alice said, diving into the story of the first time she crossed paths with Addison Hatta. "It was . . . it was a bad night. I was a mess, and this Nightmare was gonna rip my head clean off. He stopped it. I didn't believe what I was seeing, I thought I had lost my mind, but . . . there he was."

Alice remembered that moment as crystal clear as if it were last night. She remembered the stink of the alley and the Nightmare's breath. She remembered the gleam of the Vorpal Blade and the way it swallowed the dim light. She remembered the first time she heard his voice, the first time she looked him in the eye.

You wouldn't believe me if I told you, Addison had said when she asked where he was from. Then he looked her up and down like he was debating whether or not he wanted to supersize his order or something, before saying a handful of words that changed her life. *But I think I will.*

That night, she explained to Haruka, Hatta had walked her back to Grady. On the way, he asked her what had brought her to the alley. She told him about her father. She didn't cry then. She didn't do much of anything but talk and sniff. Her heart was numb, and the tears wouldn't come. It was a strange, hollow feeling, especially after having felt so many things just minutes before.

Hatta apologized for her loss and explained that was likely what drew the Nightmare to her, her sorrow, her fear. That was the first time she heard that word, *Nightmare*. Well, heard it as a name for those monsters. She had more questions. He told her the truth. She thought he was bugging, or messing with her, and she told him several times she wasn't in the mood for any of his mess. But he promised her he was sincere, even proposed that if she didn't believe his words, she should at least believe her own eyes. She'd seen what had happened, and that in and of itself showed promise.

Then, in the dull light of the EMERGENCY sign, he told her there was something special about her. That she shouldn't be able to see him with the invisibility Verse he used, shouldn't be able to talk to him, but she was. She didn't believe him until he told her to look around at the people coming and going.

She did. They eyed her in passing as she spoke to him, gave her a wide berth. She thought it was because she likely looked a mess, with her ruined wig and costume. He said it was because they thought she was talking to herself. People tended to avoid folk for that, among other, bullshit reasons.

They really can't see you? Alice had asked.

He shook his head. *Nope. At least, not at the moment. If I allow it, they can.*

Alice fidgeted. *This is really happening.*

Yep.

She looked at him. *You really killed that monster back there.*

Mmm, not for good. People like me? We can't kill them. Not permanently. That's why we need people like you.

That made Alice snort, though she looked away when she noticed his eyes on her. *What do you mean?*

Humans with a strong connection to where I'm from. Where those monsters are from. Humans who can see us when we mean not to be seen. Hatta glanced around before drawing back a step. *I need to get back. It was a pleasure, milady.* Hatta bowed before starting off the way they'd come.

Will I see you again? Alice called before he'd gotten too far.

He turned and smiled. *You'd be the only one who could.*

And with that, he was gone. The rest of the night was a whirlwind of emotions and tears, from her mother and grandmother as well. They went home. Nana Kingston spent the night with them. Alice didn't sleep at all, instead she stayed up, talking to Courtney on the phone, telling her everything.

"That is unusual," Haruka remarked after Alice finished her story. "Being able to see him like that."

Alice shrugged. "Lots of unusual things happen to me." She shoveled more food into her mouth. Despite the worry eating away at her, she ate like a woman starved. "How long before we're good to go?"

Haruka shrugged. "With everything that is happening, we need to make sure we are ready to deal with this Black Knight. I'm still not entirely sure what is going on with him."

"That's an even longer story." One Alice told in as much detail as she could. She was so wrapped up in her explanation, she didn't even notice Romi had returned until the woman dropped what looked like a bedroll onto the kitchen counter.

"I knew it was only a matter of time before the past came around again. It always does." Romi took a slow pull of another vape device, lights twinkling on this one. "Can't say I expected this particular brand of bullshit, though."

Haruka saw to cleaning up the now empty plates as Romi set the mat on the table and rolled it out. Figment Blades of various sizes lined the inside, strapped in place, their silvery surfaces gleaming.

Alice instantly reached for the daggers, though drew up short. She pitched a questioning glance at Romi. These things weren't the easiest to come by, and she didn't wanna just take someone's stuff. Romi waved her on, and she pulled the daggers free. They were a bit heavier than the ones she was used to, the blades slightly longer, but thinner.

As Alice tested the weight of the weapons, Romi typed something into her phone. "So. You all thought you would reform the Eye, take it and the only known royal—who isn't in a coma—halfway across the world to locate the missing Heart, both of which are wanted by someone calling himself the Black Knight, who you very recently double-crossed. And no one expected this sudden development of him busting your door in, possibly looking for payback?"

Alice drummed her fingers against one dagger's handle. "Well . . . I guess? We . . . there's this whole thing with my friends missing, and—"

Romi held up a hand. "I took this gig because it seemed like the best way to avoid all of the mess that followed the war. Hang out with some humans—you guys are weird but funny—travel back home now and then, slay a few monsters, just carve out a nice little life for myself. Now the mess I crossed the Veil to evade is literally sitting at my table. No offense."

"None taken." Maybe a little taken. She did call her a mess.

Alice busied herself with the plate Haruka had left behind. The Dreamwalker had made herself scarce after putting the dishes in the sink, Alice noticed.

Romi chewed on her food, managing a few bites without saying anything. After a couple awkwardly tense minutes, she cleared her throat with a faint burp. "I see you fancy daggers. I'd pick a sword, too. Just in case." She stepped away from the counter and through the living room, toward a back hall. "Help Haruka pack provisions. She's downstairs."

The door slammed shut, and Alice winced. She sat in the silence for a minute or two before setting down the daggers and pushing to her feet. Even though Romi said Alice hadn't done anything wrong, she got the distinct feeling the Gatekeeper wasn't too happy about her being here. Then again, she didn't know how she'd feel if someone with an indirect connection to trauma from her past showed up with drama at her heels.

She finished eating, dumped her dishes, then made her way downstairs. Glancing once toward the empty bookshop, she turned back down the hall that led to the bathroom and, farther on, the Gateway. With no idea where she was going, she cleared her throat, then called Haruka's name.

After the third time, the girl responded, "In here."

Alice followed the voice to one of the doors that had been closed earlier. It stood open onto what looked like a large pantry, the walls lined with shelves and freestanding cases filed along the room like bookcases at a library. Each one was stacked with stuff Alice recognized, like bottled water, freeze-dried foods, packs of snacks, and things that reminded her of what her Dad would take with him when he went camping with friends from work. Then there were other items in jars of different sizes, boxes here and there, different containers and junk.

"Ah." Alice searched the spaces between the shelves for signs of the other girl. "Romi sent me to help you. I think she's sick of me."

"She's sick of everybody." Haruka's voice came from somewhere on the right, and Alice followed it until she found the girl kneeling next to three hiking backpacks that looked fairly full. In fact, Haruka zipped up the third one and stood. "Don't take it personal."

"I'll try not to. You need a hand?" Alice gestured at the bags.

Haruka handed one over. "That's yours. For the journey."

"Thanks." She slung it over one shoulder, surprised at how light it was despite the fact that it looked like it should weigh at least fifty pounds. "And thanks for offering to be my guide. Partner? To help me get to where I'm trying to go."

Haruka shrugged. "I'm a guardian, like you. Things sound like they're getting bad. And it's all hands on deck, as Romi would say."

"Still, thanks."

Haruka led the way out of the room, turning off the light and closing the door behind them. "Don't thank me till we get there. Something tells me it's gonna be a rough ride."

Sixteen

HERE THERE BE DRAGONS

Alice spent the next couple of hours helping get things ready to cross over and recounting everything that had happened from the night the Black Knight first jumped her to when Haruka found her lost in Wonderland. She left out the personal bits, but it was still weird talking about everything out in the open after keeping it secret for so long, even if she was telling it all to people who were technically in on the whole thing.

Thankfully the Duchess had been keeping Romi and Theo, the guardian of the Southern Gateway, up to date with the basics: who the Black Knight was, what he wanted, and how they planned to keep it from him. Also thankfully, the Duchess had left out the bits where Alice had messed up royally more than a couple times.

Haruka asked a couple of clarifying questions, and Romi

had stayed eerily silent, simply readying the weapons they would take with them. During that time Alice had also called her mom to explain what was going on, as best she could. Mom wasn't too thrilled to find out she was somewhere in Tokyo—in fact she didn't believe Alice at first. It wasn't until Romi got on the phone that Mom was convinced she wasn't being pranked. Even then, it was . . . a lot.

Alice chewed at her lower lip while Romi spoke into the phone.

"Yes. We are doing all we can to get her home. Not without a passport. Yes. Yes. Our magic does not work that way. No. The embassy will want to know how she got here in the first place. They might arrest her for being a spy or something. Yes. It could take a day or two, the passage of time is strange between realms. Because our world doesn't have a sun, so there aren't actually days scientifically speaking but . . . no. Yes, she is eating. I can't promise that. Here she is."

Romi extended the phone, her face scrunched up in annoyance.

Alice took it with a silent apology before holding it to her ear. "Hello?"

"Some parents worry about losing they child in a mall or something, I lost mine through a . . . the hell you call it?"

"Veil. Or . . . portal, works."

"A por—a *portal* Alison!" Mom huffed. "Got me feeling like I'm in the damn *Twilight Zone*. What in the hell am I supposed to do with you being able to *fall* clear through to the other side of the world? No. No, no, this isn't . . . this can't . . .

oh my god . . ." Mom's voice cracked and whined as she broke into tears.

Alice's throat tightened at the pain in her mother's words. "I-it's okay. Mommy, it's okay, I promise." She sniffed and swiped at her eyes. "Don't cry, you'll make me cry."

"It's either cry or scream. Or choke somebody, but I can't be in jail while you in *Japan*." Mom mumbled something that sounded like a prayer. Alice heard at least one mention of Jesus.

"Listen, why don't you go stay with Nana Kingston until I get home?"

"What? Why?"

"The Black Knight has already showed up at the house, twice now. You shouldn't be there by yourself." *And I can't get ahold of Addison to have someone look after you.*

Mom scoffed. "So I'm just supposed to hide while you're playing Xena?"

"That's not—"

"This is *my* house, I'm not gonna be chased away by some hoodlum in a Halloween costume."

Alice barely held back a groan. "Mom."

"—tore my bedroom up, smashed my furniture all to hell."

"Mom."

"And your grandmother's place isn't even big enough for—"

"Mom!"

The line went quiet.

Alice swallowed. "He's dangerous. You saw what he's capable of. He's still out there, still hurting people, and I don't want you getting caught up in this. It's only for a couple of days, just . . . please. Go."

For a long stretch of seconds, no one said anything. Alice rubbed at her eyes, the beginnings of a headache settling in behind them.

"Okay, baby," Mom said softly. "Okay. I'm sorry, I just . . . I got no way to get to you, to protect you if anything happens."

"It's okay, Mom. Really." Alice smiled. "And I'm the one that does the protecting now."

Mom snorted a little laugh. "Whew. We still have to talk about all . . . that when you get back here. You be safe, Baby Moon, you hear me?" There was an almost desperate edge to her voice that slipped into Alice's heart like a knife.

"I hear you. I love you."

"I love you, too."

Mom hung up first, still muttering about Japan. Alice handed Romi her phone with a thanks, then excused herself to go get ready. There wasn't much to do, just throw on her clothes and grab the pack that Haruka had helped her prepare. Romi stepped out to see to a few things with the store, since they were going to be gone for a while.

Alice and Haruka stood outside the room that held the Gateway, waiting. Alice checked over the daggers at her hips. The sword pressed into her back shifted when she adjusted the lightweight pack. Magic, Haruka had explained when she asked why they didn't feel like they were holding anything. And why didn't Hatta have access to this backpack magic? Or was he holding out on her? Jerk. The familiar line of teasing thought was somewhat soothing.

Part of her longed to go back to that, to before all of this ridiculousness. The part of her that knew it wasn't possible told her to gut up—she had a job to do, and getting nostalgic wasn't gonna help. Besides, that was just last week, not some bygone era. That part of her was the mean part, Alice decided.

Romi finally came around the corner, carrying her own bag. Alice couldn't see any weapons, though.

"Let's go." Romi led the way into the room, waiting until everyone was inside before shutting the door. She looked to Alice. "Going to lose your shit again?"

Alice glowered. "Probably."

Romi held out a bottle of a faintly milky substance.

"Potion?" Alice asked as she took it.

"Sort of. Made from ginger. Should take the edge off."

"Thanks." Alice slipped the bottle into a side pocket just as Haruka flipped the lights off.

◊ ◊ ◊

Her stomach churning, Alice drank the ginger tonic like a woman dying of thirst. The sweet but biting flavor slid against her tongue and down her throat. Hopefully it would quell the nausea.

"Are you going to be okay?" Haruka hovered nearby while Romi had wandered off a short distance, puffing on her pipe as she went.

"Y-yeah." Alice finished off the tonic and stored the empty bottle in her pack. "It'll fade." She pushed to stand and found her feet held her, even if she was a bit wobbly.

Haruka fell into step beside her, and together, the two of them trailed away from the Gateway and after Romi.

For a while, they moved in silence, with Alice taking in the new surroundings. It was amazing how Wonderland, as surreal as it was, could manage to look so . . . normal. If you counted yellow trees as normal. And it was disconcerting how the beauty of this place concealed so much pain, death, and evil. Evil she was once again off to fight.

Shaking herself free from her thoughts, she turned to Haruka. "Can I ask you a question?"

Haruka looked up from a book she was reading. While walking. At the same time. "Yes."

"How did you become a Dreamwalker?"

The look that passed over Haruka's face was pained but brief. She shut the book and focused her attention ahead.

"Sorry," Alice offered hurriedly. "I didn't mean to pry."

"No, no, it's fine."

"Save story time for later, ladies. We're here," Romi called over her shoulder.

The three of them stepped from the brush of a lightly wooded area they'd entered maybe an hour ago, and Alice's mouth nearly hit the ground.

A cluster of buildings sat in a large clearing, some of them very clearly houses. Smoke rose from chimneys here and there. It was a village.

"Where are we?" Alice asked as they approached, the smell of food and the sound of voices carried on the wind. Someone was shouting in a language Alice didn't readily recognize.

"Vindighter," Haruka said. "Home of the Fury keepers."

That made Alice stop short as she recalled when Haruka first mentioned the Furies. "Excuse me, what?"

"Fury keepers." Haruka smiled as she and Romi kept going. "They who keep Furies?"

Alice raced to catch up to them just as they entered the village. It was practically out of a storybook, with the main street wide and open, moving toward a distant square. Stalls lined the various streets along with shops, people calling out to one another in passing. A few children played nearby. There were so many faces, brown, pale, dark, light. So many colors, styles, and textures of hair. A little boy with dark skin and pink locks waved at them excitedly as they passed where he sat in a stall filled with what Alice assumed was fruit and vegetables. She waved back, smiling faintly.

Several other people noted their passing, nodding and waving to Romi and Haruka. Some people waved at Alice. Others just stared. She was definitely a newcomer.

"You look shocked," Haruka said as they entered a sudden stretch of road that opened up, and the stone beneath their feet split off into several directions.

"I've never been to a village here before." She'd gone to Legracia, but that didn't really count. "It's incredible."

"This is one of the smaller ones."

Alice followed the two as they departed the hustle and bustle of the square, heading off between the buildings and along a quieter street. Eventually their path opened onto a space within the large meadow, one that was fenced in by wood, metal, and something that shimmered faintly in the daylight. What looked like a ranch house and stable lined the far fence, but out in the field rested a wonder Alice could not have imagined.

Lying sprawled or coiled against the grass were two large, serpentine creatures. One with black scales that glistened radiant colors as they shifted in the light, the other with pale blue scales that washed green. They each had clawed front feet and birdlike back legs that ended in long talons. Wide, feathery wings of silver stretched along the black beast, its head that of a great cat. The blue one had gold wings, equally feathery, and a long, reptilian head. They were huge.

"Those are the Furies?" Alice asked, unable to keep the awe out of her voice, not that she really wanted to.

"Those are two of them. There are about a dozen total, counting adolescents and fledglings. Most are probably in the stables." Haruka was beaming. She waved, and Alice turned to spot a round girl with amber skin and dark brown hair drawn back into a tail of bushy curls.

The girl approached along the inside of the fence and tilted forward to lean against it. She wore the fanciest pair of overalls Alice had ever laid eyes on.

Haruka called out in Japanese, and the girl responded in kind, a wide smile breaking across her face. Romi chuckled. Alice was lost, but smiled anyway. The whole thing had a somewhat infectious cheeriness about it.

"Willanae, this is Alice. She's the Dreamwalker from the Western Gateway." Haruka gestured to Alice, who raised a hand in an awkward little wave.

"Hey."

"Hi!" Willanae chirped.

"Alice, this is Willanae. Her family looks after the Furies in this area."

"I can barely handle two cats—I can't imagine what taking care of these things is like," Alice said. She'd never seen any, or even heard of them before.

Willanae giggled. "They act like cats, sometimes. Big ole snaky cats."

"They're beautiful. I've never seen anything like them . . ."

There are more things in heaven and earth, Horatio, than are dreamt of in your philosophy. Addison's voice filled Alice's ears, and something in her stomach fluttered while something else in her chest tightened. She hoped he was okay.

"I'd be surprised if you had." Willanae said. "Most wild Furies keep to themselves, and there's one other ranch in Luma Valley." She had the faintest accent, but Alice couldn't place it. It sharpened her words and dropped a couple consonant sounds. It was almost a mix of Australian and . . . Southern, maybe? "And call me Willa, it's nice to meet you."

"You too." Alice fidgeted with the straps of her pack as Willa turned her attention back to Haruka and Romi.

"I didn't expect to see either of you so soon. Everything okay?"

"Yes. And no. But nothing you need to worry about, the usual stuff," Romi said.

"This isn't a simple visit, then?"

"Nope. Here on business." Romi set her hand against the fencepost, which was about as high as Alice's chest, and leaped over it in one fluid motion. "How's my boy?"

"Same as when you left him." Willa stepped in with Romi,

and the two of them started toward the black and blue Furies napping out in the field. "A little grumpy because I'm out of findel fish."

Haruka ducked between two of the horizontal slats, and Alice did the same, then followed everyone toward what she now saw were very large creatures, much larger than she originally thought.

"Awww, my poor baby. I brought him some apples." Romi slung her pack off of her shoulder and fished a paper bag from within.

"You're gonna spoil him with all of these exotic goodies." The words were chiding, but Willa's tone was decidedly not.

"That's the point. Chou!"

The blue Fury blinked its large eyes open, then popped its head up, glancing around.

"Chou-Chou!" Romi called in a high-pitched squeal.

The creature rumbled as it scrabbled to its feet. Its long, thick tail that ended in what looked like a large club thumped loudly against the ground, and it bounded toward them.

Alice froze, her eyes wide, everything in her screaming to run. *"That's* Chou!?"

"Yup," Haruka said as the big thing stumbled a bit, its lanky body trying to both run and slither along, its belly dragging just above the grass. It slid to a stop in front of Romi and dragged a large, purple forked tongue that was almost as long as the woman herself against her body.

Romi laughed as it nearly pushed her over, then she threw her arms around the Fury's snout, cooing something in Japanese. Chou purred—at least it sounded like a purr—his tail still thumping. It pounded even faster when she dug into the paper bag and offered up an apple. The tip of that purple tongue curled around it and drew it between some of the biggest, pointiest teeth Alice had ever laid eyes on.

"That's how we're going to get to Findest?" Alice asked.

"Yup," Haruka repeated.

"Come say hi," Romi called back to them. "He won't bite. He's a big baby. Aren't you? Aren't you a big baby? Yes you are!" She offered up more apples for Chou to slurp up like grapes.

That was when Alice realized she hadn't moved since she learned just who Chou was. Swallowing thickly, she stared after Haruka, who had no problem striding up to this creature that could likely swallow her in two bites. She, too, said something in Japanese and petted at the Fury's snout.

Alice took a slow breath and forced her feet to move. With a potent mix of awe, excitement, and terror, she approached Romi and her freaking pet dragon thing.

Romi watched her with an amused look on her face that Alice did not appreciate one bit. "Come on. Offer your hand, just like with a dog. Let him get a good whiff of you."

"No thanks!" Alice forced a smile. "I'm good."

"Furies can be easily offended," Haruka started. "If you don't want to upset him, you need to let him get to know you."

"You are on his field. S'only fair." Willa lifted a finger. "And they don't like it when people are rude."

Alice hesitated, wiping her hands against her pants as she swallowed thickly. *No, nonono. Oh god, I'm gonna die.* "Just . . . uh . . . like this?" She held her hand out.

"Palm down," Willa said, also looking way too comfortable.

These things were huge, and the black one some distance away had sat up to eye them as well.

Alice flipped her hand over and inched forward. Chou watched her with large, glasslike eyes, the pupils at their centers shaped like diamonds. The thumping of his tail slowed and he leaned his head forward. Alice thought her heart might stop dead in her chest, or burst out of it.

Chou nudged at her fingers with his wet snoot and took two powerful sniffs. Then he opened his mouth, and right when Alice figured, *This is it, this is the end,* that purple tongue moved along her face, wet, sticky, and scratchy.

The thumping picked up again, and Alice blinked before she reached up to squeegee dragon spit from her face. She held her breath, her stomach gurgling, bile burning her throat. "N-nice . . . nice Chou . . ." She flicked the slime from her fingers and swallowed a groan.

Gross!

"He likes you." Romi's smile was megawatt bright. "Good."

"Awesome," Alice said tightly as she lifted the hem of her freshly laundered shirt—it still smelled like lavender—to wipe at her face. "Why'd I have to get slobbed up, now?"

"Oh, it's always best to let Furies get used to you before you ride them." Willa patted the side of Chou's long neck like he was a horse.

Alice froze in the middle of cleaning her fingers, the tightening in her chest returning for a whole new reason. "Wait, what?" She had never ridden a dragon before, and after ten years of Harry Potter movies, she couldn't say the thought that it *might* maybe sorta be cool hadn't crossed her mind, but now that she was staring down an actual dragon thing, Fury, whatever, she was having second thoughts.

"We're going to *ride* this thing?" Alice looked back and forth between Chou, who was still nuzzling Romi as she fed him apples, and Willa.

"Technically, I'm going to ride him," Romi said. "You and Haruka will ride in his gondola."

"His what?" Alice asked.

"It's like a basket that he holds on to for transporting extra passengers," Willa offered in a cheerful tone, as if that explanation helped quell *any* of Alice's worries.

"So he's going to carry a big basket with us in it," Alice gestured between herself and Haruka. "While flying however many hundreds of feet in the air."

"That's right," Willa said.

"And he won't just . . . drop it?"

"He wears a harness that keeps hold of you, tucked nice and snug under his belly."

"Great," Alice murmured, looking to the Fury. "I mean, he's pretty long. Couldn't we all just ride tied to his back or something?" That sounded way safer.

"Furies sort of slither while they fly. The motion can easily throw a rider if they're too far back from the safe zone just behind the head." Willa patted Chou some more, earning another low purr. "Don't worry, you'll be safe with this one. Safer than you would be with any of the others, especially Ben there." She gestured over her shoulder to the black Fury that had lain back down but continued to eye them. "Cantankerous old-timer that he is."

"His name is Ben?" Alice asked.

"Mmhm."

Alice wasn't sure why that surprised her. Probably something to do with all of the weird names in Wonderland.

"Short for Bentalandion," Willa finished.

There we are.

"Don't worry, I ride with Romi all the time," Haruka offered. "It'll be okay."

"If you say so." Alice looked to Chou, who honestly reminded her of a big dog the way he acted with Romi. A big dog that could swallow her like a Swiss roll. If this was the fastest way to Findest, then so be it. "When do we leave?"

"I need to get everything set up, then get Chou strapped in," Willa said. "I would've had everything ready if I knew you were coming."

"Last-minute mess," Romi said, shooting a brief look at Alice. "Would've warned you ahead of time, if we could."

"It's not a problem, you'll just have to wait, is all. How long will you be gone, so I know how much feed to send with you?"

"Two days there, two days back, maybe a day handling our business, make it a week even. Just in case." Romi fed another apple to Chou before holding up her hands as he sniffed along her body, searching. "Sorry, buddy, that's all I got."

"A week, huh? Awfully long time to spend on something that's not a problem." Willa arched an eyebrow but smiled at Romi. Her round face just lit up with it.

"You know me, I like to be thorough." Romi patted Chou once more before stepping back. "You be good for Willa while she gets you strapped in." The Fury huffed, and Romi wagged a finger in his long face. "Hey, no back talk. You behave. Oooh, you're Momma's Chou-Chou." She hugged his snoot once more before backing away.

"Come on, Chou." Willa tugged gently on a large whisker and Chou turned around to follow her toward the stables. "Go inside and make yourselves comfortable. Neasig made tea."

Alice watched the big beast lumber after Willa, who looked like a toy next to him, before following Romi and Haruka toward the house.

"I thought you said Chou was temperamental," Alice said, recalling earlier statements from both of them.

"He is." Romi glanced over her shoulder at Alice. "Unless you bring him treats. Then he's a big softie."

"And apples are his favorite?"

"Anything from the human world is his favorite, though he's particularly fond of apples and cotton candy."

Alice glanced after the blue beast once more, then her gaze trailed over to where Ben lay with his head on his claws, his eyes following them even at a distance. If Chou was temperamental, that one had to be downright nasty.

"Who does Ben belong to?" she asked.

A tension fell over Romi. Her shoulders hunched, and her fingers tightened on her pack straps. Alice didn't miss the little glance Haruka threw at her, either.

"He *used* to belong to the Red Queen," Romi murmured. "But then she up and disappeared. Now he's just here, with his kin. He doesn't belong to anyone and won't let a single soul ride him."

Alice frowned, looking at the creature in a new light. No

wonder he was cantankerous, or whatever Willa had said. His person was missing, had abandoned him, for all he knew. Alice felt a twinge of sympathy for the beastie.

"Did anyone ever think to maybe use him to try and find her?" Alice asked. "Like how dogs can sometimes find their way home or to their owners if they move across town?"

"We *tried*," Romi stressed. "But once she went missing, he didn't have much interest in doing anything other than eating, sleeping, and playing with the fledglings. He's seen five broods hatched and raised in his time here."

"That's a lot of broods." At least it sounded like a lot; she had no idea.

They reached the house, a long, single-story structure. Romi knocked before turning the knob and sticking her head in. "Neasig? Willa said you made tea." Without waiting for a response, Romi strolled right on in. Haruka followed.

"I did! Fresh pot!" a low voice called from somewhere deeper in the house.

Alice hesitated, hearing her mom's voice in her head about how rude it was to enter someone's house without being invited. Shoving the thought aside, she followed as well.

The place had looked like a simple house on the outside, but inside it resembled a cozy cottage. Wood beams towered overhead in a slant that definitely wasn't there from the outside. Worn planks made up the floor, covered in colorful plush rugs here and there. A fire of white flame danced in the hearth, and everywhere, hanging from the walls and resting on every flat surface, were little wood carvings of different types of Furies. They were kinda cute.

Haruka and Romi shrugged out of their packs and left them and their shoes in the little slat just inside the door. Alice followed suit.

The three of them made their way into what looked like a modern-esque kitchen. Standing at the counter was a wisp of a man, tall and thin, with caramel curls around his pale face. His bright brown eyes moved to Alice and widened just slightly.

"Oh, hello! I don't believe we've met." He spoke with the same mixed accent as Willa.

"I'm Alice." Alice lifted a hand in greeting. "I'm from the Western Gateway."

"Why, you're a long way from home, Alice." The man poured four cups of tea from a little green pot that didn't look large enough to hold half that much. "It's a pleasure to meet you all the same. I'm Neasig. Sugar? Mea juice? Fay jam?" He held up a tray with three fancy dishes, one filled with sugar, the next with a purple liquid that smelled of smoke, and the last with a green gelatinous substance that stank like glue. Each dish held a spoon for dipping.

Haruka and Romi politely declined, but Alice doctored her tea a bit.

"The Western Gateway." Neasig spooned a heap of sugar into the brown cinnamon-smelling liquid and stirred. "That would make you Addison Hatta's charge?"

"Yeah." Alice wrapped her hands around the warm cup, but didn't take a drink just yet. "You know Hatta?"

"Of course." Neasig smiled, but there wasn't much joy behind it. "Everyone knows of the knight. Wherever Queen Portentia went, he was beside her."

"So you were at court with Hatta and the Duchess?"

"Heavens no." Neasig gave a little laugh. "I've always been here, with my family, looking after the Furies that might one day be chosen by one of the royalty as their own, or any soul who might be fortunate enough to form a bond with one. Like Chou and Romi, here."

Romi snorted as she sipped at her tea. "He followed me home. And was cuddly."

Alice smirked at that, then looked back to their host. "So you knew Hatta before . . ."

"Before the war." Neasig nodded. "Yes."

"Is it true that he helped the Black Queen try and destroy my world?" Her voice was soft, quieter than she liked. She sounded like a child afraid of being scolded.

Romi tensed and continued to sip at her tea.

"It's true that he has been through quite a lot. More than he's willing to admit to himself, I'd wager." Neasig took a small sip of his tea. "But he has found new purpose in training talented individuals like yourself."

"Is he the reason the Red and White Queens were able to defeat the Black Queen?" Alice wasn't about to be steered away from her line of questioning. She realized it probably made a lot of people uncomfortable to talk about that time. Addison himself had said that sometimes you just wanted to leave the past in the past, but the past had come back to bite them all in the ass. The time for secrets and silence was over.

Neasig shifted, clearly not enjoying this line of questioning. "He was crucial to the efforts that led to victory. But, as you said,

he was part of the reason war had to be waged in the first place."
He waved a hand and turned to busy himself with putting things
away. "Enough of that dreadful business, now. Let's move on to
more pleasant conversation, mm? I have a question, which is just
what are you all doing here again so soon? Well, not you, Alice,
as this is your first time." He smiled an uneasy smile.

"It has to do with that dreadful business," Romi said, and
then went into an explanation of the goings-on of the past few
days. She told what she could, with Alice filling in details here
and there. As they spoke, Neasig's expression slowly fell, and
his white skin grew even paler.

Alice was glad Romi did most of the talking. To be honest,
she was tired of explaining this business with the Black Knight
over and over again.

"Well." Neasig swiped at his forehead with a napkin. "That
is unfortunate."

That was putting it lightly.

"You two haven't noticed anything strange during your fly-
overs, have you?" Romi asked.

He shook his head. "Nothing worth noting, but I'll be sure
to take a closer look now."

"Not too close."

Whatever Romi was going to say in addition to that was
interrupted when the front door slammed open behind them
and Willa barreled into the house. "Nightmares!" she shouted.
"In the village!"

Romi spat a curse and leaped from her seat. Haruka was
right behind her. Alice jolted forward as well, her body buzzing.

For some reason, the boy she'd waved to in passing popped into her mind. She hoped he and his family had gotten to safety.

"How many?" Romi barked as the three of them pulled on their shoes.

"I counted at least five!" Willa panted, her face flushed deep with the barest hints of red, her hair a bit wild from running.

Alice grabbed the sword from her back, the daggers still at her hips. She pushed down on the fear that tried to rise from her middle—*five Nightmares?!*—and was out the door first, Haruka behind her. Romi brought up the rear, the three of them racing for the village.

The pitch of screams and growls reached them before a flash of darkness drew Alice's attention. "There!" She pointed. A Nightmare big as a bull but with six legs and a crocodile snout barreled into a stall, sending fruit and wood flying.

"Another to the east," Haruka called. "More farther in."

"You two, take the big one on the right. I'll get the one on the left. Make it quick, then on to the next."

"Got it," Haruka said.

Alice veered right, straight for the bull Nightmare currently chomping on what was left of the produce it hadn't smashed under its claws. She brought the sword up and leaped. Her body cut through the air in an arch, and she threw her weight forward into the descent, aiming to drive the sword home. The Nightmare whirled, catching sight of her, then skittered backward faster than something so bulky should be able to move. Alice caught herself in a roll, coming out of it and bouncing to her feet just as Haruka drove into the beast from behind. She brought her sword across its flank in a series of quick strikes, landing three before the beast whirled and lashed out with its wide tail.

"Look out!" Alice shouted, but Haruka had already darted to the side, just barely avoiding being swatted. Its tail was big as a log, and the beast swung it like a jackhammer. Getting tagged probably felt like being hit by either one.

Gauging the reach on that thing, Alice moved in, thrusting her sword into the monster's side. It howled and kicked at her with its thick legs. One caught her in the calf, and pain danced up the back of her leg. She dropped to one knee but didn't let go. She twisted the sword and brought it up, throwing her weight into pushing the monster into the remains of the stall and pinning it in place. She wouldn't be able to hold it for more than a few seconds.

"Haruka!"

The other Dreamwalker leaped into the air and came down onto the Nightmare's back, her sword sinking in between its shoulders. There was a crack. It yowled, then went limp. As it began to dissolve, Alice pulled away, her injured leg nearly giving out. She glimpsed torn skin, three wide wounds, but not very deep. Already the tingle of their healing set in. That . . . that was new.

Haruka spared her a glance, brows raised as if to ask if she was okay.

Alice nodded, looking to the wound again.

She didn't have time to dwell on it. More screams farther in town had her and Haruka breaking into a run in that direction. Surprisingly, the pain in Alice's leg wasn't enough to slow her.

They rounded a corner to find two smaller Nightmares tearing into what used to be a man. Alice's tea galloped up her throat, over her tongue, and pushed against the back of her teeth. She spun to throw it up over the stone street.

Her gagging drew the attention of the Nightmares, two catlike creatures with gaping mouths and needlelike teeth. Alice's stomach roiled, but she spit out the last of the sick, tears stinging her eyes, as she hurtled forward, sword coming up in a swing.

She fell into step with Haruka easily, able to read the other girl's motions and certain Haruka was able to read hers. They danced around each other and the Nightmares, making quick work of them, the bodies popping and fizzing away, staining the earth black. They'd have to be purged, but there were other monsters to deal with first.

The stink of rot and death filled Alice's nose, the yellow pus of the monsters' insides staining her blades, her hands, her clothes. She swallowed the nausea pushing around her insides. "You okay?"

Haruka was inspecting a tear in her own sleeve, now stained red with her blood. She nodded and the two of them turned to move farther into the village. Alice spotted Romi atop a Nightmare. Something metallic gleamed where it was wrapped around its neck, held in place as she twisted it tighter. A whip, Alice realized as Romi lifted the sharpened handle and plunged it into the beast. It crumbled beneath her, and she slid off of its disintegrating remains.

"That was the last one," Romi panted.

There should have been a swell of relief, the beginnings of

celebration, even, but the sound of cries and sobs dampened all of that. Alice turned, looking at the destruction around them. Most of the stalls and some of the buildings were broken open. A quick count showed at least eight bodies lying still on the road, possibly more. There were . . . pieces . . .

People cried over their fallen loved ones, next to them, shaking them, holding them when they could. The burn in Alice's chest reached her eyes and closed off her throat.

"What was this?" Her voice cracked as tears spilled over her cheeks.

"This is how things were, before." Romi drew her whip in, winding it around her arm. "When the war began. And now it begins again."

Seventeen

MY LADY

The Black Knight stood at the mouth of the road as the Fiends tore through the town and its citizens. Strange, he'd expected a response by now. Maybe the Fiends he'd sent ahead to scout the area had been wrong about Alice being here, and all of this was for nothing.

Well, perhaps not entirely. As bodies fell, more Fiends rose, numbers to bolster Her Majesty's forces.

"She's here." A slithery voice sliced through the air at his left. "The Dreamwalker."

He scanned the chaos, trying to catch sight of her. "Where?"

"There." One of the Fiends paced at his side, its eyeless head fixated down the road.

In the distance, a Fiend shrieked as it was flung to the ground, dissolving in its death throes. Alice Kingston stood over it, a sword in her hands and fury on her face. The anger wasn't quite as potent as when he'd glimpsed her across that field, or when he'd gone to her home, but it was close.

The Black Knight nodded, his fingers clenching into fists at his sides. "Take her."

The Nightmares bounded forward with a roar. He remained where he stood, observing the fight. He'd never been able to simply watch; usually he faced off with her as her opponent. She tore through one of the creatures, her ferocity formidable, her form impressive. She twirled her weapons around her body in fluid, deadly motions. Familiar motions. He knew that fighting style . . .

His vision blurred. Pain danced between his ears as a flash of white crossed his sight, followed by a flare of red. The battlefield flickered, faded.

He blinked, trying to focus. Images pressed in against and on top of each other. One moment he was watching Alice tear her way through his forces, and the next . . . *he stared as a woman with long burgundy hair braided to her scalp dove in and around attacking creatures. Her red armor blazed in the daylight. She looked toward him. Their eyes locked. "Humphrey!" she shouted, waving him forward.*

My . . . lady . . . ?

Turning, the woman roared as she charged one of the creatures and leaped into the air. Alice was the one who dropped from the sky as the vision shifted again. An outline of the other woman's armor flickered around her. A howl split the air. Alice spun, her sword lifted. The pain in his head intensified to throbbing.

He shut his eyes. Someone screamed behind him as a Nightmare ran them down.

Wrong. This is Wrong. He knew it, and here he was anyway. There was nothing to be done.

You did something before.

But his lady willed it.

She's not my lady.

"ALICE!"

His eyes flew open. His entire body went cold.

Eighteen

ALL

A million questions flew through Alice's mind, but before she could voice even one of them, a shrill scream split the air. She, Haruka, and Romi whirled to spot . . . Alice didn't really know what she was seeing. The man that had been attacked by the Nightmares she and Haruka had slain was crawling across the ground. His trembling fingers scrabbled at the stone. His broken body left a trail of meat and red and black—thick, oozing black that bubbled over him, consuming him.

Haruka gasped something in disbelieving Japanese.

Another scream. Another body was crawling along the street. They all were, pulling themselves up, their bloody flesh falling away, darkness pouring in over them. One of them threw back their head, fangs erupting from gums with a spurt of blood and ooze, the skin of their face peeling back from a muzzle as it formed with the snap and crack of bone. Then it roared, shakily pushing up onto two legs.

"Nani, kore?" Romi hissed under her breath. The other bodies were turning and rising as well.

"Nightmares!" A woman came racing in from the far side of town. "Nightmares are com—" She screamed as the newly formed monstrosity closest to her pounced, ripping at her with talons. Romi lashed out, her metallic whip catching it around the neck. She yanked and the beast flew toward them. Alice spun into a slash, slicing through its thin middle. It hit the ground in halves, its legs kicking.

Chaos erupted around them as the other bodies rose, attacking those nearest. Screams and howls went up around them. Alice tightened her grip on her sword to try and stop her hands from trembling.

"Look!" Haruka pointed in the direction the woman had come running.

Alice's insides ran cold.

At least a dozen Nightmares poured along the street, a mix of the ones she was used to fighting and these new horrors.

"We can't fight that," Haruka gasped.

"Come on." Romi turned and raced back the way they'd come, toward the ranch.

Up ahead, long, slithery bodies of various colors and sizes took flight. The Furies, Alice realized. Willa must be turning them lose to save them.

Just then, the girl came running from the stables, toward the house. Neasig emerged, and the two of them raced over to a couple of red Furies, climbed onto them, and took to the air.

At least they're safe.

Something slammed into Alice from behind and took her clean off her feet. Pain radiated through her body with the blow, then again when she hit the ground, tumbling across it.

Her face pressed into the dirt.

"ALICE!" Haruka screamed.

A shrill wail filled her ears. Something sharp pierced her back.

Mama . . .

Nineteen

I S

The Black Knight flung himself forward, the rush of the ether parting as he vanished, spun through nothingness in a blink, then dropped into existence. He slammed into Alice from above, his back against hers, placing himself between her and the attacking Nightmare. It roared and bore down on them with a wicked, razor-sharp tail the length of his arm. He couldn't block the blow, but he could deflect it. Instead of skewering them like fish, the tail ripped at his side.

Pain tore through him.

Alice jerked beneath him and screamed.

The knight brought his sword around and drove it into the monster from beneath. It bucked and drew back, the tail pulling free.

"Ah!" Agony spread through the rest of him. He rolled to

the side and onto his knees. Alice clutched at her hip, pushing up similarly.

"W-what . . ." Her eyes lifted from her bloodstained fingers. Confusion and pain twisted her face.

Biting back a groan, he pushed to his feet, staggering as a feeling like fire chewed at his nerves. He wouldn't be able to put up a fight in this condition.

Alice swept around, knocking his feet from under him. He went down with a surprised shout, air forced from his lungs as he landed on his back. "Ahh . . ." A feeling like thunder erupted through his head when something connected with the side of it hard enough that his helmet cracked.

A foot planted itself on his chest. The end of a blade tapped the front of his helmet.

"Where are my friends?" Alice demanded, her voice shaking.

He shook his head. Her friends? His thoughts whirled, tumbling over one another. Friends. His friends were dead. What was she talking about?

"Where are they?" she screamed at him, the pressure on his chest increasing.

He couldn't breathe.

"Alice!" A girl raced toward them, sword lifted. Another Dreamwalker, from the look of it.

He had to get out of here.

Pulling at whatever strength that wasn't literally bleeding from his torn side, he felt his form waver, then fall away entirely. The world faded in a rush.

Twenty

CHAOS

Alice nearly toppled over when the Black Knight vanished and her foot connected with solid ground.

No . . . She stared at the bare spot, the Nightmare popping and fizzling nearby as the last of it collapsed inward. "No!"

"Alice." Haruka took hold of her arm and pulled. "We have to go."

Alice searched the chaos for signs of him. People continued to run. Bodies littered the road, Nightmares and people. The road was awash with fluids.

Then she spotted it. Lying against the ground, near where the Nightmare finally faded, the Vorpal Blade, slick with yellow. Impossible, yet there it was.

"We have to go!" Haruka yanked.

With a frustrated shout, Alice darted forward to grab the

handle of the blade. Heat raced through her palm, but she only tightened her grip and turned to follow the other Dreamwalker.

Romi was already across the field, fastening something to Chou, who shifted, his wings beating every few moments. All the other Furies had already taken flight, little more than colored dots in the sky.

The girls vaulted the fence and raced across the meadow. Alice's injury burned with every step, but she pushed to keep going. Haruka made it first, climbing into what looked like some sort of massive bassinet. She reached to give Alice a hand up, the two of them tumbling into the space, which was about as big as a queen-sized bed.

Romi shouted something in Japanese, and the basket jerked. Alice's stomach dropped with the familiar feeling of taking flight. With a bit of trouble keeping her balance, she finagled around onto hands and knees and pulled herself up at the edge of the basket. The wind whipped at her face and hair. Below, the ground dropped farther and farther away.

Whoosh. Whoosh. Whoosh.

Each beat of Chou's wings jostled the basket slightly as they climbed, the ravaged village eventually fading from sight.

Alice sank to sit against one side of the basket. Haruka had settled at the other end, her eyes on the black blade between them. Alice reached to take hold of it. Like before, heat moved up her fingers.

"What is that?" Haruka asked quietly.

"It's . . . the Vorpal Blade. Or at least a really good copy." Hatta had the original, which was—hopefully—still locked up safe and sound back at what was left of the pub. "The Black Knight had it." And now she did. She had no idea what that would mean, but . . . at least it wasn't in that asshole's hands anymore.

They flew for longer than Alice could keep track of. She and Haruka occasionally exchanged words, Alice talking more about everything that happened since the Black Knight first arrived, Haruka explaining what little she knew about the war. Seemed Romi was as tight-lipped as Addison and Anastasia.

Eventually a tilt and slight rush of vertigo signaled they were descending. Both girls climbed up to peer over the lip of the basket. The view was incredible, with a Technicolor rainbow of waves washing against a nearby shore, then out over the largest body of water Alice had ever seen here in Wonderland. She noticed critters moving around on the quickly approaching ground, but they all darted away before she could get a good look, though she saw some ran on two and four legs while others raced off on many more.

Great beats of feathered wings stirred the grass and dirt beneath them while Chou set them down with a slightly jarring thump. He then settled behind the basket, warbling, the sound like low, distant thunder.

Romi spoke to him in Japanese, but her tone was full of praise and love, like when people talk to their dogs or something. Alice climbed out of the basket. Her legs were a little wobbly but held. Haruka climbed out behind her just as Romi slid down from the saddle. The two of them worked to get Chou free of the harness that held the basket, then the great creature half slithered, half walked over to the edge of the water and bent his snoot to drink.

That was when Romi noticed the sword, freezing in the middle of brushing her hands off. "What's that?"

"The Vorpal Blade," Alice explained for a second time.

Romi's brow puckered. "No, it isn't. I've seen the Vorpal Blade. I've . . . I've held it."

"It's the one the latest incarnation—or whatever he is—of the Black Knight used."

"He was back in the village." Haruka stepped up beside Alice. "Led the attack."

Something Alice couldn't quite read passed over Romi's face. "How did you get it?"

"He dropped it after he . . . after he saved me." Alice shrugged when two very confused looks crossed both of their faces. "I don't get it either. But I was down, and a Nightmare was on top of me. He jumped in the way when it—he took the hit. Got him good." His blood was everywhere. "This was covered in the Nightmare's remains. He probably lost it in the fight."

"Why would he do that?" Haruka eyed the sword like it might strike on its own at any second. "Risk himself, I mean."

"Your guess is as good as mine." Alice rolled her shoulders. "I couldn't just leave it there, though. And I figured it's better in anyone's hands but his."

"That remains to be seen." The pucker between Romi's brows deepened. "Especially if it's anything like the original. Change of subject, I'm guessing neither of you managed to grab any of our stuff."

Both girls shook their heads.

Romi heaved a sigh. "Then we have no provisions. We can't make it to Findest like this."

"There's got to be somewhere to get more." A note of panic entered Alice's voice.

Romi nodded. "There are several places but that would just add more days to our journey. And, with this attack, I am wary of leaving my Gateway unprotected for so long. It is the closest—those beasts may well be drawn to it."

"Wait, you're not talking about going back, are you?" That panic intensified.

"I'm considering it, yes."

"We can't go back!" Alice tightened her grip on the Vorpal Blade. The darkness coating it rippled faintly.

Romi took a step back. "I want to help, but I can't leave the Veil unprotected. Not when that many Nightmares are roaming the wilds so close. Haruka and I have a duty to fulfill, and it's not cleaning up Addison's mess."

Alice stared as feelings of fury, frustration, and hopelessness warred inside her. Every time it felt like they were taking a step forward—

"Fine." She didn't have time to try and convince them to help her. And much as she hated to admit it, Romi had a point. "I'll go by myself. Just point me in the right direction."

Romi pinched the bridge of her nose. "You won't make it. Not like this. You should come back with us."

"You have your duty, which is fine. I have mine, too. That ain't changed." And she had the added problems of her missing friends, trying to find the Heart, and now whatever the hell had happened back at the pub. Not knowing was killing her.

"Look, I said it's fine. I get it, I promise. But I'm going. With or without you. And it would really help if I knew which way."

"You're serious?" Haruka asked quietly, watching her with a look Alice couldn't really place but that made her middle tumble slightly.

"Deadass."

Romi shook her head and muttered something in Japanese. Haruka answered in turn, and whatever she said made a smile pull at Romi's lips. "You're either very brave or very foolish."

Alice snorted. "That's such a cliché line."

"Still applies."

"I'm going with her," Haruka said. "Those things were clearly there because of her. Besides, she needs my help more than you do."

Alice blinked, frowning. That felt like a jab, though she didn't say anything. Yet.

Romi fixed Haruka with a look, and the two went back and forth in more Japanese, with Romi growing more agitated and Haruka holding firm. At least, that's how it sounded. Alice had no idea what they were actually saying.

Finally, Romi sighed once more. She did that a lot, Alice noticed.

"My protégé thinks we should still accompany you. At least part of the way, to make sure you put some distance between you and what happened. She raises a good point. Leaving you alone with that sword and no food would not be wise. There is another village one day's ride from here. From there it's four, maybe five days on foot to Findest, half that if you can find a ride. I can take you that far, but then I need to return to my Gateway. And you're coming with me." She aimed a finger at Haruka as she headed for the edge of the water, where Chou now rolled around in the shallows.

Haruka watched her for a moment, then turned back to Alice. "Sorry I can't get her to agree to more."

"No, no. This . . . this is good. It's something, which is better than nothing. Besides, she's right, too. Leaving any of the Gateways unprotected isn't smart right now." That thought sent her mind wandering to wondering about the Duchess and the Tweedles. What about their Gateway, which had definitely been left unprotected for a while now?

"I've never seen that many Nightmares in one place." Haruka folded her arms around herself.

Flashes of the fight on the football field danced across Alice's mind. The sight of half-formed monsters clawing their way across the grass piling together to form that . . . that thing? Was forever burned into her memory. "I have."

Twenty-One

AND

The Black Knight had to get away. With an injury like this, he'd be overpowered easily. He pushed through the ether, putting as much distance between himself and the battle as he could. The pain intensified. His limbs started trembling. He couldn't maintain the fade.

Dropping it, he fell to the ground and tumbled a short distance. He barely managed to push out of it to avoid breaking his arms. Landing on his stomach, he lay there in the grass, trying to focus on anything but the pain. Images flashed against his mind, solid, almost tangible.

He was on the ground, pain radiating through him. Bodies lay around him. Friends. Comrades. Blood stained their faces, flesh torn here and there, eyes gazing lifeless at the heavens.

All around him the roars of monsters and of warriors mingled as they clashed. The woman from before was nowhere to be found, but a dark figure was there. It moved through the bodies like an armored wraith, driving a black blade into giving flesh. There were screams, so shrill, so terrified, like nails against glass.

The Black Knight tried to push himself up, but he couldn't. Agony once again robbed him of strength. The wraith continued to approach, leaving writhing forms in its wake. People shifted, twisted, contorting into monsters. Spindly legs erupted from bloated tissue. Single limbs split into two or three. Claws extended from what used to be fingers.

The figure stopped when it reached him. Standing over him in silence, its helmeted head angled downward, gazing at him.

"P-please," he started, furious with himself. He'd sworn, whatever happened, he would never beg. "Don't do this." He held his hands up, a flimsy shield against whatever this thing would do.

It reached for him. Everything went white. Fingers closed around his.

The Black Knight jolted with a cry as he was pulled up. He tried to fight, but the wound in his side sent him flailing. Arms caught him around the torso and pulled, dragging him until something hard pressed against his back.

"Easy."

A familiar voice sent a chill up his spine.

Chess knelt in front of him, those dull eyes peering into his through the helmet. "You're badly injured, so go slow." He offered his hand.

The Black Knight slapped it away. "Do not touch me."

Looking unbothered, Chess stood and glanced around. "The Eye wasn't in the pub. Your target has escaped. The mission is a failure. We should return to Her Majesty for the contingency plan."

"I'm not going anywhere with you."

Chess looked down at him. Even though his expression hadn't changed, the Black Knight felt judged, and small in the face of that judgment. Anger quickly filled the wound in his pride, and he wanted to be nowhere near Her Majesty's new favorite.

"What happened on your end of things?" the Black Knight asked.

"The assault was successful in breaching the wards, but they mounted a swift counterattack and were able to escape through the Veil."

His eyebrows lifted. "So they're here?"

"The Duchess, Lady Xelon, Princes Odabeth, a human girl, and Addison Hatta."

The sound of Hatta's name rang between his ears like a bell, louder and louder, threatening to split his skull from the inside. He groaned as everything went fuzzy again. Chess's face faded, replaced with Hatta's.

He leaned in over the Black Knight, arching an eyebrow. "Doesn't look too bad. You'll have a nasty bump, though."

The Black Knight heard himself groan in response, then speak, though his lips didn't move. "I feel concussed. I'm concussed."

"Are you now?"

"Absolutely. You'll have to bring me habishums in bed and massage my feet."

Hatta snorted. "You hit your head, Humphrey, not your feet."

"You made me hit my head, so I'm holding you responsible for my complete recovery. You're not to leave my side until I'm fully healed."

Hatta chuckled. "Oh the burden," he murmured even as he leaned in.

The Black Knight felt himself drawn forward, his heart racing, his breath catching. Then something knocked against the side of his head.

The image faded, replaced with Chess's face inches from his own as Hatta's had been.

"Knight?" Chess shifted around as if trying to see through the helmet. "Knight. Are you conscious?"

"Yes, though if you get any closer, you won't be."

Chess drew back, but otherwise didn't respond to the threat. "I said that we need to go, Her Majesty expects us to return, but you didn't seem to hear me. Knight?"

"That's *not* my name," he snapped.

"What is your name?"

He glanced away, shame cooling his anger to a simmer. "Don't worry about it." He didn't have a name. He'd never had a name—Her Majesty simply called him her knight. It hadn't bothered him before, but now . . . By the Breaking, what was *wrong* with him? "Go without me. I won't be far behind."

Chess seemed hesitant, still staring at him.

"I dropped my sword, I need to go back for it. Won't take long. Go on."

Chess nodded. Stepping back, a swath of shadow rose from his feet, consuming his entire body before it, and he vanished.

Spitting a curse, the Black Knight pushed himself up and

felt around at his hips. A small medallion came free from a hidden slit in the material of his armor. He crushed the pendant in his hand, then sprinkled the Dust against his sluggishly bleeding wound.

"Dnem em," he murmured before gasping as the Verse took hold. Heat flashed along his side as flesh mended. The binding was temporary, but it would hold long enough.

Groaning, he carefully worked his way to standing, planting his feet wide in order to maintain his balance. He pressed a hand to his chest, pulling at the darkness swirling through him.

"To me," he murmured.

Almost instantly, the air began to split around him. Fiends padded forward, hushed whispers following them.

"Where . . ." His vision doubled, and he shook his head, steeling himself. "Where is the girl?"

"Gone," one of the Fiends rasped.

"But alive?" he asked.

"Thanks to you," another answered.

The relief he felt surprised him, but he pushed it aside.

"That is not what the mistress intended," a voice hissed.

"Change of plans." He tried to sound nonchalant, despite the fatigue pulling at him. "Find the one known as Addison Hatta. He is here. In Wonderland. Run him down."

Twenty-Two

PAIN

Addison had dealt with pain for as long as he could remember. Injuries when he trained to be a knight, wounds earned in service to his queen, scars from battles with the Nightmares, then with those who'd turned against Portentia, and finally when he had to turn against her himself. The pain didn't end there, either.

There was pain when Portentia's daughters locked her away, even though he knew it was for the good of all. There was pain when he was tried for treason. There was pain when the Verse for his exile was burned into him, and there was pain every day after when that Verse kept him from venturing too far or staying too long in his homeland.

As a knight, pain was his constant companion.

So when the burn of his injuries combined with the ache at his center—the exile Verse digging through him with each step—started to get to him, he knew something was very, very wrong.

"Wait," he called in a gasp, his hands pressed to the twisting in his side. "Wait."

Xelon and Courtney turned from where they both stopped a short distance ahead of him.

"I need to rest a moment." Not only was he hurting, he was out of breath, and his vision had started to wane a bit at the edges.

Courtney's worried gaze bounced between him and Xelon as the knight eyed him with those piercing white eyes of hers.

"If we stop for too long, it'll be dark before we reach the village," Xelon called.

"I know." Relieved, Addison lowered himself onto one of the boulders scattered around them. He focused on evening out his breathing. "I know." The way Xelon put that statement meant they could pause, but only for a little while. He'd take anything.

Xelon backtracked to his side and knelt next to him. "Let me see," she coaxed, then peeled his shirt up when he moved his hands. A dark look crossed her face. It was brief, but he saw it.

"That bad?" he asked.

"Bad enough." She lowered his shirt and pressed his hand back to the area. It twinged, but the sensation just melted into what was already throbbing through him. "We'll rest for a bit, but we need to get you help as much as we need to get somewhere safe before nightfall."

Addison nodded. "Just a few minutes."

Xelon pushed to stand and glanced around. "I'll see if I can't find something to take the edge off. Keep an eye on him?" she said to Courtney.

"Two eyes." Courtney moved over and settled herself onto the ground beside his boulder. She eyed him up and down, her brow furrowed. "You can't go dying on us, now. I know Xelon can carry you, but I can't handle the stress of having to tell Alice we couldn't keep her bae alive."

Addison felt the smile stretch his face, both at the mention of Alice's name and the joke. "Bae?"

"You know, bae, baby, boo-thang, boyfriend." Courtney waved a hand at him. "Whatever they call it in Wonderland." She lowered it to her lap and played her gaze over the area. "Which is where we are, right now. I never thought I'd ever see this place. I mean, I imagined it, when Alice talked about it, but I thought regular people couldn't come here."

"A human or two has been known to blunder their way through a weak point in the Veil." Addison shifted to lower himself to the ground, hissing faintly as the pain flared briefly before he tilted back against the rock, same as Courtney.

"Careful," she said, eyeing him. "I was serious about that not-wanting-to-tell-Alice-you're-dead thing."

"Takes more than . . . whatever happened to get rid of me. I'll be around for a while longer, I promise."

"Good." Courtney nodded. She fidgeted with something in her lap. A shoe, he realized, one of those ridiculously high, pointy ones. That was when he noticed her feet were bare.

"Looks like you lost one." He pointed at the heel when she looked at him questioningly.

"Oh, yeah. Back in the river. I almost went in after it; these were my favorite red bottoms." By her tone, he deduced this meant the shoe was important.

Alice had been similarly distraught when her shoes were ruined. He hoped she was well, wherever she was, likely with Romi. There was a bit of bad blood between him and the other Gateway guardian, all entirely his fault of course.

Courtney held the shoe up. "A fallen warrior, its mate served me well." Her shoulders sagged with an overly dramatic sigh.

"So you're carrying that one around as a memento?"

"I figured it I could at least use it as a weapon." She swung the heel in a stabbing motion. "Like in the movies."

Addison chuckled, and instantly regretted it as his side protested. "I'm sorry. About your shoe, that is. And that you've been caught up in all of this."

"There are always more shoes, and as long as I make it home in one piece, there's nothing to be sorry for. It's not like you dragged me here. The Duchess did that."

He laughed again and winced with a faint groan. "Don't make me laugh."

"Sorry! Sorry." She grinned. Then her attention shifted to somewhere over his shoulder and her expression fell. All color fled her face, and fear washed over it.

That's when Addison heard the growl. Strewth, he should've been paying attention! He turned, reaching up for his sword. His vision went white with the pain. He grabbed at empty air.

The Fiend came at them from the side.

Something pierced the top of the monster's head, pinning

it to the dirt just inches shy of Addison's legs. The beast bucked, then fell still, its body twitching. It started to crack and pop, collapsing in on itself.

Xelon gripped the end of a makeshift spear. She must have just grabbed it off of a tree; the branch still had leaves sticking out here and there. Looking to the two of them, she pressed a finger to her lips in a signal for silence.

Beside him, Courtney had curled in on herself, her back pressed to the rock, her hands clapped over her mouth as she trembled and panted, her nostrils flared. Tears pooled in the corners of her eyes and spilled over her fingers, but she didn't scream. She barely whimpered.

Xelon glanced over her shoulder before ducking down with Addison and Courtney behind the boulder. She shifted upward just enough to peek over the top, then dropped back down again. Addison wanted to look himself, but the wound in his side wouldn't let him.

As if sensing this, Xelon lifted two fingers, then signaled they were some distance away. Behind her, the body continued to pop and fizzle, dissolving into the ground. Without a purge, it would re-form later, but they couldn't worry about that now.

Signaling them to stay silent and to follow her, Xelon yanked her makeshift spear free, then crept away from the boulder in a crouch that was bound to exacerbate Addison's wound, but it couldn't be helped. He gestured for Courtney to go first, and when she hesitated, pulled her along with him.

Bent forward like that, it felt like his side was tearing at some hidden seam as they crouch-ran from boulder to boulder, putting distance between them and the Fiends he didn't look back for but was sure were there. He made certain to keep hold of Courtney, which slowed him as well.

Xelon stopped behind another boulder large enough to conceal the three of them and gestured for them to halt. Addison nearly collapsed against it, his side screaming. Sweat poured over his face. He wasn't going to be able to keep this up.

"There are at least two more," Xelon whispered. "I spotted them in the distance. I don't think they know we're here."

"Yet," Addison said between pants. "Can't stay here. Too exposed."

"W-what if we make a run for it?" Courtney's voice trembled just as hard as she did. "Can we reach the town?"

Xelon looked to Courtney, then to Addison, then back over the rock. She didn't have to say anything for him to know what she was thinking. If they ran, he'd only slow them down, and the noise and movement would certainly attract the Fiends; this brush wasn't dense enough to conceal the three of them.

"You can if you leave me," Addison murmured.

"No." Xelon didn't look at him.

"I'll only slow you down. If you go now, you can—"

"She said no," Courtney snapped, then covered her mouth, her eyes wide.

"We're not leaving you here." Xelon kept watch a few seconds more before lowering herself behind the rock and looking out over their surroundings.

A few more boulders dotted the area, but there weren't enough large ones to keep them hidden, and leap-frogging behind them would be painfully slow going, literally.

Xelon must have come to the same conclusion because she cursed softly. "There are only two of them. If I circle around, I can take them by surprise, one at a time."

"If you're not leaving me behind, then I'm not letting you face those things *unarmed* by yourself."

"I'm armed." She held up the stick, the end where she'd broken it off into a point spattered with ichor.

"You can't defend yourself with that," he grunted.

"You can have my shoe." Courtney thrust it toward the White Knight, who simply blinked at it, then her. "It's a stiletto!"

"Keep the shoe," Hatta murmured.

Courtney clutched it against herself, heel out as if she was more than prepared to kill something with it.

"No leaving me behind, no suicide missions." Addison shut his eyes briefly as wave after wave of agony crashed through him. "What else?"

"We run," Xelon said. "Like she said."

"I'll slow you down," he repeated.

"I'll fight them off," Xelon countered.

"We both will." Courtney looked terrified but lifted her shoe.

Addison smiled. "Good news is if these things are after us, they're likely not after Anastasia and the princess." And the Eye was safe.

"Silver linings." Xelon peeked back over the boulder. "I don't see them. It's now or never." She looked to Addison. "You going to make it?"

He shifted around into a crouch, with no small amount of

difficulty. His side was burning, and the darkness at the edges of his vision kept waxing and waning dangerously.

"Do I have a choice?" Beside him, Courtney readied herself to run.

"On my mark." Xelon held up three fingers. Two. One.

At her gesture, the three of them broke into a dead-on sprint, Xelon leading the way. Courtney hurried after her, her bare feet nearly silent in the grass. He brought up the rear, his side feeling like it was tearing open with each step.

Xelon and Courtney started to pull ahead.

His chest heaved.

His vision doubled.

"Hatta?" Courtney called, or was it Xelon? He couldn't tell over the pounding in his ears.

"Keep . . . keep going," he panted, his steps faltering in a stumble before he righted himself.

A howl split the air. The Fiends had caught their scent.

Twenty-Three

NOTHING TO FEAR

Addison willed his body to stay upright and his legs to keep moving. He didn't know how long they would hold him. Would he make it to the village? Would he make it the next five steps?

He ducked around boulders and trees, trying to keep up with Xelon and Courtney as the distance between them grew wider and wider.

Go, he urged at their backs. *Keep running. Don't look back.*

If they did, they might slow down, try to wait for him, maybe try to help him. It was too late for that, for him.

His side hitched. His legs started to give. Regret ate at him, for what he'd been unable to do: stop this imposter, help his friends, tell Alice . . .

The thought of her name brought the memory of her

voice, calling him an asshole, telling him to hold on, to come back to her. He saw her face clear as day.

I'm sorry. He wouldn't be able to return. Not this time.

His knees hit the ground. He couldn't help the pained yelp that escaped him. Courtney and Xelon turned.

"N-no." Sweat poured down his face. The fire in his side spread along his arm now. His heart pounded, his head throbbed.

Another howl rose behind him, the sound muffled by the roar of blood rushing in his ears.

Hands gripped either of his arms as Xelon and Courtney tried to pull him to his feet.

"Go," he panted.

"We're not leaving you!" Courtney's voice was thick with emotion. Even with his vision wavering, he could see the tears streaking her red face.

"Get up," Xelon urged.

He tried. Heavens above, did he try. He managed to get his feet under him, but the pain in his side robbed him of his strength. He couldn't stay up.

"Dammit!" Xelon snapped before she let him go and lifted her spear.

Courtney whimpered and tightened her hold where he rested against her.

More howls, closer this time. Hatta twisted around in Courtney's hold, trying to push her behind him.

Something on all fours came around the boulder.

Xelon jerked into a defensive stance . . . then snorted. "What in the world?"

A massive dog-looking creature with thick, long legs bounded over to the knight and loped around her in a circle. Its floppy ears slapped at the sides of its face. Hooved feet clapped at the earth. Opalescent fur rippled with light and shifting colors.

A *Bandersnatch*. The relief that flooded Addison had him sinking against Courtney.

She gave a concerned squeak, followed by a look of confusion as he started laughing.

"Are you what's been giving us such a fright?" Xelon knelt and ruffled the Bander's head between its ears. The shifting colors coalesced beneath her fingers, then rippled outward in response.

It barked and lapped at her cheek with a long purple tongue.

"Duma!" someone called from a short distance off.

The Bander barked and bounded about, yapping as Xelon straightened. She shot Addison a look that said she was just as pleasantly surprised as he was.

A young boy raced up, giggling as the Bander leaped up to lap at his dark brown face. "Duma, what are you bothering these people for?" the boy said in Xhosa, clicking at the back of his throat.

"She was no bother." Xelon responded in kind. "We are actually happy to see her. We thought something else was following us."

Courtney blinked, her expression still confused, though she seemed to understand that they weren't in any danger, at least not from this creature. She maintained her hold on him, though, for which he was grateful.

"The Nightmare." The smile faded from the boy's face.

"You saw it?" Xelon asked.

He nodded, the golden locks on his head bouncing. "We were on our way home and saw it. We were gonna go around when Grandma noticed it was tracking something."

"That something would be us," Addison said. The boy looked to him and Courtney, his eyes widening when they fell on her.

She smiled and waved. "Hi."

"You're . . . human?" the boy asked, looking her up and down. The Bandersnatch hurried over to start sniffing at her.

She took it in stride, even laughed a little, though Addison felt her tense.

"I'm sorry, I don't understand," she said.

"You're human," the boy repeated, this time in English. "From beyond the Veil."

"You make it sound fancier than it is." To her credit, she gave another little, nervous laugh. "Uh, yeah. Yeah, I am, unfortunately. How could you tell?"

"You're dull," the boy explained.

Courtney blinked rapidly. "Dull?" She didn't sound *too* offended.

"I mean your coloring."

She glanced down at herself, holding her arms out. "Huh." Turning her hands over, she wiggled her fingers. "I guess, compared to this place, I kinda am."

"You said your grandmother is with you?" Xelon asked, also in English.

The boy nodded. His eyes lingered on Courtney a moment

more before he looked back to the knight. "Her and my elder sisters." He snapped his fingers, and the Bander went from sniffing at Courtney to lick at the boy's hand.

A sharp whistle split the air. The boy smiled and returned it, cutting the sound into three parts. "That's them now." He and Xelon turned the direction the boy had come from. He lifted a hand to wave.

"Help me up, please," Hatta asked Courtney. With her assistance, he got to his feet, his side still screaming. She curled one arm around him as he tilted against her with murmured thanks. He was able to spot the trio of women heading toward them. From a distance he could see they had the same rich, dark brown skin of the boy, and the same gold hair.

The two young girls were tall and willowy, and the older woman between them was a bit shorter, wider, the muscles in her arms flexing as she shifted her walking stick.

The Bander raced to meet them, barking happily and earning pets.

The woman looked the group over with a curious but knowing light in her brown eyes. She nodded in greeting.

"Hello," Xelon said.

"Well." The woman's brows shot up. "These are two faces I did not expect to happen upon."

"You know them, Grandma?" one of the girls asked.

"Oh yes." The woman chuckled and shook her head lightly. "Xelon Min, Knight of Legracia, and Addison Hatta, former Knight of Emes." Something hardened in her tone as she spoke Addison's name and previous title. "I don't know this one, though," she said, her eyes on Courtney.

"I'm Courtney." She waved her free hand. "Knight of . . . Gucci."

"Where is Gucci?" one of the girls asked.

"Italy, I think?" Courtney said.

"She's human, Grandma," the boy offered.

"I can see that, Effe." The woman continued to eye them carefully. "You're what that Nightmare was after, mm?"

"Yes," Addison said. "The three of us. Not her specifically."

"Did you see anyone else?" Xelon asked. The hopeful note in her voice likely meant she was talking about Anastasia and the princess.

"Not another soul. It's interesting, we don't usually see Nightmares this far south." The woman patted the Bander as he licked at her hand.

"Took us by surprise as well," Addison murmured.

"It do that?" The woman gestured to Addison's bleeding side.

"This happened before."

"Well." The woman took a breath, seeming to come to some sort of conclusion. "It wouldn't do to leave you all out here with that monster roaming around. I'm Naette. These are my granddaughters Offa and Ikebe, and my grandson Effe."

Each of them nodded as they were introduced.

"We live in Rebmest, a city nearby."

"That's where we were going. To get this one some help." Xelon moved back to Addison's side. "Is there a healer?"

"You're looking at her," Naette said with a chuckle. "We were out gathering herbs for my stores." She patted a full satchel that hung from her shoulder. The two girls wore similar full satchels, along with swords at their hips. "Lucky you, eh? Come."

Naette started along again, her grandchildren trailing after her. The Bander rushed ahead, barking and howling, circling back around in play. Effe was the only one to look back as the three of them moved to follow. Addison winced, having to rely on Courtney and Xelon more than he liked, but there was no point in being difficult; it would only slow them down, and the other Nightmares were still out there.

The going was slow with Addison's injuries setting the pace, but eventually the city walls appeared through the thin smattering of trees. Sandy stone burned light brown in the daylight. The pointed roofs of buildings jutted up here and there.

A road also came into view, gray cobblestones leading toward a high archway. There were no sentries posted, at least none he could see. The sounds and smells of a lively market poured through the gate and over the high stone. Someone played a bit of music, the beat of the drums and call of the flute light and cheerful. A sort of bright sadness settled into Addison. He'd missed his homeland all these years. He thought of his own hometown, the city square, the sweet breads he used to eat as a child, then tried to show the royal chef how to cook when he lived at the palace.

"You okay?" Courtney asked beside him. She watched him with concerned, curious eyes.

He managed a faint smile. "As well as I can be."

They entered the city to the sight of people moving about

their lives, unbothered by the presence of two knights, one injured, and a human. Colorful clothing wrapped around bodies tall and short, thin and round. Nearby, a man with bright orange hair tipped his cap and vanished from sight.

Courtney gave a little jump in surprise.

Naette and her grandchildren didn't react other than to speak to one another quietly, then greet a few passersby.

The little family led the way along the main road a stretch, then ducked down a side alley. A few twists and turns—thankfully the slow pace made it easy for Addison to stay upright—they stopped just outside of a small stone house.

Naette rapped a quick but distinct pattern against the bright blue door, and it swung open. She bade them follow before slipping inside, her grandchildren after her. Xelon went in first, followed by Addison and Courtney.

Inside, the house was much bigger than it appeared from without. A wide entryway allowed all of them room to stand with a good amount of space between them. Naette and her grandchildren went about setting their belongings aside. The old woman gave the pouches to Effe, who hurried off through the house, the Bandersnatch clopping after him.

"Welcome to our home," Naette said as she clapped a bit of dust from the front of her tunic. "Please, make yourselves comfortable."

There was a gathering of chairs and a large, plush-looking couch at the center of the room, just across from a massive fireplace. Flames crackled in the hearth, and a huge iron cauldron suspended above them hissed gently as its contents boiled.

"Sir Hatta—" Naette started.

"Just Hatta is fine." He smiled faintly. "Or even Addison."

Naette arched an eyebrow. "Very well, Addison. I'll have you come this way."

Courtney and Xelon helped him through the living space and down a side hallway. Shelves lined the high walls, full of potted plants of various colors and sizes, some bushy, some leafy, some fuzzy, some sharp. There were also jars of differing sizes full of liquids, what looked like marbles, roots, and other odds and ends.

These were ingredients for potions. For a potions master, actually. Funny, Naette didn't speak like a particularly powerful Poet.

They followed Naette into a room that had been converted into a healing chamber from the olden days. It matched the descriptions from various members of his family about the ancestral estate before . . . before. There was a tub of steamy green liquid to the side of the room and a large stone table at the center. A cushion lay on top of it. Shelves similar to those along the hall lined the walls, full of similar ingredients, some of them glowing. They bathed the room in soft green light, which was cut by daylight from small, strategically placed windows here and there in the walls and the ceiling. Purple vines crawled along one wall, and a curtain of magenta moss hung beside it.

"Let me have a closer look at that wound." Naette approached, and Hatta shifted as best he could so she could get at his side.

She gingerly lifted his blood-soaked shirt and clicked her tongue. "You're stronger than you look."

"Ah . . . thank you?"

She chuckled. "We'll get you set right. Up onto the table, shirt off."

With help, Hatta climbed up to settle in, wincing as pain continued to claw through him. It was a bit of a struggle to remove the shirt, leaving the slices in his skin exposed. They continued to bleed sluggishly, a few dirty patches from Xelon's mud bandage dotting his skin. The rest must have fallen off as they ran.

"Not to sound uncaring," Xelon started, her eyes on him, then moving to Naette. "How long before he can travel again?"

The concern for the princess poured off of her. Addison more than understood.

"Wound like that? Maybe two days. Want him to be able to get away if you run into any more Nightmares." Naette went about gathering ingredients. She called out to one of her granddaughters in Xhosa, asking her to bring the big wood bowl from the kitchen.

Xelon's jaw clenched.

"Go without me," Addison said. "I'll only slow you down. Besides, I shouldn't be here." And if he went any farther into Wonderland, his wound wouldn't be his biggest worry. So far, the Verse that exiled him pulled painfully at his chest, but the hurt from his open side all but drowned it out. Once that was seen to, he'd no doubt feel the spell more keenly. Going to Findest would only make it worse.

"I don't wish to abandon you," Xelon said.

"You're not," he countered. "I'm in good hands with Naette."

"And I'll stay, too." Courtney rubbed at her arms and forced a small smile. "I mean, like, if he shouldn't be here, I definitely shouldn't. And, no offense, but I'd really like to stay here and not be out there with any more of those things."

"No offense taken." Xelon chuckled, then looked to Naette. "Could I trouble you for supplies for my travels?"

"No trouble." Naette took the bowl brought in by Offa. "Offa, get some things together for Sir Min—she'll be traveling to . . . Where are you going, again?"

"Findest," Xelon said, as if it were the most natural thing.

Naette blinked in clear surprise. "Royal business, I assume."

"In a manner." Xelon's tone was friendly but reserved.

Naette seemed to take the hint and nodded. "Offa will get you taken care of."

"Thank you," Xelon said in Xhosa before bowing slightly. She looked to Addison. "I'll take the main road, by mount if I'm able to."

"There is a man who tends a stable toward the eastern end of town," Naette called as she set a few glowing jars along the table. "Tenant, they call him."

"Thank you again," Xelon said. "I'll send word on whatever I find."

"Likewise." Addison flinched as Naette started to clean the wound.

"And, Offa," Naette said to gain her granddaughter's attention. "Take Courtney and get her something to eat. Poor thing looks famished."

Courtney blinked before murmuring a thank-you and blushing as she moved to follow the other two out of the room, the door closing behind them.

"Well," Naette started. "Like I said, you're lucky. It's not good, but it could be much worse."

"That's promising," Addison said with a faint smile pulling at his lips.

"I was wondering what brought a Nightmare around these parts. Then we run into you, of all people." She spared him a look that he couldn't quite read clearly. "Think you can do something about it before it causes any real trouble?"

"If there are any available weapons, I could certainly make a go of it."

"After we get this taken care of." She turned her attention to the wound, continuing to dab at it with one hand and using the other to pour a purple liquid over the area that left it cold to numbing. "Not smart to go wandering around unarmed."

"Wasn't the intention."

"I suppose not. Into the soak." She helped him off of the table and over to the large tub. The water steamed, coals burning pink beneath the basin.

"You weren't expecting me, were you?"

"Of course not. This was for me, to help with some pain in my joints. But I can make another, later."

A sour touch of guilt moved through him. "You don't have to—"

"I know full well what I don't or do have to, thank you very much. Now, stop talking back to your elders."

He smiled. "Yes, ma'am."

"About an hour should do. Here. You don't have to strip down entirely, just take off the shoes."

Addison did as instructed before he climbed, with Naette's help, into the tub and settled into the hot liquid. The smell of mint and earth settled over his senses, along with a sort of misty weight. The medicinal properties of the bath likely at work.

"There you are, now. Let the bath do its work. If you need anything, I'll be about, just holler."

"Thank you. Truly." He released a slow breath and relaxed against the back of the tub, his eyelids growing heavy. He let them fall shut as Naette shuffled toward the door and out of the room.

His mind started to drift, his senses swimming. The heady scent of the bath filled him with each gradually slowing breath. For once, his mind was calm. The part of himself that told him to give in to the darkness scratching at his thoughts was quiet. And he was thankful.

◊ ◊ ◊

"You look comfortable." The sharpness in Naette's voice scraped across Addison's sleep-addled brain. He didn't even realize he'd drifted off.

He forced his eyes open and sat up slightly. "I am." He lifted one hand to rub at his face. "How long was I asleep?"

"Long enough. How's that bath working?" She eyed him down the length of her nose.

"Pretty good." He slipped one hand to his side to test the

wound. It was still very sensitive, but the worst of the pain had dulled. "Seems to be doing the trick."

"Good, good," she murmured, then clapped her hands together. "Let's start the next phase." Naette vanished, then reappeared across the room, grabbing a jar of something that glowed blue. She eyed it briefly, then put it back in place. She examined a few more jars before vanishing and reappearing near another shelf, searching through it similarly.

Addison stared, blinking slowly. "You're a Tirip," he murmured.

"I am." She finally found whatever she was looking for, nodding before vanishing again. She appeared next to the tub to pour it in. "This ought to help."

The water started to bubble slightly as if heated, though the temperature didn't change. Steam rose into the air, carrying the scent of rosewood and something earthy.

"There we are." She smiled. "Deep breaths, now." She stoppered the jar and vanished once more, appearing across the room in order to return the jar to its place.

Addison drew in an obedient breath, then another. "I was once friends with a Tirip." He stammered, his tongue thick and clumsy with the words. Something was wrong. "What's . . . what's happening?" Panic drummed sluggishly in his mind as he struggled to lift his arms, slapping weakly at the rim of the tub in attempt to grab it.

Naette came over and took one of his hands between hers, her touch warm. She rubbed his fingers. "No need for fear. It's an effect of the bath." Her voice dipped, softening. "The worse a patient's injuries, the more energy their body expends to heal them. The bath helps speed up that process. You're pretty banged up, so it puts you to sleep to do its work. Don't worry, I'll keep an eye on you so you don't drown."

Well, that was somewhat comforting. He wanted to say thank you, but all he could manage was a low groan.

Naette chuckled, patted his hand, then let it slip back into the bath. "One last thing." She stepped over to the small window on the far side of the room. She pushed it open and drew a breath. "There. That'll keep things from getting too steamy in here. Back soon."

And with that, she was gone.

Addison shut his eyes and sank deeper into the bath. The tingling along his skin gradually intensified, especially around his wounds, almost to the point of discomfort. Still, it was better than literal sidesplitting agony.

Click. The latch on the window fastened.

It was a struggle, but he forced his eyes open, expecting to see Naette. Instead the Imposter stood over his bath, helmeted head angled to the side. "Enjoying ourselves?"

Water went sloshing when Addison jolted as fear sharpened to a fine point, the only thing in focus, before darkness finally crept in and consumed him.

Twenty-Four
WHAT'S IN A NAME

Addison didn't move nor open his eyes immediately upon waking. Instead, he kept still, kept his breathing even, and tried to discern all he could with his limited senses. It was difficult, with the steady burn of the exile Verse twisting up his insides this far from the Gateway.

He was no longer in the bath, but instead sitting up, in a chair of some sort. His arms were pulled behind him, and his shoulders and wrists ached slightly. He was likely bound. He resisted the urge to test the bonds. His feet didn't feel bound, but that didn't mean anything.

"I know you're not asleep," a familiar voice called from nearby.

Leaning against the table toward the wall in Naette's medicine room, the Imposter tapped his fingers against the tabletop. "There he is."

Addison twisted his wrists slightly. Fibers dug into his skin, some type of rope.

"Are you comfortable?" The Imposter tilted his head to the side. "Not too tight, I trust."

Addison swallowed, trying to think past his thumping heart and frazzled thoughts. The remnants of whatever had put him under were still clinging to the edges of his senses. He glanced around. As he'd assumed, he was trussed up in a chair, his arms behind his back. His legs were free.

So many questions raced through Addison's mind, but only one managed to free itself. "Where is Madeline?"

"The Poet is fine. In one piece and everything. My lady has need of her, so she is well protected. For the time being."

Grunting, Addison relaxed his shoulders even as his fingers worked furiously at his bindings, searching for a weakness in the knots. "And who is your lady?"

Silence stretched between them as they stared at one another. At least, Addison stared at the Imposter, who could have drifted off to sleep behind that helmet for all he could tell.

Finally, the Imposter drew a slow breath and straightened. "Does the name Humphrey mean something to you?"

Addison's spine snapped straight. It'd been years since he heard that name. Even now it attempted to conjure memories he'd rather stay buried. He narrowed his eyes. "Why?"

"Ahh, so it does." The Imposter drummed his fingers on the table. "Was he important to you?"

"Why?" Hatta asked a second time, forcing the question through clenched teeth.

In his experience, true coincidences were few and far between, and usually an act of nature. It started to rain while you were in a shop that sold umbrellas, or you got a flat outside of a tire shop. This? This was bound to be something more. The Imposter showed up, Portentia's name was invoked for the first time in years, and now Humphrey?

"Did you do something to him?" Hatta pressed as his hands continued to work at his bindings. "Like you did with Madeline?"

"Do something to him?" The Imposter plucked a sphere from the table's surface. He turned it over in his hands, the glossy surface shifting colors between blue and purple. "And I told you, she's fine."

"Why should I believe you?"

"Granted, I have attacked you, injured your allies, helped facilitate the capture of another, but I have not lied. I'm quite proud of myself for that one."

When he reached to set the orb down, he winced. He shifted to try to conceal it, but Addison had seen it. An injury on his left side looked to be giving him trouble. And it didn't look like he had his sword on him, nor did Addison see it sitting anywhere nearby.

"I'm sure you are." Addison froze when he felt the bindings finally loosen. His fingers curled to keep them in place.

"Look, I'm only here for answers. Just tell me what I want to know, and I'll be on my way."

Addison sniffed and nodded. "Counteroffer. How about you kiss my arse, then tell me what you've done with my friends before I beat you to within an inch of your slimy existence."

"Don't you mean *or* you beat me to within an inch of my slimy existence?"

"No." Hatta twisted free of the bonds and bolted up from his chair. Pain radiated from the wound at his side, but he pushed through it, driving his fist toward the Imposter's helmeted head.

The bastard jolted before throwing his arms up to shield himself, and that was when Addison twisted with the fake and hammered into the Imposter's injured side. He yowled like a wounded animal, doubling over, which put him just where Addison wanted him. Addison gripped his helmet and smashed it against the edge of the table.

The helmet shattered, pieces scattering across the floor. The Imposter slumped to the ground, groaning. Kneeling, Addison snatched at bright red hair, visible now that the helmet was gone, yanked the Imposter around, drew back his fist, and froze.

Shock played through him like icy fingers beneath his skin as his mind warred with what his eyes were telling it.

His thoughts swirled, trying to make sense of things, to understand just what he was looking at, but it kept coming back to a single word. *Impossible.* And yet, he knew that face as sure as he knew his own.

"H-Humphrey?" The name fractured on his tongue, his voice breaking with it.

The Imposter's eyelids fluttered with another pained sound as he forced them open. Those impossibly blue eyes rolled around, dazed for a moment before fixing on Addison and widening.

Addison loosened his hold immediately and lowered his hand. "I—I don't understand . . ."

Humphrey grimaced as he pushed himself upright. Addison reached to help, only to have his hands slapped away.

"Don't touch me."

"All right! All right." He drew back, staring. Of all the possibilities for who was under that helmet, this was not a guess he would've made, could've made.

All the times he'd imagined this moment, imagined seeing the other again, what he would do, what he would say, how he would apologize for everything that happened during the war, and after. Then, when Humphrey went missing, he thought he'd never have the chance. The guilt had eaten at him almost as badly as the Madness.

And now, with the impossible opportunity before him, his words abandoned him. He drew a slow breath and gathered his chaotic thoughts. There had to be a reason for this, for Humphrey—of all people—to do all of this.

Humphrey stared at him, his expression unreadable, but those eyes. Addison could always tell what he was thinking or feeling just by looking into those eyes. What he saw cut him deeper than any blade. Humphrey had been upset with him before, angry, furious even, and hurt, but he'd never been afraid. Until now.

Lifting his hands, Addison drew back to give Humphrey some space. "I'm not going to hurt you."

"Why not?" Humphrey swallowed. "It's like you said, I attacked you, I attacked your friends. I'm your enemy, why wouldn't you hurt me?"

A stab of hurt tore into Addison's chest. "This is—I don't . . . I don't know what's going on, why you're doing any of this, but it—you're . . . You have to know, no matter what was going on between us, I would never raise a hand to you. Not you. Not even for her."

"That's not an answer." Humphrey's eyes danced with fire. "Why won't you hurt me?"

"Because." Hatta's mouth went dry. He knew the words, knew the memories behind them, knew the emotions they stirred. He thought that part of him was long dead, until Alice awakened it. *Alice* . . . He drew in a slow breath. Oh yes, he knew the words, though he hadn't spoken them in so long, hadn't thought he ever would again. And now they slipped free. "I love you."

Twenty-Five

ALL IS DARKNESS

Alice gripped the rail around the inside of the basket like the oh-shit bar in her Mom's car. She couldn't help but think how disappointed twelve-year-old Alice would be right now. Here she was, being flown through the air by a mythical creature, which was likely as close to dragon riding as she would get, and she hated it.

Oh, it hadn't been so bad the first time, when her adrenaline had been pumping after she'd nearly been torn to shreds by a small army of Nightmares. Now? Every slight jostle felt like she was being tossed like a salad. Her stomach did front flips, back flips, side flips, all the flips. Twice she was sick over the side of the basket. Afterward, Haruka made sure Alice drank a few gulps of water from the small canteen that had, luckily, been clipped to the back of her belt. To prevent dehydration.

Now Haruka watched her with a careful though surprisingly unbothered expression. "Going to be sick again?" she called over the sound of wind and the beat of Chou's wings.

Alice shook her head. Slowly. "When are we landing?"

They'd been flying for hours. The sky shifted through the colors of the day around them. Alice spent most of that time hunkered in a corner of the basket, her head between her knees.

"Won't be long," Haruka said. "Chou will need to rest. And to eat."

As if on cue, the basket jostled, and Alice's stomach gave a little drop. They were going down. Alice closed her eyes and breathed through the worst of it. She jumped when Chou landed, then again when the basket hit the ground.

Haruka stood and offered Alice her hand. "Here."

Alice took it with thanks and, with the other girl's help, got to her feet and then climbed out of the basket. Romi stood nearby, talking in baby talk to Chou. It might be Japanese, but the funny voice and intonation was universal.

"Are you all right?" Haruka stood near Alice, though her gaze swept the surrounding area. Always alert, that one.

"I'm good." Even though her stomach was less than happy, she'd had worse. She straightened and glanced around as well. They were in a small patch of clearing within a . . . puffy jungle. Seriously, the bushes and trees looked like they were made from bunches of cotton caught on branches, with silvery flowers sticking out amidst the green tufts. A nearby tinkling signaled water running over the glasslike rock that sometimes formed in Wonderland riverbeds. Running water meant maybe food, though she wasn't much of a fisher.

"Think there's anything edible swimming around in there?" she asked.

Haruka looked to Alice, then in the direction of the river. "Maybe. Want to have a look?"

Alice nodded as she straightened. Haruka called out to Romi as they headed for the river. She waved a hand, having finished unhooking Chou from the basket and rubbing at his neck as he went in on some grass.

They reached the edge of the river, and Alice went to her knees faster than in prayer. She leaned in and splashed water against her face, wrinkling her nose at the slightly vinegary smell.

"I don't see any fish," Haruka said, moving along the bank.

"That's okay, I—"

The water surged as Alice's reflection broke the surface and latched onto her arms.

Alice screamed and tried to yank away, but Reflection-Alice's hold only tightened. Her skin was ruddy, the veins bulging and black along her fingers and arms. Her face was bloated, her hair a wild tangle of coils around her head.

"Don't," Reflection-Alice rasped as she used her hold on Alice to pull herself from the churning waters. "Don't!"

Alice twisted and pushed, trying to break free of her reflection's death grip. "Let me go!"

Reflection-Alice's hands were like ice, cold and hard, unforgiving in their hold. Her nails dug into Alice's skin, tearing it. She pulled, dragging Alice headfirst into the river.

Kicking and screaming, Alice tried to go for her sword. She twisted against her reflection's hold, but every time she broke free, fingers clamped down in a new place, capturing her all over again.

"Don't!" Reflection-Alice cried out.

She pulled Alice deeper into the water. Water spilled into her nose and mouth, pushing past the back of her throat. She coughed and gagged, her lungs joining the struggle. She couldn't see. Everything was water, sand, and Reflection-Alice's dingy skirt, wrapping around her. Choking her. The current pulled at her flailing limbs, slowing them, robbing them of their strength. A panicked throbbing set in at the base of her skull.

Her fingers curled around the hilt of her sword, and she swung. The water parted as light exploded from the blade. Reflection-Alice vanished. Alice lay against the riverbed, stones pushing into her back, stabbing at her. Droplets rained against her face and shoulders. For a split second, the river was empty, the water just gone. She whipped her head around, fear pounding in her ears.

Romi and Haruka stood on the shore, their weapons drawn, their faces lined with confusion. Then the water rushed back in, stealing Alice's breath all over again and sending her tumbling, but the hands were gone. The skirts were gone. Her reflection was gone; she was free. She kicked, pushing toward the surface. She broke through, gasping and hacking as she crawled free. Romi and Haruka came running.

"Alice!" Haruka shouted.

"Are you all right?" Romi called.

Haruka reached her first, kneeling beside her, hands on her shoulders. "What happened?"

What happened? Alice couldn't form words at first, too busy trying to breathe and cough up the oddly sweet water she'd swallowed. "D-did you see her?"

"Who?" Haruka looked to the river.

Alice shook her head. "Sh-she, she pulled me in. She pulled me under!" Alice pushed back from the edge of the water even farther. "I couldn't get away!"

Haruka and Romi exchanged a glance.

"There was no one there," Haruka murmured. "You just started screaming and jumped into the river. Then you pulled that sword, and . . ."

Alice blinked, rubbing at her face, chest still heaving. She followed Haruka's gaze to where the Vorpal Blade rested against the grass, the black blade looking like a slice of nothing splitting the ground. "No. No, she . . . she was there! I saw her. I *felt* her nai—" She held out her arms to show them the scratches from nails tearing into her skin. Nothing. Not so much as a light bruising. Her arms were perfectly fine.

"Alice." Romi squeezed her shoulder. "Nothing was there. I swear to you."

Alice whimpered as she looked back and forth between them. She looked to the now calm river. A massive groove hollowed-out part of the opposite bank. She'd done that. With the Vorpal Blade.

"This isn't happening." Alice shook her head. Weird dreams? Fine. Even though she wasn't supposed to be dreaming at all. Okay. Being able to see things most people can't see, but those things actually exist? Led to the weirdest year of her life, but fine. Still cool. Flat-out hallucinations? Acid trip, wandering the desert hallucinations? No. Just no. Even in Wonderland. *Especially* in Wonderland.

"You haven't eaten in a while," Haruka pressed gently. "And you were injured."

Said injury was already mostly healed, and barely registered as a boo-boo. Alice swallowed thickly, shame burning through her as she brushed her hands together, more for something to do with her now trembling fingers than anything else.

"Visions in Wonderland are not uncommon." Romi straightened. "This world works in mysterious ways. We'll rest here. Night will rise soon. We'll continue at daybreak."

"I think you may have scared off any fish," Haruka said with a faint smile.

"I'll take care of food, you two see to a fire." Romi jogged in the direction of the trees, where Chou chewed on the leav— puffs in the branches.

Haruka's hand dropped into Alice's line of sight. "Come on." Her voice was quiet, understanding.

Shame still burning through her, Alice took that hand and the help up. Neither of them spoke as they returned to the basket, where Haruka dug a lighter from a small compartment that held some pots and pans. Still working in silence, the girls gathered some branches and grass, picked a relatively earthy spot, and got to work.

It didn't take long for the girls to get a fire started. Romi returned with armfuls of tufts. At her direction, the girls roasted them on the ends of sticks like marshmallows. They smelled like oranges and tasted like honey-glazed ham. The weirdest, most delicious thing Alice'd ever eaten. Romi explained that they didn't hold much nutritional value, but they would help take the edge off of their growing hunger. For a time.

Night fell with Alice stealing glances at the river every so often.

"Still haven't seen anything," Haruka murmured from where she sat nearby. "What happened, again?"

Alice shook her head. "I'm not sure. I *thought* sh—someone grabbed me." No way she was about to try and explain that she was attacked by her damned self; that would only make things sound wilder. "They pulled me into the river and held me under." She ran her hands over her bare forearms. "Scratched me. I *felt* it." That was the part she couldn't shake. You don't imagine pain like that. Or maybe you did, here. That was the point of this place, right?

"But you're okay?"

"I'm fine." Alice didn't understand it any better than Haruka was kindly trying to. "At least physically. I don't know, maybe . . . maybe this place is just messing with me. It is Wonderland."

Haruka smiled at that. "Here." She offered one of the remaining sticks Romi had set in the ground with cooked, smoky meat leaves. "We've got a long day tomorrow, don't want to stop if we don't have to."

"Thanks."

After dinner, Alice offered to take first watch. She didn't think she would be able to get to sleep right now, anyway. With orders to wake Haruka when the Breaking began, she settled in near the fire. Romi and Haruka slept in the basket. It didn't look much more comfortable than the ground, but Romi insisted it was.

Two hours down and nothing happened. Alice spent the time looking over her loaner sword for any signs of damage. Nothing out of the ordinary. The silvery glass of the blade glittered in the blue moonlight. Alice used the hem of her shirt to clean it, slipping just close enough to the river to dip the cloth in before hurrying back to the fire.

Once it was as good as it was going to get, she went through a few practice stances, acclimating herself to the weight, the heft, the reach. She'd already used it in battle once, but you could never get too familiar with a weapon, especially when your life depended on you using it. That was something Hatta used to say a lot, in a lot of different ways.

Damn. Even while practicing in the middle of nowhere, after nearly being drowned by her reflection, she couldn't keep her mind from wandering his direction. She remembered the screams over the phone, the sounds of destruction. God, she hoped he was okay. She hoped all of them were okay.

Sliding the sword into the sheath, she took a low breath to try and calm her anxious nerves.

"Alice."

She froze. Every inch of her went stone still. That wasn't Haruka. Or Romi.

That did not just happen . . .

Her heart pounding, her eyes wide and darting about in the darkness, she searched the edges of the fire's light.

Nothing.

Careful, her senses straining, she made her way over to peek into the basket. Romi and Haruka were stretched along the bottom, their chests rising and falling slowly with the lazy breaths of sleep.

A cool, runny feeling of relief swept through her.

I'm hearing shit now?

"Alice."

The voice was sharper that time, clearer. It drew her name out, beckoning.

She spun, her hands gripping her sword, ready to draw it.

That was when the firelight flickered and a flash of flame against black caught her attention. The Vorpal Blade lay in the grass near where she had been sitting. Its surface seemed to ripple in the night, the light of the fire reaching out but never touching the surface, snuffed out just a few inches shy. Except, just barely, a hint of light shot along the length of the sword.

Alice bent to retrieve the dark weapon. The pommel rested cool against her palm. The sword itself was lighter than anything this size had any business being. Like she had with the Figment Blade, she swung. The black blade arched through the night, the shuttering of light as it passed through air giving the impression it had sliced the very air for the briefest of moments.

"Alice!"

She spun to face the river, fear swimming through her. She'd definitely heard someone call her name this time, and swallowed the want to call out, demand to know who was messing with her. That was how people died in these situations, hollering in the forest at some strange sound or noise.

You better act like your Black ass done seen enough of these movies to know better. Strangest pep talk ever, but with a measured breath she drew on another memory of Hatta, during her first trip in Wonderland.

You are the most dangerous thing out here right now.

Her fingers tightened on the Vorpal Blade as her gaze swept her surroundings, slower this time. Her eyes passed over the river.

"Alice, quickly!" The water splashed along with the words. Had that happened last time? She hadn't been paying attention.

Sword out, she inched her way toward the water's edge. As she approached, the image of the sky reflected on the water's surface stretched out before her. Shining brighter than the moon, Reflection-Alice waited beneath the waters. She wasn't the rotting vision Alice had seen earlier, and that alone was the only reason Alice dared to draw closer.

Their eyes locked, and the familiar warm brown of her father's eyes, her eyes, gazed back at her. They even crinkled slightly at the edges when Reflection-Alice smiled.

"At last," Reflection-Alice breathed.

Alice glanced around, over both shoulders, back at the basket, then to the river. "The hell is going on?"

"I've been trying to reach out to you, but my voice is silenced so far away from the source."

"The what now?"

"The source. It is how I am able to manifest in such ways as this." Reflection-Alice lifted her hands, indicating herself.

"Right." Alice looked her reflection up and down. "This . . . Who're you? I mean, you look like me, but you ain't me. Not for real. 'Cause I'm me." Okay, now she was starting to sound like the locals . . .

"I am, but I am not. Much like you are both yourself and not at all who you think you are."

Alice shook her head, lifting a hand. "No, just . . . This vague, mystic stuff, I don't . . . I ain't got time for that. Just once I'd like a straight answer."

"I'm sorry. I'm not myself, you see. And I'm barely you at all, but just enough for us to meet like this."

"But you've been here before." Alice finally lowered the sword. "In a dream. I thought you were a dream. Then . . . you were at the pub. You gave me the Eye."

Reflection-Alice nodded.

"You're . . . You were there when . . . when I fought the Black Knight." Alice had been turning what she remembered from the fight in the football field over and over in her mind, trying to see if there was any way she could've known, any way she could've saved Chess. In the end, she wasn't exactly sure how she'd saved herself.

Xelon had explained that everything was covered in that black pitch, the place full of it to bursting. She thought everyone was done for, until an explosion of light and warmth cleared the area. When the light faded, Xelon said Alice was left lying in the grass, Hatta not far off. The two of them found Chess's body, then a half-conscious Alice, got them both into the car and back to the pub.

Later, Alice tried to remember. She recalled the light. A voice. Her voice.

Reflection-Alice nodded again. "I have been here from the beginning."

"When I became a Dreamwalker?"

"Much longer."

Alice blinked and nodded this time, mostly to herself. "I've lost it." She gave another nod. "I'm in the woods, in the middle of the night, holding a devil sword, and literally talking to myself."

"As I told you, I have always been with you. Our connection is stronger here, my voice louder."

Alice eyed her reflection. "Was . . . that you earlier? Trying to drown me?"

Reflection-Alice shook her head.

"So I *did* imagine it."

"Yes and no—ah!" Reflection-Alice gasped and clutched at her chest.

"What! What is it?" The sight of herself in some sort of pain was . . . trippy AF.

"I've wasted too much time." Reflection-Alice met her gaze. "I came to warn you. You cannot do this. The path you're on will lead to nothing but darkness and despair. Turn away."

"Turn away? W-what turn away, I can't—you mean going to the castle?"

"You must let love in, or the cycle continues." Reflection-Alice started to fade. "Trust your heart when your eyes deceive you. Believe in the truth of yourself, or swords will shatter. Hearts will break. Heads . . . will roll . . ."

"Wait!" Alice stepped forward, her feet sloshing at the bank. The waters were clear, her reflection gone.

"Alice?" Haruka stood in the basket, clutching her Figment katana. She blinked, glancing around, her hair a bit disheveled but her gaze alert.

"Nothing." Alice murmured, stepping back. "Sorry. Thought I saw some . . . some fish. Didn't mean to wake you."

Haruka made a noise at the back of her throat, though she didn't sound irritated or anything, despite having been woken up at least a whole hour early. The golden lines that would split the sky had just started to crawl across the vastness of the heavens.

"You can go back to sleep. Not your watch yet," Alice said, embarrassed.

"Once I'm up, I'm up." Haruka climbed out of the basket, munching on one of the leftover meat puffs. "It's fine. You should get some sleep, though."

"Not sure I'll be able to." She peeled her wet shoes and socks off and set them near the low-burning fire.

"You should try." Haruka eyed her up and down, a considering look on her face.

Alice's face heated in turn.

"If not, let me look at your wound." Haruka pointed.

For a second, Alice wasn't sure what was being asked, then she jolted with realization. "Oh! Um, okay." The fire in her face intensified as she shifted around and lifted her stained shirt. It was covered in Nightmare gunk, a bit of blood, mostly the Black Knight's. She tossed it aside, thankful for the cami beneath, and wondered why she hadn't taken it off already.

It says something when you're so used to being covered in crap that you don't actually remove it when you can.

She shifted around to place herself in front of Haruka, angling her body over to expose her side to the light. It stung a little, the shifting, but was otherwise fine.

"Oh!" She jumped slightly when Haruka's touch brushed her skin.

Haruka yanked her hand back. "What?"

Alice shook her head. "Nothing. Just surprised. Tickles . . . a little . . ." Well, that wasn't awkward as hell.

Haruka chuckled faintly and Alice felt like her cheeks were going to spontaneously combust.

"How! Um . . . how did you become a Dreamwalker?" Alice blurted, eager to change the subject. "I asked before, and you started to tell me, but we were interrupted." She hoped she wasn't being rude, just . . . weird, and . . . Haruka was hot, okay? And it was getting hot out here, and they should just talk about something else maybe?

For the stretch of a minute or so, Haruka didn't say anything, and Alice desperately wanted to find a rock to crawl under. The hell was wrong with her? Getting in other folks' business. The look on Haruka's face the first time said this probably wasn't something she wanted to talk about, but Alice just *had* to press. She wasn't trying to be hurtful, just . . . Haruka seemed . . . nice? No, that wasn't it. It was more than that. The other girl was like Alice, out here, fighting all of this.

Yeah, the twins were, too, but this was different. Dee and Dem had each other, and they were dudes. Guys were expected to be the hero, the warrior. Girls were the damsel or the prize. Well, Alice wasn't anyone's damsel, and she wasn't anyone's prize. Haruka *definitely* wasn't. And she seemed like . . . like a kindred spirit. One Alice kinda wanted to connect with a bit more, if she was being honest with herself.

"Nightmare killed my mother," Haruka said, so suddenly it made Alice jump. "Not a Nightmare, but a man under the influence of one. It had gotten through. I didn't know that was what happened, only that he broke into our house and stabbed her while I was at school."

Alice's insides twisted. She knew what it was like to lose a parent, though . . . Her dad died of natural causes, messed up as they were. She couldn't imagine him being murdered. "I'm sorry."

"I was at the police station when Romi found me. She felt it was her fault, what happened. They had missed one, and this was the result."

"They?" Alice pressed gently.

"Her and Touma. He was called before me." Haruka tapped her fingers against her thigh. "They fought together for years, prevented so much. But . . . not that. As a result, Touma felt it was time to step down. He had a husband, children. His time wasn't his own like before, and he had responsibilities. So I took his place. To prevent this from happening to anyone else for as long as I could."

Something inside Alice bubbled faintly, but not unpleasantly. The way Haruka talked, the conviction in her voice, made Alice's spine straighten just a little bit more.

"I'm sorry for your loss," Alice said, her mind drifting toward her own mother. She wondered what she was doing now, how she was handling Alice being gone now that she knew where she was and what she was doing. Would knowing all of that alleviate any of the fear that she might get that call? That someone, not even the police, would show up at her doorstep to tell her her baby was gone? She hoped so. If only a little. And she hoped not too much time passed in the human world before she saw her again.

"Thank you."

Alice wondered briefly if Haruka's father was still in the picture, if he was somewhere, worried about his daughter the same way Alice's mom was worried about hers. It sent a slight twinge of guilt through Alice, but Haruka had chosen this, just like she had. She hadn't heard Haruka mention needing to go home or check in, so it was anyone's guess, really.

"What do you do when you're not doing *this*?" Alice asked, hoping to change the topic to something lighter.

Haruka grinned then. "Do you know *Sailor Moon*?"

Alice's eyes widened.

By the time she noticed the broadening lines in the sky that signaled the start of the Breaking, she and Haruka were deep in discussion of the finer details of what turned out to be their favorite show—subbed, not dubbed. Haruka's ever careful fingers had kept up their dance around the healing wound on Alice's side. She'd cleaned it up and now pressed a damp mixture to it.

"Bit of chewed Jack." Haruka pointed. "Those little needle things in patches near the water. Will act as a bandage and pull some of the venom out a bit faster."

The stuff was cold and tingled slightly. "So, all good?"

"All good, for being just shy of maybe taking out one of your kidneys."

Alice snorted. "The Black Knight took the worst of it."

Haruka pulled Alice's cami down and lightly patted her side. "That's strange. Him taking the blow for you."

"Then killing the Nightmare."

"He must've been badly injured to leave that behind." Haruka jerked her chin at the Vorpal Blade where it lay in the nearby grass.

"Blood loss makes you do wild shit." Alice set a hand over her side, barely resisting the urge to scratch. It was itchy now, for some reason. "Guess I'll try and sleep."

"Good idea," Haruka murmured.

Alice climbed to her feet and took up the Vorpal Blade. She glanced at the basket. "Do you think this being near Romi will cause any trouble?"

Haruka rolled her shoulders. "The way I understand it, it's useless if you don't know how to use it."

"I guess that would be the literal definition." Alice waved and headed for the basket. Chou slept curled behind it, rumbling faintly. Climbing in, she settled into the spot across from Romi, who slept without a sound.

Her body was exhausted, but her mind was running every which way with any random thought that popped into it. Mostly she wondered what her reflection was talking about when she said all that stuff about love and trusting your heart.

Maybe it meant something about the actual Heart. Or maybe she was hallucinating.

Setting the Vorpal Blade between herself and the side of the basket, she folded her arms into a pillow and shut her eyes. Darkness. All was darkness. Would there ever be light again?

Twenty-Six

MEMORIES

"**B**ecause I love you."

"You *what?*" The Black Knight's eyelids fluttered as his mind short-circuited. He hadn't heard that right. Clearly, he'd imagined the last bit, but what the devil did that say about him?

He glared up at Addison Hatta, who'd gone from trying to crack his skull open to claiming he didn't want to hurt him, when there was absolutely no reason for the other to want to do anything but tear him apart. And yet . . .

Hatta just continued talking, like he wasn't spouting utter nonsense. "Or at least I used to." He pursed his lips, his brow furrowed. "I know I fucked up, and I'm paying the price for that. And I know what I did hurt you, but . . . strewth! For you to pretend you don't even know me? To do all of this!" He flung his hands into the air. "With how much you hated what I'd become, you just went and did the same thing?"

"I am *nothing* like you!" Anger poured through the Black Knight. "You're a coward. A traitor, who murdered Queen Portentia and allowed her usurpers to take her place. Then you drove her remaining forces into the Nox."

"W-what?" Hatta stared like he wasn't sure exactly what he was hearing, or like no one had ever confronted him for his crimes. "Murdered? Portentia wasn't—"

"It never occurred to you we'd retaliate, did it?" The Black Knight felt a smile twist his lips, satisfied with the shock on Hatta's face. "That we'd ever grow strong enough to come back from the brink. But we have, and you will all suffer as we did."

Hatta continued to stare at him, his lips pressed into a thin line. After a moment he tilted his head, his expression suddenly thoughtful. Something in the Black Knight shuddered, as if it recognized that look. But it couldn't. He didn't.

Instead his mind pulled at one of his earlier visions: Hatta standing over him, Hatta pulling him to his feet, Hatta leaning in and . . .

"Who is we?" Hatta's voice jolted him from the memory.

He blinked rapidly. "What?"

"You said it never occurred to me that 'we'd' retaliate. That 'we'd' grow stronger. Who is we?"

The Black Knight lifted his chin. "Those loyal to the true Queen of Wonderland."

"Which can't be Portentia, because she's dead. According to you. So who will rule in her place?"

"Her Majesty," he offered almost reflexively. "She who is most loyal."

"Does Her Majesty have a name?"

Of course she had a name, he wanted to say, but when he tried to conjure it, his mind went blank. He could recall her face and her title—Her Majesty, his lady—but no name.

"You don't remember your name. You don't remember *her* name. What *do* you remember?" Hatta leaned in, his gaze curious, searching.

The Black Knight attempted to draw back, but the table hemmed him in. A pinch of pain twisted between his eyes. "I remember you betrayed us . . ." He hated the way his voice faltered.

"How?" Hatta pressed. "When? Do you remember where it happened? What happened? Do you remember any part of the war? Any of the battles? Do you remember life before it all started?"

He tried to. He tried to recall any of the details Hatta demanded, but all he found at the back of his mind was darkness and pain, an emptiness that allowed the questions to ricochet off one another.

"What about the Red Queen? Do you remember her, your duty to her? To serve her, protect her."

The pinched feeling between the Black Knight's eyes began to spread through the rest of his head. "I . . . I don't . . ."

"She was your queen, and you followed her into oblivion, surely you remember that!" Frustration edged Hatta's tone.

But he didn't. Try as he might, he couldn't recall anything before waking in the darkness, rescued from the swimming black by Her Majesty. He was lucky to be alive, she had explained. Few others made it out in one piece, but he was strong. He was resilient. He had fought bravely by Portentia's side until the end. An end brought about by the traitor, Addison Hatta.

Now, with Her Majesty's strength, he could fight again, in Portentia's honor. He could take the mantle of the one who had betrayed them, and he could secure the throne and Wonderland's future from the usurpers. He could be her knight.

And he accepted.

"You . . . you don't remember anything, do you." Though Hatta's words were soft, they leveled an accusation at him like a sword, cutting through the Black Knight's muddled thoughts.

His fingers twitched, wanting to reach for his own weapon in order to defend himself, but it was gone. The weight of his recklessness in coming here unarmed and seeking . . . he didn't even know, started to press in around him.

"I remember *you*." The Black Knight's heart was racing. It pounded so loud in his ears a part of him feared Hatta would hear it, or somehow sense how afraid he was.

And he *was* afraid. Afraid of how none of this made sense, and yet every bit of it did.

"But you don't remember the truth." Hatta reached for him.

The Black Knight smacked his hand away again. "I said don't touch me." There wasn't as much force behind his demand this time. "If you're going to kill me, get it over with."

Pain flickered across Hatta's face. He shook his head,

adamant. "I said I would never hurt you, and I meant it, but you have to let me help you, Humphrey. I don't know what's going on, but something's clearly wrong, with this, with you." Hatta glanced toward the door. "There's a healer here, a woman who might be able to . . . I don't know, but I can't leave you like this." He extended a hand once more, but this time simply held it between them.

The Black Knight stared at that hand. It couldn't be true. It had to be a lie. But if it was, why couldn't he *remember*? And why hadn't he tried to before now?

Hatta sighed. "Either way, you can't sit there all day."

A sudden stab of pain shot from the Black Knight's skull through the rest of his body. He doubled forward, his head in his hands, as pressure built behind his eyes.

"You can't sit there all day." The words echoed in his mind, growing louder and louder, folding in over one another. *You can't sit there all day. Can't sit there all day. Sit there all day. There all day. All day.*

"You can't lie there all day," Hatta said, his words thick with amusement.

The Black Knight blinked his eyes open. The purple Wonderland sky stretched over him, orange clouds thick against the daylight. A shadow fell across his face and he glanced to the side to find Addison Hatta standing over him. The silver of his armor seemed to glow faintly. Two women stepped up on either side of him. The woman on his left, her dark hair pulled back from her face and bound in a tail, wore white armor similar to his. The other, her hair a pile of bright red curls atop her head, wore a plume of skirts in various shades of purple folds falling to the ground.

"I wasn't planning to be here all day," the Black Knight heard himself say. "Just most of it."

Hatta's smile widened, and it sent his stomach spinning in the best way. "Well, you'll have to come back to it. We've been summoned." Hatta extended a hand.

Taking it, the Black Knight pulled himself to his feet. It was then that he noticed he too wore armor, the same red as the woman. "Nothing serious, I hope."

"Her Majesty likely wishes to discuss potentially assigning us to her daughters," the woman draped in skirts said. "I hear she feels looking after the four them puts a strain on our captain."

Hatta grunted as he slid his arm around the Black Knight's shoulders, and he in turn curled his arm around Hatta's waist.

"I'm more than capable of seeing to my duties," Hatta grumbled as the two of them started across the field of long yellow grass the Black Knight had been stretched out in. A palace twinkled in the distance.

"Maybe so," the woman in armor said as she fell into step beside them. "But the princesses are getting older and will likely start going out on their own. You can't be with all of them at once."

"I fear for whoever is assigned to the youngest. She's the one who needs looking after." The Black Knight felt his lips quirk in a smile, still unable to control them, his tongue, or any part of his body as all of this simply . . . happened.

The armored woman returned his smile. "Odette is a handful,

always running off with her games of hide-and-seek with her 'friends.'"

"*The friends none of us can see?*" Hatta asked.

"*It's just the one,*" the woman in skirts corrected.

"*Well. None of it matters. You three are the finest knights in the land.*" Hatta glanced over each of them, then pressed a kiss to side of the Black Knight's head. "*The princesses will be fine, no matter the assignments.*"

"*Humphrey . . .*" a distant voice called.

Darkness closed in.

"No . . ." He strained against the growing black. "No, I want to see. I have to see!"

"Humphrey."

The image faded, leaving the Black Knight floating in shadow and emptiness.

"Humphrey!" Hatta's voice rang clear now.

The Black Knight jolted as his eyes flew open. He glanced around, chest heaving, mind panicked.

Hatta sagged with a sigh of relief. "Strewth." His hands tightened where they had hold of the Black Knight's shoulders. "I don't know what's going on, but I'm going to get you help. Naette!" He called, looking to the door. "Courtney, someone!"

That's when the Black Knight jerked back, drew his knee in, then planted the bottom of his boot in Hatta's chest.

With a pained grunt, Hatta toppled over backward and tumbled a short distance away. He started to push himself up at the same time the Black Knight scrambled to his feet. His side burning, his head thundering, he bolted for the window.

"H-Humphrey, wait!" Hatta wheezed.

The Black Knight didn't so much as glance back as he dove through. The instant he hit the ground in a roll that propelled him to his feet, his side screaming, he let go of the hold on his physical form. The last thing he heard as the ether swallowed him was the sound of Addison Hatta's voice, shouting his name.

Twenty-Seven

SOME FRIEND

Addison groaned as he rolled onto his side. His lungs strained against the blunt force trauma of Humphrey's surprise attack, like they'd forgotten how to take in oxygen for a moment. He coughed, the taste of blood coating his mouth. His wounds burned, torn open again, no doubt.

"H-Humphrey." He forced the word free, trying and failing to push himself up as the other dove out the window. "Wait!"

Finally, he managed to get his feet under him enough to stumble over to the window. Catching himself against the sill, he stared out into the small alley between this house and the next. Empty. Humphrey was gone.

"Shit." Frustration pulled at Addison, but also relief, and a strange . . . sort of joy? Humphrey was alive. After all these years wondering, forcing himself to accept the "truth" of the other's likely death, everything was upended. He was alive, and in trouble. Something had clearly happened to him, to his mind, for him to be doing any of this. They two of them hadn't parted on the best of terms, but it wasn't anything either of them would be trying to kill each other over. Whatever was going on, this lady had to be at the center of it all.

A sudden, stabbing sensation shot through Addison's torso, completely derailing his train of thought. He needed to get help, or he wouldn't be around to puzzle any of this out for long.

Arm wrapped around his middle, he made it to the door and pushed out into the hall. "Naette," he called, moving along with a hand braced against the wall. "Courtney!" Where was everyone?

Sharp barks pierced the air right before Duma came around the corner, jumping and yapping. Addison smirked faintly at the Bandersnatch as she raced over to circle his legs, sniffling at him. He dropped a hand to rub at her head. "Hey, girl, y-you know where everyone went?"

She barked again before trotting back down the hall. That was when he heard voices on the air, drawing nearer.

"I knew pretty much from the beginning," Courtney was saying. "And she told me about Wonderland, but I never thought I'd see it with my—Hatta!" Her and Effe came around the corner holding baskets and sacks with sprouts of green and blue sticking out of them. She hurried to put her parcels down, then ran over to his side, getting up under his arm just as she had out in the forest. "What happened?"

Addison grunted, partly in pain, partly in relief. "I had a visitor."

"I'll get Grandma!" Effe put his bags down and raced back the way he'd come. Duma bolted after him, still barking.

"Went to get dinner?" Addison asked, nodding to the bags and baskets on the floor when Courtney looked at him with her face scrunched in confusion.

She shook her head. "Ingredients for potions and more healing thingies. Naette wanted to grab some since we were at the market looking for a horse for Xelon. Come on, let's get you back to the healing room."

"Ahh. So she's gone?" Addison winced as they shuffled around to face the other way, then back down the hall.

"She wanted to get to Findest as soon as possible, in case Odabeth was already there." Courtney smiled. "It's kinda cute, those two. But you and Alice are still my favorite couple."

"Are we?" He chuckled.

"OTP, baby." Courtney pushed and held the door open with her ankle so they could get through.

When they finally made it across the room, he sank into the chair he'd been tied to earlier. "Sorry," he murmured.

"What for?" Courtney asked.

He pointed at the splotch of fresh blood on what looked like a new shirt.

She held the fabric out to inspect it. "Oh. No worries."

"Oh my," Naette breathed from the doorway. Her wide eyes traveled around the space, taking in the broken vials and toppled plants. "What happened in here?"

"Company. The Imposter paid me a visit."

Courtney's eyes widened. "That asshole was here?"

"Yes. And . . . it turns out that asshole is my friend." Hatta dropped his head back, his eyes falling shut. What little adrenaline that had pumped through him was fading, and pain and exhaustion started to chip away at him.

Fingers peeled away his shirt and poked near his wound. He flinched but did his best to hold still. "Some friend, to leave you in this condition," Naette said from nearby. "You're almost worse than when we first found you."

"He wasn't exactly himself." Hatta shook his head slowly. "Stars, how did I not see it?"

"See what, exactly?" Naette asked.

"Humphrey! The Imposter! Being one and the same." The way he spoke, the way he acted. Looking back on everything, it couldn't have been clearer, yet he hadn't recognized the other at all.

"Don't move so much," Naette chided.

"If this guy is your friend, why is he trying to kill us?" Courtney asked.

"Something's . . . wrong. He didn't remember me, at least not entirely. Christ, he didn't even know his own name." Addison couldn't get the image of Humphrey out of his mind, sitting there in front of him just staring at him with such anger, such hatred. "Something happened to him. I don't know what, but it wiped out everything that he was and turned him into . . . this." A tightening sensation crawled up his throat, and Addison swallowed the burn of tears as he pressed a hand over his face. "I should've gone looking for him. For both of them. Exile or no exile. He would've searched for me. He would've . . ." He bit into his lower lip to keep it from trembling.

A hand fell over his. He didn't open his eyes but figured it had to be Courtney, with Naette still working diligently on his reopened and now worsened wound.

"This is my fault," he murmured. "I knew, I *knew* Humphrey wouldn't just disappear like that. Not without telling someone. And I let them convince me of the worst."

"People keep secrets," Naette said as she pressed something cold and wet to his side. "Even from those they're close to. Especially from those they're close to."

"Maybe it was for a mission," Courtney offered. "Something need-to-know?"

Addison shook his head. "He only had one mission at that point, serve and protect the Red Qu—" He froze, his eyes flying open. Courtney was right. The only conceivable reason Humphrey would vanish like that without telling someone would be if he was ordered to, and the only one able to give such an order would've been the Red Queen.

"I serve Her Majesty," Humphrey had said. His lady. The Red Queen.

Which meant Alice was headed right for—

"Sharp poke," Naette said before a needle pressed into his arm.

Shivers spread through him from the injection site, warm and runny. A trickling sensation settled over his mind, muddling his thoughts. He blinked against a sudden swell of dizziness. "What?"

"You need something stronger than the bath." Naette massaged the spot on his arm. "I was out of this particular tincture, but a trip to the market rectified that. Oh, mind your head. It'll make you drowsy."

"N-no . . . no wait . . ." Something . . . important. About Alice. He was losing it. "Alice." His eyes rolled shut again.

"Hatta?" Courtney called, worry pitching her voice higher.

"Don't worry," Naette said, her voice dipping, slowing. "Heeeeee'llllllll beeeeee alllllllll riiiiiiiiiiiiiight."

Alice . . .

"Geeeeeeeeeeeet hiiiiiiiiiiiiiiiiiim toooooooooooooooooooo thhhhhhhhhhhheeeeeeeeeeeeeeeee—" The voice trailed off, swallowed by a buzzing in his ears.

Hands tugged at his body as he sank deeper and deeper.

No . . . He tried to pull away, but the darkness had hold of him. It crawled through him, stealing his strength, robbing him of his senses. Sounds melded together. Voices mingled. His thoughts scattered as his mind drifted, and everything faded to black.

Twenty-Eight
NO PROMISES

Alice gripped the oh-shit bar inside the basket and groaned. Haruka patted her thigh. The other girl had elected to sit beside Alice this time, pressing against her gently to offer some "solid ground" while the basket jostled. Alice couldn't tell if it was helping at all, but she was glad for the comfort.

"Are you sure you do not want to look? Just briefly." Haruka pointed up. "The view is stunning."

Alice leveled a scowl at her. Honestly, sitting in this thing was hard enough; standing would probably be hell. "That's okay. I can miss a bit of stunning."

Haruka shrugged and tilted her head back against the basket, closing her eyes. Alice did the same.

Deep breaths . . . She drew them in through her nose, then pushed them slowly out through her mouth.

Her stomach flubbed in defiance. Ugh, she was gonna be sick. Again.

Pushing up and around on shaky legs, she got to her feet, then made to lean out over the edge, and froze. Gone was the brilliant pink of the Wonderland sky and the wide, swaying Technicolor grasses and plant life below. Instead the heavens fissured, lines similar to the Breaking but harder, jagged, tearing the sky open. Dust spilled loose, along with fragments of the sky itself, falling toward the lands. There were only two colors spread out before her, the black of shadows and the red of fire.

All of Wonderland burned.

"What—" Alice croaked, the word stuck in her throat.

Her heart pounded. Her breathing kicked up as she tightened her hold on the edge of the basket. What was this? What was happening?

"There!" something shouted.

Alice lifted her gaze just in time to see a creature fly at her, beating batlike wings, furious. It parted its beak with a shriek and dove, snatching at her with huge, birdlike talons. Alice jerked back with a shout, her legs colliding with Haruka's feet.

Her back hit the rim of the basket. Her center of gravity pitched upward. She went over the side.

Fingers grappled at her legs but couldn't get purchase. Haruka's panicked face appeared over the edge of the basket. For a split second, Alice could see the fear in her brown eyes before she dropped away, plummeting through the air.

A scream of her name followed her.

For a moment, there was nothing but the sound of wind in her ears, the thrum of her heart, and the numbing feeling of having nothing. Nothing to grab, nothing to stand on, just her and the empty air. Her mind blanked, not sure it believed what was happening. Above her, Chou roared as he dove.

Spread your arms. She did so immediately. She didn't remember where she'd heard that this slowed you down, but it was better than nothing. That physical action shook her loose of the shock that had stolen her ability to think. It also opened her mind up to the gnawing fear that rocketed through her. She was falling. She was falling!

She turned, looking down. Big mistake. The ground rushed at her. Chou wasn't going to make it. She was going to die.

No!

A hurricane of white exploded against her vision. Her body jerked, hard, like something had hold of her. She blinked, her eyes watering as the world slowly came into focus. Ribbons of light poured outward from the Figment Blade at her back, just like it had when she fought that massive Nightmare on the field. They circled her, their motion slowing her descent, but it wasn't enough. *What the hell?*

A pulse of black flickered in the corner of her eye. The Vorpal Blade was still at her hip, and darkness danced along the edge. It seemed to cower in the face of the Light's brilliance, at least until a few of the ribbons brushed against the shadows. They pulled at the black tendrils, coaxing them free, darkness bleeding into light until the dueling energies swirled around her. That's when Alice noticed she was slowing down. But it wasn't enough. She was still coming in hot.

She had to do something! But . . . there was really only one thing she could do. Stamping out all apprehension of being possessed or swallowed by the black, she reached for the Figment Blade. And for the blade so black.

The instant her fingers wrapped around the hilt, darkness shot free like electricity, mingling with the light. Together, the two formed something . . . different. They coalesced, their color shifted, graying out, and then hardening. An orb of crackling energy solidified around Alice, and she slammed into the bottom of it with a grunt and a jab of pain where she hit her shoulder and her face. The coppery tang of blood slid along her tongue. She shifted, freeing her arm. Her grip on the Vorpal Blade faltered and, with a jerk, the bubble dipped. So did her already upset stomach.

"Ack!" She tightened her hold, and everything steadied. She was safe. Floating in the air. In a . . . a light bubble. The trembling in her middle spread through her limbs. "Oooooh my god: Ohmigod. Okay . . . what is . . . okay . . . you're . . . fine?"

"Alice!" Romi brought Chou around, circling her before the Fury beat his wings to hover. It sent her little bubble bobbing, but it didn't go anywhere.

"Are you all right?" Haruka asked, her panic as clear in her voice as it had been on her face.

"I . . . I think so . . . What is this?" She gestured with her free hand at the bubble.

Haruka blinked. "You're . . . asking me what your . . . magic bubble is?"

"No, not—well . . . I guess? Romi?"

Romi frowned. "I'm not sure."

Alice shifted, glancing around. Why did the weird shit—and this was Wonderland, so that was saying something—always happen to *her*? She was stuck in the air, which was a helluva lot better than falling to her certain death, but now she couldn't go anywhere. Careful, she turned in a slow circle, eyes widening as the bubble, orb, thing turned with her.

"Whatever it is, it looks like you can control it," Romi said, an intrigued lilt to her voice.

"Okay, but how?" Alice lifted the Vorpal Blade to slip it back into her belt, but gave a surprised shout when the bubble rose into the air. Then it dropped when she held her arms out for balance. That was when she noticed the Vorpal Blade was coated in a faint shimmer of black.

"Dafuq?" She drew the blade close to get a better look, then yelped when the bubble dipped toward the ground without warning.

She flung her arms out to brace herself, and just as suddenly the bubble stopped. Alice went stone-still. Her heart jumped in her chest like a nervous rabbit. Her hands shook, though held steady. "What is HAPPENING!"

Romi brought Chou down to circle her, the three of them stopping to hover in front of her again.

"The swords," Romi called over the rush of wind. "When you move them, the bubble moves."

When I move . . . Alice's gaze bounced between the weapons. Similar to the haze of darkness around the Vorpal Blade, a shiver of light clung to the Figment Blade. They were . . . powering this thing?

"Try again, only don't point down," Romi said.

"Okay, okay. Let's see." Alice released a slow breath. "Don't point down." Made sense. She tightened her hold on both hilts, and brought them forward.

The bubble jerked forward.

Alice screamed.

Chou had to dive to get out of the way.

Alice flailed, trying to catch her balance, and that sent the bubble bouncing every whicha-damn way. Alice tumbled around inside like so much dirty laundry.

Haruka and Romi were both shouting, but she couldn't make out what they were saying. Chou darted in and out of her sight. So did the sky. Then the ground. Then the sky. Then the ground—ugh, she was gonna be sick.

She dropped the swords to press both hands over her mouth as the contents of her stomach raced toward her lips. That's when, mercifully, the bubble came to a stop.

Curled on her side, her face pressed to the cool surface of . . . she had no idea what this thing was made of, she groaned. "Whyyyyyyyyyyyy."

"Try again," Romi said from somewhere above her. "Carefully."

Alice took a few deep breaths before prying herself up. Both blades rested at her feet, still pulsing gently. Swallowing the bitter taste coating her tongue, she reached with trembling fingers to pick them up.

The bubble shuddered, but didn't go anywhere. Okay. She could do this. Just no sudden movements. Shakily, she brought the swords together. With a few *very* gentle test swings, she figured out the directions and gently made her way toward the ground. It was start-stop the whole way, and by the time she landed, her stomach was roiling.

She dropped to her knees, her head spinning, and released the blades. The bubble shattered into a million glittering pieces that were carried off by the wind.

Beautiful . . . Alice smiled as she watched the shards float away. Then she took a deep breath and promptly puked.

Chou touched down nearby, and Haruka vaulted out of the basket, hurrying over to her, asking if she was all right.

Alice assured her she was. Shaken all the way up, but in one piece, though her stomach was in shambles. "I'm never gonna be able to eat again . . ."

"What happened up there? You . . . practically jumped out of the basket," Haruka murmured.

Ice slipped through Alice, her insides churning for a whole different reason now. "I—I . . . I saw something." She explained her vision. How it looked, sounded, even smelled real. And when that thing dive-bombed her, she just reacted.

"You're fortunate to have both swords on you," Romi said as she stroked her chin. "From the look of it, you needed them for . . . whatever that was."

"And what was that, exactly?" a familiar voice called.

Alice glanced up just as the Duchess emerged from the trees. Behind her, Odabeth shuffled into view. Both of them looked like they had seen better days, their hair braided back, their clothing stained, but they were alive. That was what mattered.

Pushing down on her nausea, Alice leaped to her feet and raced toward the two of them. Or, she tried to, but her legs didn't want to cooperate. She managed to hobble over with a shout and a laugh.

"You're all right!" Alice threw her arms around Odabeth. The princess made an adorable little noise and returned the hug with a quick squeeze, like it was the first time anyone had forced physical affection on her.

Smiling, fatigue pulling at her features, the Duchess clasped Alice's arm like the warriors in those movies. "We are in one piece. And it is good to see you are also well."

Drawing back, Alice searched the forest expectantly, but no one else emerged. Her smile faltered, and her gaze bounced between the princess and the Duchess. "Wha—it's just you?" A twisty feeling settled in her stomach.

"I am afraid so," the Duchess murmured, moving past Alice and toward the others.

Odabeth fell into step behind her.

Just them. No Addison. Alice's chest tightened and heat rose behind her eyes. He wasn't here.

But that didn't necessarily mean he was *gone* gone. Anastasia would've definitely said something.

"Okay then." With her heart somewhere around her ankles, Alice glanced at the woods one last time before hurrying back to the others.

"What happened?" she asked as she caught up to Odabeth and Anastasia. "There was this loud noise while I was on the phone with Addison, and the line went dead."

"Your friend assaulted the Looking Glass." The Duchess breathed the words, her exhaustion clear.

Alice nearly stumbled. "You mean Chess." The twisting intensified.

"He attacked with Fiends in tow," the Duchess continued. "We were unprepared."

"Is . . ." Alice looked from the Duchess to Odabeth, then back again. "Is everyone . . ."

Odabeth remained oddly silent. She clutched at the straps of her pack, her shoulders hunched forward, her posture sunken, as if the very act of remaining upright took every ounce of her strength.

"Everyone was alive when we last saw them," the Duchess said.

Alice wanted to ask for clarification, but they'd reached the rest of the group. Romi bowed deeply to Odabeth, speaking softly in Japanese. Odabeth dipped her chin and responded in kind. Haruka mirrored Romi's greeting. The itch to ask questions, the need to know what happened to the others, to Addison, crawled through Alice, but she didn't interrupt.

The Duchess gripped Romi's arm the way she had Alice's.

Romi smirked. "You look like shit."

"Better than how I feel," the Duchess murmured.

"Not to be rude," Alice cut in, the words practically bursting from her lips. "But what happened? Why is it just you two? Where's Xelon? Where's Addison?"

Odabeth's tired expression wilted under a grimace. "We . . . don't know. Chess overwhelmed us, and we ran. We made it to the Gateway, but—" She looked to the Duchess. "Something went wrong."

"Something interfered with the crossing, and we . . . fell

through. The princess and I landed close to one another, but there was no sign of the others."

Alice's heartbeat kicked around her ears. Worry gnawed at her insides. She swallowed the sour taste at the back of her throat.

The Duchess shrugged off her pack and let it drop to the ground, then lowered herself to sit beside it. "We searched briefly, but we were out in the open, exposed, unarmed. I had to protect the princess. We made our way to a nearby village, got some food, got some rest, and decided on our next steps."

Odabeth tilted against her pack as well. "It was Anastasia who suggested we carry on with the original plan of going to Findest. She said it's what Addison would do, and if he was with the others, he would lead them there."

Romi made a gesture as if to say, *Told you so.* "I figured as much. It's why we're here, escorting Alice."

A faint smile pulled at the Duchess's lips. "It's been a while since our military days, but we're all still thinking the same, it seems. As a unit."

Romi snorted. "I'm a bookseller, not a soldier, Anastasia. And the instant I see Addison, I'm going to let him know just how little I appreciate being pulled into this nonsense."

"So . . . Hatta's all right?" Alice asked, twisting her fingers together.

A look crossed the Duchess's face that sent a chill through her. "He was injured when we fell through. It looked . . . not the best, but Addison is a survivor. In truth, I'm more worried about what the exile Verse will do to him the longer he stays here."

A buzzing settled between Alice's ears. The exile Verse. She hadn't even considered—

"But," the Duchess quickly cut in. "Like I said, he's a survivor. And if he's with Xelon—" The Duchess reached to set a hand over one of Odabeth's slightly shaky ones. "They're both likely doing fine."

Romi grunted but didn't say anything.

"Your other friend, Courtney?" Odabeth started. "She was there during the attack. She may be here somewhere as well."

"Courtney's in Wonderland?" Alice blinked. Was that even possible? Well, clearly it was, but . . . did that make her a Dreamwalker? And what effect would it have on her when they got back home? What effect would *she* have while she was here?

A million questions poured through Alice's head, a dull ache pushing in behind them.

"Well." Haruka clapped her hands together. "It sounds like we've all had a pretty long day. Why don't we set up camp for the night and get a fire going for supper."

Odabeth let out a relieved breath, smiling faintly. "That sounds amazing."

Alice didn't want to stop, not now, not after hearing that Addison and Courtney were out there somewhere, possibly heading for Findest as well. And Addison was injured!

A hand fell to her shoulder, and she nearly jumped out of her skin. She glanced up to find Haruka smiling down at her. "Let's grab some firewood."

"Y-yeah. Yeah." Alice climbed to her feet and, leaving Romi and the others to set everything up—and forage something for Chou to munch on—the two of them meandered toward the edge of the forest where Odabeth and the Duchess had emerged moments ago.

Working together, with Alice gripping branches and Haruka cutting them free, they'd be able to gather a nice bit of wood to maintain a fire pretty quickly. Alice wrenched at a stubborn branch, yanking again and again and again until it ripped free of the tree with a crack. She stood there, panting, clutching the stick in shaking hands.

"I'm still with you."

"What?" Alice glanced up from where she'd been staring at this stupid stick.

Haruka closed the distance between them. "Whatever you decide, I'm still with you." She closed her fingers over Alice's trembling ones. "I saw the look on your face when the Duchess explained what happened. I know how much you probably wanted to run out there to find your friends." Her touch gentle and warm, Haruka peeled Alice's fingers from their death grip on the wood, then massaged them where the skin had gone angry red. "I also know you probably don't want to hear this, but all of this new information doesn't change anything. It doesn't change their current situation or ours. We still don't know where they are, and our best bet is to go to Findest. Finding those two proves it."

Alice wanted to protest, but there was no point. Haruka was right, about this and about her not wanting to hear it.

"But I understand what it's like to know people you care about are in danger, to want to do everything you can to help them. If you want to go searching for them, I'm with you. If you want to continue to Findest, I'm with you. But we will only have supplies enough to do one." Squeezing Alice's hand, Haruka bent to gather up the branches they'd piled together.

For a moment, Alice didn't know what to do or say. She simply stared, the burn behind her eyes filling the rest of her face. She could still feel the warmth of Haruka's touch on her skin.

Finally, she bent to help gather the branches. "Thank you."

Haruka nodded. "Make the decision in the morning. Let's eat. I'm starving."

"Me too," Alice murmured, smiling. They carried their load over to where a fire now flickered amidst a cleared patch of dirt, dug in just slightly. Odabeth sat on a rolled-out mat, managing to look impossibly regal but at the same time incredibly uncomfortable. This was probably the roughest few days of her life. She toyed with the silvery chain around her neck, the indent of the Eye poking up beneath her shirt.

The Duchess and Romi spoke quietly to one another, glancing up as the girls approached. Soon there were roasting spits in place holding what looked like blue beets over the flame. The smoke that came off of the fruit was pinkish and smelled oddly like cinnamon.

As they all settled down, and the sky began to darken, Alice turned Haruka's words over in her head. She *did* want to go look for Addison and Courtney. But Haruka was right, she still had no idea where to even begin.

A voice pulled Alice from her wandering and worried thoughts.

"What was that ball of light, Alice?" Odabeth asked.

"I . . . I don't know. Looootta weird shit has been happening." Alice explained that she'd fallen from Chou's basket, and why. She even talked about when she was certain her reflection had pulled her into the river last night. "Lately, I've been able to shoot these . . . I don't know, light boomerangs from my blades. The bubble is brand-new, though. Is . . . is this something Dreamwalkers can do? Any of it. The ones who aren't me, I mean."

The Duchess and Romi exchanged another look.

"Dreamwalkers have been known to do amazing things. Usually ones who have been at it for some time, but never anything like this. Not that I am aware of." The Duchess took a swig from her canteen.

"It's a neat trick," Romi added. "But not one I've ever seen, either."

"Have you ever seen anything kinda sorta like it?" Alice asked.

Both women shook their heads.

"But each Dreamwalker is unique," the Duchess offered. "Some are stronger than others, some faster, some more . . . acrobatic."

"Yeah, none of this sounds at all like slinging light from their swords," Alice countered.

"Touché." The Duchess took a bite from her blue beet. "You are peculiar, Alice Kingston. According to Addison, you always have been. You were able to see through his invisibility Verse. You were one of the few trainees he's ever had that learned so quickly, maybe even the fastest. Perhaps these abilities are simply the natural progression of your skill as a Dreamwalker."

Alice grunted. "The twins are better Dreamwalkers than I am. So's Haruka!"

"I don't have a bubble, though." Haruka bit into her beet and winked with a grin.

Alice coughed faintly, her cheeks warming. "I'm just saying, shouldn't one of them be able to do all this . . . never-done-before stuff?"

"Maybe." The Duchess narrowed her eyes slightly. "But they're not. And as fond as I am of the boys, I doubt their first time wielding a weapon as powerful as the Vorpal Blade would yield such . . . nondestructive results."

Alice snickered. The Duchess had a point. The Tweedles were skilled, no doubt, but nowhere near subtle.

"To be honest," Anastasia continued, "I'm shocked you were able to wield that thing at all. The Vorpal Blade, at least Addison's, was very particular about who it answered to."

"Mmm." Alice stole a quick glance at the blade where it lay in the grass nearby, the faint shiver of darkness around it ever present.

"She's right. Wielding a sword like that? Requires some serious skill." Romi tossed her now-empty stick into the fire. The purple flames gobbled it up. "Or maybe it's not raw skill. Maybe your Muchness is unlike anything we've ever seen." She pulled on a vape pen and released a plume of bright yellow smoke into the air. "You're much Muchier than you clearly believe."

"Maybe," Alice murmured, suddenly uncomfortable with all this contemplation of her skill or lack of skill or whatever. She turned her attention to her meal, biting into the fruit. It tasted tart, like coffee, but then had a caramel-like finish. Wonderland fruit was so weird.

"On to other matters—the journey to Findest." Anastasia glanced around. "We're not far, less than two days."

"We could cut that time down with Chou," Haruka said as she offered Alice a bit of her leftover meat leaf.

Alice took it with thanks.

"Afraid not." Romi shook her head. "Chou was doing all right with the three of us, but if we add two more bodies, he won't *do* at all. Especially having already gone as long and as far as he has." She patted the Fury's huge head where he nuzzled at her side. "It'll be on foot from here."

"That won't be a problem," Anastasia said.

"I figured it wouldn't. One more thing." Romi took another drag of her pen. "I won't be going with you. With whatever the hell is going on here, I've left my Gateway unprotected long enough. I need to get back."

The Duchess nodded. "I understand. I have . . . similar concerns."

"Haruka and I will leave in the morning," Romi said.

Haruka poked at the fire with a stick. "I'm going with Alice."

For a moment the only sounds were the gentle whistle of the wind, the *whuff* of Chou's breathing, and the tinkling crackle of the flame. Romi let a pearl of purple smoke curl from her lips. "Nanitte?"

"Doko mademo ishho ni iku 'te Arisu ni yakusoku shitano." Haruka glanced up at Alice. "I promised I'd go with you. I mean to do just that."

Romi arched an eyebrow. She gazed at the girl for a moment before releasing a breath and murmuring in Japanese.

The two of them went back and forth for a moment. At one point Odabeth and the Duchess both glanced at Alice, then back to the conversation, and she had the sneaky suspicion that something had been said about her.

"Well, it seems you'll have an extra sword for this excursion, Anastasia, against my council and Haruka's sense."

Haruka held Romi's gaze, though there was no heat or anger behind either set of dark eyes.

Romi tapped a bit of ash from her pipe onto the ground—Alice hadn't even noticed her swap it out with the vape pen—before taking another drag. The tobacco, if that's what it was, burned blue in the growing dark. "I can hold the fort on my own, but not indefinitely. Get the job done and get back safe. Wakatta?"

Haruka gave a quick nod. "Hai."

"If you could," the Duchess started, "reach out to the boys to tell them to get home, soon as they can. Use Ghost Protocol. They'll know what it means."

Alice blinked. "What, like the movie?"

The Duchess smirked. "I'm afraid not. And I'm certain this was in place long before humans developed cinema."

"Wait." Alice frowned. "If they go home, who's going to look for Chess and Maddi?"

The Duchess pursed her lips. "I'm afraid the search will have to be called off for now. We have our duty, Alice," she cut in before Alice could protest. "It is to defend the Veil, not to look for our comrades, no matter how much we may wish to. The protection of your world, and ours, comes first. Madeline knew this."

"Chess didn't," Alice grumbled before she could stop herself.

"I know." The Duchess set a hand on Alice's shoulder. "And I'm sorry, but it must be this way. Now, let us focus on the task at hand. The faster we get it done, the sooner you can pick up the search."

Reluctantly Alice nodded. She was getting sick of so many people being right about things she didn't wanna do.

"You all need anything else when I go?" Romi asked. "Check your mail, drop off your dry cleaning?"

The Duchess chuckled and said something in Russian.

Romi spoke back in the same before stretching her arms above her head. The group spent the rest of the growing evening in soft conversation about the goings-on of the past few days while they finished their meal. Then a watch order was decided and everyone settled in for the night. Alice didn't expect sleep to come so easily, but she was exhausted and out cold until Romi woke her for her rather uneventful turn at watch.

Morning came, and after a quick breakfast of more blue beets, Romi gestured for Chou to rise, which he did after stretching like the world's longest dog. Haruka said good-bye to the large beast, and Alice even took a moment to scratch his ears and say thank you. Romi wished them all haste of smooth passage before, with great flaps of Chou's wings, she took to the sky. The three of them watched her for a moment before Anastasia put away the last of their rations and hefted the pack onto her back. "Let's go."

She took up the lead, the three girls falling into step behind her.

Alice's hand went to the weapon at her hip, out of habit and a need for familiar action to calm her nerves, but she stopped before curling her fingers over it. The Vorpal Blade wasn't hers. Yes, she'd used it, and she would in a fight if she had to, but she didn't want to get too familiar with it.

"We should reach the castle before nightfall tomorrow." The Duchess glanced back at them briefly. "If not, we will camp at the edge of the castle grounds and begin the search the following morning. It would not do to wander Findest in the dark, to face whatever lies therein."

"I thought the place was supposed to be empty," Alice said.

"True. And the Black Knight should be no more, yet he challenges us. The Fiends should be gone, but their numbers flourish. How things should be is turning out to be dangerously different from how they are." The Duchess looked towards the sky, likely gauging the time. "There could be nothing waiting for us at the Royal-less Palace. Or we could run afoul of something most sinister. I'd like to be prepared for either outcome, wouldn't you?"

Alice snorted. "I'd like to go more than forty-eight hours without something trying to maim me, maul me, stab me, claw me, or eat me."

The Duchess released a heavy breath. "I make no promises."

Twenty-Nine
WHAT MATTERS

Addison jerked awake, his eyes flying open. Stone stretched over him, smooth and polished, rising into a low dome. He was in bed, in a small bedroom, the walls bare.

Moonlight poured in through the window, mixing with the flickering haze of a fire in the hearth. A small desk sat against the far wall, and on it a mortar and pestle, along with a few other items he recognized as healer's tools. He didn't recognize this place.

Why was he in someone's house he didn't recognize? And why the hell did his head *hurt* like this? He lifted a hand to press it over his face, then winced when a sharp pain shot along his left cheek. He touched gingerly at the puffy area beneath his eye. That was when he noticed the bandages around his arm. He stared for a second before playing his gaze over the rest of his body, also wrapped, clear down to where a blanket was flung over his hips.

Despite the numerous injuries, he didn't seem to be in any immediate danger. So what was this sense of urgency buzzing through him, this undercurrent of . . . fear? It was as if some part of him was on edge, aware of something he couldn't pick up on consciously, at least not yet.

Just as his mind started to fill in the important information, the door swung open and Naette stepped through, holding a tray. "Oh good, you're up. Saves me the trouble of waking you. You need to eat something." She moved to set the tray on the small table near the head of the bed. The smell of something rich and meaty hit his nose, likely the chunky-looking stew in the bowl. There was also a glass of water.

"Mmmm. How long was I out?" He pinched the bridge of his nose and rubbed at it.

"A handful of hours." Naette uncorked a vial and poured a brown liquid into the water. She stirred it with a spoon until the liquid seemed to vanish entirely, leaving the water clear. "For any lingering pain," she said, setting the glass down again.

"That's all there is." He shifted to sit up. It was slow and achy going. "Where am I? How did I get here?"

"You're in the recovery room." The old woman shuffled over to add another log to the fire from a pile of red wood. The flames jumped, the edges going crimson briefly. "After the visit from your friend, I had to put you in another, stronger bath. You're lucky we came home when we did, much longer and you may have bled out on my floor."

An uneasiness moved through Addison. "Why don't I remember . . . any of that?"

"Funny thing about trauma—the mind tends to find ways to block it out." Naette glanced up from the fire, the flickering light casting shadow and ember across her dark brown face. "It's either that or the drugs."

Hatta chuckled then winced. His ribs were less amused. "Gave me the good stuff, then?"

"Nothing but the best for my patients. I have a reputation, y'know. And you really should take better care of yourself."

"You'll be happy to know I don't plan on making a habit of getting blown up and stabbed."

"Fantastic. Now drink." Naette flapped a hand at the glass as she settled into a nearby chair.

He reached for the water with murmured thanks. Lifting it to his lips, he paused when a ghost of a thought fluttered across his mind, a flicker on the periphery of his memory. Something to do with Alice . . . but it was just outside of his reach. Frowning, he took a few swallows. It tasted faintly of peppermint and stint vine.

There was a knock at the door.

"Come in," Naette called as she took hold of the tray.

Courtney poked her head in. "Oh good, you're awake."

"Barely," Addison murmured as he settled back against the pillows and Naette placed the tray in his lap.

"Eat." Naette plucked up the glass. "I'll get more tonic."

"Thank you."

Naette nodded, then moved to slip past Courtney, who side-shuffled awkwardly. She waited until Naette closed the door behind herself before approaching. "How're you feeling?" She settled into the chair the old woman had abandoned.

"Like hell." He tucked into the meal, delighted to find Naette made an excellent Jubjub stew.

"Well, you look better." Courtney heaved a sigh, twisting her fingers together where they sat in her lap.

"Something on your mind?" he asked between spoonfuls. Damn but he was hungry.

She frowned. "Did Naette tell you, you were talking in your sleep?"

He shook his head, watching her as he continued to eat. She fidgeted, much the same way Alice did with her fingers or her sleeves, only Courtney shifted like she couldn't quite get comfortable.

"You kept saying you had to warn Alice. It sounded like something bad was about to happen."

Addison paused, frowning.

"I know it was probably a dream, but . . . you sounded really scared," Courtney murmured. "Are you okay?"

"Fine. Save for the fact that we don't dream. Not like humans do, at least."

He set the bowl on the tray and put it aside. "What did I say? Exact words, if you can."

"U-um . . . well . . . you said, 'Alice. Have to warn. Have to stop the red. Trap? Trap the Heart.' I think. Or something close to it. I know it doesn't make any sense . . ."

Courtney's voice faded as Addison's mind latched onto her words. Alice. Warn Alice. A trap. The Heart. Red flashed across his mind, a sharp pain following. His foggy thoughts suddenly solidified.

Everything came together like the pieces of a puzzle. Humphrey had *known* Addison had the Eye, because the Red Queen told him. She was there when her sister gave the Eye to Addison to hide in the human world. And then she took the Heart and vanished. There was no telling what had happened between then and now, but whatever it was, it was awful enough to strip Humphrey of his very self and cause the Red Queen to forsake her charge. The Eye and the Heart were never to be brought together again.

The Heart. The Red Queen had the Heart. And—

Addison threw aside his blanket. "Where are my clothes?"

Jumping slightly in her chair, Courtney glanced around. "I—I . . . I don't know. I . . . They're all bloody. I think they were washed—what's wrong?"

"Alice, Xelon, Odabeth, they're all walking into a trap." He hesitated a moment before pushing to stand. His knees buckled, and he caught himself against the edge of the nightstand.

"Whoa!" Courtney reached for him. "You shouldn't be moving yet!"

"Didn't you hear me?" Addison gritted his teeth, staring into Courtney's wide, shocked eyes. "It's a trap! Humphrey is the Imposter. He used to be the Red Knight, but then he and the Red Queen went missing, and the Heart went missing with her. Now, years later, he shows up demanding the Eye from me. Only two other people knew I even had it, the White Queen—who's in a coma, thanks to him—and the Red Queen. Back at the pub, when the princess used the Eye to locate the Heart, it showed her Findest. The Red Queen's palace. If it's there, it's because she's there. It's a trap." He shook his head, disgust at himself curling his lips. "I should've seen it. I should've *seen* it!"

Courtney stammered, glancing around the room as if she might find answers hiding in the corners. "What . . . what do we do?"

"I have to go after them. Hopefully, I'll get to them before—"

"What are you doing out of bed?" Naette stood in the doorway, another glass of water in her hand.

Addison shoved himself upright. Thankfully, his legs held. "I have to leave." He explained to her what he had to Courtney, that his friends were walking into a trap, and taking one of the Black Queen's artifacts with them.

Naette, impressively, remained calm. At least, outwardly. Her brow crinkled just so, and she stepped forward to hand the glass over. "Your injuries have had a chance to heal a bit more than before, but they are freshly sealed and easily reopened. If you go and you get into another fight, I won't be there to patch you up afterward."

Addison polished off the tonic and set the glass aside. "I'll have to risk it. We can't just let this happen. Not again . . ." He had a chance to stop it this time. To do something to prevent the horrors like those before, horrors he helped raise.

And there would be horrors.

Addison reached to take one of Naette's hands in his. She blinked at their fingers then at him, her expression curious.

"You and your family have already done more than I could ever hope to repay," Addison said.

A smile pulled at her lips. "True."

"And I hate to ask more, but . . . I have to do this. But I can't do it in this condition. Is there anything more that can be done?"

Naette pursed her lips and sighed through her nose.

"I can make a potion that *should* give you strength enough for the journey. But once it wears off, it will weaken you in other ways," Naette said. There was an ominous lilt to her voice. "Ways that will bring you dangerously close to the brink."

"I'll cross that bridge when I come to it," Addison murmured.

"That bridge is death, Sir Hatta. I would not treat it so flippantly."

"There is nothing flippant about this. I know full well what I am risking. This is worth it. Alice is worth it." He shook his head. "I caused . . . so much pain during the war. M-more than I could ever hope to repay. But I can make the right choice this time. Help me. Please."

For a stretch of seconds, Naette merely stared at him. Her expression was blank, her eyes betraying nothing. He had no idea whether or not she would help him, and for a moment he feared she would not. But then she nodded. "Very well. Though I cannot in good conscience let you go out there like this alone."

"He won't be alone." Courtney set her jaw and jutted her chin out as she glanced at him. "Because I'm going, too."

Addison almost laughed. In fact, he felt a faint smile pull at his face, but hid it as he shook his head and rubbed at his mouth. It wasn't ha-ha funny, just . . . funny. "You can't do that."

"Course I can. We walk out the door, head in the same direction, it's not that hard."

"No, no, what I mean is I'm potentially heading into battle. I'm already halfway on my ass, it won't take much to knock me the rest of the way, I won't be able to look after you."

"And? You think I don't know that?" Courtney folded her arms over her chest. "And I didn't ask you to look after me. I'm going to look after you, since you missed that bit. My best friend is out there in this. She has been for so long, and I just . . ." She took a quick, shaky breath. "She talked about how dangerous this shit was, and I didn't really listen, but after seeing those . . . *things* at my school? Then at the bar and . . . dragging *my* ass halfway through this place, I at least owe her going the rest of the way. And Chess, he's . . . he's out there, too. I can't just do nothing!" Her voice cracked. With a frustrated whimper, she wiped at her eyes and sniffed before schooling her expression. "I want to fight."

Addison released a slow breath. He knew what Courtney was feeling to some degree. What it was like to have someone you loved, in the thick of things, and not be with them. Not be able to protect them.

No, he knew *exactly* what Courtney was feeling, because that someone was the same someone for both of them. Alice was her best friend and his . . . He didn't have a word for what Alice meant to him. Not yet. And the thought of losing her before being able to define it?

Oh yes, he understood the want to do something, anything, to help. But he also understood how trying to help could actually be a hindrance when you didn't know what you were doing. Courtney had heart, but heart couldn't carry a weapon.

"Alice trained for this. Weapons training, combat training. Broken bones, bruises, all of it. She was at the pub for months before she ever set foot in Wonderland, then she spent from then until now facing down a very real danger time and again. She is an experienced warrior." He reached to set a hand against her trembling arm, squeezing lightly as her sniffles increased. "Your other friend . . ." There were a few theories.

Whoever this Chess was, whatever he was, there was a fighter in there somewhere, and a damned good one. To think he'd been at Alice's side this entire time, and Addison had never known . . .

"He can hold his own in a fight."

Courtney snorted a laugh that sounded one part humor, two parts incredulity. "Clearly."

"He's also part of this now. He doesn't have a choice. But you do. And, quite frankly, I'm not going to be the one to explain to Alice I brought you along and wittingly placed you in the line of danger."

This time when she laughed, it was all genuine, though soft.

"Because if this battle doesn't put me fully on my ass, she will."

"True." Courtney gave one final, long sniff as she rubbed at her bright red face. Her eyes continued to water and her throat worked in a swallow.

Addison rubbed her arm lightly, offering what comfort he could.

"I'm okay," she sighed, nodding. "Or I will be, when all of this is over." She swiped at her nose, then wiped her hands against her pants. "I still wanna help. I can pack things, or mix stuff, just . . . gimme something to do." She flapped her hands, her fingers curling.

"You and Effe can go into town and get supplies and a mount for Sir Hatta." Naette had made her way to the door, but paused to watch their little exchange. Understanding shone in her gaze as well. "I'll work on making sure he's on his feet as best we can get him. Then it's up to him to stay that way."

"Thank you," he said with a tip of his head, but whatever happened to him didn't matter. His main concern was getting to Findest. Whether or not he survived, well . . . That far into Wonderland, if the Red Queen didn't finish him, the exile Verse would. Its grip on him had been a painful undercurrent beneath more severe injuries, but now that they had been seen to, he could feel the Verse's effects keenly.

It was a feeling like fingers around his heart slowly tightening, squeezing, choking the life out of him. It thickened each breath he took, like the air was too thin. It made him dizzy, the pain a constant drain, like his bones were brass and his blood was lead. Things would only get worse from here, but that didn't matter, either.

It was almost laughable, how the punishment for his past crimes was the only thing standing in the way of making things right. How he'd survived all the terrible things he wrought only to die doing what was right.

Or maybe not funny, simply just. A fair price. Either way, he didn't have time to feel sorry for himself. He didn't have time for much at all, so long as it was enough to get him to Alice . . .

Whatever happened after that, he'd have to live with it, for however long, or short, that was.

Thirty

FINDEST

Alice was damn near about to pass out from exhaustion by the time they stopped to make camp shortly before nightfall. They divided up the watch, with even Odabeth offering to take a turn. The night passed without incident, and they set off the next morning.

No one really spoke as they walked along, with the Duchess in the front, Odabeth after, and Alice bringing up the rear. Haruka stayed back with her, and the two exchanged a few words now and again. Had either of them ever been this far in? Had they been inside the Red Palace? No, for both of them.

Their party stepped out of the forest and the Duchess lifted a hand for them to stop. "We're here." The palace sat on a small rise, cliffs on three sides, waterfalls spewing into a vastness they couldn't see from here. It was beautiful, but different from what she remembered seeing in the mirror.

"I have not been here since I was a child," Odabeth murmured, her hand clutching at the Eye where it rested beneath her shirt.

"Eyes up. Stay alert." The Duchess set a hand against her hip, over the whip Alice hadn't noticed before. Romi had a whip, though hers was more chain-like than this.

Haruka likewise took hold of her weapon. Alice went to do the same, then realized she was reaching for the Vorpal Blade. She paused before switching to the Figment Blade.

Carefully, quietly, they crossed the overgrown grounds with nothing but the noise of the animals and the chorus of waterfalls following them. They circled to the gate that opened into the main courtyard. When they passed through, Alice . . . wasn't sure what she was seeing. The cliffs vanished, and plains spread out around them. *This* was the image she remembered from the pub's mirror.

"What?" she asked quietly.

The Duchess glanced back at her and smirked. "The hidden battlement. The Red Queen was quite adept at illusion Verses. That this one has lasted even in her absence is a testament to her power."

They kept going, approaching the looming doors at the front of the structure. Their steps echoed faintly as they climbed the stairs. Like at the White Palace, they moved to the side of the massive doors and instead found a set of smaller ones. The Duchess looked them over quietly, as if to ask, *Ready?*

Everyone nodded, and she pushed her way inside.

Alice wasn't sure what she expected once they entered

the Red Palace, but it wasn't this. The place was near perfect! The portraits, the trappings, the furnishings, all of it was pristine and polished. It was like everyone had gone to bed just last night and would rise at any moment to start the day.

But that wouldn't be the case. There was an emptiness here, a quiet that was more like a scar against the atmosphere, so different from the life at Legracia.

Like Legracia, the crystal ceiling allowed light to pour into the palace and along the halls. A carpet muted their steps as they proceeded.

Haruka ran her fingers gently over a table as they passed. They came away covered in a layer of fine white dust. Alice blinked, shocked. None of the items around them looked dusty, but sure enough, when she touched them, her fingers came away coated in the same powder. Weird.

The Duchess led the way to the throne room, and Alice couldn't help the faint gasp that escaped her. Her mind instantly went to when her parents took her to Disney World as a child and she couldn't help being a little disappointed when she passed through the castle for the first time. It was nice, but small, and kind of plastic-looking. This? This was a palace, a real palace, a real throne room, tall and elegant, the walls lined with tapestries and gossamer curtains. The room was huge, and their steps echoed around them, taking on an almost musical quality.

At the far end of the room, the throne sat empty, abandoned, royal-less.

They stopped at the center of the room, along the red rug

that led toward the throne. Alice wrapped her arms around herself as a shiver slid up her spine. She thought she felt a breeze the way her skin prickled.

"All right, Your Majesty," the Duchess murmured.

Odabeth nodded and set aside her pack. Haruka took hold of it for her.

The princess pulled the Eye free and took a slow breath.

Watch out . . .

The words were a whisper against Alice's mind, but she heard them clear as day. "Wait." She grabbed Odabeth's wrist, interrupting the Verse. The princess blinked in surprise and confusion. "Something . . . something's not right," Alice murmured, her eyes flickering over their surroundings.

The Duchess turned to glance around as well.

Alice was starting to feel a bit silly when a sound floated in from one corner of the room, filling the space around and above them.

Laughter.

The voice finally grounded itself as the shadow of the throne shifted along the floor as if alive. It bubbled and rose, reminding Alice of the ground the night she first met the Black Knight, how the black had taken on a life of its own. Only, instead of forming a Nightmare, it formed an archway, and through it stepped a woman.

Shadow fell from her body, sliding along it like liquid, giving her the appearance of having been sculpted from it. Blood-red hair fell along her pale, white shoulders and down her back. Her beautiful, elfin face was pulled into a disdainful expression, the smile on her lips sharp like a blade. Red fabric painted her body the same color as her hair. And her nails, long, lethal-looking things, tapped at her hips where her hands rested against them. Her eyes, red as coals, fixed on Alice. The shadow archway behind her spilled black mist a few feet into the room, lightning flashing at the woman's back.

Alice had stared into those eyes before, in the In-Between.

"Smart. For a human," the woman snarled. Her gaze swept over them, then landed on Odabeth. "I've enjoyed our little game, flushing you all out like mice, watching you scurry. But I've been denied long enough. Give me the Eye." She lifted a hand.

"Behind, Your Highness." The Duchess pulled her whip free and stepped in front of Odabeth. It uncurled against the carpet, spikes along the length of it and the morningstar tip gleaming in the faint light.

Alice drew the Vorpal Blade.

The woman's eyes shifted to the black blade.

"So . . . that's what happened to my knight," she murmured.

"*Your* knight?" the Duchess asked.

"Mm." The woman tapped her nails against her chin. "Mine. I've started a collection. I think I'll add this one to it."

She snapped her fingers twice. The shadow arch behind her shifted. Two figures stepped through, the first one stumbling forward as she was shoved at sword point.

Odabeth gave a strangled gasp at the same time Alice's chest tightened.

Xelon, her face twisted in pain, shuffled forward. She

clutched one arm below a red stain in the fabric. Red stained the ends of her white hair where it fell around her shoulders. Behind her, Chess pressed the tip of a sword between her shoulder blades.

Where Xelon's expression was angry and defiant, his was blank. He was a shadow of the boy who had met her outside her grandmother's building what felt like an eternity ago, the same boy who came to her broken and confused, and had kissed her. Those violet eyes of his were dulled, almost dead. But he wasn't. He was standing there whole. Or was this another trick, another inky lookalike, like the one from the school parking lot?

Alice's throat closed. Her eyes stung. If this was Chess, he was a shell. Maybe the real Chess was lost in there and she could get him out, but seeing him like this? She took a few quick breaths, fighting back tears.

"What do you think?" The woman reached to trail a long nail against Xelon's arm. "She would make a marvelous addition, yes?"

The White Knight yanked away from her and spat on the ground at her feet.

The woman stared at that spot, her nose wrinkling slightly. "Mmmph. Chester, darling."

He drew back the sword.

"No!" Alice shouted.

"Don't!" Odabeth cried.

Xelon jerked as Chess cracked the pommel of his blade against the back of her head. She dropped to her knees, and he pressed the tip to her back again.

"Leave her alone!" Odabeth screamed, moving forward. Alice reached to hold her back as the Duchess threw out an arm.

"Stay back, Your Highness!"

"No need to be dramatic," the woman crooned. She stepped over to Xelon and slid her fingers into those white strands, twisting them in her fist. "It's simple, really. Give me the Eye, or I kill this one. And maybe that one." She jerked her head toward Chess, who didn't react whatsoever.

"Don't do it," Xelon spat, then hissed when the woman yanked at her hair.

"Don't be rude," the woman warned.

Xelon glared up at her before shifting her gaze to Odabeth. "Don't give it to her."

"I—I can't . . . I can't watch you—"

"You can do anything, beloved," Xelon murmured. "Be strong."

Odabeth whimpered, tears spilling over her amber cheeks. For a moment Alice didn't know what would happen. They'd done so much, been through so much, to save people. And now . . .

The woman rolled her eyes and let go of Xelon's hair, shoving her away.

"Fine. Then I will put an end to one nuisance and take the Eye for myself. Chester."

Alice's eyes widened as Chess lifted his weapon. Odabeth screamed. The Duchess started forward at a run.

Alice felt something inside her shatter.

Chess's sword came down.

Thirty-One

LATE

Alice's breath caught as Chess brought down his sword. It crashed against another blade, the sound tearing through her ears. It wasn't the howl of metal on metal but the scream of glass. Alice's eyes widened, and her heart leaped in a rush, a smile pulling at her face.

"Haruka!"

Chess jerked in surprise, giving Haruka just the leverage she needed to throw him back. That was when the Duchess unfurled her whip and twirled it around herself in a flourish.

Crack!

The whip launched itself across the space. The woman screamed as she stumbled back, her hands going to her face.

Chess reached for her, but she threw him off with a shriek.

"Don't *touch* me!"

By now, Xelon had regained her feet and hurried down

the stairs, Haruka guarding her back. She raced to a frantic Odabeth's side. The princess reached to pull uselessly at her bindings.

Brandishing the Vorpal Blade, Alice stepped forward to join Haruka on the stairs. Her eyes moved between Chess and the woman, wanting to call out to him, to tell him he didn't have to do this, he could fight it, but the words shriveled on her tongue when the sound of laughter began to build.

"You dare . . ." The woman straightened, her hands still pressed to her face. Blood ran red streaked with black and glistening between her fingers. She drew them away to stare, revealing the wide smile on her equally red lips. The skin of her cheek was split open where the Duchess's whip had torn into it.

Alice's hand went to her mouth as her stomach rolled. The flesh of the woman's cheek was black beneath a layer of pale skin. The gash poured red and black down the woman's neck, painting her skin: Portrait of a Bloody Lady.

"You dare to strike your queen?" Her voice echoed faintly.

The Duchess scoffed. "I plan to do more than that."

The Bloody Lady ran her tongue against her red-wet fingers, and Alice cringed.

"I had hoped to delay things, to watch you all suffer as traitors should." The Bloody Lady curled those same fingers into a fist. "But I grow tired of your impudence." She lifted her hand into the air.

Alice tensed, waiting for some sort of attack. Instead, the shadows around them began to shift and twist. Then came the snarls, low growls that rumbled menacingly. Fiends crawled into being, stepping out of the dark. They padded forward, hackles raised, maybe six or seven of them. At least . . . she thought they were Fiends. They were small, lithe, and on all fours like Fiends, but as they shifted, Alice noticed that their proportions were off. Their limbs were a bit longer, their torsos shorter. Their claws weren't claws at all, but long and fingerlike, tipped with needle-thin talons. Their faces were flat, round. Black lips pulled back from feral snarls and jagged teeth, but that wasn't what sent an icy jolt of fear through Alice's body.

It was the eyes.

Each fiend had a pair of eyes at the center of what were clearly faces. Watchful eyes. Humanoid eyes.

"Oh my god," Alice whispered.

Haruka whispered something in Japanese Alice was fairly certain was a curse.

"Behind me, Your Majesty," Xelon said.

"What . . . what did you do to them?" Anastasia breathed, fear and disgust ripening her words.

The Bloody Lady sneered as she peered at them down the length of her nose. "You don't like my pets? Poor things, first such harsh judgment from my knight, and now this?" She extended a hand and one of the . . . not-fiends crawled beneath it, butting its head against her palm like a cat. She stroked red nails against the inky skin. "Well, such rudeness simply will not do. Let's be done with this. Chester. The princess."

Faster than Alice had ever seen him move before, Chess flung himself toward Xelon and Odabeth, sword lifted. Alice sidestepped to meet him, their blades locking. Around them, the Not-Fiends leaped on the attack.

Haruka dove forward with a swipe at the one nearest her.

The Duchess's whip came to life around her once more, lashing out at the monsters. Xelon placed herself in front of Odabeth, despite being bound. The princess drew her own short sword and gripped it in shaking hands.

Alice twisted around to break free of the lock, facing her opponent, her heart crumbling. "Chess!" This close, she hoped to see some sort of recognition in those dull violet eyes, some sign it was him and not whatever he had turned into. But he stared at her blankly.

"Please don't do this," she begged.

Lifting his sword, Chess lunged. His shadowy blade hummed when it collided with the Vorpal Blade. Alice twisted in with his attack, working to block and defend. She couldn't bring herself to go on the offensive. This was her friend! He . . . he wasn't himself! She couldn't hurt him.

"Chess! You don't have to do this!" She jerked to the side, barely avoiding losing a kidney.

He said nothing, instead bringing his blade around for another attack. And another. Driving her back, slowly, steadily. Her arms ached with the force of his blows. Her heart ached as she realized she wouldn't be able to keep this up. She was going to have to stop him, even if it meant hurting him.

Around her the room dissolved into a maelstrom of flashing blades, slashing claws, and gnashing teeth. Alice's mind swam as it tried to balance defending herself, watching out for her comrades, and not hurting one of her best friends.

So when Haruka cried out in pain, Alice's brain sputtered

for the briefest moment, caught between focusing on her own fight and looking to the other Dreamwalker.

Just long enough for a blow to slam into her chest. It drove the air from her lungs, and sent her hurtling backward. Pain flared along her body as her arms and legs banged against the stairs. Her weapon went clattering as she threw her hands out to try and stop herself.

Ears ringing, her head spinning, she tried to breathe around a feeling like fire in her lungs.

"Chester!" the Bloody Lady shouted. "Bring me the Vorpal Blade."

Alice lifted her head. The room spun, but she could see Chess stalking toward her, his movements jerky, as if he didn't have full control of his body.

The Vorpal Blade lay a short ways off. Chester stumbled toward it. Gritting her teeth, Alice pushed into a run. She couldn't reach the blade first, but she could reach Chess.

She tackled him, the two of them going down hard in a tangle of limbs. As Alice scrambled to try and get up, he scrabbled to catch hold of her.

His fingers caught in her hair, and she shouted before driving her fist into his stomach.

He wheezed but didn't let go. Kicking, she tried to break free, but he had hold of her shirt. She should have been able to get away easily, but whatever that witch had done had made him stronger. He was taller than her, and heavier. His fingers clamped onto her arms and squeezed hard enough to send jolts of pain through her, like glass pressing up from beneath her skin. He twisted and drove a knee into her stomach.

Pain ricocheted through her entire body, and she stopped fighting. When Chess let go, she rolled onto her side, arms wrapped around her middle. Her diaphragm struggled to do its job, and she coughed as her lungs were suddenly without air. Her vision fuzzy, she watched as Chess crawled the short distance to where the Vorpal Blade lay against the ground. He scooped it up, then turned back toward the throne. Alice pushed to her feet. Her legs felt like overcooked ramen.

"Ch-Chess . . ." She stumbled after him, snatching at his shirt.

He whirled on her, sword lifted. She caught his wrist and squeezed as he brought it down. She felt the bones grind, but he didn't bat an eye. Twisting, she used the momentum of his swing to bring him around, wrenching his arm up behind his back. The sword came free, and at the same time, Chess pressed into the bend. With a queasy feeling in her stomach, Alice heard something in his arm snap. She *felt* it.

He wriggled free and came at her with his good arm with a punch that could probably have taken her head off. She drew back, bending to snatch up the Vorpal Blade as she went.

Straightening, she swept her gaze around the room. Three black bodies lay motionless. The Duchess and Haruka each faced off with a pair of Not-Fiends, with Xelon and Odabeth between them. Around the floor, the darkness curled and hissed, giving birth to more monsters. They were going to be overrun.

Fingers pulled at Alice, and she turned to face Chess just as Xelon shouted, "Your Highness, no!"

Light filled the room. Chess threw his good arm up to shield his eyes with a pained shout. Alice yanked away from him, twirling to catch his legs with her own and sweep them from under him. He hit the ground in a heap, and she was on top of him, pinning him with his good arm twisted up against his back. He jerked with another cry, and she felt her heart break.

"I'm sorry!"

"Enough." Odabeth's voice echoed around them, bouncing from the walls, the high ceiling.

The light faded, revealing the princess, luminescent, the veins in her arms pulsing golden, as they had been in the pub. At the center of her brow, the Eye blazed.

Around her, the Not-Fiends rolled and bucked as their bodies cracked and sizzled, the light burning their flesh. They hissed and yelped as they withdrew to the edges of the room.

Haruka and the Duchess stared at the princess with twin looks of shock on their face that mirrored the same in Alice.

Behind them, the Bloody Lady stared as well, but her face held an entirely different expression. There was no fear or wonder as she beheld the illuminated Odabeth, but a manic sort of joy, her lips splitting into a smile.

"There you are," she murmured, pressing a hand to her chest. Her fingers began to blacken, her skin taking on an inky quality before her nails dug into her flesh, peeling it away. As bits and strands of tissue came free, a stone revealed itself, embedded in her skin. Jagged black edges cut into tissue, angry red around the lines where the stone had clearly been broken away or in half.

The Duchess's gasp was audible. "The Heart . . ." she whispered, her voice shaking.

Where Odabeth was light and brilliance, the woman became shadow and blood. The red of her hair, of her dress, painted her now, slick against her skin, similar to the way pitch oozed to form Nightmares.

The princess looked to the Duchess in surprise, and that was all the Bloody Lady needed. She flew forward, her feet barely touching the ground. Odabeth tried to pull away, but one black hand caught her around the throat. The other curled fingers around the Eye. "This is not a toy for little girls," the Bloody Lady snarled, and yanked.

The jewel came free with an audible snap. In an instant it was over. The radiance playing through Odabeth flickered out as her body jerked, then fell still, her feet dangling where the Bloody Lady had hold of her.

At that point, everything slowed. Xelon screamed, the sound long and loud in Alice's ears. The Duchess raised her whip. It unfurled and shot through the air. It wrapped around the wrist that held the now-dimmed Eye. The Bloody Lady turned, releasing her hold on Odabeth. The princess dropped to the ground. Xelon scrambled toward her as fast as she could, still bound.

Alice pushed herself to her feet, eager to help, but the cold press of a razor's edge made her freeze.

"I wouldn't," an oddly familiar voice hummed.

The Black Knight stepped around from behind her, holding the hilt of the sword pressed to her neck. At least she thought it was the Black Knight. He wore the same armor, and sounded like him, though the voice was clearer because of one major change. His helmet was gone, and Alice found herself staring at the face of a boy who looked around nineteen, with bright red hair and eyes so blue they practically glowed.

"I'll take that." The Black Knight wrenched the Vorpal Blade from her hand. "On your knees."

Swallowing thickly, her entire body shaking with enough rage it made her vision blurry with tears, Alice lowered herself to kneel.

To the side, Chess managed to get to his feet, one arm still hanging useless at his side. Behind him, Haruka and the Duchess had drawn in even closer to the unconscious Odabeth and bound Xelon. Not-Fiends, still hissing and snarling, closed in around them.

"This is a mess." The Black Knight waved a hand, and the creatures drew back but maintained their positions surrounding the four of them.

"Alice," Haruka called when she spotted her.

"I'm all right," Alice said.

"And if you want her to stay that way, you'll drop your weapons." The Black Knight tapped the flat of his sword against Alice's shoulder.

Across the room, the Duchess's face had gone slack. Her mouth hung open as she stared at them, her eyes wide.

"I said drop your weapons," the Black Knight repeated.

Alice hissed when the blade bit at her exposed skin.

The Duchess released her whip, the handle smacking the ground. Haruka dropped her sword with a clank.

"That's it. Let's all just take a breath." The Black Knight played his eyes over them before looking toward the throne. "What do you want us to do with them, my lady?"

Near the throne, the Bloody Lady played her blackened fingers over the Eye, her attention so focused it looked as if she'd forgotten everything else that was going on.

"My lady?" the Black Knight called.

The Bloody Lady remained fixated on the Eye.

"My lady," he tried again, louder that time.

The Bloody Lady looked up, surprise dancing over her face at first before she scoffed. "Glad you could finally join us, useless lump."

The Black Knight's jaw tightened. "What would you like us to do with your prisoners?"

The Bloody Lady glanced around at them with a strange sort of disinterested annoyance. It was like she had come home to a mess in her living room and she had no idea what happened. "Lock them up."

◊ ◊ ◊

Alice trudged along as she and the others were marched down a corridor, with actual Fiends on either side of them—Alice couldn't believe she was glad to see the wolf-like creatures—and the Black Knight at their back. Those . . . abominations had stayed with the Bloody Lady.

Stone walls rose on either side of the hall, chipped and

cracked with age. The once-plush carpet was nothing but tatters and strips along the floor. This part of the palace wasn't as pristine as where they entered.

Haruka fell into step beside Alice with Xelon following behind, the chains of her bonds clanking. The Duchess, her arms full of unconscious princess, brought up the rear. The Black Knight kept his sword at her back.

"How could you?" The Duchess's voice, quiet as it was, cut through the silence like a knife.

Alice turned to find she'd stopped walking.

"Move." The Black Knight nudged her with the tip of his blade.

She didn't even flinch. Instead she turned to face him. "How could you do this?" Her voice wavered, thick with more emotion than Alice had ever heard come from her. "After everything we went through, everything we lost?"

The Black Knight stared at her, his jaw tight, his eyes bright. "Move." He chewed on the word, forcing it from behind clenched teeth.

"What happened?" Her words were a plea, begging for understanding. "Tell me, what is all this? Hum—"

Smack! The Black Knight's hand collided with the side of her face, and her head whipped around. Shock played through Alice and across the Duchess's expression. The Black Knight's had gone stormy. "Move. Or I run this through your heart."

The Duchess gazed at him. Alice's body trembled where her muscles had tightened, ready to throw herself forward.

"You already have," the Duchess murmured, before facing

forward again. They started walking, and she stared straight ahead, her cheek bright red.

Alice's mind whirled. What the hell was that about? Anastasia was lucky that asshole didn't kill her! They were all lucky, actually, to still be standing. How long would that luck last? What was going to happen now that the Bloody Lady had the Eye and the Heart? And just who was she?

The Fiends leading them veered off, and soon they were headed down a spiral of stone stairs. At the bottom, another dimly lit stretch of space was lined with metal bars. Cells, Alice realized, surprised at how . . . well, surprised she was. She'd never been in an actual palace dungeon before. It was just like in the movies.

"Stop," the Black Knight called before stepping around them. He moved over to a cell and pressed his hand to the wall. The stone flickered red beneath his fingers before the door swung outward. "Inside." He gestured with the Vorpal Blade.

Alice scowled as she went, not breaking eye contact. The others filed in behind her.

"Don't do this," the Duchess murmured after the door clanged shut behind them. "I . . . I don't know what is happening here, but we can talk through this."

The Black Knight glared at her through the bars before a smile pulled at his lips. "Enjoy your visit." He turned to go back the way he had come. The Fiends drew back, pressing into the surrounding shadows and vanishing.

"Visit?" Haruka asked just before a faint, raspy sound drifted from the deepest part of the cell, awash in shadow.

Everyone whirled. Alice stared, willing her eyes to adjust, hoping that maybe, just maybe, the noise had come from another cell, or perhaps the castle settling like an old house.

For a stretch of seconds, nothing happened, and no one made a sound.

Then, ever so slightly, something shifted in the darkness.

Thirty-Two

NO CHOICE

Once he was out of sight of the prisoners, the Black Knight relaxed his posture. His wounds continued to sing, his body wanting to give out.

Rest, his shaky knees said. *You need rest.*

Instead he trudged his way up the stairs and back through the dim halls of the Red Palace.

His eyes trailed over everything, every inch, every stone, every crack, every frame, every fading portrait. None of it was familiar.

He was surprised to find a small part of him had wanted it to be.

"You're the Red Knight," Hatta had said. "You went missing, same as the Red Queen!"

Missing. For a period of time that would explain why he couldn't remember any of his past. It didn't bother him before.

Before, all he knew was he had a purpose and a duty to his lady, the woman who had freed him, had told him he would have the vengeance his heart so craved.

Freed him from what, exactly? He couldn't remember that, either. His faulty mind angered him, his lack of knowing frustrated him, because now he wasn't sure who he could trust . . .

And that scared him.

Even so, he marched along to the throne room, stepping over the body of a felled Nightmare. Seated on the throne, Her Majesty had reverted to her natural form. The darkness and shadows had receded, though she was still covered in blood. An angry slash in her cheek bubbled faintly with pitch, the wound slowly closing. Her skin had taken on a sickly color, appearing ashen, grayed. Yet she still held herself with a regal grace as she angled around to face him as he approached.

He bent forward in a slight bow, the wound in his side screaming. "M-my lady."

"Where have you been?" Her expression was calm, serene, but the bite in her voice was anything but.

"I was waylaid during my retreat. I underestimated my enemy and paid for it dearly." His side throbbed as if in agreement.

"Do you think you've paid enough?"

"I . . . forgive me, Your Majesty."

"Mmm. Bring me the sword." She held out her hand expectantly.

The Black Knight drew the blade and climbed the few stairs to the throne, his injury panging him the entire way.

He then presented it with both hands. She took the blade and waved a hand dismissively. Reluctantly, he backed down the stairs to his previous spot at the base.

She laid the blade over her lap, the fingers of one hand tracing the surface while the fingers of the other curled and uncurled, again and again where she held the Eye, which pulsed faintly in her grip, like a dying star.

"I am glad you've achieved your goal in obtaining the Eye," he murmured.

"Yes, no thanks to you. Imagine being raised for a single purpose and failing so spectacularly at it I had to trick my enemies into bringing it to me."

Indignation flared within him. Before, he would've remained silent in the face of her onslaught, finding he deserved such punishment, but something . . . a part of him newly awakened . . . did not want to stand for this. Even so, he kept his tone as even as possible. "I did all you asked, Your Majesty. I learned of the Eye's location from the White Queen, I poisoned her and Addison Hatta so they would have no choice but to seek out a cure in the Heart, which meant restoring the Eye, as you wanted—"

"And at every turn, you somehow managed to let that girl get the best of you." Her tone sharpened once again. "She was to be a means to an end. And yet, for some reason, you've gone out of your way to . . . I don't know what you were doing, exactly, other than jeopardizing my plans. It causes me to wonder if you are indeed loyal. If you're strong enough to do what needs to be done."

"I am, Your Majesty."

"Oh? Let's find out." She tilted her head to the side. "Chester."

Chess stepped into view from where he had no doubt been skulking behind the throne, waiting at her beck and call. His arm was still broken, but shadow slithered along the length of it, slowly righting the injury. The sight repulsed the Black Knight. Grave as his own wounds were, he never wanted that muck near him.

"I have a gift for you," she purred, before extending the Vorpal Blade to Chess.

The Black Knight blinked in confusion, then incredulity. "I . . . You said the sword's power would only respond to my call, Your Majesty."

"Are you questioning me?"

He dropped his chin. "No, Your Majesty." But to see his sword in another's hands? No, he'd seen it in Alice's. She'd even wielded it against him. To see it in *those* hands . . . twisted something inside him he couldn't rightly understand.

"You aren't very good at keeping track of your things." Her eyes bore into his. "So I have no choice but to take them away."

"Am . . . I to go unarmed, Your Majesty?" He barely managed to temper his voice.

"I suppose not. Chester, give me your old sword."

Chess handed over the blade in a manner similar to how the Black Knight had presented the Vorpal Blade. Her Majesty took it by the hilt and flung it from herself the way one might fling soiled clothing. It landed with a clang at his feet.

"Go on," she cooed, when he didn't move to retrieve it.

Shame and indignation, and no small touch of anger, pouring through him, he bent to take up the weapon.

"Good. Now, then, about your loyalty to me. Let's test it. You can christen your new sword by driving it through Alice's heart."

His body stiffened as ice slid down his spine.

"Then you are to bring me her head. Do this, and I will question your fealty no longer."

It took a moment before he could manage the words. "Y-yes, Your Majesty."

She smiled and tilted toward Chess, beckoning him with a curl of her finger. "Chester will accompany you to make sure her friends don't give you too much trouble, and that you do as you're told. If, for some reason, you fail, Chester will finish the deed. It should be simple enough, with the Vorpal Blade."

A look crossed Chess's face that mirrored the apprehension in the Black Knight's heart. "I—I . . ."

She froze, her eyes lifting to her new pet. "You?" she coaxed gently, her expression anything but.

"I . . ." Chess's lips twisted as he fought for the words, but he couldn't manage them. His brow furrowed. He blinked, his eyes brightening just a tad. Then he glanced around, uncertainty clouding his expression.

Her Majesty reached out to press a hand to his torso. "What was that, Chess?" Her fingers flexed, and the shadows crawling over his broken arm pulsed.

And with that, his face settled back into complacency. The light left his eyes. "Yes, Your Majesty."

"Yes indeed." She pushed to her feet, still grasping the Eye.

The Black Knight was thankful for her fixation on it, otherwise she may have noticed the way every muscle in his body tightened when she brought Chess back under her control. Had she ever done that to him? Was she doing it now?

"Oh, and one more thing." Her Majesty gestured between them. "If you fail, Chester will kill you as well. Am I clear?"

"Yes, Your Majesty," the two of them replied together, Chess under her sway and the Black Knight out of reflex. It shocked him, how easily he agreed to his own execution merely because she willed it so.

No . . . This wasn't right. He wasn't sure what was anymore, but this certainly wasn't.

"Good. And also bring me the Poet. Now that I have the Eye, her real work begins." She stepped around the throne and toward the archway at the far end of the chamber. The shadows slid after her like obedient dogs.

Chess descended the stairs and came to a stop just in front of him. He stared with those dulled eyes.

"You're going to let her do this?" the Black Knight whispered, when he was certain she was out of earshot.

Chess didn't respond. The shadows around his arm continued to pulse.

The Black Knight sighed. "Seems you have no choice in the matter." Tightening his grip on the metal sword, he turned to head for the door, Chess on his heels. "And neither do I."

The two of them exited the throne room and moved into the long corridor that would take them to the dungeons. If he was going to save Alice's life, and his own, he had to do something before they reached the lower chambers. There, Her Majesty's "pets" kept watch.

"Or perhaps we do," he said evenly, just loud enough he knew Chess would hear. He didn't respond, though. "We don't have to do this. We can convince Her Majesty to spare them. Tell her they could best serve her alive." He cursed himself for being unable to keep the desperate edge from his voice.

The torches through the halls were cold. The glass and mirrors that reflected natural light throughout the palace fogged and dingy. This place was bleak, hollow, much like the growing fear tearing at his chest. Oh, he was afraid, well and truly terrified for the first time he could remember. It ate at him, slowly taking him over. But not only fear for himself, fear for Alice. For what would happen once they reached the dungeon. They approached the stairs leading down. It was now or never.

"I don't know what Her Majesty is doing to you," he murmured. "But . . . it doesn't last." He was proof of that.

Chess made some snorting noise, indignant. His feet scuffed against the carpet.

Clang. The Vorpal Blade hit the floor.

Confused, the Black Knight whirled. His eyes went wide.

Thirty-Three

COMPLICIT

Addison had not laid eyes on Castle Findest in almost two hundred years, but the memory of it was clear as crystal. The high spires still glittered in the sun, but the overall appearance of the place was dulled, dimmed, lacking life. Even in the heat of the day, the stone walls appeared cold, foreboding. Lush as the surrounding woods were, very little grew on the palace grounds. A fire had once burned here as bright and lively as the Red Queen herself, but that light had long left this place, same as she.

Or so everyone thought.

Drawing the horse to a stop, Addison dismounted. He patted her neck, the turquoise hair shimmering beneath his fingers. "Thank you for the ride."

The horse sniffed. "I still don't think going in there is a good idea." Her tone was two parts disapproval, one part fear.

"There has been a taint in the air for some time now. Other animals no longer linger. Even the plants have started to withdraw."

"How long has the taint been present, exactly?"

"Mmm. It is relatively recent." The horse shook her head as she turned this way and that. "A shame. This place was lovely once."

"It still is." Addison drew the sword he was able to procure from the town smith from its place strapped to the saddle. It was a simple blade but would serve his purposes. "Hopefully we can keep it from being lost completely."

"I wish you well in your endeavor." She turned to go, then paused. "Will you need a ride back? It's a fair distance on two legs."

"I don't wish to impose." And he doubted he would be making the journey at all.

"There is no imposition, Sir Knight."

"Just Addison is fine," he murmured. That name, that title, he wasn't worthy of either any longer. "But . . . there are others who may need help, even if I don't."

"Mmm. Very well. I will do what I can."

"I appreciate it." He set a hand to his chest and bowed.

The horse dipped her head before turning to trot back down the overgrown road.

Wincing, Addison dug his fingers into his chest a little. Naette's potion was working wonderfully, but the ache near his heart remained. Something told him no potion, no tonic, no salve would soothe this hurt.

Sword in hand, he headed for the side entry to the palace.

The massive doors were shut and sealed from the inside. He pressed his way into the receiving hall and couldn't help the way his breath caught just slightly.

Everything was exactly as it had been when he last visited. The high ceilings of glass and crystal that let in the daylight, tinting it the faintest red. The trappings and furnishings ever pristine. It was, as always, picture-perfect, but it lacked the one thing that always made such places sing softly

Life.

There was no staff, no gathered courtiers, no laughter or singing. The palace was all but a glorified husk, a pretty corpse.

Releasing a slow breath, Addison pressed on. Down one hallway, then the next, silent as possible. Gradually the sparkle faded. The walls and carpets grew weathered. Time may not have touched the grand entry, but it slithered through other parts of the palace.

He moved carefully, slowly, senses straining for signs someone was here. Natural shadows lined the halls. A hush filled the empty space. There was a sense of age and yet agelessness that clung to every facet of the palace, as if it lay dormant and, with the right Verse, could be awakened again.

The majesty of the grand palaces of Wonderland was much to behold. There was power at these nexus points, though neither Legracia nor Findest would ever rival the wonder of Emes.

He would have to be nostalgic later. Now he was focused on locating Alice, or anyone else who might be present. Xelon had to be here somewhere, at the very least.

Coming around a corner, he went still when he heard the distant roll of voices.

"We can convince Her Majesty to spare them. Tell her they could best serve her alive."

Addison recognized Humphrey's tenor tone, and his heart stuttered. Humphrey could be talking about any number of people, or he could be talking about Alice and the others. Either way, he couldn't leave whoever this was to their fate.

He shifted along the wall, pressed against the shadowed stone, and waited.

Humphrey stepped past first, a slight limp to his gait. Chess followed, shadows crawling along his body. Addison slipped forward, coming in behind him, moving silently, swiftly.

"I don't know what Her Majesty is doing to you," Humphrey said. "But . . . it doesn't last."

Addison launched himself forward, his arm going around Chess's neck. The boy was nearly a head shorter than him, making it a bit easier. He gagged, dropping his sword in order to claw at Addison's arm.

The blade hit the ground with a *clang*.

Humphrey spun and froze. His mouth opened as if to say something, but he didn't. He glanced up and down the hall swiftly before looking back to them as Chess struggled in Addison's arms.

The boy twisted and bucked, fingers clawing at Addison's sleeve. Addison rode the attempts to throw him off, tightening his hold until he felt the other start to go still. Catching Chess's weight when the boy went limp, he carefully lowered him to the ground. Kneeling beside him, he reached to check his breathing and pulse. Not dead. Good. Alice and Courtney would be quite cross.

Addison glanced up and right into Humphrey's shocked face, then smiled. "Hey."

Humphrey's mouth worked noiselessly for a second before he looked to Chess, then back and forth between the two of them, lips pursed.

"Where are the others?" Addison asked as he hooked his arms under Chess's and dragged him the short distance to a nearby pillar, propping him up against it.

"What are you doing?" Humphrey hissed.

"Rescue mission. Sounds like you were thinking the same."

"I . . . wasn't . . ."

Addison glanced up and down the hall for any signs anyone or anything had heard that brief scuffle. "Sure you were. If you weren't, you wouldn't've have let that happen."

"I didn't—"

"You didn't stop me. You could've, but you didn't. Ergo, you let it happen."

Humphrey puffed his cheeks but didn't say anything.

Gone his memories might be, but he was definitely still himself in there, and that was a comforting thing.

"While I appreciate your assistance with step one, there's still a lot of work to be done," Addison said. "Where are your captives?"

Humphrey glared at him, his expression stormy, his lips tight.

Addison fought back a smile. The other knight used to get that same look whenever Addison did something to irritate him. But this wasn't hiding the other's greaves or putting dew milk in his tea. "You're already complicit in this rescue, you may as well go all the way."

"Am I?" Humphrey snapped. Then his eyes went to the Vorpal Blade. It still lay where Chess had dropped it.

Addison tensed. If Humphrey went for it, he wouldn't be able to stop him.

Humphrey flexed his fingers. "Let's test that theory."

Thirty-Four

REUNITED

Alice's whole body went rigid as she waited for whatever lurked in the shadows to pounce. If it was a Nightmare, none of them had any weapons to defend themselves. If it was something else . . . Well, Alice didn't really want to imagine what else would be skulking around down here.

The shadows shifted again. Everyone froze.

"A-are . . . the ravens flying?" a small voice chirped, just before feet shuffled and a familiar face came into the dim light.

"Oh my god!" Alice stumbled the short distance across the cell and threw herself down beside the mousy girl. Her knees banged against the cold stone, but she didn't care about the pain. Her friend was alive!

Maddi was never much of a hugger, but she wrapped her arms around Alice and squeezed.

Alice could feel her trembling, shaking so hard it sent shivers through her.

"L-lot . . . lost . . . and shadow . . ." Maddi's voice quivered as well, soft and withdrawn. "In a past. Far gone, n-no, no!"

"It's okay." Alice sniffed and drew back, wiping at her face. "It's okay, we're here."

Alice hugged Maddi again before withdrawing so the Duchess could do the same, smiling and speaking softly to the bartender. Behind them, Xelon had gone to her knees, the unconscious Odabeth lain against her. Haruka stood near the door, her eyes flickering between the group and the stairwell.

"Trapped," Maddi breathed. "Trapped, a flutter, a wing and stutter."

"Are you all right?" Alice asked, not understanding a word the other girl said, but her frightened tone spoke volumes.

"Moonlight . . . moonlight song!"

The Duchess settled beside them, her gaze intent as Maddi babbled her usual, though now frightened, babble.

"She says that woman, the one we fought, has been experimenting with Slithe and corpses. She's . . . trying to raise an army of undead Nightmares, one that—" Her head whipped around to Maddi, and she said something in quick Russian.

Maddi nodded, her head bobbing.

"An army that what?" Alice pressed. Undead Nightmares sounded bad enough, but something told her that situation could be made worse.

"That can't be purged . . ." The Duchess trailed off, her eyes wide.

"Is that possible?" Haruka asked.

The look on the Duchess's face said not only was it possible, but that she'd seen it before.

Maddi continued speaking, snapping the Duchess out of her stare.

"She says . . . Chess was one of those experiments."

Alice's stomach plummeted. Did this mean he was really dead?

"But the process was unstable," the Duchess continued. "So, because of Madeline's service as Master Mixologist to Queen Portentia, that woman sent Chess to capture her. She believed Madeline could help perfect the procedure. Maddi worked for her, but flubbed it here and there to buy time until she was rescued. She *did* manage to stabilize Chess, but doing so keeps him under the woman's control, because of the Slithe. It's . . . different from normal Slithe, bound to that woman's essence somehow. Madeline doesn't know if there's a way to sever the connection without . . . without killing him."

Tears brimming, Maddi looked to Alice. She sniffed and winced. "I—I . . ." Another flinch as her lips worked. "So . . . s-sorry . . ."

Her own tears spilling over her cheeks, Alice leaned in to wrap her arms around the other girl, squeezing. "It's not your fault."

"Pardon me for interrupting a tender moment."

Alice drew back, fury coiling through her, as she and everyone else turned to find the Black Knight peering at them through the bars. He stood with his sword drawn, the black blade resting against his shoulder in a casual threat.

"Her Majesty wishes a word, Alice," he murmured, his tone heavy.

"Tell her majesty she can kiss my ass."

"Happy to, but I'm afraid if you don't comply, I'll have to start poking holes in your friends, and neither of us wants that."

Alice stiffened.

"Just come quietly, and they'll be spared." He pressed his hand to the wall, and the door popped open slightly.

For a moment Alice thought about rushing him. They had more numbers, they could overpower him, get the sword. But then she noticed the shadows lining the walls, shifting, glowing eyes blinking in and out of sight, a fanged growl here and there.

This place was Nightmare Central; they'd probably be torn apart before they reached the stairs.

"I come, and they don't get hurt?"

"Not by me."

Alice pushed to her feet. She started for the door, only to draw up short when Haruka stepped in front of her.

"You don't have to do this," Haruka murmured. "We can fight."

"Maybe we can, but not right now. I'll go see what she wants. You guys try and come up with something to get us out of here."

"You know I can hear you, right?" the Black Knight called.

Annoyed, Alice hugged the other Dreamwalker, then stepped past her and to the Black Knight's side. He closed the door, which locked with a clank, before turning to lead the way toward the stairs.

The two of them climbed in silence, which was a bit strange. Usually the Black Knight was . . . chatty. But this time he just seemed somber. Alice still wanted to beat his entire ass. He'd nearly killed her friends, kidnapped them, torn up her house with her mom inside! If she didn't manage anything else, she was going to kick his teeth in.

At the top of the stairs, the Black Knight moved a few steps into the hall, then stopped. Alice did as well, tensing as he heaved a sigh.

"I'm sorry, kitten, but you're not going to see Her Majesty."

She didn't like the way he said that. "Then where am I going?"

"Home," a familiar voice said. "If I have anything to say about it."

Her heart leaping, Alice whirled and came face-to-face with Addison. Shock locked down her tongue, but her body moved on its own, hurrying to throw herself at him. Her arms went around his neck, and she buried her face there as well.

His arms wrapped around her in turn, and for a moment she was safe. She was okay. And he was squeezing her. But then she drew back, wiping at her face, her mind going a mile a minute.

"W-what are you doing here? H-how . . . but . . . the exile . . ." That was when she noticed how pale he was, how dull his eyes had grown, the edges rimmed in orange. "Oh my god . . . you're . . . you're dying . . ."

"Can't worry about that now, we have to get out of here."

Alice stared, blinking, her mind trying to make sense of what was going on. Then she remembered the Black Knight and whirled to find him standing nearby, his arms folded over his chest. Her head whipped back and forth, confusion building. And if that wasn't bad enough, that's when she caught sight of Chess slumped over unconscious behind a nearby pillar.

She pointed. "What—"

Hatta took her shoulders and brought her around to face him. "I know, it's a lot, but we don't have time. The woman behind all of this, it's the R—"

"The Bloody Lady?"

"Who?"

"She's all red and covered in blood."

Hatta blinked rapidly. "Sh . . . she's not the Red Queen?"

Alice shook her head as her shoulders hunched. "I-I . . . I don't think so, no one recognized her."

Hatta's brow furrowed. He muttered about something not making sense, but then shook his head. "Fine. This . . . Bloody Lady, then. Humphrey says she has the Eye."

"Humphrey?" Alice asked.

"That's Humphrey." Hatta gestured to the Black Knight, who waggled his fingers.

Again, Alice glanced back and forth. "So y'all for real *know* this asshole." First the exchange with Duchess earlier, and now this? The hell was going on around here?

Hatta flinched. "Yes. It's . . . complicated. He used to be the Red Knight, but then he went missing at the same time as the Red Queen. We're still not sure what happened to either of them, and Humphrey doesn't remember anything before he woke up as the Imposter, and . . . Long story short, he's on our side."

Alice really didn't know what to say to that. She just stared at Hatta, then stared at the Black . . . Humphrey, then at Hatta again. "So, what, we're good now? Let bygones be bygones?"

"You don't have to let anything go, princess," Humphrey said. "But we can't do this right now. The . . . Bloody Lady— strewth that's a ridiculous name—"

Alice glared. "Then what's her actual name?"

He fidgeted. "I only know her as my lady."

"I thought she might be the Red Queen, but . . . it seems I was mistaken," Addison said.

Alice nodded. "Then Bloody Lady it is."

Humphrey sighed. "The Bloody Lady plans to raise an army to exact a vengeance I thought I wanted, but now I . . . I'm sure that's not something that'll end well for any of us."

Alice scoffed. "Oh, so now that your ass is on the chopping block, too, you feel a way about all this nonsense."

"Total memory loss shifts a person's priorities. Are we going to stop her or argue about it?"

Alice continued to scowl. "Is Chess all right?"

"Far as we can tell," Addison said.

"Besides the being-half-dead thing," Humphrey murmured.

"*Must* you?" Hatta asked.

Humphrey said something else, but Alice had stepped away and over to her unconscious friend. The last time she saw him, he'd been trying to take her head off. Now he was just lying here, shadows crawling over him, his face slightly drawn up as if in pain, and—if Maddi was right—there might not be any way to free him without . . .

Alice straightened and turned to face the two of them, who'd fallen silent as they watched her. "So what's the plan?"

"Take her by surprise. Use numbers to overwhelm her," Addison said.

"With the number of Nightmares at her command, doubtful." Humphrey frowned. "And with both the Eye and the Heart, if we don't do this right, we're all dead. I can get close enough to get the Eye away from her. Then we might have a chance."

"What about everyone else?" Alice asked.

"They'll have to stay where they are," Humphrey said. "For now."

"Why?" she shot back.

"I was ordered to come get you. Well, your head. If I let the rest of them out, she'll be alerted long before we reach her."

"Faster than when you show up without my head?" Alice ran one hand along her neck.

Addison reached to weave his fingers between hers. "They're safe where they are. Safer than we're about to be, at any rate."

"And if we fail?" Alice asked, her voice faltering. *If* I *fail* . . .

"It won't much matter either way," Humphrey said.

Alice shook her head. "We can't just leave them trapped down there. There has to be something we can do."

Addison released a slow breath.

"Nothing that leaves everyone alive." Humphrey frowned and sheathed the Vorpal Blade against his back. "I . . . might be able to buy a few minutes, but only a few. You'll have to move fast."

"What about you?" Addison asked, an odd note of concern in his voice. Alice had to remind herself that this was a friend of his essentially back from the dead. She was quite familiar with that particular feel.

"What about me," Humphrey murmured. He shook his head when Addison looked to protest. "I can make a quick getaway if I need to."

"You can't face her alone," Addison pressed.

"You're in no condition to help me," Humphrey fired back.

"Addison's right," Alice said, much as she hated it. "You're injured. I can tell by the way you move."

Humphrey snorted. "Thought it was because you're the one who injured me."

"Little column A, little column B. But you can't do this by yourself. And it's too important to risk it. I'll go with you. Addison, you can get the others and get out whatever way you got in."

Addison shook his head. "No, I can't—"

"Look at you." Alice gestured at him. "You're about as bad off as he is, if not worse. You can't fight."

"But he can?" Addison scoffed.

"I honestly don't care what happens to him." Alice folded her arms over her chest.

"Offended," Humphrey murmured.

Addison lifted his hands. "It doesn't matter. I can't just watch the two of you go off to face her." He reached to take Alice's hand, his thumb stroking against the back of her fingers.

Alice gazed up at him, her heart in her throat. She wanted nothing more than to press into his arms, her lips to his, but now wasn't the time. And they had company.

"You have to. I know it's hard, but we don't have any other options," she said.

"And we don't have much time," Humphrey said. "Whatever we're going to do, we need to do it now. She's bound to start wondering where I am."

Addison didn't look happy but nodded, his lips pursed. "Fine. But you had better come back to me. The both of you."

Humphrey gave Addison a look Alice couldn't quite decipher before he turned to her. "Now I need to figure out how to get you across this castle, alive, without alerting her."

"Let me save you the trouble."

Alice spun toward the sound of a voice. The last thing she saw was the Bloody Lady standing at the end of the hall, her skin so sickly it appeared white. She lifted a hand, and everything went black.

Thirty-Five

WHAT YOU GONE DO?

Pain jolted through Alice, white hot.

"Ah!" Her eyes flew open. She twisted to try and sit up, but her body wouldn't move.

It wasn't the restrictive press of something holding her down, just . . . when she tried to wave her arms or flex her fingers, nothing happened!

She floated, her arms and legs spread, caught as if in water.

All was darkness and shadow save for the occasional flash of crimson lightning.

"W-what . . ." Her voice echoed around her and between her ears. "What's happening? Where am I?"

Panting, pain singing through her body, she pulled even harder. Nothing.

"Help . . . help!"

Panic started to set in. Chest heaving, her vision waned.

"Alice . . ." The voice was soft, careful. "Alice, you have to focus."

Another flash of lightning. Another stab of pain. She screamed.

"Alice." The voice pressed in, closer now.

She shook her head, gritting her teeth as red crackled, popped, and fizzled along her body. God, it hurt.

"Alice!"

She jerked, her eyes fluttering open. Hovering in the darkness was . . . well, her. Dressed in the same glowing skirts of white light, Reflection-Alice stared at her, her expression saddened.

"Get up, Alice."

"I—I can't. I can't move!"

"Hatta, Humphrey, they're fading. Even now, the Bloody Lady turns them to her will."

"N-no . . ."

"They will be lost. Unless you stop her."

Tears burned hot against Alice's face. "I—I can't. I can't stop her, she's too strong."

"Yes, you can."

Alice whimpered.

"We can. If you finally trust me." Reflection-Alice drifted forward. She pressed a hand to Alice's chest and, with a sudden rush of warmth, Alice's limbs fell free of whatever had been restricting them.

She flailed, her balance thrown off, but she was able to bring it back under her control. She wiggled her hands, holding them up in front of her face. Then she looked at her reflection, who watched her with such a strange expression.

"Who . . . who are you?"

Reflection-Alice smiled. "Let's say . . . I'm your Muchness."

Alice's eyes widened.

Reflection-Alice nodded. "That part of you that believes in you, even when the rest of you doesn't."

"My . . . You look like—"

"Well, it's how you imagine yourself at your most powerful, so it is not much of a surprise."

"Moon Princess. Right." Alice swallowed, glancing around. "W-where are we?"

"Where I've always been." Reflection-Alice reached to set a hand to Alice's chest. Warmth spread from where her fingers pressed gently. "The Bloody Lady is using the Eye and the Heart to try and corrupt you. I was able to hide us away in the deepest part of your heart, but . . . that meant going somewhere you didn't want to."

Alice was about to ask what that meant when the darkness behind Reflection-Alice began to peel backward. Light filled that small space, and at its center rested her dad's smiling face.

"Hey, Baby Moon! What you up to?"

Something inside Alice cracked open. "D-daddy?"

Another section of the black peeled open. Another image of her father, still smiling. "Hey, Baby Moon!"

One after the other, visions of her father's face faded in, surrounding her. Some smiled. Some laughed. Some frowned. And they each called out to her.

"Why so down?"

"Don't do me, little girl."

"Alice."

"Fix your face."

"Alice."

"Hey, Baby Moon."

"Alice!"

Alice pressed her hands to her mouth as the sadness filling her threatened to spill over. He . . . he was everywhere.

Reflection-Alice gestured widely. "This is where you keep him. Here you are at your strongest, but also your weakest. Here your heart is most guarded. But here, if the darkness reaches you, is where it can pull you under."

Reflection-Alice's words barely registered as memories of her father swirled around them. Memories of their time together, of him teaching her to ride a bike, to sew her first costume. Memories of them watching Saturday morning cartoons, of him shouting at a football game, of him calling out to her.

"Sup, Baby Moon?"

"Alice whimpered. She didn't want to be here. She wanted to be anywhere but here.

"You can't let it overwhelm you."

"No!" Alice pressed her hands over her ears. She didn't want this. It was too much.

Crimson lightning arced through the black. Reflection-Alice glanced around, a look of fear crossing her face.

"Alice, we don't have time."

Alice shook her head, drawing back when her reflection

reached for her. She didn't want to be touched, she didn't want to be here, she didn't want any of this!

Crash! The lightning struck one of the memories. It shattered. Pain spiked through Alice's head. She doubled over, clutching it.

"Alice!" her reflection called. "You have to get up!"

Another arc of lightning, another window shattered. Now the space around them began to fill with lightning.

Reflection-Alice spun in a circle, glancing around at the chaos pouring in. "She's going to break through . . . Alice, get up!"

Why . . . what's the point . . .

"Alice! Ah!" Reflection-Alice jerked as lightning struck her. It darted across her, shrieking and crackling.

The pain in Alice's head intensified.

He's gone . . .

"But you're still here, Baby Moon."

"Daddy?" Alice squeezed her eyes shut. "I can't do it . . ."

"Yes, you can. You can do anything, don't you know that?"

"I can't do this."

"But you already did. You're here because you did it."

"I can't!"

"Breathe, Baby Moon."

Alice drew a shaky breath. Pain radiated through her body. Someone screamed. Maybe her. Maybe Reflection-Alice. She didn't care.

"Again."

She took another breath.

"Again."

And another.

"That's my girl."

"It . . . it hurts, Daddy. It hurts so much."

The darkness faded, and Alice found herself wrapped in one of the remaining memories of her father. The sun was bright in the sky; the air smelled of fresh cut grass, dirt, and summer; and Alice sat on her father's lap, where he held her after picking her up from the sidewalk. A small bike lay to the side, its wheels spinning. Pain radiated up Alice's leg from where her knee was split open, bleeding freely. Little Alice blinked up at her father through tears.

He sighed as he dabbed at the tender skin around her wound. She whimpered and gave a little squeal.

"She okay?"

Alice recognized her mother's voice. She stood in the doorway to their house, a towel in her hands, her face scrunched as she squinted into the sun.

Alice's dad glanced over his shoulder and up the driveway. "She's good, Tina. I got it."

He looked back to Alice and smiled.

"It hurts," Alice murmured, wiping at her snotty nose.

"I know it hurts, baby. And I'm sorry. I wish I could make the pain go away, but I can't. It's gonna have to heal on its own." He finished cleaning the wound, then taped a bandage into place. "There. Now, ready to try again?"

Alice glanced at the bike and fidgeted.

"No?"

"Mmph."

"Why not?"

"What if I fall again?"

"You might." Dad nodded. "Might be worse next time. But you might just keep going. Then you might just get better. Then? You might be the best." He smiled, tickling her other knee. "My girl, best bicycle rider in the neighborhood."

Alice giggled. "The world!"

"The world!"

She smiled, then looked at the bike again. An ugly feeling twisted in her stomach. "I'm scared . . ."

"That's all right. It's okay to be scared. I was scared when you fell over. My heart near jumped out of my chest." He set his hand over it. "But we can't let fear control us. We can't let it make decisions for us, neither. You wanna learn to ride a bike?"

Alice nodded. The heavy balls at the ends of her braids bounced against her shoulders.

"Don't let fear take that from you. Don't ever let fear steal anything from you, because it'll sure try. Sometimes fear lies and tells you you can't do something when you can do anything."

Alice rubbed at the edge of the bandage lightly. "But . . . but what if I'm really scared?" She stole another glance at the bike.

Dad sighed and scratched at the bushel of hair along his chin as his nose scrunched. He was thinking. "If you're ever really scared, I want you to take a deep breath. Like this." He inhaled, then exhaled slowly. "Go on."

Alice mimicked it.

"Again."

She took another breath.

"That's right. When you're really scared, just breathe, Baby Moon. Then you say to yourself, I am Alice Kingston. Go on."

"I am Alice Kingston."

"And I am afraid."

"A-and . . ."

Dad nodded.

"And I—I am afraid."

"But fear cannot stop me."

Alice blinked. "But fear cannot stop me."

"Now, all together. I am Alice Kingston, and I am afraid, but fear cannot stop me."

"I am Alice Kingston, and I am afraid, but fear cannot stop me."

Dad smiled wide. "That's right. Can't nothing stop you, and that's the truth. Remember that, and that I love you, and you'll be all right."

"And Mommy, too?"

"Yeah, I guess Mommy loves you, too." He chuckled, kissing Alice's forehead. "Okay. You're afraid you might fall again. But?"

"But fear cannot stop me!"

"That's my girl. So what you gone do, Baby Moon?"

Alice looked to the bike . . . and smiled.

Her eyes fluttered open. All around her the shards of memories floated in the black, illuminated by arcs of lightning stabbing through the darkness.

"A-A-Alice . . ." Reflection-Alice was coming apart, her body fissuring the same way the memories had. "Alice . . . g-g-get . . . get up . . . Alice . . . Alice . . ." She was fading.

Pushing against the cold and hurt pouring through her, Alice reached out to latch onto her reflection's hand. With a sound like shattering glass, Reflection-Alice solidified. She gasped, her glow returning. Panting, Reflection-Alice glanced around, then at her. She smiled softly. "You did it . . ."

"I did . . . and I'm still afraid . . ." She held out her other hand.

Reflection-Alice took that hand. "But?" Her light poured down her arms and into Alice's, filling her. Warmth spread through Alice's body, like feeling returning to sleeping nerves. Her skin tingled. Her heart pounded. Both of them glowed now, brighter and brighter. Alice knew this light. It had filled her hands and then her sword. It had come to her rescue when she slayed the Nightmare in the football field. It had cradled her when she fell from Chou's basket. It was her. This entire time, it was her. It was *hers*.

"But fear cannot stop me," Alice whispered.

Reflection-Alice smiled. "It never could." Then her entire body went white, bright and blinding, until there was nothing left but her shine. That shine poured into Alice through where they held hands, flowing up her arms, filling her from the top of her head to the soles of her feet.

What you gone do, Baby Moon? Dad's voice echoed all around her.

Thirty-Six

THIS

Alice opened her eyes. She stared at stone overhead, the stone on either side of her. Stone pressed against her back, cold and unyielding where she lay on the floor. Her body was heavy, clumsy, but under her control as she struggled to sit up.

To her left, Humphrey lay on the ground, unconscious. Ribbons of shadow pulsed where they circled him, binding him. Red lightning jolted through him, his body jerking. To her right, Addison was similarly trapped. Fear spiking through her, Alice threw her body forward, crawling toward him.

"A-Addison . . ." She reached him, hands pressing his face. His skin was pale and cold to the touch. He didn't respond when she shook him. "Addison! Ah!" Red lightning zapped her fingertips, stinging them.

"I-impossible . . ."

Alice spun. At the far side of the room, the Bloody Lady tilted heavily against a pillar. Her skin had nearly washed white, her bright red hair like flames around her head. Her eyes had darkened to complete pools of black. Her veins stuck out bright red beneath her skin, a webwork of bloody coils and curves, like she had been tattooed with it. She looked . . . like a wraith, a pale shadow of herself. At the center of her brow, the eye pulsed dimly, flickering, dying. Whatever she'd done, it'd clearly taken a lot out of it and her.

The Bloody Lady panted with effort. "You . . ." She clutched at her chest.

That was when Alice saw it, the faint pulsing of red between her fingers.

"You *dare*!?"

The Heart pulsed again. A sort of buzzing filled Alice's ears. Her own heart fluttered.

The Vorpal Blade went snicker-snack . . .

There, on the ground between them, the Black Knight's sword lay against the stone. Darkness hovered along the edge, but there was something else. A faint hum shivered along the length of the blade, wavering. Alice reached for it.

"Who are you to deny me?" the Bloody Lady snarled.

Her knees trembling, Alice pushed to her feet. "I am Alice Kingston . . ." The hilt of the Vorpal Blade warmed in her hand.

"You . . . are nothing." The Bloody Lady flexed her fingers, and darkness spread between them. It crackled with red lightning. "I don't know how you broke free of my Verse, but I will suffer your impudence no longer." The pulsing around the Heart increased.

So did Alice's heartbeat. "And I am afraid."

What you gone do, Baby Moon?

Before Alice could think, she was moving, legs wavering but holding, her joints aching with the sudden force of her strength. Her eyes stung. Her chest tightened as her lungs struggled to take in air for the briefest moments. Heat bled through her body, to the palms of her hands. The Vorpal Blade went white. She swung.

The Bloody Lady screamed as she flung up a hand. The blade collided with a wave of darkness that had formed like a shield. Alice lashed out with a kick aimed beneath the shield, driving her foot into the woman's stomach. As she stumbled back, Alice drove forward with another swing of the Vorpal Blade. The Bloody Lady threw out another shield, but this time Alice was ready. She angled the blade to glide along the darkness, then used the momentum to swing around in another swipe. The Bloody Lady scrambled backward, barely avoiding being cut in half.

She pressed a white hand to her stomach, her chest heaving. The Heart pulsed. The Eye flickered. "No." The Bloody Lady shook her head, her eyes wide, the red lines in her flesh bulging. "No! I have . . . the Eye, I have the Heart! I am fear incarnate! How . . . are you doing this? You cannot . . . unless . . ."

Alice took a slow breath and shifted her stance, gripping the sword with both hands. "Fear cannot stop me." Alice clenched her fingers. The light in the Vorpal Blade brightened. With a swing, it burst forth from the blade, driving toward the Bloody Lady, who raised her arms, another shield at her fingertips. But she hadn't seen Alice dart forward, hiding in the arc's wake.

The light had concealed her, and now she was too close for the Bloody Lady to do anything about it. Her dark eyes flew wide as Alice drove the sword into the woman's chest.

The Bloody Lady gasped, the sound a mix of pain and surprise. The power in her fingers sputtered away. The stone at the center of her chest cracked up the center.

Alice snatched at the Eye. Her fingers latched on. Pain tore through her hand, a feeling like holding broken glass, but she didn't let go. Instead, she tightened her grip and yanked. The Eye came away with a crack. The Bloody Lady's eyes, the pupils rimmed in flame and shadow, found Alice's.

"You," she snarled, her voice a rasp.

Alice, her entire body trembling, twisted the Vorpal Blade where it dug into the woman's body. SNAP! The handle came away with Alice, the blade protruding from the woman's chest.

Alice stumbled back, nearly falling over. The Bloody Lady grasped at the broken blade with both hands. With a squelch, she pulled it free and let it clatter to the floor, coated in pitch and blood. The same welled up past her lips. Clutching the wound in her chest, she stumbled backward, her breath hitching, before she crumpled to the ground and lay still.

For a moment, nothing and no one moved. The only sounds in the room were Alice's labored breaths as her chest heaved. She stared, her nerves buzzing, her muscles tight. Was that it? Was it over? She needed to make sure.

Ever so slowly, her fingers trembling, she extended the jagged edge of the sword toward the dead woman. Then took a step. And another. And another, until she stood over the body.

Still, nothing happened.

Okay. Okay . . . Alice tightened her grip and raised the broken blade overhead. One more time through the heart should do it.

Fwoosh. With a sound like water slouching down a drain, the surrounding shadows leaped forward. Two Not-Fiends slithered past Alice. She jumped back as the creatures swarmed around the Bloody Lady, hissing and snarling. Alice held the broken sword in front of her. She didn't know if she could use it to kill these creatures, but she would sure as hell try.

Only, they didn't attack. Instead, they nosed at the body, giving soft sounds that were almost whines. Then they laid on either side of her, stretching their bodies to press against hers. Alice stared, not . . . entirely sure what to do, what she even *could* do, especially on her own. That's when the Not-Fiends, their inky forms prostrate, started melting.

Skin slackened and slid loose, pouring outward and over the Bloody Lady, swallowing her up until she was cocooned in darkness and there was nothing left but a large mass of gently writhing shadow. Alice's stomach churned at the sight. The mass gave a loud *crack* that made her jump, then it began to dissolve, soaking into the ground. The shadows hissed and steamed, not unlike a dying Nightmare.

Alice stared, eyes wide, as all of it vanished from sight, leaving nothing but a dark stain against the stone.

For a moment, she didn't move. She didn't speak. All she could do was breathe. Then she looked to her throbbing hand, her fingers split where they clutched the Eye. It was cracked, but whole. The hilt of the Vorpal Blade shivered in her other hand, the darkness falling from it, melting away to reveal a polished, bright red stone where the tang of the sword was snapped into pieces.

"A-Alice?"

She glanced over her shoulder and met Addison's slightly darkened gaze. Stumbling toward him, she dropped the Eye and the hilt and reached to curl her arms around him. The shadows and the lightning had faded, but he still looked like hell.

"You did it, milady . . ."

To the side, Humphrey groaned as he started to come around. Chess did the same.

"Go on," Addison said.

Alice pressed a kiss to his lips, then hurried over to drop beside her friend. "Chess?" she called softly, her hands hovering over him.

Chess rolled onto his back, hissing as he winced. His eyes found hers, and Alice started. They were . . . bright. Impossibly bright, glowing even.

"Alice . . . what . . ." He glanced around, then moved to push up, flinching.

"Go slow," she murmured, reaching to help him. To the side, Addison was doing the same with Humphrey, who sat up with a hand to his head while Addison said something she couldn't quite hear.

Braced against one hand, the other pressed to his middle, Chess lifted his gaze to her. Those violet eyes of his practically shimmered with emotion. He shook his head, shifting backward slightly. "I . . . I'm so sorry."

"Chess . . ."

"I saw . . . what she made me do. I heard it. I didn't want

to do any of it, but I . . . she . . ." His throat worked in a thick swallow.

Alice swallowed as well, trying to ease the burn rising at the back of her throat and pushing behind her eyes. "It's okay."

"But it's not!" He flinched and pressed a hand over his face. "I tried to fight it, fight her, but it was like I was drowning, and no matter which direction I swam, I couldn't come up for air." His voice trembled, and when he lowered his hand to stare at his fingers, she noticed the rest of him did as well. "I wasn't strong enough. I couldn't control myself."

"You did, at first. When you . . ." *Kissed me.* "First came back. That time in the parking lot."

Chess shook his head slowly. "I wasn't in control then. Not much. I was supposed to go after someone. A . . . princess?"

Odabeth, Alice figured. That was who he went after when he tore into the pub. Did he remember doing that? "You were yourself, at least briefly."

"Not enough for it to matter."

Alice set a hand to the side of his face. "Enough that you were still in there. And you're here now. We'll figure out the rest. Here, let me see." She reached to gently peel his shirt up. Beneath the fabric, his skin was still torn, ragged, and bleeding black. Her throat tightened at the sight.

"How bad?" Chess murmured.

"You're alive." Alice lowered the shirt. "That's what matters." *Maddi will be able to do something about this*, Alice told herself. And she clung to that as she glanced to where Addison and Humphrey were struggling to their feet. "You two all right?"

"In one piece, for the most part." Addison winced, pressing

a hand to his chest. His face twisted with pain, and he blinked, as if confused.

Alice stiffened. "What's wrong?"

"Nothing," he said, a bit too quickly. "Just a bit banged up."

He took a step that ended with him faltering and dropping to his knees.

Humphrey scrambled to catch him as Alice clambered toward them.

"Addison? What's *wrong*?" She pressed in at his other side, helping keep him upright. "And don't you even think about telling me no 'nothing.'"

A smile pulled at Addison's lips. It was tight, his expression still pinched. "No harm in . . . thinking." He lifted his gaze to hers, and Alice nearly recoiled. All of the color had been bled from his irises, the black of his pupils cracked across the whites. The amber ring flared brighter than before. It was like his insides were turning to ash and embers right in front of her.

"What is this?" she breathed.

"Naette's potion wore off." Addison flinched.

Alice shook her head. She didn't understand this, any of it.

"The Verse . . . my exile. I'm too far in." He chuckled faintly. "The potion was staving off the worst of the effects—now the Verse is . . . basically melting me from the inside."

"Potio—exile . . ." Her mind tumbled over Addison's words, picking out their meaning and then tripping right into a full-blown panic.

He was too far from the Gateway. He was still in exile. There was no way to get him back in time. He coughed, so hard it shook his entire frame. His hand came away stained red and black.

"N-no." Alice pressed in closer as he sank toward the ground, his skin paling out to a sickly gray right in front of her eyes.

"I-it's all right, milady." His chest heaved. His breaths came quicker, the sounds thick and wet. "It's all . . ."

"What do I do?" This couldn't be happening. "Tell me what to do!" She wouldn't let this happen! She pushed his hair out of his face as he struggled to breathe.

"Pardon," Humphrey said, his voice tight. Alice had forgotten he was there, standing over them. "He needs to be pardoned, or it will kill him."

Pardoned? How were they going to—"Odabeth," Alice realized. In the next instant she was on her feet, yanking Humphrey after her. "Go get the princess, she can do it."

Humphrey turned and limped toward the stairs.

Alice dropped to her knees once more just as Addison gave one last rasping breath before falling still. "Addison?" Her insides went cold. "Addison!" She gripped his shoulders and shook them. When he didn't respond, she shook harder, her vision blurring, her eyes and throat burning.

Voices drifted up from the stairs. The Duchess, Maddi.

"They're coming. You have to hold on, okay? H-hold on, they . . . they're . . ." She bent to press her face to his motionless chest. "They're coming . . . Don't you leave me. Don't you . . ." The fire in her eyes filled the rest of her. The burn spread, merciless, unyielding.

Someone dropped in at her side. She didn't bother opening her eyes to see who. Hands pressed in against his chest, fingers brushing hers.

"Addison Hatta," Odabeth said, her words rushed and airy

around panted breaths. "You are hereby pardoned of all crimes against Wonderland. I release you."

Alice straightened, swiping at her eyes and nose.

He didn't move.

Seconds ticked by.

He didn't . . . move . . .

"N-no." Alice's voice crumbled. Pieces of her broke away, scattering like dust. "No, you can't—Addison. You hear that, you're pardoned. Addison!"

Odabeth sat back, her face pinched with sadness.

"It requires two," the Duchess said from somewhere behind Alice, her voice cracking. "Two royals banished him. The pardon requires—"

"No!" Alice screamed. "He's dying. Do something . . ." But no one moved. Everyone just stared at her, wearing sadness like masks.

Not again . . .

A hand fell to her shoulder. "Alice," Haruka murmured.

Alice shook her off. The action flung her face-first into the memory of that night . . . She stood in the waiting room, the doctors saying there was nothing more they could do. Her father was gone. Her mother reached for her, and Alice . . . Alice ran. Away from the hospital. Away from the truth. Into the night. Into the dark. Into the monstrous fear.

Into Hatta.

With a shaky breath, Alice brushed dark green strands from his pale face. "W-well done . . . Sir Knight . . ."

Thirty-Seven
PARDON?

The last time Addison felt pain like this, he stood on the terrace of the Western Gateway. The stone was bright and blazing in the daylight. The silvered trees glittered and sparkled. It was beautiful, a gorgeous backdrop for his shame to play out.

"Addison Hatta." The White Queen drew her shoulders back and lifted her chin. She stood on the platform with him. Beside her stood her sister, the Red Queen. The two wore equal expressions of schooled indifference, but their eyes betrayed their pain. This hurt them.

"Your crimes against Wonderland are numerous and severe," the White Queen continued.

Behind her, Romi stood in her bright white armor, her glare sharp where it bore into him. At her side, Humphrey stood in his red armor, his lips pursed, his gaze aimed at the ground as his *chest heaved in silent breaths. Anastasia . . . she was not here, her sentence already carried out.*

"The damage you've done, the harm you've caused, the lives you've broken can never be made whole again. The punishment for these charges is death." The Red Queen lifted a sword. His sword, still in its sheath.

Addison bowed his head. He knew what was coming next.

"However," the White Queen said, "given your service in the defeat of the Black Queen, which was instrumental in bringing about the era of peace we've entered, your life will be spared."

"But you are hereby banished from this realm for the remainder of your natural life," the Red Queen said. She extended the sword.

He took it without a word.

The White Queen lifted her hand. The Red Queen took it. Then they spoke as one.

"Now by our will we bind your heart,

And from these lands you must depart."

The pain was instant and bone deep. It drove through him, tearing a scream free, robbing him of his strength enough to send him to his knees. The queens continued to speak, but he couldn't hear them over the sound of his thrashing heart and his own agonized groans. Darkness hazed his vision. It stole his breath. The voices mingled and swirled, filling his ears.

They called his name. Insistent.

"Addison . . . Addison!"

He forced his eyes open. His vision was still blurred, but the pain had started to subside. Someone leaned in over him.

"He's coming around."

"Oh thank god."

"I thought we hadn't caught it in time."

Addison blinked to clear his vision. Three faces solidified above him: Alice, Anastasia, and Odabeth. The princess
looked haggard but relieved, her bronze face sallow, bags sag-
ging slightly beneath her eyes. Something flickered between
her fingers where her hand was pressed to her chest.

Anastasia and Alice wore twin expressions of concern,
reaching to help sit him up.

He winced as something in his chest tightened. "What . . .
happened?"

"The exile Verse nearly killed you," Anastasia said.
"Fortunately, the princess was able to give you a reprieve."

"I'm surprised it worked," Odabeth said. "Two queens cast
the verse, two must break it. Usually. But . . . here you are.
How do you feel?"

"Like Bandersnatch shite—oomph!" Addison nearly toppled
over when Alice flung herself against him. His arms curled
around her as she squeezed at him, mumbling about how he
was a stupid, head-ass, reckless, something to do with fornica-
tions with someone's mother. He held her as she sniffed and
sobbed quietly for a minute or two then she drew back, allowing his eyes to fall to where she wove their fingers together. He
smiled faintly. "Hey."

"Hey," she breathed, wiping at her face.

Behind her a young Japanese woman stood with a sword
at her hip.

Humphrey and Chess were also awake, looking as haggard as he felt.

"What happened, exactly?" Addison asked.

"Well, I got my Muchness in order." Alice smiled faintly. "But that's about the only good news there is . . ."

Thirty-Eight

FOOLISH

"**H**umphrey."

The Black Knight paused. That name again.

It was so strange to know it likely belonged to him, but to feel nothing when hearing it.

And yet he responded when the woman known as Anastasia called to him.

He looked up as she approached. He'd separated himself from the group to give them a moment to compose themselves and to deal with his own . . . whatever was happening in his head. So much and so little. It was a frightful thing, not knowing who you were, barely knowing who you were not.

"Yes?" he answered.

She paused and eyed him in a way that left him feeling . . . exposed. "You truly don't know me?"

"No." He looked away from her then, uncomfortable with the intensity of her stare. He wanted to apologize, but what for?

"Mmm. I know this may seem like a lot, but . . . Actually, no, I don't know what this may seem like for you. Any of it. I can't imagine how confused and lost you must feel—"

"Not helping," he murmured.

"But I want you to know that we're going to figure this out. What happened to you, what happened to the Red Queen, how . . . that woman claimed the Heart."

At the mention of Her Majesty, a sense of . . . foreboding rose around him. It was a looming thing, like being caught in the eyes of a predator watching him from the edge of a forest, unseen, unheard.

Anastasia lifted her hand as if to reach for him, but thankfully did not. "It'll take time—these sorts of things do."

"Have much experience with magic-induced amnesia? If that's what this even is."

She chuckled faintly. "I should've known. No one else wields a wit half as sharp." She sighed softly. "Think about the offer to come with us. There's nothing for you here." She gestured to the dingy walls and halls around them.

This place . . . it was the only home he'd known. It was here that Her Majesty had awakened him. Freed him from a prison, she'd said. Where he, she, and others loyal to the true queen had been locked away long ago. And he'd hung on her every word. Her Majesty. His lady. To think he followed a woman and didn't know her name. And he'd been so sure of his duty to her, of his purpose. But now? Now he saw that he was simply a means to an end. Everything he knew, everything she had told him, was a lie.

"Maybe." He closed his eyes. While he was certain he could no longer trust Her Majesty's words, he didn't know if he could believe Anastasia and the others. He couldn't even believe what was in his own head.

But he didn't have anywhere else to go, and there was no staying here. The subtle shifting of shadows in this place set a fear inside him, and not because of the Nightmares. In fact, there were no Nightmares—they seemed to flee when Her Majesty's body vanished. Something about the place still left him uneasy.

"Are you all right?" Anastasia asked.

He laughed. "I simply am, right now."

"What do you mean?"

"I'm Humphrey. Maybe. I'm also the Black Knight. Either way, I am a traitor." The very notion turned his stomach, even though a part of him was certain he'd made the correct choice. A small part of him that had grown bolder and louder since . . . well, since the night he first met Alice on the road to Ahoon.

His mission had been simple: attack the girl, implant the Verse, sic a Nightmare on her. But when she'd been injured, when she'd been calling out, part of him was desperate to answer. To . . . protect her. And that drive had only intensified over the following days until it culminated in him throwing himself between her and a Nightmare's barb.

"That woman did something to you to make you into this—"

"Perhaps." It was likely true. He had seen her do the same thing to Chess, but the difference was Chess had come back to himself. He remembered who he was before. The Black

Knight . . . Humphrey . . . remembered nothing. Just . . . feelings.

Anger. Devotion. Hatred. Loyalty . . . love?

"I love you," Hatta had said.

Humphrey didn't want to believe him. It would be so much easier if he didn't believe him. But he did. And because he did, he knew he wouldn't be able to leave them. Not yet.

"I'll go with you." He lifted a hand. "For now." It was the only thing that made sense, and possibly the only way he was going to even begin to try to figure things out. It was also fifty different kinds of foolish, essentially turning himself over to people who'd seen him as a hated enemy only moments before, but for the first time that he could remember, it was fully his choice.

Thirty-Nine

CONTINUOUSLY CURIOUSER

Alice stood behind Addison as he stared at the broken throne. Stone and glass littered the ground around it. Moss and overgrowth covered the high glass ceiling, strangling the light as it tried to enter the throne room. Now that the Bloody Lady—seemed the name had stuck—and her minions had dipped, some of the gloom had lifted, but it was still a far cry from the brightness that filled Legracia and had probably done the same for this space once.

"How fitting that this place would be where everything would come together, seeing as how it seemed to be where it all fell apart," Addison had said after he and everyone else were brought up to speed.

The Bloody Lady wasn't the Red Queen, like Addison had feared—which was why his fool-ass came racing out here, nearly getting himself killed in the process. But she wasn't anybody any of them recognized, and neither Chess nor Humphrey knew her name. They both called her my lady or Her Majesty. Freaky.

"Is everyone ready to go?" Addison asked quietly.

"As ready as we can be. I can't believe you just know a bunch of talking horses." Or maybe she could. Wonderland, after all. Did this mean *all* animals could talk, or just some? Was Chou just the strong, silent type?

"That was all Phinny's doing." Addison smiled. "She's an old friend."

"Seems you have a lot of those." Speaking of old friends, there was one in particular Alice wanted to talk about. Or not talk about, really, but try to understand just what the hell was going on. "So the Black Knight is actually Humphrey? Who's . . . the missing Red Knight."

She wasn't certain, but she thought she saw him flinch. "Mmhm. A shock. When he vanished, I . . . we feared the worst." He looked to her, his expression slightly pinched. "Apparently, something far more sinister was in the works. Humphrey was brave and loyal. Much smarter than me, if you hear him tell it. For him to end up like this . . ." Addison shook his head as his shoulders sagged beneath the weight of his unspoken words. "I think I hurt him most when I chose to continue to serve Portentia after it was clear she was choosing a path of darkness. In fact, I know I hurt him most. So much so, his anger toward me survived whatever that woman did to him. But he'd never do something like this. No matter his pain. He's truly lost himself, and . . . I don't know how to help him."

Hesitation played through Alice, listening to Addison talk

about someone else like this, hearing the emotion in his voice, seeing it on his face. But she pushed past it and moved to take his hand. He squeezed her fingers. "You two were . . . clearly close." She hoped she didn't sound like some jealous thot, though she couldn't help feeling like one. Mostly the jealousy part, not the rest of it.

Addison sighed. "We were involved, intimately, but that is long over. I'm not even sure we were friends, by the end of it. I'd betrayed him, after all. Betrayed Wonderland."

"I'm . . . sorry." She didn't know what else to say. Hell, she didn't know why she was saying that. Her mind swirled with images of Addison and Humphrey together. Not like that! Well, kinda like that? And it wasn't like she had any room to be all up in her feelings about this, not when she'd kissed Chess and . . . the butterflies in her stomach really got to going around Haruka . . . She was a mess. They were both a mess.

"Don't be," Addison said. "My mistakes are mine to live with. To pay for."

Alice nodded. She'd have to pay for hers, too.

"Besides, I may regret the choices I made, but I don't regret the path they led me down." He looked to her, a smile pulling at his lips. "Or who they led me to."

Those butterflies she was thinking about a second ago went wild as Addison leaned in. She met him, their lips brushing, sending a tingle of heat down her spine. She pressed into the kiss, molding her mouth to his, chasing the taste of him. When they broke away, she pressed in at his side, her head resting on his shoulder.

Her eyes trailed to the throne, same as his had before. "It feels like I failed my duty again," Addison said.

"What do you mean?"

"Humphrey is not himself, and this Bloody Lady is in possession of the Heart. This likely means the Red Queen is gone. I know it wasn't my duty to defend her, but . . . it had been, once."

"You thought the same about Humphrey, and here he is."

"True, but I'm reluctant to look for twice the miracle."

Alice could understand that. But she would hope for him. For the others. "About that, the Heart and whatnot, I thought only a member of the royal family could use it."

"Mmm. From what you described, doing so drains her severely. She's likely forcing its power somehow, nearly killing herself in the process."

"Curiouser," Alice said.

Addison blinked before smirking. "And continuously curiouser."

She heaved a sigh before snorting, toying with his fingers then weaving hers with them. "You aren't the only failure here, you know. I was supposed to find the Heart. It was my plan. Now it's wherever those things took her body. Without it, you and the White Queen can't be cured."

He pursed his lips, nodding. "No, we can't. But I made my peace with my condition long ago. As far as the White Queen, hopefully Maddi and Naette can treat her, the way Maddi treats me. If not, well . . . Princess Odabeth will take her mother's crown and be the last remaining member of the royal family."

Alice hoped they could help Odabeth's mother. She'd meant it when she said she didn't wish the pain of losing a parent on anybody, and that was before she and the princess were friends.

"On to more cheerful subjects—Chess is doing well?" Addison asked.

Alice nodded. "Whatever the Bloody Lady did to Humphrey, she started it on Chess. We were able to get to him before he lost his memory, though. He's sorry for everything he did, but up and breathing. For now." Her voice softened on those last two words. "Odabeth is too weak to use the Eye, if it'll even work on him. So we have to wait and see what happens."

"Between Maddi and Naette, we'll be able to keep the Slithe from completely consuming him." Addison curled his arm around her shoulder and pressed a kiss to her temple. "I promised we'd take care of him, milady, and we will."

"I know."

"It's strange, though. I had no idea your friend was such a capable warrior." Addison arched an eyebrow.

Alice snorted. "That makes three of us, including him. Could the Slithe have . . . I don't know, given him powers, like with me crossing into Wonderland?"

"It . . . maybe?" Addison rubbed at the back of his head. "Slithe has not been put to use like this before. Perhaps it was the Bloody Lady's puppetry of him."

"Maybe . . ."

Alice fell silent when he turned to guide them through the palace to where everyone was preparing to journey to some nearby town where Courtney was waiting for them. There they would resupply and prepare to part ways. Alice, Addison, Maddi, Courtney, Chess, and . . . Humphrey would make their way to the Western Gateway. Xelon and Odabeth would return to Legracia, along with this Naette, to tend the White Queen. The Duchess would accompany Haruka to the Eastern Gateway before returning to her post.

The Black Knight was gone, the Bloody Lady's plans— whatever they were—were foiled, and everyone was in one piece, for the most part. That . . . that was more than Alice could've hoped for.

THE BEST PEOPLE

"**A**lice Kingston, stop running in my house!"

Alice flinched, drawing up short where she'd been racing down the stairs, taking them two at a time. "Sorry!" Thanks to the construction going on to fix the damage caused by a "particularly rowdy burglary," the carpet on the steps had been pulled up, and now Mom could hear Alice no matter where she was in the house. It was like she was five again, damn.

The trade-off was she was getting a new bedroom. Humphrey had apologized when she told everyone at the pub about it. He'd apologized for a lot over the past few days, and was still working through his shattered memory to piece together his life. It had to be hard. She felt kinda sorry for him.

Once she reached the bottom of the stairs, Alice hurried for the kitchen at a trot—technically not a run—groaning at the smell of fried eggs, bacon, and something decidedly sweet baking. Usually everything smelled like paint and saw-dust unless Mom was cooking, which was pretty much all the time now. It helped her de-stress. She was still coping with her daughter being a superhero. It was cute, and funny.

"Smells so good."

"I know, because *I'm* good. Wash up, it's almost ready." Mom stood at the stove, robe still tightly wrapped around her body, hair tucked in a bonnet. She glanced over her shoulder as Alice bypassed the veritable buffet spread out over the island in order to grab a yogurt cup.

"Wha—that's it?" Mom held her hands up, gesturing at the food with a spatula. "I made a whole breakfast."

"I know, but I promised Courtney a Belated B-Day Brunch." Though she did grab a bit of bacon, taking a large bite out of it before leaning in to kiss her mom's cheek with greasy lips.

Mom *ugh*ed as she wiped at the grease with the back of her hand. "Her birthday was last week."

"And I missed it, remember?" Alice also snagged a piece of toast.

"Mmhm. Where y'all going?" Mom turned back to her pan.

"Yonnie's."

Mom's brows shot up. "Bring me back a strawberry bagel."

Alice smiled. "Yes, ma'am." Her phone chirped. She glanced down at the cracked screen. "Court's here. Back soon!" She turned and hurried for the door.

"Stop. Running. In. My. House!"

"Sor-ry! I love you, bye!" Alice called over her shoulder as she slipped outside.

Courtney's Camaro waited at the bottom of the driveway. Alice hurried to jump into the passenger seat.

"Hey!" Court beamed.

"Hey," Alice said, a little out of breath

Court's eyes dropped to Alice's chest. "That . . . is gorgeous."

Alice smiled as she fingered the rose charm dangling from the end of the chain around her neck. "Thanks. My grandma gave it to me." Luckily she'd tucked the jewelry case it came in away in a drawer the night she got it, otherwise it might've gotten damaged in the fight with Humphrey, or lost when she literally fell into Wonderland. "Said it's been passed down through generations."

Court's lips pulled into a pout. "My grammy never gives me family heirlooms."

"Maybe not, but she gave you a Porsche!" Alice had learned about the birthday present a couple days ago. It was still tucked away in the Marroné garage, bow and all. "And you don't even use it."

"I mean, I will! I'm just attached to this one." Court patted the dash affectionately. "A girl's first always holds a special place in her heart." She batted her lashes dramatically.

Alice groaned, and the sound was echoed from the back seat. She turned to where Chess was stretched across the leather. "Hey," she said, fidgeting slightly.

He waved. Things had been a little weird since . . . well, since he was freed of being controlled like a puppet by an otherworldly entity. And then there was the kiss. Alice pushed the memory aside and did her best to ignore the faint burn in her cheeks.

"I thought you were still feeling a bit down," she said to him.

"Uh, Yonnie's." He held his hands up. "I'd crawl out of a casket for those omelets."

"Me too," Court sighed as she pulled onto the highway. "Though I think they got rid of the spinach one you like."

"They what?" Chess sat up straighter in his seat. "When?" The indignation in his voice made Alice snicker.

"I think a few weeks ago?" Court peered at him in his mirror as he sank down in his seat.

"Is nothing sacred?" he muttered.

Alice smirked as Court tried to cheer him up by telling him all the new flavors of jam they had for the season. Alice's phone vibrated in her hand. She glanced down to find a text from Dee. It was him and his brother, making faces. Well, Dem was making a face. Dee was glaring at him for it.

Beneath the photo a message read:

Dee: All clear. The only nightmares are the ones I'll have after looking at Dem's stupid face.

Alice smiled. Another message popped up in the group chat, this one from Haruka.

Haruka: Truly terrifying.
Dem: Hey!
Dee: She understands.

Alice grinned. She'd started the group chat after they finally returned home. With the twins going back Russia, and Haruka to Tokyo, she didn't want to lose touch with any of them. It was supposed to be an official Dreamwalker chat, but it quickly dissolved into general shenanigans.

She tapped out a response.

Alice: Will go check the field again after school. I think the purge got everything but I wanna make sure.
Nothing to report until then. Though I offer condolences for having to look at Dem's face.
Dem: 😞
Dee: Baby.
Dem: *leaves chat*
Haruka: 😂

"What's so funny?" Courtney's voice cut in.

Alice glanced up. "Mm?"

"You over there giggling to yourself. What is it?" She stole glances in Alice's direction, mostly focused on the road.

"Oh." Alice rolled her shoulders and shrugged. "Work stuff."

Both Chess and Court went still, eyes widening slightly.

Alice barely managed to keep from laughing. She couldn't blame them, but the sheer terror that crossed their faces was kind of funny. "Don't worry, nothing serious."

"Good," Court sighed as her grip on the wheel relaxed.

"By the way, I need to run a quick errand after school. That cool?"

Court narrowed her eyes. "Is it in this world? Like, on this earthly plane?"

"Yes," Alice said, finally giving in to laughter.

"I guess that can be arranged."

Alice's phone chirped again. She glanced down, expecting another message from the group, though Haruka's name flashed across her screen.

Haruka: Did you see the latest episode!? Can't wait to talk tonight!

Her stomach flipped a little before Addison's name pushed up beneath that first message.

Addison: Hey luv. Think you can come by when you have a moment?

She tapped out a response to Haruka—doing her best to ignore those damned butterflies—then asked Addison what was wrong.

Addison: Nothing at all. Just wanting to see your lovely face.

She smiled, a bit of warmth spreading through her.

Alice: You could've started with that, got me worrying for nothing.
Addison: Apologies. Maddi wants me to tell you that she would also like to see your lovely face.
Alice: Aight, I'll come through. You're lucky I like you. 😵
Addison: Luck has nothing to do with it.
Alice: You're bananas, you know that?
Addison: I hear all the best people are.